TIME JACK

A Novel By John Whitfield

Also by John Whitfield
Under Pseudonym Divine G

Novels:
Baby Doll (Published by Q-Boro Books)
Money-Grip (Published by Street Knowledge Publishing)
Money-Grip 2 (Published by CreateSpace)
Enigma of Love (Published by Divine G Entertainment)
The Canarsie Connection (Published by Divine G Entertainment)
No Other Love (Published by Divine G Entertainment)
TGONG (Published by Divine G Entertainment)

Short Stories:
Averted Hearts (appearing in *The Game*, published by Triple Crown Publications)

Stage Plays:
Peak-Zone (appearing in *Exiled Voices, Portals of Discovery*, published by New England College Press)

TIME JACK ®

ISBN-10: 1-940765-17-X
ISBN-13: 978-1-940765-17-4
Createspace Edition

Paperback & ebook editions published by Divine G Entertainment
Written by: John Whitfield
Edited by John Whitfield
Cover layout/Design by KooziArts, LLC
For information contact: Divine G Entertainment
Email: divinegentertainment@gmail.com
Website: https://www.divinegentertainment.com

Dedication

This novel is dedicated to the number one person in my life: Good ole mom. She is the one person who has proven time and time again that no matter what the situation she will always have my back. This novel is dedicated to you for being there when times have gotten extremely rough, rocky, raw and real. Once again, thanks for all the support, love and understanding.

PRELUDE

Calvin Thompson's sweat-covered face glistened like a melting Hershey's chocolate bar as he barked commands. "Decrease the pitch!" He was dressed in a white lab coat and stood inside a topless control station behind a plexi-glass window, watching a machine the size of an overgrown phone booth. Four other scientists, all similarly dressed, sat behind consoles, adjusting computerized devices connected to the machine. Calvin's anxiety resonated from every part of his body as he nervously rocked back and forth on his heels with his arms crossed. "Take it easy!" He shouted when he heard a surge. "We're not in a race!"

The anticipation in the laboratory had almost reached pandemonium. As Calvin looked on while a mixture of frustration, hopelessness and bewilderment raced through his body, the machine hummed loudly and violently. What was causing the flaw to persist in this manner!?

Every so often sparks flew from the base of the machine.

Eric Seabright, Calvin's assistant, shuffled over to Calvin and shouted over the noise. "It's not the pitch! We have to increase the energy flow in the distributor! It'll balance out the defect!"

Calvin turned and met Eric's excited stare. That was a very risky maneuver; if too much energy was introduced too quickly, and a surge took place, the Gallium Phosphide Crystal could explode and not only destroy the machine, but possibly the entire lab. This was the reason Calvin repeatedly discarded this approach whenever the thought crossed his mind. Calvin faced forward and resumed watching the machine as his thoughts ran wild. Could this really be the root of this defect? he wondered. After hastily weighing the situation and the consequences, he decided to take a chance. Eric's suggestion had to be clear confirmation that he was initially on the right track.

"Demetrius!" Calvin shouted as he turned to the curly haired Latino man, who had a smooth facial complexion and even features. He

1

sat behind a console, resembling a NASA space station. "Slowly increase the energy level in the distributor!"

Demetrius's brown eyes widened in shock as he looked up to meet Calvin's no joking stare. After a moment, his trembling fingers began activating the computer dials.

Calvin held his breath.

The humming increased and the whole laboratory tremored as if an earthquake had activated.

Calvin turned, saw Eric was enthralled with excitement, and for the first time it dawned on him; this could be one of Eric's tactics to sabotage the experiment. Eric tried to conceal his desire to gain control of the project, but Calvin's keen ability to read peoples' ulterior motives was as brilliant as a God given gift.

Suddenly, the Time Machine made an ear torturous squealing sound and the smell of burning plastic appeared. The sparks coming from the base of the machine were now flowing steadily.

Calvin calculated what the sound and smell represented, and terror bolted through his body. He realized he made a monolithic mistake that would cost him his career. The Time Machine was going to explode!

Just as Calvin frantically spun around, about to scream for Demetrius to decrease the energy, and before he opened his mouth, a sudden, tremendous flash engulfed the lab.

CHAPTER # 1

Calvin entered his office as his head spun with fury at what he had done. How was he going to explain this!? He flopped down in the seat at his desk and started cursing himself for allowing his overzealousness to cause him to make a decision that brought about this uncomfortable moment of painful mental aerobics. Even though he subconsciously knew his actions were appropriate in light of the greater good that will occur down the road, his heart, on the other hand, seemed to be telling him that his sacrifices might not be worth it. That voice in his head reminded him that he was losing something far greater than success. He didn't want to hear this, so he struck out against the invading thought by opening the project file on his desk, hoping it would help take his mind off the guilt and pain he felt in his chest.

The second he laid eyes on the Board of Directors' statement in response to his progress report, explaining how the energy increase repaired the flaw, he smiled cheerfully. In an instant, he was beginning to feel like his old self again. Then, he repeatedly began telling himself Dameeka would understand why he could not attend her first Junior High School theater performance, and slowly he began feeling a little less guilty. If only he hadn't promised her he was going to be there, he could have avoided breaking her little heart once again. The image of Dameeka's hurt facial expression when she looked out into the audience and saw Ramanda there alone, unleashed a pain-stricken grunt.

As Calvin struggled to convince himself Dameeka would understand, he suddenly heard Eric's hard sole shoes approaching his office. He couldn't understand how those damn shoes could make a tocking sound like no other pair of shoes he had ever heard before. He wondered if Eric had them custom-made with a unique material that made them sound that way.

Tock! Tock! Tock . . .

Calvin sighed, reclined in his seat and braced himself for the storm that was rapidly approaching. There was no doubt there was going to be some fireworks. Calvin fixed his clean shaved face, making his ceaselessly serene and friendly expression appear firm and unwavering. His contagious ready smile mutated into a lock jawed frown that was alien to him and looked as fake as a counterfeit Rembrandt painting. After all these years of mind wrecking research, and putting up with all the racism at every single stage of his career, there was no way he was going to allow some new jack, rich kid who was as spoiled as week old milk sitting in the blazing hot desert sun, to walk in on his project and take everything he worked so hard for right from under his feet. If you kind-heartedly gave an inch, they would ruthlessly take a mile!

There was a knock. "Come in." Calvin shouted.

When Eric Seabright entered, Calvin realized he underestimated his response. His boyish facial features and those stone chiseled cheek bones encased in a head full of sandy brown hair didn't look upset in the least. Eric looked so calm, Calvin's thick eyebrows crunched closer to his soft brown eyes with perplexing force. Calvin even felt his dark brown skin turning lighter as the confusion mounted.

With a pleasant smile Eric said. "We need to talk, Calvin." He waited for Calvin to offer him a seat, but after a moment breezed by without receiving it he invited himself.

Calvin locked eyes with Eric. "I'm all ears." He said, reminding himself that smiling faces tell lies, and they don't tell the truth.

"I read the board's response to the progress report and I think it's rather unfair my efforts weren't mentioned." He was struggling to keep his promise not to blow a gasket. "What happened?"

"The board writes what it wants in those reports, Eric."

Eric swallowed the built up rage in his throat as he pulled a copy of the report from the pocket of his lab coat. "This report says you told them it was you, and you alone, who repaired the glitch in the

Continuum Antigravity Infusion System." He politely laid the document on the desk.

Calvin sat up and clasped his hands together on top of the desk. "I don't want to appear as if I'm unconcern about your grievance, but I am the lead scientist and the time travel expert on this project. And you were brought in to assist me ... Yes, you did help. But I discovered the flaw and you--"

"With all due respect, we may still be in the lab trying to rectify the defect, if it wasn't for me."

Calvin sighed hard. "You actually believe without you this problem would not have been detected?" He shook his head with a smirk on his face, displaying just how pathetic he thought Eric's position was. "Has it ever dawned on you, if I could create the Continuum Antigravity Infusion System, it's apparent I could repair a minor glitch?"

With complete composure, Eric said, "I heard it was your father who created this system, and it--"

"You should do your homework, Eric." Calvin rose to his feet, allowing his impatience to take control. "I'm not going to alter the report. Your contribution was minimal. Any way you choose to look at it, standard protocol says it's well within my right to present my report in this fashion, since you are my subordinate."

Eric humbly locked eyes with Calvin's. But he really wanted to jump up and release some of his frustration. The desire to be the first official time traveler was so piercing, Eric felt a mixture of sheer terror and hatred at the thought Calvin was going to be the one. This was going to be the greatest scientific accomplishment of all times and Eric was willing to do anything to have his face represent such a phenomenal scientific achievement. He was hoping he could get the board's attention by showing them he was more qualified than Calvin to run the project, but things weren't unfolding as he would like. Although he was recognized as the second most qualified Time Travel Specialist, being number one was the only position he could settle for. What the hell was the board thinking!? How could they allow this!? Eric told himself if this were a couple of hundred years ago, he wouldn't be sitting here locked in a staring match with Calvin. He was convinced this work fanatic, arrogant Negro would be shining his shoes and begging to clean his bathroom!

With a humbled smile, Eric rose from the chair and spoke in the most respectful fashion he could muster. "Thank you for giving me the opportunity to voice my grievance. Now that you mention the protocol, I must admit you're right. I was just hoping our teamwork philosophy would allow each team player to receive credit when he demonstrates he wants what's best for the team. Sorry for the intrusion, Calvin." When he saw Calvin's head nod, he picked up the report from the desk and exited the office.

Calvin flopped down in his chair as a disturbing premonition swept over his entire being. Alarms were going off in the back of his head; each one telling him something was wrong with Eric's nonchalant response to the report. Usually he was excited and hostile about everything. That over-confident smirk and that warped twinkle in his eyes were even more troubling. When the board brought Eric in as his assistant, it only took a couple of days for Calvin to see Eric was an extremely competitive person who had his eyes fixed on taking Calvin's position. It wasn't Eric's desire to become the top man on the project that made Calvin nervous. Since the board wanted the most qualified scientist to be in charge of the project, and because Calvin knew he was the best, Eric was no real threat intellectually. But what got under his skin was Eric's money. It didn't take a lot of brains to recognize money made the world go around, and usually when people with substantial amounts of it went out of their way to obtain things, they usually got what they wanted.

☼ ☼ ☼ ☼

Eric had the expression of a man in deep thought as he headed toward Diana Fullmore, his girlfriend's office. He actually was sizzling with rage.

Diana was talking into her voice-activated computer when Eric entered. She was a brunette with matching colored eyes, and her lustrous wavy chestnut hair that fell to the middle of her back when she let it all hang out was her most notable feature. With high cheekbones and a waist that was disproportionately small in relation to her thick, muscular looking legs, Diana could turn plenty young heads despite being 36 years of age and could even pass for a model. She stopped in mid-sentence when she saw the tension throbbing from Eric's body. She rose to her feet. "I guess I don't have to ask how it went."

Eric sat in the chair next to the desk, causing Diana to sit back down. He sighed hard and said. "I can't take this shit anymore. I see the writing on the wall as clear as day. As long as Calvin is in charge of this project, he's never gonna allow my accomplishments to be recognized by the board."

"Well," Diana leaned back in her chair. "I warned you. Calvin is very over-protective of this project. He's not gonna let anyone out shine him. His selfishness is a blinding emotion that'll never allow him to give others the credit they deserve."

Eric felt like all his dreams were being shattered one by one as reality set in. The feeling of hopelessness and defeat were so overwhelming, he felt the urge to cry slowly metamorphosing into a strong sense of despair. He shifted his emotions back to the feelings he was content working with. Ever since he took this position, he'd been hoping and praying it would not come to this. But, at least he could say to his conscience and the integrity component of his mind, he tried to get Calvin to do the right thing. He sincerely didn't want to result to the use of extreme measures. A hard sigh escaped from his body because he wasn't asking for much. All he wanted was to receive credit for the work he put in. He locked his stare on Diana as he spoke. "He's giving me no choice."

Diana held back a determined smile. "Oh, you do have a choice. Life is full of choices. All you have to do is determine what are your options and select one."

Eric's mind was made up. "I didn't make this choice. He did." He rose and when he received Diana's supportive head nod, he turned and headed for the door.

CHAPTER # 2

Calvin entered his two-story, two-car garage, pool in the back, modern style home, realizing his guilt had reached its zenith. But the moment the stomach teasing aromas of Ramanda's succulent delicacies coming from the kitchen touched his senses, he felt an emotional skirmish set off inside of him. The mixed smell of roasted soybean burgers, onions, garlic, brown rice, spinach, peach cobbler and several other aromas he couldn't identify made his mouth water with delight. His pleasure didn't last long because he felt worn-out with a ton of unfinished research looming over his head. Most of the day he was entrenched in an emotional tug-o-war match; exhilarated by the repair of the Continuum System, but deeply hurt by his failure to attend his daughter's play, and it all was finally taking its toll.

As Calvin closed the door behind him, and fastened the locks, he heard Dameeka rushing down the stairs. Hanging up his jacket on the coat rank, he felt her staring eyes boring into his back. When he turned, and saw Dameeka leaning against the wall with her arms crossed, he couldn't believe how much his 13-year-old child was starting to look just like her deceased mother, Cookie, especially when she was upset. "Sorry, Dameeka."

"What happened, Daddy?" Dameeka twisted up her face, and did not wait for his answer because she knew what the excuse was. "Do you know how embarrassing it is to be the only person whose father wasn't there?" She wanted to unleash a barrage of fake tears, but she couldn't seem to get them flowing.

Calvin stood there looking like a misplaced pimple. "There was an unforeseen emergency with the project, honey." He went to her, gave her a strong hug and a kiss on the forehead. "I'll make it up to you." He was about to say I promise, but realized he was running this particular phrase into the ground whenever he found time to talk to her. "Please, baby, try to understand. This is gonna be--"

"I know, I know." She said with a mimicking voice. "This is gonna be the World's greatest invention. I understand, daddy."

With his arm around Dameeka's shoulder, they headed for the kitchen.

Dameeka wanted to lash out, but her dad completely disarmed her with his warm embrace and affection. "When you start traveling in time, daddy, I want to go with you to the time when Cleopatra was the Queen of Egypt."

"As long as you promise not to alter any of those events with your beautiful smile, we'll see what we can do."

They entered the kitchen and saw Ramanda working at the food counter wearing a white apron. Her high yellow complexion and those sensuous brown eyes and lips made her look totally out of place slaving in front of a microwave. She looked like someone whose business was best illustrated in the bedroom or on the silver screen.

Ramanda spoke without turning around. "You guys can get cleaned up, dinner'll be ready in a minute."

Calvin gestured to Dameeka to go get cleaned up and she obeyed. He came up behind Ramanda, wrapped his arms around her sexy waist and kissed her on the neck.

Ramanda spoke while stirring the pot of rice. "Your daughter was shattered when she didn't see you in the audience."

Calvin eased away from the embrace and leaned against the counter. He really didn't want to be reminded of the pain he caused Dameeka and was now becoming irritated. "I tried to get away, Ramanda, but once we repaired the defect in the Continuum System, there was nothing I could do."

Ramanda faced Calvin with excitement in her eyes. "You finally fixed it!? So that means there's gonna be a test run very soon?"

"Yes, that's exactly what it means. In fact, we're scheduled to send Blinky on a trip tomorrow."

Ramanda went to the counter, retrieved the strainer and began pouring the long grain rice into it. "Calvin, I understand how important this project is to you, but your daughter really needs to spend some time with her father. I'm doing the best I can to fill that void. I really don't think she's fully over the loss of her mom. We get along just fine, but if you were around more, it would make it a lot easier for our--"

"Dameeka assured me that she understands," Calvin hated when she rubbed in the fact he was inadvertently neglecting his daughter. "This is only temporary."

Ramanda started preparing the table and held back the urge to remind him four years of being an absentee father was not temporary. "Well, Calvin, I'll say it again; it's time to squeeze in some quality time with her. Just one day out of a month will help tremendously and make a world of a difference."

"Please, let's not start this again. I told you, Ramanda, we're at the most crucial stage of the project."

"Calvin, something has got to give. Your child needs your support." She sat down and gestured for Calvin to do the same. He refused. She really wanted to tell him she needed him as well, but the use of his daughter would obviously have a better effect and a realistic potential to bring about some results. "Some sort of sacrifice on your part has to be made. If you love her you would--"

"Don't throw that in my face, Ramanda. You know I love my daughter. This is absolutely the wrong time for this. I'm literally days from reaping the benefits of all these years of mind breaking work." He almost raised his voice too high, but caught himself. "Have you been listening to me!? I'm almost there. The first official time traveler, do you know what that means?"

"Of course, I know what it means. But whatever happened to keeping things balanced. All work and no play is a formula that'll--"

"I thought we agreed when this is over, we'll make it like it was before. Dameeka understands, why can't you?"

"Your daughter tells you she understands because she loves you, and wants to make you happy." She took a moment to collect her thoughts. "Have you ever walked in on her while she was crying? Have you ever asked her why she was crying?" Ramanda saw Calvin bowed his head. "Well, I have. And you know what she says 99.9 percent of the time when I ask why she's crying?"

Calvin sighed, leaned against the counter, and crossed his arms impatiently. He looked into Ramanda's eyes. Why was she doing this!? Why now?!

Ramanda sensed he wasn't going to answer. "Dameeka claims she cries because she's losing her dad." Ramanda rode the silence for all it was worth, maintaining eye contact every step of the way. A moment later she said. "I was thinking, maybe this weekend the three of us could go to the movies, or an amazement park like Great Adventures, even a restaurant, or just go window-shopping, anywhere as long as it's the three of us together."

Calvin bowed his head again because he felt terrible. He was so into this project, he couldn't squeeze in a measly single day with his family. When he felt himself slowly giving into Ramanda's suggestion, he heard his dad's dying request scream in the back of his mind, and he began shaking his head. He refused to let his focus be knocked off track. He came too far for this! There was simply too much on the line and too many years of hard work to waver now.

With a straight face, Calvin spoke softly. "I'll say this again. This is the most crucial stage of this project. All of my time, including work-time, spare-time and time off, must be spent at the lab and putting the final touches on this project." He paused, realizing the mere mention of the word "time" and "project" compelled him to look at his watch. He sighed, wishing there were more hours in a day. "Sorry, Ramanda, please try to understand." He wanted to give her a hug and a kiss, but the frown that suddenly appeared on her face told him to let it go. "I'll eat later. I have to get right to work on a couple things before tomorrow. If you want, you can put me a plate on the side and I'll get it as soon as I can." He rushed out of the Kitchen.

Ramanda shook her head in disgust, wondering how did Calvin's ex-wife (Dameeka's mother, Cookie) put up with Calvin's placing his work before his family, his health and everything else in his circumference. She often wondered how she, herself, was able to endure such neglect. Now that she saw their relationship intricately involved severe bouts of loneliness and never-ending rounds of minimal communication, she had second thoughts about marriage, even though she understood what Calvin was trying to accomplish.

Ramanda rose to her feet and began preparing two plates of food. Once again, it would be her and Dameeka eating dinner together. Ramanda once believed she could deal with Calvin's excessive work habits, but that was before she got a taste of genuine neglect. He hadn't touched her sexually in over a month and a half, and she was starting to realize this was standard operating procedure; one steaming hot episode followed by months of absolutely nada (nothing). Her rage was mounting daily because she needed some real, steady and hard-core affection, and if she didn't get it soon, she was going to be forced to jump ship on this relationship.

CHAPTER # 3

"Easy, Blinky," Calvin said softly to the lab monkey, who was making a loud squawking sound as he laid on a gurney with wires attached to his head, arms, chest and stomach. Calvin and Tina Jones, a short, stocky woman, with sandy brown hair, watery blue eyes and a severe case of acne, were conducting a head-to-toe exam on Blinky. Eric, Demetrius, and Diana were performing a series of last minute inspections on all the Time Machine components. When Calvin was satisfied Blinky was in excellent health, he turned and spoke to Eric. "How's everything coming along?"

"I think Demetrius discovered a minor problem," Eric was fiddling with the huge fiber optic cables in back of the Time Machine. "Hey, Demetrius, what was that you found?"

Demetrius looked up from his computer. "There's a hair fracture in the inner Cyclonic Plate." He walked over to Calvin. "Let me show you." He picked up a device resembling a flashlight from a tool cart and lead Calvin inside the Time Machine. He turned on the device and pointed the infrared beam of light at the almost invisible squiggly crack. "If you get us another Plate, we can replace it within an hour."

Calvin maintained his composure with an effort as he examined the fracture. How did this happen!? Before his anger could grab hold of him he realized this wasn't the first time such a fracture occurred. Last week they found a fracture on one of the outer plates.

Calvin sighed and headed for the phone in his office at the other end of the lab. As the scientist in charge of the project, Calvin was the only one who could order supplies and equipment. He picked up the receiver of the phone on his desk and dialed the number to the warehouse. When the line was picked up, he spoke. "Larry, this is Calvin. I need you to send me a left inner Cyclonic plate ... Yes, as soon as possible ... Okay. Thanks." He hung up, went to the Time Machine

14

to conduct a few last minute checks and to recheck everything his subordinates had checked.

About an hour later, the outer perimeter alarm went off. It had to be the Cyclonic Plate. Calvin went to the visual intercom and saw Larry had apparently hired a new deliveryman without giving him advance notice in accordance with standard protocol. "Let's see your ID?" Calvin said into the intercom as he closely scrutinized the blond haired man with a thin mustache, dressed in the company uniform. He raised his ID card and Calvin honed in on the document. "Bring it a little closer to the camera." When he saw Eddie Bartlett's information was in order, he activated the entry dial. The locks opened with a loud clank.

Calvin felt the urge to call Larry and make a big stink, but too much time had already been wasted. Plus, he knew Larry would not send anyone to the lab without first receiving the appropriate security clearance, and if his ID wasn't intact, Eddie wouldn't have made it anywhere near the fence. Calvin watched Eddie through the security monitors, heading toward the entrance about three hundred yards from the outer gate.

Eddie Bartlett saw the rumors were true. Timetron really did have a fully self-contained state of the arts laboratory that had its own security system and needed no security guards. Covering over fifteen acres of land, the complex was down in a heavily wooded valley and was surrounded by triple layered barbed wire fencing that was sensory activated and had microscopic cameras all over the outer perimeter. With a one by three feet cardboard box tucked under his arm, Eddie nonchalantly moved toward the lab, examining the trees scattered about and the plush green lawns that looked like sophisticated carpeting. He wondered if Eric was exaggerating when he said any intruder who came within two feet of the fence without authorization received a debilitating jolt of electricity that left the invader unconscious for at least an hour. Animals other than humans were exempt!?

15

Eddie pulled his gaze from the scenery and let his eyes dance upon the main building. It was a one story, white brick, ultra-modernized complex with no visible windows and had an observatory like section on the roof. Eddie squinted his eyes from the reflective glare of the sun that bounced off the gigantic satellite disk in back of the building, which stood dominantly over everything else like an all-seeing eye keeping watch over the complex. Edward secretly commended Timetron because this lab was in the middle of nowhere. With the nearest sign of human life over twenty miles away, Eddie couldn't think of a more confidential location because this area was the perfect place for conducting a project immune from pestering eyes prying into private affairs.

As Eddie arrived at the sliding door entrance, he nervously hoped whatever Eric was up to wasn't going to cost him his job. Eric sounded like he was definitely up to no good. Eddie was never the favor giving type, but five thousand dollars wasn't something a smart person with gambling debts would let slip through his hands, especially when the money provider was able to guarantee him nothing would go wrong.

Eddie entered the lab and Calvin realized he evidently knew who he was because Eddie headed straight for him. Eddie walked across the lab, and Calvin saw all the high-tech equipment mesmerized him.

As Eddie moved pass the Time Machine, he saw it resembled an oversized phone booth that could hold three adults, and had a cylindrical tube on top leading up to the ceiling. His attempt to conceal his amazement was unsuccessful.

When Eddie arrived, he smiled as he handed Calvin the box. "Good afternoon, Mr. Thompson." He then handed Calvin the electronic signature device.

Calvin smiled back. "Same to you, Mr. Bartlett." He signed in the section of the devise which said signature and handed the device back. After Eddie gave Calvin a head nod and a smile, he headed for the door he had entered the lab. Calvin headed for the counter on the far side of the lab to make sure the Cyclonic plate was intact.

Eddie carefully inspected the signature, as he moved across the lab, retracing the path he took moments ago.

Eric was assembling some tools on a mobile cart and made eye contact with Eddie as he walked by. When Eric saw his inconspicuous head nod, he felt a surge of excitement tumbled downward and crash landed in the pit of his stomach. He tamed the tight-lipped smile that almost slipped across his face. Eric scanned the area to see if anyone saw the visual exchange between him and Eddie. In one graceful sweep, he was able to conclude with unequivocal confidence that no one was paying him or the deliveryman any attention.

As Calvin helped replace the Cyclonic plate, while wielding sparks flew from the solder that mended the plates together, he slid into a daydream like trance. His mind retraced the history of time travel technology, and he smilingly basked in the thought that he was finally about to become an intricate part of it.

At the dawn of the twenty second century, Calvin bore witness it was at this point it all started to take shape. When Jonathan Moyer broke the light barrier, the field of time travel turned from a theoretical possibility into a legitimate field of science. Mr. Moyer solved the mystery behind Dark Energy and used that discovery to create an apparatus that allowed matter to travel at speeds faster than light. Although traveling at warp speeds was and remained limited to super-compressed energy, this achievement constituted a major breakthrough for the field of time travel.

Three decades later came the breakthrough that shoved time travel a huge step forward. Carl Thompson, Calvin's father, created a system that not only transformed matter into dense, super-compressed energy, but also allowed this energy to be moved great distances and then safely reconstructed back to its original state. The system responsible for such a feat was called the Gallium Phosphide Crystal. But without a way to tame the devastating force of gravity, these breakthroughs were worthless, since gravity would crush anything that did not conform to its rule of law.

As a result, Carl began his work on what came to be known as the Continuum Antigravity Infusion System. But the moment he was weeks from putting the final touches on this system, Carl was struck down by a stress related stroke. As Carl laid in his death bed, he summoned his son, Calvin, to his bed-side.

Suddenly, his father's last will and testament flashed across his mind with profound clarity and Calvin grunted as the event re-enacted itself in his third eye as if it was appearing in real time, instead of inside his head.

Calvin had entered the hospital room on trembling legs. The antiseptic smell was everywhere, and as usual, it made him nauseous because the scent was synonymous with pain and suffering. He saw his father lying in bed with wires attached all over his body while the heart monitor beeped lively. Calvin saw his dad open his eyes, turn his head with a struggle and crack a pain-drenched smile when he saw Calvin. His chubby cheeks, squinted brown eyes, ashy golden brown skin and his head full of gray hair looked worn and sickly.

Carl spoke hoarsely with a trembling voice. "Calvin, come quickly, we must talk." He coughed painfully and gasped for air.

Calvin nervously pulled up a chair to his bedside, sat and grabbed his father's hand. "You shouldn't do any talking, dad." His father's grip was strong, almost desperate and it scared him. "I was planning to come see you tonight, but Nurse Serena called me at the lab and said you wanted to see me. She said it was an emergency."

"Listen, Calvin, I'm not gonna make it. I need you--"

"Don't talk like that, dad!" Calvin felt a tremor of dread sweep over him. He couldn't fix his mind to even image his father in a coffin. "Remember you said your worst enemy is your own mind. Talking like that will kill your will to fight this. The doctors said it's a fifty--"

"Listen to me," Carl said in his *I'm not playing any games voice*. "I need you to continue my work. The Continuum Antigravity Infusion System is literally days from completion. This is my entire life's work. Everything that I stood for is in--"

"But I know nothing about time travel, dad. I'm a geneticist. Studying genes and the--"

"You're a scientist! That's all that matters!" Carl coughed explosively, and saw it almost unhinged Calvin. "You have a critical mind, my son. You can do anything, once you put your mind to it." He paused, drawing deep breaths. "I trust no one else to carry on my legacy. Before your mother died, she asked me to let you be who you wanted to be, not to force you to follow in my footsteps, and that's what I did. But I need you to do this. I--I--" Tears rolled from his eyes as he coughed explosively. The thought of all those years ending up wasted and the prospect of his life-long struggle not being accomplished seemed more painful and frightening than the fact he was winking at death.

Calvin was flabbergasted and confused. He knew he couldn't tell his father no, especially not at a time like this. "Don't worry dad, I'll do it." He knew this promise was just words because his father was going to be just fine; the doctors personally assured him of this fact.

"All contracts are in order," Carl gasped for air. After a moment, he tamed the attack with a struggle. "Go see Bill. He'll explain all the legal issues. Calvin, please, promise me you'll be the first time traveler."

Calvin spoke, while squeezing his dad's hand with a loving embrace. "I promise, I'll be the first time traveler." He saw his dad smiled and closed his eyes while his grip disappeared. "Now, you can calm down and relax--"

The loud, ringing sound that engulfed the hospital room when his dad flat-lined would echo in his mind for eternity.

Within two years, Calvin saw to it that the Continuum Antigravity Infusion System was fully operable. During numerous experiments, all compressed energy sent to various Black Holes, Cosmic Strings and Wormholes withstood all degrees and forms of gravity. The way the System worked was notoriously simple; the compressed energy was encapsulated in a negatively charged force field made from space debris taken from the rings of Saturn that possessed strong antigravity properties. When the main constituent, tycafollium, was extracted from the debris and made into a concentrate, the antigravity qualities increased. The more the substance was concentrated, the more the antigravity properties grew. Acting as an antigravity scaffolding, the casing covering the super-compressed energy would hold open a Wormhole portal long enough for the encased energy to pass through or the casing would simply repel any surrounding and ever-present gravity.

Once the gravity obstacle was conquered it was downhill from that point because time travel was well researched from a theoretical standpoint. For hundreds of years, scientists studied time travel, and fortunately, some of the theories developed turned out to be accurate. It had become common knowledge that Wormholes attached to Black Holes were time portals that could transport matter further into the future. Likewise, Cosmic Strings had the ability to send matter into the past. With everything in place, Timetron and a few other labs began a race to become the first to turn time travel into reality. After Timetron rebuilt a new Time Machine that incorporated all the new technology, and gave Calvin everything he needed to fulfill this mission, inanimate objects were the first things to experience time travel.

TIME JACK   JOHN WHITFIELD

A ballpoint pen was the very first object to be placed in the Time Machine, and sent it to the ERB Black Hole in the Andromeda Galaxy at a velocity a thousand times faster than the speed of light. After the energy passed through a selected Wormhole channel, the energy was hurled back to Earth to a time zone about two hundred years into the future. As the energy landed on the planet earth, it was reconstructed back to its original form. The same procedure applied to backward time travel into the past. Instead of using a Wormhole as the transport medium, Cosmic Strings (long, dense, thin objects believed to have coalesced out of the universe's very earliest days) were utilized. As a result, the pen, in the form of super-compressed energy, was fired at the two Cosmic Strings located in the center of our Galaxy, the Milky Way. Traveling at the speed of 93 million miles per second, the energy flew pass the parallel Strings, which in turn hurled the energy back to a time zone in the Earth's past. When the pen was brought back to the lab, it underwent various Carbon 14 tests and the microscopic dirt particles attached to the pen, confirmed the pen made contact with the Earth around the year 1005 AD as indicated by the Time Machine. Further tests confirmed the pen's molecular structure was brought back without a single flaw.

After a dozen successful experiments (transporting inanimate, inorganic objects), Calvin and his team moved on to inanimate, organic objects such as fruits, plants, and organs from animals. There were a few setbacks because some of the objects were returning with flaws in their molecular structure, believed to have occurred during the reconstruction process. On the surface the objects appeared to be in perfect condition, but upon microscopic analysis, the flaws were detected. The objects that came back without any problems were put under meticulous scrutiny and Calvin was baffled for quite some time. Finally, when Calvin took action on Eric's suggestion to increase the energy in the distributor, the defect was instantly rectified. During that experiment, a sedated dog was transported to China in the year 313 BC and returned moments later. After a barrage of tests was performed, it was determined the dog's physical integrity was in order. When the dog was awakened, and began happily licking Calvin's face, the Timetron team cheered victoriously.

But the achievement that Calvin could call his own was the time dial which allowed him to pen-down time zones by manipulating the locations and angles in which the energy passed the coupled Cosmic Strings or entered a Wormhole. For example, the coupled Cosmic Strings utilized by Timetron covered a distance of 5 million miles, which comprised twenty thousand years of backward time travel. If the energy was directed at the top section of the Cosmic Strings, the energy (or time traveler) would be transported back twenty thousand years, but if it was aimed at the bottom section, the subject would be transported back only a couple of days. The meticulous aligning of the Time Machine enabled Calvin to manipulate transportation to time zones with near perfect precision.

Another achievement Calvin took pride in was his indispensable contribution to the development of the reverse system. This component in the Time Machine initially had significant defects, but Calvin added onto this system by creating the Micron watch, a device that activated the reverse process when the subject pressed the control switch on the watch. The Micron watch encapsulated the subject and anything he or she touched inside a Gallium Phosphide field. Once the return coordinates were activated, everything within this field was converted to super-compressed energy and taken through the return process.

Calvin also created a primer chemical that was designed to offset the violent and deadly effects of the deconstruction and reconstruction processes. Many insects and mice that traveled through time without first being chemically primed had died instantly from the trauma caused by the violent demolecularization process. With the use of a Gallium

Phosphide Zirconium compound that was injected intravenously, living subjects' atoms were smoothly deconstructed and reconstructed. This compound also ensured that the time traveler's body was perpetually in synch with the Time Machine.

But, today, Calvin's excitement was at its ultimate level because they were at the final stage before they would go public. Blinky was going to be the first living organism with monitoring equipment to travel through time, and if everything went well, they would be able to prove conclusively that time travel was not only safe, but it could also be monitored with audio and visual devices.

"That'll just about do it." Demetrius said as he completed the final inspection of the replacement.

Calvin was instantly pulled out of his energizing reverie. "Let's get Blinky dressed."

As Calvin placed the Micron watch on Blinky's wrist, the monkey squabbled happily. "You like this, huh, Blinky?"

"ARRAARR! ARRAARR!" Blinky responded.

When the watch was fastened, Blinky began toying with it, apparently trying to figure out how Calvin placed it on his wrist. Since there was no visible latch like the other watches he'd wore before, Blinky was baffled by the fact.

This particular Micron watch was manufactured without a control switch in order to prevent Blinky from tinkering with the experiment.

"Let's get that backpack over here," Calvin said to Tina. The Gallium backpack was equipped with a variety of monitoring equipment that would record and take samples of the time zone Blinky would travel to. The omni-directional camera and microphone would record everything in their vicinity, while the aerometeorograph would record temperature, atmospheric pressure, humidity, and the weight and density of the air and the gases present.

Calvin and Eric put the backpack on Blinky while Diana approached with a hypodermic syringe containing the primer solution. She belatedly tried to conceal the syringe from Blinky by placing it behind her.

"AAAAAHHH!" Blinky shrieked wildly, grabbing hold of Calvin's arm in terror. "AAAAAHHH!"

Calvin gave Diana a daggered-eyed stare, and then spoke comfortingly to Blinky. "Relax, no one's going to hurt you, Blinky." He massaged Blinky's hairy neck as his voice became more soothing. "You won't even feel a thing. And if you behave yourself, we got some real nice treats for you when you get back."

Blinky was determined not to get stuck with the syringe and began thrashing as Diana eased closer. Blinky kept his eyes locked firmly on Diana.

As she drew closer, Blinky moved away and got behind Calvin, squawking loudly while waving his hairy hands at her.

Calvin gave Diana an expression that told her to stop approaching. He was glad he had a back-up plan in place. Calvin gave Demetrius a covert nod.

Demetrius inconspicuously picked up the syringe from the nearby tray.

As Blinky was watching Diana's every move, Calvin whispered in Blinky's ear to relax and distract him.

Blinky was so preoccupied watching Diana he didn't feel a thing when Demetrius injected him as fast as a bird flaps its wings.

Without having to be told, everyone took their places.

Calvin grabbed Blinky's hand, escorting him to the Time Machine, while the others entered the control station, activating a spectrum of switches. Demetrius took a seat behind the mainframe computer and turned on the preliminary power source. The humming sound came to life.

24

Calvin opened the door of the Time Machine. The pressurized value made a "sssssss" sound and a small cloud of smoke swirled from the Time Machine. Calvin kneeled and spoke softly to Blinky. "You gonna make us proud of you, Blinky. In about another half hour, you're gonna be the most famous monkey in the world, my man." He tickled Blinky's stomach. "When you get back we got a surprise for you. You with me, big guy."

"AAAHHHH!" Blinky started jumping up and down happily. "AAAHHHH!"

Calvin gave Blinky a huge hug and then ushered him inside the machine. He bolted the door. As he headed for the control station, Calvin turned and gave Blinky a wave.

Calvin entered the station, instantly barking off commands. "Activate the Gallium Phosphide Crystal." When Calvin saw the universal monitor indicate his instruction was obeyed, he continued. "Activate transport components."

The mild hum now transformed into an ear torturous streak as sparks started jumping enthusiastically from the base of the Time Machine.

Calvin saw Blinky was jumping up and down excitedly. He knew Blinky was not acting excited because he was afraid; he could not hear the horrifying noise since the Time Machine was soundproof. Calvin turned and looked into the eyes of each of his crew, seconds from giving the final command to jettison Blinky to Rome in the year 25 AD at the height of the Roman Empire. Everyone stared back, anxiously waiting with edgy expressions. Calvin looked at his watch. It was 4:07 p.m. He drew a deep breath and said, "On the count of three. One ... Two ... Three!"

There was a huge flash!

Everyone squinted their eyes in response to the brilliant light rays, despite the protective visors they wore.

The bright flash remained at an intense level for several grueling seconds and slowly subsided.

When the light receded completely, Calvin saw the Time Machine was empty. "Yes!" He mumbled joyfully.

There was a universal mutter of tight-lipped cheers.

"Activate all monitors," Calvin said when he realized there was no picture on the monitor directly in front of him.

"Everything's activated." Demetrius said.

Calvin looked at the other near-by monitors and saw there was nothing coming from any one of them. His heart tumbled from his chest cavity and landed at the base of his stomach. He quickly told himself not to jump to conclusions. Don't panic. "Are you sure they're activated?" He said calmly, surprising himself at how composed the words flowed from his mouth.

"Come see for yourself," Eric said, standing behind Demetrius, looking over his shoulder at the main monitor.

Calvin eased over to the main console. Upon arrival, his eyes scanned over each and every dial with lightning speed, hoping one of the switches was not placed at its correct coordinate. As the silence gripped the room, Calvin gritted his teeth and struggled to maintain his professionalism.

"Do you think we should pull him back?" Diana said.

"No," Calvin did not want any hastily and possibly reckless reactions. "Let's do a complete troubleshooting analysis." He moved back to the location he was standing moments earlier while the others began checking all dials. "I want no stone unturned and if that doesn't--"

"We have something!" Demetrius said excellently.

Calvin bolted back to the console. When he saw a very fuzzy imagine trying to come to surface on the screen, and then faintly heard Blinky's squawking sounds, he almost unleashed a victorious cheer. The way Blinky was squawking instantly told him something was wrong.

26

Blinky sounded as if he was in pain or in trouble. He even sounded like he was fleeing.

"Something's wrong, Calvin!" Tina said with terror in her voice.

"He's in trouble!" Eric screeched.

"Pull him in!" Calvin shouted. "Hurry! Pull him in!"

Demetrius's hand slammed down on the emergency return lever and the humming came to life with a vengeance. The lab began to shake and the sudden explosive flash appeared much brighter this time.

Calvin raced toward the Time Machine, not waiting for the energy surge to whine down. He slammed through the control station's door with Diana, Eric and Tina dead on his heels. Calvin's pace turned into a panic drenched run when he saw the machine looked empty. When Calvin reached the Time Machine and saw Blinky lying on the floor, he frantically unlocked the door and flung it open. Calvin turned and shouted. "Get a stretcher!"

Calvin kneeled and saw blood oozing from a series of injuries. Most of them were inflicted on Blinky's arms and legs. A tear almost escaped from Calvin's eyes as Blinky moaned in pain. "Hang on, big fella, we're gonna take care of you." He said softly and then noticed something in Blinky's blood-covered hand. It was hair. Calvin needed no other evidence to know Blinky was attacked by a wild beast and had fought whatever it was that attacked him.

As Diana and Tina rushed Blinky to the emergency room on the other side of the lab, Calvin stood staring into the oblivion as his mind started lashing out at him. If only he had pulled Blinky back at the moment he realized they didn't have a visual, he might have prevented this. He sighed in frustration as he headed for his office. Calvin walked pass Eric and saw he was about to say something, but upon detecting his locked jawed expression Eric had wisely changed his mind.

Calvin entered his office and turned on his voice-activated computer with a verbal command. He sat down and sighed as he accumulated his thoughts, developing a plan of action. Before he did anything he had to clear his mind because frustration and anger were his worst enemies when it came time for critical thinking. "Activate visual and audio recorder graphs." He said to the computer.

A picture of the time travel camera, a graph of its structural make-up and all its specifications appeared on the screen. As the graphs of the audio and visual devices appeared on the screen, there was an onslaught of questions jumping around in his head: What the hell is causing these problems with the visual and audio? Why hadn't they obtained a clear view, even though all dials said everything was in order? And what happened to the sound? There was simply no rational reason for any of these malfunctions! Where's all this coming from!?

Calvin leaned back in his chair and said, "Present a complete read-out of all actual and potential defects."

Calvin watched the information popping up on the screen. He could already hear the executive board's distraught response since he had assured them an accredited and documented time travel would be ready by next week. Calvin gritted his teeth when the computer said everything was working fine.

He sighed, struggling to stay calm because this was going to be an all-night situation. His intuition was reminding him these unexplained problems could be foul play, and with this in mind he instructed the computer. "Give me a complete integrity analysis of all visual and audio recorder components." As the stress mounted, so did the realization that this setback was much bigger and more substantial than he thought. It was also self-evident that this mishap was going to cost him some major points.

CHAPTER # 4

The hours flew by as Calvin sat in front of his computer hammering away at finding the solution to the visual and audio problems. He found the defects about an hour ago. The focal-plane shutter inside the camera was adjusted incorrectly and the transducer inside the audio recorder was at the wrong frequency. Once Calvin made the adjustments and ran the assimilation program, he saw the systems were working correctly. Foul play was instantly ruled out. But, when he tried to find out how these maladjustments occurred in the first place, he ran into the present difficulty. After conducting several assimilations, the flaws returned, disappeared and returned again. Calvin was so baffled by the dilemma he decided he wasn't going home until he figured out how to stop the Systems from repeatedly jumping back into the wrong alignments.

Calvin's dogmatic zeal caused him to get brain-locked on fixing the problems. Indeed, his preoccupation with solving this puzzle was so overwhelming he did not realize Tina was standing at the door talking to him.

"Calvin!" Tina shouted this time.

Calvin looked up, irritated. "Yeah? What's up?"

"I wanted to let you know we're leaving. If you haven't noticed, it's one o'clock in the morning." She pointed at the digital clock on the wall just above Calvin's numerous Degrees and Awards.

"I'll be a few more hours. Just make sure you lock up everything. I'll see you guys bright and early in the morning. Let the others know tomorrow's gonna be a rough day."

"Good night, Calvin." Tina disappeared as she closed the door behind her.

Eric was in the passenger seat of Diana's green Subaru parked in front of the lab. Diana was behind the wheel; they were waiting for Tina. The darkness of night had deepened since Eric came out an hour earlier for some fresh air. The moon and the Milky Way overhead glistened as if they had been newly polished. He saw Tina exit the lab, approaching and he opened the door. When Tina slid in the back, Diana pulled off. With the Subaru's headlights providing the only source of light, Diana drove to the main gate and brought the car to a stop. She stuck her ID card out the window so the sensory beams could activate the gate. When the gate opened, she sped through the gate. It took twenty minutes to get to the main highway.

During the ride, the three talked about Blinky, how his injuries were repaired and how he was going to be all right. They all couldn't wait for tomorrow to take another crack at conducting an error free time travel trip.

About forty-five minutes later, Diana pulled up in front of Eric's two family home. As Eric opened the door, Diana said. "See you in the morning, Eric. Make sure you're ready when we get here."

"Good night," Eric closed the door and waved as the car disappeared down the street. When the car was completely out of sight, he headed for his garage and entered. He jumped in his black Mercedes Benz, revved its powerful engine and maneuvered the vehicle onto the street. In an effort to keep his plan as clean and tightly knit as possible, he had told his coworkers his car was in the auto shop undergoing repairs.

As Eric floored the gas pedal, hoping he didn't miss the window of opportunity. It was late so he didn't worry much when he opened the engine. He nervously kept an eye on his mirrors for any signs of highway patrol, since a speed fluctuating between 90 to 100 miles was sure to provoke an unwanted stop. He arrived back at the lab twenty minutes flat and knew he had broken a record in the process. He parked his vehicle inside a thick patch of underbrush about 500 yards from the outer perimeter of the lab. Since there was no traffic in the area, there was no need to conceal the vehicle.

Eric got out the car, retrieved a bag from the trunk and jogged through the underbrush toward the main entrance. The shadows of night were clearly defined as a pale moon waxed across the midnight sky. When Eric arrived, he pulled a pager looking device from his pocket, pointed it at the satellite disk and hit one of the control dials. Then he pulled another gadget from his pocket and saw the screen on the instrument indicated all cameras were looped and the sensory alarms were under his control. The gate opened when he pressed another key on the pager looking device. Eric entered and jogged toward the lab. The smile appeared when he saw Calvin's car. Pulling in deep breaths of air, he got his wind under control before slowly entering the lab.

☼   ☼   ☼   ☼

Calvin's head rose from the computer when he thought he had heard a noise. He held the position for a moment. When he heard nothing, he continued what he was doing.

☼   ☼   ☼   ☼

Eric tiptoed as he set the trap. He took from the tool cabinet a systonic wrench made of gold, platinum and other expensive metals and placed it inside the Time Machine, dead center on the floor. There was no way Calvin was going to walk by and not see this five-thousand-dollar wrench lying on the floor of the Time Machine. Eric was equally certain Calvin was absolutely not going to allow it to remain there either. The tool cabinet was about ten feet from the Time Machine and Eric headed for it. Eric picked up a stool as he approached the cabinet. He opened the door, sat the stool inside, stepped in, took a seat and closed the door until a crack remained. He repositioned the stool, making sure he had a perfect view of the Time Machine.

Calvin nodded sleepily and realized he was losing the fight to keep the inevitable sleep at bay. He struggled to remain fully alert, but the laws of nature were taking control. The four cups of coffee didn't help much. There was a bottle of pure caffeine pills in Tina's desk, and Calvin was tempted to go get himself a few, but he vowed never to result to the use of any form of drugs to remain awake. He let loose a huge eye-watering yawn. He looked at his watch. It was 2:58 am.

Calvin calculated the amount of work he had left before the problems would be solved and realized tomorrow he could complete the repairs within two hours. If he continued under this condition, he knew there was a chance he could overlook something of extreme importance. And with that thought in mind, he decided to call it a night.

As Calvin walked pass the Time Machine, he looked at it with a feeling of tremendous pride flowing freely through his veins. After all these years, he was finally fulfilling his promise in a tangible fashion. He stopped suddenly when he saw the systonic wrench on the floor of the Time Machine. He headed for it, realizing someone had negligently forgot to put it back in the cabinet. As he approached, Calvin suddenly felt odd, almost as if something was wrong. But, the sensation didn't last long because this wasn't the first time one of his subordinates left expensive tools lying around.

Calvin entered the Time Machine, and as he kneeled to pick up the wrench, he heard rapid movement. Just as he turned (he was so startled by the sudden movement, he spun around and went into a karate stance), the Time Machine door slammed shut.

When Calvin saw it was Eric, and he was wearing a wicked grin on his face, his bowels and bladder became weak. Terror gripped him, obstructing his ability to think clearly. He was afraid to even imagine what was about to happen. "What the fuck are you doing, Eric?" Calvin banged on the bulletproof, shockproof and even explosion-proof glass. When he saw Eric wailing with laughter, Calvin fought to contain the murderous rage that erupted inside of him. He quickly realized losing control was not going to help the situation. His eyes were riveted on Eric as he pulled something from his pocket and laid it on one of the mobile tool carts. It was a piece of paper.

Calvin noticed Eric's lips were moving and was talking with a smile. Calvin focused on Eric's lips trying to decipher what he was saying. As Calvin heard his heartbeat booming in his chest, he realized Eric was saying . . . "Have a nice travel?" . . . "Hope you like to be a . . ." Calvin wasn't able to interpret the last part because Eric turned and headed for the control station. A thunderous burst of realization exploded in Calvin's mind. Oh, God no! This can't be happening! This is murder!

"Eric!! You Motherfucker! Don't do this!" Calvin screamed at the top of his lungs, but knew it was a complete waste of time. He pounded on the glass in desperation.

When the barely noticeable humming vibration appeared, Calvin flinched and noticed he was sweating profusely. A million and one horrible things ran rampantly through his mind as he struggled to calm himself down. He didn't want to believe he was about to be turned into super-compressed energy without first being exposed to the primer chemical. Could he make it to wherever Eric was sending him without being chemically primed?! That inner voice told him "hell no!" He had no Micron watch and no monitoring backpack!

Calvin instantly realized he was going to die. The pain inflicted on a subject when traveling time without being primed was so profound the entire brain of a lab mouse had exploded during one of their experiments. This particular incident danced wildly in his head as his whole life flashed before his eyes. His father's face and the promise he made to him screamed with such seething force inside his third eye Calvin almost fell to pieces with tears.

Suddenly, Calvin realized whatever was going to happen was simply beyond his control. Falling apart was not going to alter his predicament. He drew his chest up and held his chin up high. If he were going to die, he'd might as well do it with dignity. The thought of giving Eric the satisfaction of seeing him fall apart helped him pull it completely together. He saw Eric in the control station working diligently with his head bowed.

When Eric looked up, Calvin saw Eric's crooked smile. Calvin's eyes were clouded with fear, hate and rage. In an attempt to torment him, Calvin saw Eric smilingly raise his hand in the air with the index finger in a pointing position and held it there for a moment. With the other hand Eric waved by-by.

With his head still held up high, and a proud, honorable facial expression, Calvin braced himself as he watched Eric's finger descend very slowly. This bastard was squeezing every punishing moment out of this malicious attack on his integrity, Calvin realized. If he was gonna do it, just do it and get it over with, you bastard! Against his will, images danced around in his mind and he wanted to plead with Eric not to do this. There were many faces he would never see again; his daughter, and Ramanda took priority. Then there were those who he had let down because he allowed himself to get trapped like this. His Wife, Cookie, his mother, and his dear old dad flashed cross his consciousness with the ferociousness of a spiraling hurricane. Calvin couldn't hold back the tears.

Eric's hand continued downward.

Calvin wiped the tears from his eyes, swallowed hard and reactivated his dignity stance.

Eric's hand was almost there.

Calvin closed his eyes and held his breath.

SSWWWUUOOOSSHH!!!

There was a brilliant flash when Eric's finger finally made its touchdown.

From Calvin's standpoint, the flash was the brightest light he had ever seen in his life. The explosion felt like it not only shattered his eardrums, but also every cell in his body. He never thought it was conceivably possible to experience the level of pain he felt at the moment of the flash. All in a fraction of a second, just before Calvin plunged into the ultimate darkness, he felt every single cell in his body being ripped apart, while his molecules and atoms were simultaneously compressed into a violent whirlpool of twirling energy. In a vicious fury everything Calvin was made of was sucked away into the transport valve.

When the energy surge subsided, Eric saw the Time Machine was empty. As he exited the control station, on his way to make absolutely certain Calvin was gone, he grabbed his bag and was already visualizing his career and world fame skyrocketing beyond comprehension. He could see his face on every major magazine and newspaper on the planet!

Eric looked inside the Time Machine. Calvin was gone. "Yes!" He muttered victoriously. "Daddy, you low life fuck! If you could only see your son right now, you wouldn't be talkin' that shit!" He was seething with joy.

Eric pulled himself together and began fixing everything to make it look like Calvin conducted a time travel without the aid of the others. He already had the letter with Calvin's signature, which was placed on the tray earlier. The timer connected to the send lever was already in place, which would explain how Calvin could activate the main send lever without any assistance. Now, he had to rig-up the pressure bolt on the Time Machine door.

Eric took a device from his bag about the size of a dictionary and had four electronic suction cups on each of the four legs. He plastered it on the Time Machine, directly over pressure lock bolt and attached the two metal rods to the bolt. With a built-in timer, the device would slam the bolt in place, thus, creating the appearance that Calvin stepped inside the Time Machine, closed the door behind him and the device had activated the pressure lock bolt. It took Eric ten minutes to get everything in order.

Eric stood with his hands on his hips, looking at the Time Machine, unable to quench the urge to continue smiling. Eric laughed. It was a deep throaty chuckle. He couldn't believe how good he felt. With gleeful euphoria circulating through his veins, Eric realized the feeling had a fierce intensity to it. He sighed happily, turned and exited the lab.

CHAPTER # 5

The following morning, Eric, Diana and Tina, as usual, arrived at the lab around 7 o'clock. When they entered Demetrius approached them with a horrified expression. "You guys are not gonna believe what happened."

"What's wrong?" Eric sounded just as shocked as Demetrius.

As Demetrius walked over to a stool about several yards from the Time Machine and took a seat, Diana made eye contact with Eric and gave him that knowing expression.

Tina's heart was thundering in her chest. "What is it, Demetrius?"

"Calvin conducted an unauthorized time travel last night."

With squinted eyes, Tina said. "What are you talking about unauthorized?"

"Calvin got inside the Time Machine and left."

"Oh, my God," Tina said, "But--but how do you know this?"

Demetrius pointed to the letter on the mobile tool cart.

Tina headed for the letter with Diana and Eric in pursuit. She was about to pick it up.

"No!" Demetrius startled Tina. "The board told us not to touch anything. Read it but don't move it or lay a finger on it."

As Eric, Diana and Tina hovered over the letter reading it, Demetrius continued. "I checked the mainframe." He shook his head in disbelief. "He traveled without a Micron watch; he wasn't chemically primed, nor did he have a backpack."

"What the hell was Calvin thinking?" Eric said as a hand went up to his head to signify his distress. "What is he trying to prove with a stunt like this?"

Tina was shaking her head doubtfully. "This doesn't make sense. Calvin would never jeopardize this project and he certainly would not attempt a time travel without the appropriate equipment."

"Well, this letter confirms he made the attempt," Diana said as she sat on a near-by stool. "It's definitely his signature. The letter looks like it came from his computer."

Eric spoke while pacing. "There's no question Calvin did a time travel without our assistance. What we need to do now is find out how we're gonna continue this project without Calvin--"

"Wrong," Demetrius said. "What we need to do first is find out if Calvin is still alive. We gotta go inside the configuration System to find this out. Calvin and the board are the only ones who have the password to get in that System."

Eric stopped pacing. It felt like he was struck by a heatwave. "I thought a subject could not travel without being primed. Over at Continuum-tech no subjects of ours ever survived."

"Yes," Demetrius said. "That is the norm, but here at Timetron there are exceptions."

"Before you and Diana came aboard," Tina said. "There were a few experiments where subjects were not primed and survived both an outgoing and incoming transport."

Eric struggled to keep an unemotional, straight face. This was bad news in every sense of the word. Demetrius's earlier comments twirled inside his mind. Go inside the configuration system? A password that only Calvin and the board possesses? How can they put up with all this secrecy?! Continuum-tech would never allow such practices. It's obvious if you can't trust the people around you, they should not be amongst you in the first place. He guided the discussion to another topic to tame his mounting anxiety. "Did the board say when they'll be here?"

Demetrius looked at his watch. "They should be here any minute." He rose to his feet. "This is gonna be an intense inquiry." He sighed. "I hope they don't terminate the project on account of this mishap."

Ten minutes later, the seven person Executive Board of the Timetron Corporation arrived. The convoy of five limousines and six minivans with an army of bodyguards and lab technicians created the appearance as if the President of the United States of America was inside one of the vehicles. Dressed in sleek business suits, the multiracial board entered and shook the hands of each one of their scientists.

James Simpson, the CEO, a white man with sandy brown hair and noticeably blue eyes was the first to speak, "Where's the letter?" He said to no one in particular.

"It's right over there, sir," Demetrius pointed.

James gave a head nod to one of the lab technicians who took several pictures of the letter from various angles and positions. When he finished, he picked it up and gave it to James, who began reading it.

Meanwhile, the other technicians were inspecting the Time Machine, the timers believed to be set by Calvin and the control station. They were taking photos and examining all the equipment thoroughly.

Eric was trembling inside as the letter was being passed to each executive board member. He hoped and prayed he did not mishandle anything because the way the tech-team was working they were bound to find it. Now he understood why Timetron was leading the way in time travel technology. These people were extraordinarily well organized, which frightened Eric even more when the thought really began to sink in.

After all seven board members read the letter, Keith Wilson, the president, a black man with salt and pepper hair, and slightly overweight, shouted to a technician. "We need a hard copy of the most recent operations?"

The technician hastily went inside the control station and within a minute he returned carrying several documents. He handed it to Keith Wilson.

Robin Choi, the Vice President, a Korean woman with petite features and a perfect English vocabulary said, "I guess we can start our meeting."

The group proceeded down the corridor to the conference room with James in the lead. Following behind James were Sydney Smith, the Executive Director; Mark Phillips, the Operations Manager; Karen Koenigstein, the Special Projects Director; Albert Coppola, the Finance Director, and the other board member. Everyone else followed in the board's footsteps.

The speechless atmosphere was ear shattering as they breezed down the corridor, making a right and then a left turn.

They entered a huge expensive looking conference room that had thick carpeting and a small platform with a long counter that seated seven people; down below were a dozen cushioned chairs. The seven board members took their seats on the platform behind the counter, while Demetrius, Eric, Diana and Tina sat in the seats below, directly across from the board. The image resembled a Congressional Hearing.

James asked a question before anyone was comfortably in their seats. "Did Calvin inform anyone of you of his intentions?"

They all responded no.

After Keith Wilson glanced over the recent operations documents, he passed them to the next board member who did the same. The documents were passed on until the entire board got a brief look at them.

Mark Phillips spoke, "Has anyone noticed if Calvin was experiencing any unusual stress?"

They all indicated Calvin was not under any abnormal stress.

Suddenly, the humming sound appeared. The mainframe computer was turned on and it felt like the building trembled.

Karen Koenigstein spoke, "Do you believe you can function without Calvin?"

They indicated they could.

James said, "This project must continue while our investigation into Calvin's disappearance is proceeding. The last progress report indicated the only problems involved the visual and audio recorders. Although these defects are not catastrophic issues, any human time travel must meet the utmost criteria of safety. Eric, we have decided to put you in charge until Calvin returns."

Eric displayed no outward response, but inwardly he sighed with soothing relief.

James continued. "We'll provide you with a copy of the universal manual which explains in depth your duties and responsibilities as the lead scientist. This matter concerning Calvin is to be dealt with in the strictest of confidentiality."

Albert Coppola added, "In other words, no one is to talk to anyone about anything involving Calvin's disappearance. We will inform his family of what has occurred."

"May I ask a question, please?" Demetrius said.

"Of course, Demetrius," James said.

"With all due respect, we would like to know if Calvin is still alive. The configuration system should be able to tell us if the subject died or lived during the transport."

James said with a straight face. "Yes, Calvin is alive."

Eric felt a flash of terror, but it started to fade some when he realized without a Micron watch Calvin was stuck.

Demetrius continued. "What efforts are being made to bring Calvin back?"

"None whatsoever," Keith Wilson said. "Until all components are functioning without any complications, there will be no human time travel."

"For your edification," Sydney Smith said. "This board believes Calvin may be conducting an experiment on a Backlash component within the Time Machine."

41

"Backlash?" Eric muttered, realizing whatever it was it definitely sounded like something he was not going to enjoy hearing. "What do you mean by Backlash component?"

Demetrius, Tina and Diana all nodded in unison, expressing their ignorance of the Backlash component.

"Well," Robin Choi said, "Calvin placed a component in the Time Machine which he called Backlash. It's basically a safety mechanism for subjects who travel time without a Micron watch or other equipment."

Eric suddenly felt faint.

Mark Phillips continued, "Four months after a faulty time travel, two portals will open about a thousand miles from the transport return landing location, one eastward and the other westward, thus, enabling the subject to return to the time zone in which he originally transported from . . ."

Eric wiped away the tiny beads of sweat that suddenly appeared on his forehead and struggled against the hyperventilating sensation.

As the board explained the Backlash system in further detail, Demetrius saw Eric's nervous response and he wondered why Eric was suddenly becoming very uncomfortable with this particular topic? For the first time a cloud of suspicion loomed over Eric. Nah, impossible! He wouldn't dare try something like that! He couldn't pull it off even in his dreams.

Demetrius's doubt grew further when the mystery behind the Backlash component started working itself into the equation together with the fact Calvin was a very adventurous person. When Demetrius remembered Calvin served in the Mediterranean War as an infirmary Lieutenant and saw plenty of action on the battlefield, he began to realize he was probably misinterpreting Eric's nervousness. Then it dawned on him Calvin was so obsessed with time travel technology he would not hesitate to engage this sort of adventurous experiment.

When all the other circumstances started working on Demetrius's mind, including the letter with Calvin's signature and the two timers that were strategically positioned, all suspicion instantaneously faded until there was no more.

☼   ☼   ☼   ☼

Calvin's whole body felt alien as he lay flat on his back motionlessly, staring up at the rapidly changing night sky. The twilight and the pitch darkness were fleeing the onslaught of the sun. The current hue of the light blue sky was magnificently beautiful and he wondered how this was the first time he noticed the sky could take on such beauty. There were trees all around him.

But despite the pleasing images unfolding before his eyes, Calvin was afraid to budge one single muscle. The pain that rushed through his body moments ago when he awoke from the deep sleep, and tried to move, had brought tears to his eyes. The stream of tears rolled down the side of his temples and into his ears. When he tried to move a second time to confirm what he was experiencing, it felt like a blowtorch was placed upon every cell in his body. This was the clearest warning signal he'd ever received in his life, and it told him in the most explicit language that he'd better not move.

His calculations told him his cells needed time to reconstruct themselves, since there was no primer chemical present in his body. Despite the mind-boggling pain, he was grateful because it indicated he made it through alive and intact without being chemically primed.

The rasping of the crickets and the not too far away hooting of owls in the forest were fading, gradually being replaced by the chirping calls of small birds. As the sun began to dominate the sky, as did his urge to get up dominated his thinking, Calvin started wondering where Eric transported him. Without turning his head, he could tell he was in a forest, some kind of wooded area. On all sides of him there were withered trees with small fresh leaves trying to sprout from their branches. It was almost springtime as it was where he'd come from. At least the Time transport kept him in unison with the seasons. Then the ramifications of what Eric had done to him began to register. An intense anger started to formulate.

SSSHHRRR!!

The sudden noise caused Calvin's heart to flutter. His involuntary flinch brought a blinding sheet of pain, but he noticed he was able to move his legs and wiggle his toes without the infliction of too much pain.

SSSHHRRR!!

The noise was getting closer; he was sure of it.

Calvin's eyes grew wide with terror and his mind started running wild. Images of what happened to Blinky flashed across his mind when he heard a grunting sound, similar to that of a wild animal. The thought of being eaten alive by some wild beast took center stage in his mind. He was on the verge of panicking. The movement and grunts were moving toward him! He was unable to control the burning urge to panic. Turning his head ever so slightly in the direction of the noise, the pain exploded in his neck. He cringed from the seething pain and saw nothing but trees. To his surprise he could still hear the approaching noise.

SSSHHRRR!!--SSHHRRR!!--SSHHRRR!!

Whatever it was had suddenly started running toward him. Its paws sounding like those of a charging horse as it cut through the underbrush.

Calvin drew a deep breath (he instantly decided he'd rather deal with the searing pain than be eaten alive). He clinched his teeth and forced himself into a sitting position.

AAAAHHHH!!

Calvin screamed so loud and so long, it stopped the wild boar dead in its tracks. With two huge fangs protruding from the sides of its mouth, and a set of skin crawling gray colored eyes, the mangy, evil looking pig stood about twenty yards away. It looked over Calvin as if it was seriously reevaluating its ability to commence a successful attack.

Calvin moved again and the explosive scream was even louder. With tears rolling down his face, while breathing like an insane bull, Calvin saw the pig was now more afraid of him than he was of it.

When Calvin got on his hands and knees, then struggled into a standing position while screaming every step of the way, he saw the huge hairy looking pig was stepping backwards, moving away from Calvin. Realizing these screaming episodes had terrified the wild boar, Calvin yelled directly at it.

AAAHHHH!!!

The wild pig suddenly retreated and fled in the direction in which it originally came.

A gallon of sweat dripped from Calvin's body as he stood wobbling. The sound of the fleeing pig was becoming less distinct as the seconds passed. He realized thankfully the pig apparently wasn't hungry or else it would have attacked no matter how afraid it was.

Breathing deeply, Calvin closed his eyes to stop the spinning sensation. Suddenly, he felt himself being pulled in two different directions; he wanted to lie back down, but also wanted to remain standing. The pain turned him into a confused wreck. After contemplating the situation for a moment, he decided to remain standing because the thought of going through that level of pain all over again was simply too terrifying to imagine.

About five minutes later, Calvin sensed the pain was subsiding or maybe his body was beginning to adapt. Whatever the reason for the disappearance of his suffering, it felt wonderful. He continued breathing deeply and before he knew it, he was moving various parts of his body without the thunderous flash of agonizing distress. Although his vision was still blurred, and that drunken sensation was still present, at least the main problem was over and done with, and that, without question, was the horrifying pain.

For the first time he took a hard look at his surroundings. He was definitely in a wooded area. As Calvin took a few baby steps, he almost stumbled. Slowly limping over to a tree, he held on to it when he arrived. He turned, propped his back on the tree and just stood there looking around. The sun was now rising on his right and that's where he would be headed, east. Then, something shiny on the ground caught his attention. It was not too far from where he laid moments ago. It was the Systonic wrench Eric used to bait him inside the Time Machine.

Calvin waited about twenty minutes and walked over to the wrench. He noticed he was no longer stumbling, nor was he disoriented. After picking up the wrench and placing it in his front pants pocket, Calvin realized he was almost back to a normal state of being. He decided to get moving and started walking through the forest. The blood circulating through his body pulsated with excessive force. The fresh smells of the vegetation were all around him. Even the air smelt unusually clean and refreshing. Thoughts of the Backlash component surfaced, but other issues demanded it be placed at the back of the line. His stomach was growling and he was thirsty. These were known side effects of the molecularization process; nutrients and water were leeched from the body during the reconstruction process. Also, a nagging question was demanding to be answered: Where was he?

He needed to see a person, a vehicle, a house, anything that would give him an idea whether he was in the past or future. Every so often the thousand miles he had to travel within four months in order to get back home crossed his mind. But after his subconscious reminded him, once again, that the Backlash issue was worthless without first knowing exactly where he was, what vehicles were available and what type of obstacles may get in his way, the issue was repeatedly put on the back-burner. Dameeka and Ramanda appeared in his thoughts and numerous dreams started bursting in thin air. He realized he was going to be late for a whole lot of dinners, but he knew that wouldn't be anything unusual.

A half hour later, Calvin came upon a huge open field and about thirty yards in front of him was a huge patch of tall grass about six feet high, a few inches taller than him. Calvin looked both ways and the grass seemed to reach out into the horizon as far as the eye could see. Then, suddenly, on his right, far off on the horizon about a mile away, he saw something moving slowly in a westward direction. It was a horse-drawn wagon and seconds later it disappeared into the forest. Horses and wagons were certainly a thing of the past. He was somewhere back in time, no question about it. It was too early to tell whether or not this was good or bad, he thought as he re-entered the forest and headed in the direction he saw the wagon.

About twenty-five minutes later, he arrived at what looked like a frequently used dirt road. He looked down the road westerly, but the horse and wagon was long gone. Calvin closely examined the tracks in the dirt; the horse hooves and wagon tracks were as vivid as the pain he experienced earlier. On both sides of the road were fields of what looked like wheat or some sort of tall gold colored weeds. He started walking down the dirt road in the opposite direction the wagon was traveling. That wagon came from somewhere, he concluded. Plus, Calvin was bent on heading east.

After ten minutes of hard paced walking, Calvin saw another wagon approaching. He sought cover in the wheat or weeds on the side of the road. The smell of the rich quality dirt was strong. He found a place where the plants were very tall, kneeled on one knee and waited. The need to conduct a further investigation of the time before developing a plan of action was obvious. The clothing Calvin wore was from the late 22nd century and would look totally out of place in a time where horse-drawn wagons were the main source of transportation.

The wagon was pulled by a brown chestnut colored horse Calvin saw as it drew closer. When the wagon eased pass him, his eyes absorbed everything as if his mind was a Polaroid camera. He even heard the white woman expressing her dissatisfaction with a girdle she'd just purchased. She was talking to a white man wearing a straw hat, who kept a firm grip on the reins that constantly tapped across the horse's back. Calvin's mind started working diligent as all the history lessons that all time travelers were required to master began to resurface with profound clarity. By the look of the man and woman, Calvin was able to nail it down to the late 18th century or early to mid-19th century, somewhere in the southern region of the United States. The heavy southern drawl in the woman's speech was without question a unique attribute of the southern region of the United States, which enabled him to rule out any other English speaking countries. Now, he needed to nail down an exact date and location.

As he got back on the road, heading in the direction the wagon came from, Calvin started scooping up dirty and smearing it on his clothing in an attempt to make them look partially with the time. It didn't take long to figure out this was a waste of time because the dirt would not stick to the advance dirt-proof fabric. He took off his jacket and shirt because they were simply too advanced for the time when compared to the outfits wore by the people on the wagon. He discarded the clothing and continued onward.

About an hour later, the wheat fields on the sides of the road faded into small trees and thick underbrush. Calvin maintained his hard-pressed stroll. Fifteen minutes later, he smelled the distinct odor of salt water in the air. Apparently an ocean was up ahead; obviously it was the Atlantic or a river connected to it.

Oh no! Calvin muttered because that meant he'd been moving in the wrong direction! The Backlash portals would open a thousand miles from the landing location, which meant the eastern portal would open in the Atlantic. The thought of turning around and heading west was strong, but the hunger pains in his stomach and the devastating need for water told him it was too late to turn back now. There had to be a store somewhere up ahead in light of the nagging woman's comment about the girdle she'd bought, he concluded.

Suddenly, after a slight northerly turn in the road, Calvin saw what looked like a small town up ahead. As he got closer, he saw it was definitely a town and it wasn't all that small after all. There were numerous wooden buildings scattered all over the area. About a couple miles beyond the town, Calvin saw the huge body of water. Maybe it was the Atlantic Ocean, he surmised. The vague image of huge wooden ships could be seen with a struggle. People, both white and black were moving about the dirt-covered streets. Horse and mule-drawn wagons moved about in full force. When Calvin saw black men carrying huge wooden crates and baskets, dressed in rags and were barefooted, while following behind white men dressed in suits, he realized this was a time in American History when blacks were slaves. The inhuman nature of such a brutal and savage system was so unbelievable to Calvin it never crossed his mind when he made his earlier calculation regarding his current whereabouts. This new revelation changed the situation in a significant fashion, he suddenly realized, because this circumstance was definitely going to be a major obstacle. A nervous anxiety gripped him and would not let up.

As he stood near a huge Sycamore tree, his mind pulling up information he had studied about this time era, Calvin suddenly realized there were free black people during this time in America. In fact, there were black slave owners and they were all over the region, in almost every single one of the 13 colonies. At least that's what the history books

49

indicated. Overhead, the sun was now dancing with blistering force and Calvin wondered why it was so unusually hot for a spring day? The heat was beaming down upon Calvin's head and he felt himself becoming weak with hunger and severe thirst. With this knowledge of free blacks tumbling in the back of his mind, he headed for the town with the intention of presenting himself as a free black man.

The minute he entered the town, the people began watching him with the most perplexed expressions. It was as if they had literally seen a space creature. Both blacks and whites looked on with mouths hung open and eyes wide with mesmerizing confusion. What is attracting all this unwarranted attention? Calvin hastily began looking at his clothing, his pants, and his tee shirt. When his eyes landed on his black soft sole shoes, he wondered if they were the root of this attention. There was nothing he could do to change what he was wearing since taking off his shoes was definitely out of the question, so he shrugged his shoulders and continued onward.

Calvin saw chickens, roosters and even pigs running around freely. He knew if the people of this town were aware of how unhealthy it was to keep these sorts of animals in close proximity to their living environment, they would alter the way they were doing things. Mingled with the foul odor of human and animal waste, the delectable smell of cooked food was heavy in the air. Even though he didn't eat meat, the aroma of the burning animal flesh hovering on the cushions of air smelled delicious. In light of these current unfortunate circumstances, Calvin realized he was more than likely going to be forced to start back eating meat.

As he carefully scanned his surroundings, Calvin saw a black man dressed in rags pumping a lever on a water pump, filling a wooden bucket. Calvin almost ran for the water. He saw his abrupt movement frightened the onlookers. With crusty lips, Calvin said to the black man, who was so black, he looked blue. "May I please have a drink?"

The black man nodded, picked up the bucket and stepped away from the pump.

Calvin kneeled, put his mouth under the faucet and began to pump the lever. The water tasted so good. It soothed his stomach so beautifully, he was making grunting sounds of pleasure as he sucked and slurped the water. He put his whole head under the water, allowing it to flow all over his face. When he finished, he pulled away and released a huge burp. "Excuse me." He wiped the water from his face and noticed a small crowd had formulated. The gossiping whispers and pointing fingers were becoming more intense by seconds. He felt like he was on a stage and his audience was waiting for the next scene.

Calvin made eye contact with some of the people. Most of the women were wearing bonnets while the men wore hats (some made of straw, others made of felt). Calvin didn't want to appear as if he didn't know what he was doing so he casually headed for the store that had a decrepit sign above the entrance that said, "Wally's General Store." He politely said, "Excuse me" and "Pardon me" to the people as he eased pass and noticed they seemed even more shocked when he spoke.

Calvin entered the store and the bell attached to the door came to life.

"May I help you?" A white man, apparently the storeowner, drawled from behind the wooden counter. When Wally got a good look at Calvin, his eyes explicitly broadcast his deep-rooted bewilderment.

"Do you have a calendar on hand?" Calvin said politely.

The storeowner pointed suspiciously at the wall behind Calvin on the right hand side.

Calvin turned and headed for the bulletin board. It was 1831. Tuesday, April 3rd. Upon further observation of the materials posted on the board, he saw a letter from a community religious group that said "We the people of Savannah, Georgia." Once he saw this he read no further. Calvin's mind raced as he calculated the circumstances. He had until August to get to the Backlash. What State was a thousand miles from Savannah, Georgia? He was going to need some time to make that determination, but he was absolutely certain he would be heading west.

As Calvin was mapping out a crude plan of action inside his head, the doorbell jingled. When Calvin turned his head, he saw three white men had entered. Two of them were heavily bearded and all three of them were staring at Calvin with rocks in their jaws. They reeked of danger and even smelled terrible, as if they hadn't bathed in months, or maybe even years.

The three men nonchalantly approached Calvin and surrounded him, while inspecting his clothing and footwear with jealous, hateful smirks.

"Where's yous from, boy?" The stocky and heavyset man with a reddish-brown beard said.

Calvin was momentarily stumped; he never thought of what he would say if he was asked where he was from. He was also knocked off balance by the smell of the man's breath. By the stench, he could tell there was an evil spirit roaming around inside this man's body. "I'm from New York."

"So yous one 'em free niggers, huh?" The tall, clean shaved man said, envying the apparent intelligence resonating from Calvin's vocabulary.

"Yes," Calvin responded with a questioning look. The use of the word nigger deeply irritated him, but he struggled not to show it. "Yes, I am."

"Let us sees yo' papers, boy." The black bearded man with gray eyes and filthy clothing said, moving closer to Calvin as if to intimidate him.

"Ah," Calvin was truly stumped now. He wanted to step away from the foul smelling black bearded white man, but the clean shaved one was standing behind him. "I--I lost them during my trip here to Georgia and--"

"What's that in yo' pocket, nigger!?" The clean shaved man said with countrified excitement. "This nigger here is carrying a weapon!"

Calvin cursed himself for failing to get rid of the wrench. "Ah, it's not a weapon." He was about to reach for it. "This is only a--"

"Don't you dare!" The red bearded man said through gritted teeth. "Put yo' hands where I can see 'em!" He shouted, reached in his pants pocket and retrieved a rope, which caused the others to become even more excited. "You knows niggers ain't 'posed to carry weapons."

The clean shaved man reached inside Calvin's pocket and confiscated the wrench.

"It's not a weapon, it's a--"

BLAM!

The red bearded man slapped Calvin almost into a spin. "Don't you sass me, boy!"

BABLAM!

Calvin impulsively slapped him back even harder. The impact flung red beard into a full spin as his hand instantly shoot up to his face and clamped on his left cheek. His eyes bulged with a mixture of astonishment and genuine pain.

The other two white men were immobilized with shock. Their eyes and gestures were overflowed with sheer disbelief.

The clean shaved man took a swing at Calvin, but he stumbled awkwardly when Calvin ducked it. "Hold still, nigger!"

The black bearded man tried to tackle Calvin, but Calvin sidestepped the clumsy maneuver, causing the man to crash into a shelf containing boxes of lime and other products.

Before Calvin was able to spin around to see what happened to red beard, he felt a blow to the side of his head. It staggered him. Before Calvin recuperated from the blow, another punch landed on the back of his head. Calvin stumbled forward, but quickly regained his footing. He turned, ran and flying kicked the clean shaven white man.

BRRAASSHH!!!

The clean-shaven man crashed through the glass window. When he landed outside, he was partially unconscious. The crowd outside was awestruck.

"Stop right there, nigger!" Wally, the storeowner, shouted. He was aiming a rusty smoothbore musket at Calvin. "Don't make me say it again, boy!"

Calvin slowly and nervously raised his hands. In a flash, and before he knew what hit him, the two white men grabbed him and his hands were tied behind his back with a rope. The bad breath red bearded man started grandstanding in front of Calvin and then spit in his face. Calvin reflectively kicked him square in the testicles.

AAAHHHAA!!

Red beard screamed explosively as he crumbled to the ground.

Calvin was about to kick him again, but he received a heavy blow to the back of the neck and a firm knee to the gut, which landed him to the floor. The second he hit the floor the mass stomping boots rained upon him, most of them to the head. Calvin heard red beard grimacing as he rose to his feet. After receiving a few dozen stomps and kicks to the head and other parts of his exposed body, Calvin felt himself being snatched to his feet. Before he gained his footing, he was whisked out of the store. He was bleeding from a series of cuts and bruises on his face and was sporting a black eye. His legs were weak and weary from the pain of the beating.

As he was escorted pass the terrified onlookers, the red bearded man whispered in Calvin's ear. "If'en you don't know, boy, it's a crime to strike white folks in Georgia, punishable by death or life-time servitude." His voice suddenly rose ten notches. "'Course you ain't gotta worry about the humiliation of life-time servitude 'cause I'm gone kill you, nigger!"

Calvin wanted to puke from the wretched rotten tooth odor oozing from red beard's mouth, but when those comments about killing him registered, Calvin felt a fright that almost brought tears to his eyes.

CHAPTER # 6

Eric popped the antacid pill in his mouth. He sat on Diana's sofa in a state of complete turmoil. Without touching the glass of water sitting on the coffee table in front of him, Eric dry swallowed the pill.

Diana looked at Eric and shook her head. She was sitting in the armchair, dressed in a purple sweat suit.

Eric sighed. "Four months is not a very long time." He shook his head. "We gotta take another crack at that Backlash System. There's gotta be a way to--"

"We examined every component," Diana picked up the glass of wine, took a sip and held onto the glass. "All variations were considered. We have to face reality. If we remove the energy frequency on that Black Body energy Oscillator, the Gallium Phosphide Crystal is gone."

Eric gritted his teeth because he did not want to be reminded of the fact he was boxed in. "I disagree. That packet of energy Calvin labeled BKFR has several antiparticles within it. If we rearrange the energy--I'm not talking about extracting it--I think it'll throw off the Backlash enough to prevent Calvin from transporting back here."

Diana was growing weary and angry with Eric's off the wall and completely reckless theories. "Listen, Eric, I understand the life threatening nature of this situation. And it's clear if Calvin returns and reveals what you have done to him, you'll be charged and likely convicted of attempt murder, among many other crimes. I understand these disturbing prospects, which is why I am here, Eric. But please don't let your eagerness obstruct or interfere with your professional, scientific judgment. Simply put, if you touch any component of that Backlash it will destroy the Crystal. Calvin manufactured the system with full intentions of preventing anyone from altering any aspect of the System." She sat her glass on the table. "Do you really think that flashing warning signal, which explicitly says any attempt to alter the coordinates will result in a full System failure is a joke?"

There was a long silent pause.

Eric laid his head back on the sofa, staring at the ceiling. He began massaging his temples with the tips of his fingers to relieve the tension. He didn't want to admit it, and was hoping his devil's advocate game would miraculously uncover a way to re-adjust or reprogram the Backlash System. But that was not going to be the case, he realized as reality set-in. In actuality, he knew the Backlash System was untouchable the moment he looked at the entire System's Configuration. That damn Calvin!

Eric sprung to his feet and began pacing when that overwhelming feeling of being boxed in started growing. It felt like he was in a coffin, buried alive and all his air was gradually disappearing. At these moments, he always remembered the wrong things. Eric thought of his brother, Milton, who was an astronaut currently on an outer space mission building a space station just beyond Pluto. The rage was mounting. Then, his sister, Arlene, came into the equation; her award-winning work helped to create the first computerized robot that could practically think and respond as if it possessed human cognitive attributes and emotions was chipping away at his aspirations. He was boiling with fury by the time his father's degrading statement indicating he was "the dumb one in the family" resurfaced.

Diana saw Eric was locked in a personal thought and was apprehensive about disrupting it. But she hated to see him in pain. "As long as we keep looking there is a chance we might find something."

"Calvin can't return here. We can't let that happen!" Eric punched the palm of his hand, startling Diana. "When do you think the board is gonna approve an accredited time travel?"

"Once the visual and audio components are working correctly, I would say a trip will occur within a couple of months."

Eric sat back down. He didn't know why in the hell he didn't just get rid of Calvin the good old fashion way; hire a hit man. Directly on the heels of this mental discourse, Eric's whole thought process stopped abruptly. A sudden look appeared on his face that said he found the answer to what he was searching for.

"What is it?" Diana asked.

Eric bowed his head and remained silent for a moment. Then, suddenly, his head shot back up and he said excitedly, "We know Calvin can't return back here, right? . . . We know where Calvin was transported . . . We also know how he looks and have pictures of him . . . We know where the Backlash will open and how much time he has to get there . . . We know--"

"Alright, alright," Diana hated these little mind teasing games. "We know a lot of things. Cut to the chase."

Eric held the thought for another moment, realizing it could actually work. When he saw Diana getting angry, he said. "We're gonna send a hit man back into time to kill Calvin."

Diana shook her head pitifully. "Are you out of your fucking mind, Eric? This is as crazy as altering the Backlash coordinates. Tell me how are you going to transport a hit man to the past without Demetrius or Tina finding out? If they catch wind of what you're doing, they will go straight to the board and I wouldn't blame them because heads will roll if the board finds out about any unauthorized time travels."

With a smile, Eric laid back comfortably on the sofa and kicked his feet up on the coffee table. The more he thought about it, the more he realized this plan could work. "I want to ask you one thing and I think it will answer, or better yet, dispel your pessimism. . . What would happen if the atomic spectra was increased until the photons in the Antigravity Infusion System were about to experience a gravitational collapse, but just before that happens, the antiparticles are put in harmonic motion and simultaneously camouflaged with a series of electromagnetic fields

58

while a tiny, discrete amount of Black Body radiation is emitted around the Gallium Phosphide Crystal until all monitors indicate all readings are at stable configurations?"

Diana worked the equation over in her mind. This time she nodded her head. When she made eye contact with Eric and saw that twisted smile of his, she said, "Smile all you want, but I charge time and a half for all my overtime efforts."

SWAAP!!

The whip seared across Calvin's bare back so many times he had plunged into unconsciousness twenty lashes ago.

Before the lashing began, Calvin was stripped naked, both arms wrapped around a tree as if he was hugging it and his wrists were firmly tied with a rope. Calvin decided he was not going to scream and holler. He couldn't give these redneck racists the satisfaction. But the moment the whip touched his back, he instantly realized holding back a yell would eventually become impossible. By the seventh lash, Calvin was hollering, screaming and cursing while Eric's face flashed across his mind each time his back exploded with an indescribable pain. If he got the chance, he would kill Eric for this!

SWAAP! . . .

Calvin's lifeless body flinched explosively with every whip lash as he laid slumped against the tree.

The community judge had "sentenced" Calvin to receive fifty lashes and be placed on the audition block to be sold to the highest bidder. Fortunately for Calvin, Judge Stratford didn't believe in "destroying property" for the sole purpose of satisfying some poor white trash's inclination for revenge. According to Judge Stratford, "this town needed all the money it could get," and killing a "healthy nigger with a good strong back is an economic sin." But in order to quench the three men's so-called "thirst for justice", the Judge gave them the opportunity to enforce the fifty lashes. Unfortunately for Calvin, fifty lashes turned into whatever the three thought was appropriate, since they couldn't count very well. They based the number of lashes on how tired their arms became and how loud Calvin screamed.

SWAAP! . . . SWAAP!

"Hold it!" The black beard man said to the red beard man who was about to bring the whip down again. "I think we oughta make sho' we ain't kill this nigger. He ain't holler in quite a while."

Red beard was breathing hard and sweating profusely. He was about to panic when he realized Calvin looked like he was dead. The judge said Calvin was to be sold, not killed. "Go throw some water on him. This nigger can't fool me. He's playin' possum."

When the bucket of water struck Calvin in the face, he was catapulted from a world of triple darkness and into one of fiery pain. He snatched air into his lungs as if he was coming up for oxygen after almost drowning. Instantly, it all came back to him. He was being whipped and had passed out. His back was scorching with agony, and his mind was cloudy with great hopelessness. Whoever said pain was a sensation people could develop a desensitization to, was a goddamn liar! Calvin thought as he struggled to pull air into his pain-stricken body. There was not a drop of energy left in his body.

When the rope was cut, Calvin collapsed to the ground as if he was a sack of lifeless potatoes. Lying on his stomach, Calvin closed his eyes because the unconsciousness was grabbing hold of him again. He fought to stay awake, but the 61 gapping whip wounds on his back were sapping the precious elements of life from his body. As blood oozed from the whip wounds, so did his ability to remain conscious. He fell to sleep within seconds of hitting the ground.

☼   ☼   ☼   ☼

Demetrius pulled his red Corvette up in front of Calvin's home and exited the vehicle. He had received a call from Ramanda after the board paid her a visit. She was very upset by Calvin's disappearance and wanted to have a talk with him. Since she insisted the phone wasn't the appropriate vehicle for such a discussion, Demetrius knew she was planning to blow this matter out of context. He hit the doorbell.

The door was opened.

"Come in, Demetrius," Ramanda said, waving him inside the house.

Demetrius entered and went to the living room. When he saw Dameeka sitting in an armchair with a depressed facial expression, he approached and said playfully. "What's the sad eyes all about?"

Dameeka shifted in her seat. "They said there's no guarantee my father will be coming back."

"Your dad is gonna be all right," Demetrius massaged her shoulder. "So don't you go worrying yourself, you hear me?"

Dameeka gave him an insincere nod.

Ramanda gestured for Demetrius to have a seat as she sat on the sofa. "They showed me that letter they claim Calvin wrote. Demetrius, you know I'm very good at reading people's writings. That's not Calvin's letter."

Demetrius sighed because she was right. Ramanda was up to her usual activities. She was his older sister and made no bones about letting it be known who ran the show. She was picky, paranoid, pessimistic and pushy, which was the reason he insisted Calvin go out with her. A strong man needed a strong woman to boost him to greater levels of excellence was the persuading proposition he promoted to Calvin and it apparently worked. This argument had substantial truth to it when coupled with the fact Ramanda would inherently bring out the best in

61

him, since she was absolutely appalled with any form of weakness, especially with regard to the men she chose. "Listen, Ramanda." Demetrius gave Dameeka a glance and then laid his glance on Ramanda. He went back and forth with the glancing eye exchange.

Ramanda saw what Demetrius was trying to hint at. "Dameeka has a right to hear this. Calvin is her father. She's not an infant."

Demetrius shrugged his shoulders and said. "All the evidence at the lab indicates Calvin conducted an unauthorized time travel. Foul play was ruled out. There were timers strategically placed and all the facts point to--"

"I don't care what those facts point to." Ramanda said firmly. "Calvin had some difficulty with that new guy. What's his name, I think it's Eric Sea . . . Sea something."

"Eric Seabright," Demetrius said. "They had some minor disagreements. It was nothing serious. For a person to send a black man back in time to the 1800's there has to be some kind of intense hatred. I didn't see that kind a hatred in their relationship."

"Say what you want," Ramanda said. "But I think Eric is behind Calvin's disappearance. I called you over here because I want you to keep an eye on Eric. I can feel it in my bones. Calvin is in trouble and. . ."

Dameeka looked on with excited eyes. She liked when Ramanda got revved up about an issue because she always let her get involved in the juicy stuff.

Ramanda paused a moment and said, "Calvin may have been obsessed with this time travel stuff, but he was not crazy enough to travel time without the appropriate equipment. Especially when the equipment is sitting right there in his face." She shook her head enthusiastically. "He wouldn't do it and you know it Demetrius."

"That's right," Dameeka added. "My daddy wouldn't do anything to hurt himself."

Demetrius wanted to give them a rude awakening by going off on a tantrum about the Backlash System, but he realized they did point out some valid facts. Plus, Eric was acting very strange lately. Demetrius rose to his feet. "Say no more, sis, I'll do my own little investigation and keep you guys abreast. Is that all?"

"Yes . . . For the moment."

CHAPTER # 7

With a chain serving as a leash around his neck, Calvin was dragged onto a platform where a group of casually dressed white people stood below waiting with a mixture of cheerful and serious expressions. It was a windless, gray and dreary overcast day with forbidding clouds dancing in the sky, blocking out the rays of the sun. The atmosphere fitted Calvin's mood perfectly. Calvin was barefooted, partially starved, and had not brushed his teeth, nor combed his hair since he transported here, 37 days ago. If hell had a look to it, Calvin fitted the description. But his spirit was not broken. In fact, it had become a little stronger and a lot more determined.

As Calvin labored not to make eye contact with the potential buyers, he realized he never thought there would come a day when he could say he knew how it felt to truly hate other human beings. From Calvin's perspective, there were literally no words within the human language to describe the level of degradation and brutality the institution of slavery inflicted on black people. Even the most radical literature he read was either sugarcoating what went on or they were just plain uninformed. Wild animals and household pets were treated far more humane than blacks. There were incalculable hangings, rampant rapes, massive mutilations, limitless whippings, savage assaults, and maniacal murders. One incident that that stunned Calvin beyond comprehension occurred during a public execution when two slave overseers tied a slave's legs and arms to two horses and forced the horses to rip the slave in two. The most disturbing aspect of this incident was the blood-thirsty applauds of the white audience. The complete denial of adequate food, water, clothing and any form of medical treatment was so commonplace, death was lurking everywhere at all times.

"We got top prime niggers!" The auctioneer shouted. "Now on sale to the highest bidder!"

The potential buyers got in single file and began their inspection of Calvin.

Calvin felt the ultimate disrespect when the white people began forcing apart his compressed lips to expose his clenched teeth, and with their bare hands probed him all over; under his armpits, on his chest, arms, back and even his genitals. When a stocky, blond hair man who had a face full of freckles began caressing Calvin's genitals in an excessively perverted fashion with a degenerate smile, Calvin was seconds from breaking his jaw. The thought of undergoing another whipping was the only thing that stopped him.

As the potential buyers left the platform and took their positions below, Calvin saw the freckled face freak had a slave with him who was standing behind him with his head bowed like all blacks were required to do when in the presence of whites.

"Four hundred dollars!" The auctioneer shouted. "Do I hear four hundred dollars!?"

"Four hundred!" A white man in a black suit shouted.

"Can I get five hundred!?" The auctioneer continued. The speed of his speech quadrupled. "Five hundred, five hundred, five hundred!"

"Five hundred!" The perverted freckled face man shouted.

Calvin couldn't believe he was actually praying for the auctioneer to continue and he prayed even harder that someone besides the pervert would win the auction.

"How about six hundred?!" The auctioneer shouted. "This a strong and healthy nigger, with years of service in him. Come on, lemme get six hundred!"

"Six hundred!" The man in the suit shouted.

The bidding continued back and forth between the two until it reached nine hundred. Calvin crossed his fingers when the pervert was hesitant to go any further, after the man in the suit agreed to nine hundred.

65

"Nine hundred fifty!" The auctioneer shouted. "Nine fifty, nine fifty, nine fifty!"

The pervert looked at Calvin with a frustrated expression. Calvin saw he wanted him bad, but didn't have the money. Thank goodness!

"Nine fifty!" The pervert shouted.

Calvin sighed in anger, looking at the man in the suit as if to say "come on, you can do it!" But the man waved his hands at the auctioneer indicating he was not going any further.

"Going once, going twice, sold!"

As Calvin sat in the back of the moving wagon amongst sacks of grain and wooden crates filled with glass bottles, he shook his head in disbelief. The pervert's name was Dick Gilbo? He thought this had to be a cruel joke. His slave, the driver of this double black horse-drawn wagon, was called Virgil. Calvin was so distraught by the situation he found it difficult to think of anything else besides how he was going to dealt with Dick if he made any homosexual advances toward him. The only comfort came when he realized they were traveling west, which drew him closer to his destination. The date was May 10th, which meant he had only 83 more days to get to the Backlash zone. Ever since the day he arrived, Calvin was counting the days as if his life depended on it, and under the circumstances, it obviously did.

During the two-day ride they had made two stops at two plantations, rested throughout the night and in the morning continued onward. The Indians he saw during the trip were a sight for historically oriented eyes. By the way they walked, Calvin saw they really were a very proud and dignified people. Based on his research, Calvin knew these particular Indians in this region of the Country were either Creek or Cherokee.

Calvin realized they had reached their destination when he saw a group of black children running toward the wagon as if they were happy about the arrival. Calvin felt his heart dropped when he saw the children looked worse than skid row derelicts. They were sickly looking and to define their clothing as rags would be an outrageous understatement.

The wagon came to a stop and Calvin pulled his focus from the approaching children and saw a large white house with small shabby shacks, the slave living quarters, beside it. Just beyond was a huge field with over two-dozen slaves plowing, planting seeds, and picking cotton. In the westward direction, Calvin saw there was a huge forest.

"Come on," Virgil said to Calvin as he dismounted the wagon. "Gots to show you round."

Calvin turned and saw Dick had turned around and was watching him with a blank, almost zoned out expression.

"Richard," A white woman with long black hair, wearing a long white dress shouted as she pranced toward the wagon. "We were so worried about you."

Calvin broke away from the staring match and jumped from the wagon. The sores on the soles of his bare-feet reopened again for the hundredth time and he cringed as he followed Virgil toward the shacks. There was no way his feet would ever adapt to such treacherous treatment. The thought of getting a major infection in his feet continually kept him in a state of terror because if such a problem occurred he would likely have to start counting his days. No penicillin, poor diet, contaminated drinking water and no way to keep the wounds clean spelled amputation and eventually death. If he didn't find a way to make himself some footwear, he was planning to demand some shoes.

Virgil playfully ruffled the malnourished children's nappy heads and sent them off.

As Calvin followed Virgil toward the shack, he saw Dick turned around and stared at him with that blank expression just before he entered the mansion with the woman. Calvin wondered if the woman was Dick's wife or girlfriend and whether she knew Dick was fruity?

They walked past the first group of five shacks and stopped at the next group of shacks that looked even worse than the first group. Calvin instantly realized the first group was either a front of some sort or was reserved for slaves who received special treatment, like the house slaves. Suddenly, a foul odor struck Calvin's nose. He turned and saw the pigpen several yards away. There were chickens, roosters and a dog running around freely. Ten paces later, they stopped in front of a shack that had huge holes in the walls that were supposed to be windows.

"This in where yous be sleepin'." Virgil said. "The head oberseer, Massa Harvey, a be here to talks to you. Be careful now, 'cause he's a mighty evil one."

Calvin gave Virgil a head nod and watched him head back to the wagon. Calvin stood with his hands on his hips, closely observing the immediate area. On the far right, he saw an old black man, crawling on his hands and knees, inside what appeared to be a garden. With a head full of pure white hair, the man looked like he was wearing a wig. Calvin saw the frail old man get up with a struggle and began limping slowly toward him. About a minute later, he arrived with a missing tooth smile.

"How's you doin' chile, my name Jake the gardener." The old man patted Calvin on the shoulder. "You our new nigger, huh? What cho name is, chile?"

"My name is Calvin," He tried to sound countrified like everyone else, but realized it sounded fake and ridiculous. He saw the twisted frown on Jake's face.

"What's wrong with cho voice, chile?" Jake moved closer to Calvin as if the act would help him figure out the problem. "You sound funny."

Calvin decided to speak in his usual voice and dialect. "I was trying to fit in. I was trying to change the way I speak, trying to sound like everyone else."

"Oh my God!" Jake was aghast. "Yous one 'em free niggers, ain't yah!? You sound like one of em' up north white mans I seen preachin' at the church house!"

Calvin realized he may have created a problem and started looking around nervously. "Relax, please calm down, Mr. Jake. You gotta promise me you won't tell anyone about this . . . Please."

Jake looked at him suspiciously. "You means ta tell me, Massa Dick don't knows yous a smart nigger who talks like a white man?"

Calvin nodded, still looking around to see if anyone was nearby. "So you'll keep quiet?"

Jake laughed. "Yeah, chile. I's keep quiet. If'en that's one thang ole Jake can do is keep his ole mouth shut." He headed toward the shack. "This yoh cabin?"

"Yes," Calvin said as he followed him.

They were almost at the door when Jake suddenly saw a white man with a black pirate's patch on his left eye, heading toward the garden. He turned quickly and started limping away. "Gots ta go, chile. Talk to ya later." He stopped abruptly and whispered. "What's yoh name?"

"Calvin," He whispered back and watched Jake scurry away. Jake started talking to the white man and Calvin turned, pushed the door open and entered. The place was empty except for what he guessed was supposed to be a mattress. It was spread out on the dirt floor in the far corner. The place reeked of spoiling fruits and vegetable, which caused Calvin to wonder what was the source of the odor. He hoped it wasn't the mattress. Upon inspection, he discovered it was. Inside the mattress were corn silk, leaves, and a variety of other unidentifiable rubbish.

THUMP!

The hut door slammed open.

69

Calvin turned in a flinching fashion and saw the medium built white man with the pirate's patch covering one eye. He noticed the man looked much more threatening at close range.

"So yous our new nigger, huh?" James Harvey said, and then spit a glob of brown chewing tobacco on the floor. "I have one rule here. You work, you work and you work some mo'. If'en you trys to escape, I don't give lashes when we catches you. I cuts off body parts. If'en you do what you 'posed to do 'round here, you'll be fine. Yah hear me?"

Calvin nodded, while trying to imitate the way blacks acted around white people; eyes lowered, head bowed, accompanied with nervous gestures. He just hoped they knew what a deaf-mute was because that's what he officially became after that exchange with Jake.

"Let's go!" Harvey said.

Calvin followed him out the door, foot shuffling along the way. He felt a stabbing pain in his chest as he followed Harvey toward the huge field. His pride was shattered. He had to repeatedly tell himself over and over again, if he intended to survive long enough to escape he would have to continue these little degrading games. But the more he had to shuck and jive, shuffle and bojangle, and pretended to be weak and afraid, the more he was convinced he was going to kill Eric for this. With the thought that Eric might become the first time traveler working inside his head, he felt something indescribable growing inside of him. However, he welcomed all these abject thoughts because they provided an intense motivation that made him believe he could literally move a mountain.

☼ ☼ ☼ ☼

Tilling the field and planting seeds was a lot harder than it looked, Calvin discovered after Harvey assigned him to be a "field nigger." It was not only back breaking work, but was finger blistering and muscle

70

draining. The beaming sun only magnified the misery twenty folds. A minute felt like an hour, an hour felt like a day and he really did not want to know what a week or a month of this torture felt like. His whole body felt burnt out as he raised and brought the hoe down into the ground. After spending a lifetime of acquiring all sorts of scientific knowledge and working in a number of supervisory positions, his current behavior (working the field) was so alien to him it felt like he died and was reincarnated; better yet, it was more like a never-ending nightmare.

Calvin saw some of the shirtless slaves had huge gruesome scars on their backs, and wondered did his back look as grotesque as theirs? When Calvin rubbed his fingers across his back, he could feel the coagulated bubble like scar tissue, but he was unable to see the wounds with his own eyes. The scar tissue felt horrible, which meant they probably looked even worse.

Calvin wiped the sweat from his forehead and noticed one of the field slaves started looking around nervously, saw no overseer in the immediately area, stopped working, took a piece of corn meal from his pocket and started eating. This reminded Calvin that he also had a piece of corn meal in his pocket and did the same. Calvin was amazed by the fact that slaves weren't even allowed to take a simple break to eat.

As Calvin ate the stale corn meal, he continued closely examining his surroundings. The forest beyond the plantation attracted his attention and he gazed at it with an excitement circulating through his body. He also had noticed the overseer, Harvey, had two assistants who rode horses and kept muskets and pistols on them at all times. There was a tool shack that Harvey controlled and Calvin saw this was the place where the assistants retrieved the guns. The first chance he got he was going to conduct a thorough investigation of the shack. He figured in a couple days, he could master the rhythm of how the plantation was run, and then he could start preparing for his journey. He'd been carefully counting the days and with little more than two months to get to the portal (he'd finally calculated the location would be in present-day Oklahoma) it was evident there was no time for any foot dragging activities.

Calvin's attention was suddenly pulled from the shack when he noticed movement in his peripheral vision. He turned and saw a little black child on the roof of the huge white house. The child was so agile and expertly coordinated as he jumped from one section to another Calvin initially thought the kid was a monkey in human clothing. Everyone else acted as if he was invisible and nothing was unusual about his behavior. Even the overseers didn't pay him any attention.

Calvin saw the child found a comfortable seat above the second floor window and started eating peaches he had stuffed in his raggedy pants pocket. Calvin smiled. This was something he hadn't done in a very long time and it felt weird when he realized what he was doing.

About a minute later, Calvin saw Dick, the pervert, come out of the mansion and instructed the child to come down. From a distance, Calvin heard Dick say, "Jim Roof, get yoh behind down here right now. I wants to see you." When Calvin saw the child shake his head "no" with a terrified frown, while displaying a mixture of anger and fear, he had almost reached the point of blowing a gasket. This freak ass motherfucker better not be molesting that child?! The kid was no more than ten years old! The rage caused Calvin to unconsciously move toward the house and then suddenly stop abruptly. His conscience told him to do something, but his rational mind told him it would be suicide.

The other field slaves were startled by Calvin's sudden behavior. They were not only deeply confused, but were scared shitless because when one slave messed up, sometimes they all got whipped. They were even more frightened because they could see Calvin was angry at the way Dick was talking to Jim Roof. They all sensed a mass whipping was looming heavily on the horizon and they were on the verge of panicking.

Calvin gritted his teeth when he heard, at a distance, Dick threatened Jim Roof with a "whippin'" if he didn't come down. He was boiling with fury as the child reluctantly climbed down from the roof. Calvin held the rage in check as the child was escorted to the back of the house. With his stomach turning in disgust at the thought of what was going to happen to Jim Roof, Calvin noticed the overseer, Harvey, had saw what Dick had done and he mumbled angrily under his breath. Calvin inconspicuously tossed the corn meal and resumed working when he noticed he had attracted the attention of the gun totting assistants.

Harvey slowly moved the horses toward Calvin and gave him a deadly stare. When Harvey passed Calvin while examining the slaves working, Calvin turned to see if Jim Roof had come back, but what he saw stopped him in his tracks. He stopped on a dime and the hoe almost slipped from his grip. He rapidly blinked his eyes to make sure his vision was functioning correctly. One of the other field slaves gave Calvin a nervous glance, trying to signal him that Harvey was watching with angry eyes, but Calvin was paralyzed with disbelief. The woman he was staring at had a bucket in her hand, heading toward the well. She had smooth jet-black flawless skin, appealing brown eyes and petite, but shapely African bodily features.

Harvey didn't like what he saw. "Hey! Get yoh ass back to work!" He shouted at Calvin and instantly made a mental note to keep an eye on "this nigger" because he wasn't gonna have anyone "getting eyes" for his number one bed buddy.

Calvin pulled himself from the sight of the woman with a heartrending struggle. As he resumed hoeing the soil, all he could seem to do was repeatedly mutter to himself, "It can't be! Impossible!"

CHAPTER # 8

Eric was behind the wheel of his black Mercedes Benz, carefully structuring his response to Diana's question. Because of the extensive amount of time that had elapsed since he decided to utilize a hit man, Eric didn't want to offer a knee jerk reaction. "Well," He sighed as he steered the vehicle around a close curve in the highway. The headlights on high beam displayed miles of emptiness. At 2:10 in the morning this was no surprise. "If the price is right he should agree."

Diana was becoming truly tired of Eric's fantasy world type of optimum. "Why does that sound like a broken record? That's what you said a month ago when you tried to get that man named Alvin Graham to take this job."

Eric took his eyes off the road and laid a momentary stare on Diana. "I really think this guy is the one. I hear he's one of those adventure and thrill freaks. This type of job is right up his alley."

"I don't know how much longer I can put up with all this--this--" She grappled for the right word. "This sneaking around! And conspiring and--and watching every step we take, cleaning up behind everything we touch, thinking not twice, but a dozen times before we speak. I just can't continue living like this."

Eric reached over and massaged her thigh. He knew all she needed was to be shown she was appreciated, loved and needed. "Diana, please, I can't do this without you. Look at what lies on the horizon. When all this becomes water under the bridge, we'll settle down as husband and wife and be the most famous couple the world has ever seen."

Diana wanted to blurt out the fact she wanted to get married right here and now! Not next week or next year, but right this goddamn minute! She sighed. "You know I would never abandon you. I just got a bad vibe that's telling me if we don't stay on top of this we could lose each other. I say that to say, I think another problem might be lurking in the wings."

Eric sighed and didn't have to be told it was Demetrius's odd behavior because he saw it as well. He didn't want to get her riled up which is why he never brought it up before. In any event, he'd been formulating a plan, and a real good one at that. "Don't worry about Demetrius. When the time is right, he'll be dealt with. Right now, he's no real threat. Since the board is about to close the investigation and has went on record stating no foul play was uncovered, as long as we walk light we'll be all right."

Twenty minutes later, the Mercedes drove down a deserted street and pulled up in front of a bar that had a closed sign dangling from the window. This was the instructions given by Larry Drugan. Eric killed the engine and seconds later, from the shadows of the alleyway emerged a figure. It had to be Larry, Eric surmised. The figure drew closer, heading straight for the Mercedes, crossing the street with a swagger in his walk. Eric saw Larry had a muscular built under his brown leather jacket and black dress slacks. With a square jaw and huge watchful brown eyes, Larry could easily pass for the epitome of an old fashion, twentieth century organized crime hit man.

Eric opened the door, and Larry slid into the back seat. Eric turned and stuck his hand out. "It's a pleasure to meet you, Mr. Drugan."

Larry shook Eric's hand, making certain he created a good impression by trying to break a couple of Eric's fingers. "Call me Larry."

Eric dove straight into the issue. It took Eric five minutes to explain the circumstances surrounding the contract hit. One of the stipulations was, Larry had to start the job right this minute. The other was he would receive $50,000 up front and $50,000 upon completion.

Larry laid back in the seat, in deep thought. This was probably going to be the most exciting, deeply fulfilling and thoroughly challenging contract he'd ever performed. Shit, if anything, he was going to make history because he was going to be the first time travel assassin. This couldn't have come at a better time, since he thought he'd done every kind of job there ever was. "You say this time travel stuff is safe? I'm not gonna come back with body parts missing or parts in the wrong place; like my dick on my nose or my eyes in my asshole." He chuckled.

"It's a 100% safe," Eric said reassuringly.

"If you raise it from 50 to 60 gees up front and upon completion, you got yourself a deal."

Eric was so enthralled, he almost blurted out his agreement to the terms. He fought the impulse, because if he reacted hastily, it would imply he was desperate and not in control. He paused for a moment. "That's a considerable jump. I tell you what; if you can guarantee us you'll bring us his head, you got a deal."

"My work is always guaranteed." Larry stuck his hand out and Eric shook it.

☼   ☼   ☼   ☼

Demetrius was in the deepest level of sleep, dreaming about an argument he was having with his girlfriend, Rebecca. A sudden ring resounded and the dream was shattered as Demetrius snatched himself from the dream world.

It was the alarm he had set.

In an attempt to catch Eric and Diana engaging in misconduct, he had planted a series of microscopic sensory devices and cameras all around the lab.

He flung the sheet off him, jumped out of the bed and headed for his computer that sat on the table on the other side of his bedroom. He hit a button and the screen came to life. Demetrius took a seat when he saw Eric, Diana and an unknown man heading toward the lab. His finger activated the control key that instructed the camera to take pictures. He sighed in frustration when they entered the lab because he knew he should have tried harder to find a way to plant a microscopic camera inside. He had tried to plant one in the control station, but there was simply too much traffic in the lab and everyone seemed to be watching everyone.

Demetrius got comfortable because he was going to wait until Eric, Diana and the unauthorized man were leaving and take more pictures. About an hour later, Eric and Diana exited the lab without the man. Demetrius shot to his feet. "I know they didn't do it. No, fuckin' way! They can't be that stupid!"

☼   ☼   ☼   ☼

Larry Drugan slowly opened his eyes. "Well, I'll be goddamn!" He shouted joyfully as he spun around in a circle, realizing he was no longer in the Time Machine and was now in a forest. The sound of crickets, barking animals at a distance, the smell of fresh woodlands and the sight of the quarter moon and stars were like a sensory overload. He couldn't believe he didn't feel a thing. It was like he faded into a graceful unconscious state and suddenly returned to his original state. The only thing he felt was a tingling sensation all over his body and then there was an amazingly bright flash.

Larry was transported to the exact spot Calvin laid in pain 40 days ago. The date was May 13th and Larry was convinced 80 days was far more than enough time to complete this job.

Larry pulled a high-tech compass from his bag, found out what direction was west and started walking. With a knapsack flung over his shoulder, and wearing clothing Eric went to great lengths to make sure were in accordance with the time, Larry put the compass back in the bag and pulled the map from his back pocket and looked at his handwritten notes. The nearest town was about four miles. He stuffed the map back in his pocket.

Larry enjoyed the weight of the knapsack on his shoulder because it reminded him of what was inside. There were not only dried foods and bottles of water, but also a small arsenal of high-tech weaponry of the era he came from. The two featherweight laser guns were the items that stayed on his mind as he swaggered through the woods. He suddenly remembered the first time he used a laser gun. It was at a firing range in upstate New York about a year ago. Those damn weapons cost so much money only government agents could afford them, and if a civilian were caught with one, he would automatically receive a life sentence in prison. The mere thought he had one in his possession, and he was in a place where the law couldn't touch him, the temptation of seeing the laser in action was driving him crazy. Plus, he just loved the way the laser ripped through things with remarkable ease.

He stopped, dug inside the knapsack, pulled out the laser gun (it resembled an oversized pack of cigarettes with finger slots) and held it in his hand, savoring the way it felt. His jovial smile grew broader with every passing moment.

He aimed at a tree about twenty feet away and pressed the firing button.

SSHHAAHH!!--BLAAMM!!

The yellowish orange colored laser beam ripped through the tree. Upon impact, explosive sparks appeared and the tree fell crashing to the ground. Splinters were flung every which a way and the smell of burning wood was heavy in the air.

Larry's mind was saturated with glee as he went to the tree to inspect the damage. He was shocked when he saw the trunk of the tree was well over two feet thick, yet the laser beam cut it down as smoothly as a red-hot knife piercing through a stick of butter. Now he was over-anxious to see what the laser would do to the body of a man, in particular, Calvin Thompson.

He continued onward. He pulled the picture of Calvin from his back pocket, and with the help of the moonlight, he reinforced the image of Calvin's face that was already chiseled onto his third eye.

CHAPTER # 9

"Plant your feet firmly like this," Calvin was showing Jim Roof a karate move. They were in the back of Calvin's shack and the sun had set about two hours ago. The burning torch provided them with inadequate light. After Calvin received confirmation that Dick was molesting Jim, he felt an intense duty to at least try to show the kid how to fight back. "Then you kick out like this." Calvin cut loose a snap kick.

Jim mimicked the maneuver with graceful excellence. Calvin recognized little Jim was naturally flexible and followed instructions extremely well. But he was too timid, docile and had no confidence whatsoever. Riding on the heels of this analogy, Calvin realized he had to re-harness himself in this time period because Jim was growing up in a world where he was taught he was inferior and it was natural for him to respond in this fashion. How else would he be expected to act? Calvin suddenly wondered if teaching Jim to fight back was a wise thing to do. Maybe being docile, timid and insecure was a survival instinct appropriate under these circumstances? He shoved these invading thoughts from his mind because he knew this defenseless child was being raped and he simply could not standby and do absolutely nothing.

"This is what you call a roundhouse," Calvin spun his body while simultaneously snap kicking at the imaginary target. Jim tried it, but he needed a little practice.

For the pass four days, Calvin had been preparing for his journey. The date was May 16th, and with a less than three month deadline looming over his head, Calvin knew it was suicide to take things in stride. This was strictly time for aggressive action. In the wee hours of the night, he prowled all over the plantation. He checked just about everything, from the position of the shacks in relation to the forest to the kind of pad-locks on the hut used to secure the tools and weapons. He not only examined the plantation's entire perimeter, but also conducted a special inspection of the western area. When he stumbled onto a secret dog kennel in the south section of the plantation, Calvin thought he had messed up royally because the dogs started barking. Luckily the dogs did so well before he reached the kennel, which enabled him to race back to his shack without being detected. The following day after these preparations, Calvin felt like a zombie due to the lack of sleep and rest.

Calvin threw a rapid combination of kicks, punches and chops. When he returned to the original stance, he felt dizzy. He needed to sit down. "All right, let's take a break." Breathing exhaustibly, Calvin walked over to a two-foot tall tree stump and took a seat. Jim sat on the ground directly in front of him with his legs crossed like a student of Buddha. Calvin suddenly noticed he was undergoing a déjà vu experience when he realized he used to sit the same way when he was a kid about Jim Roof's age and his father used to return home with amazing stories of what happened at the lab.

"They says you was a free man," Jim said. "How's it feels to be free?"

Calvin was at a loss for words. How do you explain freedom to a child locked into this horrific predicament? "Well, I would say it feelings good. There's no one forcing you to do things you don't wanna do." He saw Jim smiled and that made him smile as well.

"Before they kill my momma, she says her daddy was free. Say he was brought over here on one of 'em big ole ships. I's forgets the place she say he was from--"

"Africa," Calvin interjected. "That's where most black people come from. A place called Africa." Calvin put special emphasis on the word Africa and the pride resonated as the word was spoken.

Jim squinted his eyes. That wasn't the word she said. He thought the word sounded like Gambi or something like that. "It's 'cross the waters, right?"

81

"Yes, it is," Calvin saw Jim pick up a twig and started drawing circles in the dirt. There was a burning urge to know how Jim ended up at this plantation. From what Mary Sue told him, Jim hadn't been here very long. "What happened to your mom, Jim? How did she die?"

"They hung her on a tree when we's was with Massa Thomas, over yonder." He pointed south. When he saw Calvin nod his head as if to say continue, he said. "Massa Thomas say she kill his observer, Jimbo, with some poison, but she didn't. That's when Massa Thomas sold me to Massa Dick 'cause he kills my momma. He say nigger boys 'comes dangerous to whites who kill they momma."

Calvin's heart instantly filled with grief as a thick penetrating silence took over. He wondered what he would do if someone killed his mother? One thing he was certain of, he would definitely seek revenge. This also confirmed that plantation owners weren't stupid. But what touched Calvin the most was, it was evident Jim was sold to Dick for the sole purpose of breaking his spirit. His being here was designed to destroy him by preventing him from becoming a man. This profoundly infuriated Calvin. At this moment, while he was in this frame of mind, Calvin felt he could have started an insurrection and could have put Nat Turner's endeavors to shame.

Jim locked eyes with Calvin, and said. "Can I's go with you when you leave, Calvin?"

Calvin wasn't sure if he heard Jim correctly because of his heavy countrified accent and he was hoping he didn't hear what he thought he heard. "What did you say?"

"Can I's come with you when you 'scape?" Jim said.

Calvin's heart suddenly began to pound. "How did you know I was planning to escape?"

"I's was up in that tree over yonder when yous talk to Jake," He pointed at the tree about thirty yards away, next to the garden.

Calvin sighed with partial relief. "Did you tell anyone else?"

Jim lowered his head and was now staring at the ground, giving the appearance he felt ashamed and had done something wrong.

Oh, no! He went and ran his mouth. Calvin felt his escape plan unraveling before his eyes. Numerous historical events emerged from the archives of his memory bank. The insurrectionists in New York in 1741. Gabriel Prosser, who almost pulled off a successful revolt, but was executed on October 7, 1800. Denmark Vessey was another black man who came close, but on July 3, 1822 he too was executed. Then there was Nat Turner, a preacher who carried out the bloodiest slave insurrection in American History. After killing 57 whites, Nat Turner was hanged on November 11, 1831. Even John Brown, a white abolitionist, was unable to persevere and after organizing a mob of men, black and white, and took control of an arsenal at Harpers Ferry, he fell victim to the system on December 2, 1859 when he was hanged at Charles Town.

Calvin sighed as he stared silently at Jim Roof, already formulating a backup plan because every single one of these historical events had one thing in common: a house Negro bent on dismantling the insurrection by running to "massa." What if his escape plans got into the hands of that House-servant Anne? She would tell Dick as sure as day and night are inseparable. Without success, Calvin tried to push the thought to the back of his mind.

Calvin's patience was slowly dissolving. "Come on, Jim, tell me who else you told this to. I won't be mad with you."

Jim looked up with thankful eyes. "You won't be mad at me?"

"That's right."

After a moment Jim said, "I's told Mary Sue . . . 'cause I's figured since you gots eyes on her, yous was gonna take her with you. I's wanted her to take me too, but she ain't knows 'bout it."

The mere thought of Mary Sue turned his heart into jelly. She looked like a carbon copy of his wife Cookie and that day when he first laid eyes on her it was like he was locked in a vivid dream. After he formally met her, he saw she even had similar attributes and characteristics as Cookie. The way she nervously fiddled with her hands as he spoke to her, and that attentive look in her eyes when she was interested in a topic was amazing. If there was such a thing as parallel world twins, Mary Sue was Cookie's without question. But he was devastated at the thought he couldn't take her with him. "Did you tell anyone else?"

"No."

Calvin decided he was going to see Mary as soon as possible to make sure she hadn't told anyone else. "I need you to promise me you won't tell anyone else about this."

"I's promise," Jim said. "But I's wanna go with you. Can I's go?" His eyes started watering when Calvin took too long to answer.

Calvin saw the tears formulating in his eyes. He hated to break the child's heart, but there was no way he could take Jim with him. Not only would he be a burden and might slow him down, but the Backlash portal would only bring back what it had initial transported. If an organism not transported from the original transport zone attempted to enter the portal, it would be rejected. Jim or anyone from this time would have to be exposed to the chemical primer and possess a Micron watch to get to the time Calvin came from. It was obvious none of these necessities were available and he did not have the facilities, materials or resources to create them. "If I could take you I would, but I just can't. Please Jim, you have to believe me."

Jim was sniffling loudly with eyes filled with tears and he made no attempt to wipe away the runaway streams of water.

Calvin felt the urge to embrace his little friend and comfort him, but he fought back the emotional surge. There was no need in making this matter worse than it already was. He couldn't bring him; it was as simple as that. It was a feeling Jim would eventually get over.

At a distance, Calvin saw an approaching figure coming from the direction of the garden. It moved very slowly and it was evident who it was.

When Jim detected the figure, he rose to his shoeless feet and headed toward the shack he shared with a field slave woman, named Sally. Jim turned and said as he walked away, "I's see you 'morrow, Calvin."

"Good night, Jim," Calvin felt relieved because another minute with Jim crying like that and he would've been joining him.

Maintaining a slow, steady and determined pace, Jake arrived breathing slightly hard. "Ooohhh weee, Chile! I sho' ain't like I used to be."

"Here, rest yourself." Calvin gave Jake the seat on the tree stump.

Jake sighed with excessive force as he sat down. "Was that ole Jim Roof just left?"

"Yeah."

Shaking his head pitifully, Jake said, "Poo' chile." He always tried to imagine the humiliation and the pain Jim Roof was forced to endure, but his mind couldn't seem to grasp it fully. Jake shifted cringingly in his seat because he knew Jim's backside was probably sore and raw all the time. That day, about two years ago, when he saw Jim Roof walking around with blood soaked breeches had left a permanent scar on his soul. "It's a damn shame what that poo' child is goin' throughs."

There was a long silence as the crickets sang their song and the lightning flies sparkled up the area.

"I wanna help you 'scape, Calvin," Jake said. "When I was a youngin', I tried ta 'scape. But got caught three times. Theys cut off my big toes and my . . . " He pointed to his crotch area.

Calvin was thunderstruck. "You mean to tell me they cut off your penis?"

Jake squinted his eyes. "P . . . what!? What the hell's a Peus!?"

"I mean, your uh—um--your thang," Calvin pointed to his own crotch area.

"Yeah, they cuts off everything down there. Killed me from ever havin' chilluns. They was gonna cut off my digga-lang, but I guess the grace of God was on my side."

Grace of God on my side!? Calvin could only imagine what Jake thought constituted a lack of the grace of God on his side. How could they cut off the man's testicles for Christ sakes!? Calvin instantly realized Jake's awkward limp was due to his having no big toes. "Did you ever find out what you might have done wrong to cause you to get caught?"

Jake contemplated the question, staring at the fields abroad. "I was startin' ta thank white folks had magic." He chuckled. "Even afin I got all the way to a place called Virginia, them patrollers come up outta nowhere." Shaking his head, he stared up into the heavens, wondering why God didn't let him get to freedom that time. He had traveled so so far, prayed to God every step of the way and was so so close to freedom. He looked Calvin straight in the eyes. "But I knows you gotta head north. It's this way." He pointed. "You say yous goin' that ways is wrong." He pointed westward. "Theys ain't nobody helpin' niggers that way. All yous gonna find is more plantations and mean ole white folks. Now, up north, theys all kinds of people who says slavery is wrong. And theys even helpin' niggers 'scape, whites and free niggers." He still thought Calvin was lying when he said he was from the future. He assumed Calvin was playing some kind of game with him or was trying to conceal where he was from. "I don't care where's yous from, but that way is trouble. 'Cause I like you chile, that's why I tell you, yous gotta go that way, north."

Calvin wasn't about to explain the Backlash opening again because it was apparent Jake didn't believe him. Calvin didn't blame him because if he were in Jake's shoes he wouldn't believe it either. "I thank you deeply for all the advice, Jake. I'm sincerely grateful. North. I'll think about it and get back to you." He saw his last comment put Jake at ease.

"Talk 'round here says yous been sweet on Mary Sue ever since you laid eyes on her," Jake said teasingly. "Chile, if I was a youngin', I'd be layin' some big eyes on that woman. But I sho' might have ta kill Harvey for soilin' that girl."

Soiling!? Calvin suddenly felt a conglomeration of horror, anger, sorrow and revulsion well up inside of him. The subtext of this word "soiling" was strong and almost obvious, but he still needed to know precisely what it meant. "Are you telling me Harvey's raping Mary Sue?"

"I don't knows what's raping is, but if it means he's forcin' her into his bed, then yous on target."

Wrapped in a silent cocoon, Calvin was emotionally shattered. That filthy, nasty, rotten tooth bastard couldn't be assaulting Mary! She was an African princess with the prettiest face he'd seen since being transported to this living hell. Calvin had to find a seat because his knees were getting weak. When a picture of Harvey penetrating Mary flashed across his mind, his shock changed to sheer rage. He could visualize himself blowing Harvey's brains out. He was about to start pacing, but quickly told himself Mary was not Cookie, over and over again until he felt the anxiety slowly becoming bearable.

"Chile, yous look like yous need this here seat." Jake chuckled. "Boy, you sho' falls in love 'bout as fast as a jack rabbit make babies." He chuckled harder.

"How long has this been going on?" Calvin pretended to be unaffected.

"Ever since Harvey laid eyes on her." Jake paused. "Massa Dick brought Mary here afin he swapped her 'cause her ole Massa couldn't pays his gamblin' debt. I hear Harvey even lets Massa Dick pay him less money, justin' to bees with Mary."

Calvin was pissed off, but tried to maintain his composure.

"Way yous actin' that means you takin' Mary long with you. I sho' hope so."

Calvin remained silent and wanted to blurt out a comment indicating he couldn't do that. It was obvious no one in this time zone would understand, so he kept his mouth shut.

Jake took Calvin's silence as a yes, and he smiled broadly. "You says yous from the future and that's where yous goin' back? Then yous better let's Mary Sue knows about the future 'cause she's got her heart set to go with you."

"How do you know this? Has she been telling this to any of the other slaves?"

"I don't thank she says any thang to these big mouth niggers 'round here. She's a smart chile. I just knows she been actin' funny, like she's thankin' 'bout leavin'. I tried three times and I knows when a nigger's 'bout to 'scape. Since you and Mary be sneakin' 'round, I figure yous takin' the chile with you. And she sho' needs to get away from that mean ole Harvey." Jake smiled when he saw the mere mention of Harvey brought on a massive wave of tension in Calvin's whole body and Jake was loving every minute of it.

Calvin's mind was made up. "I'm gonna go talk to Mary. I'll be right back."

"I be right here when yous get back." Jake said and then mumbled under his breath as Calvin moved away. "And while yah at it, I sho' hopes you puts some fire to Harvey's cracker ass."

Calvin was standing in front of Mary's window, looking in. He saw she was sitting on a cot. She was sewing a shirt with two burning candles sitting on a nearby wooden cabinet. "Mary!" He whispered.

Mary looked up.

"It's me, Calvin."

When she saw it really was Calvin, she lit up with a tremendous smile. She tiptoed to the window, lifted the screen, and crawled through it.

Calvin helped her onto the ground and realized this was the first time he'd ever touched her. She was so soft and womanly, just like Cookie. Whispering he said, "I wanna talk to you. Let's go over here."

Calvin silently led the way, heading toward an old wooden bench near the Peach trees Jim Roof climbed and retrieved his treats. If it wasn't for the light emitting from the quarter moon, they would not have been able to see their hands if they were placed before their eyes.

Mary sat down first and then Calvin did the same with a slight hesitation.

Calvin wanted to come straight out and tell her that he could not take her with him. But the thought of breaking her heart was too much for him. When the silence became almost ridiculously too long he said, "Mary, have you heard of my plans."

Mary's heart fluttered with intense joy. She was right! He was going to take her with him! Thank God! "If'en in yous talkin' about the 'scape, yes."

"Have you mentioned it to anyone else?"

"No!" she started nervously fiddling with her hands.

After a moment, Calvin said, "Did I ever tell you where I was from?" He knew the answer, but he had to ease into this sort of thing.

"No." she said. "But I hear you from up north. The ways you talk, I knows yous from the place where niggers is free." She knew he was going to get her to freedom because he was so smart! He was even smarter than all the white folks she'd ever seen.

"It's very hard to explain this, but I'm not from this time." He wished he could see her facial response clearly because her bodily

89

response was not telling him how she was digesting this information. "I'm from the future. Hundreds of years from now people will have the ability to travel time. They'll be able to go into the past or the future." He knew she was probably responding as if he was speaking a foreign language, but he continued anyway. "I was sent here by a disgruntled--I mean a person working under me who hated me and wanted to get rid of me. In his effort to do this, he sent me here without the appropriate equipment. Now, in order for me to get back to the future, I have to go to a portal where I'll enter it and be returned to the place I came from. Now, I would love to take you with me, Mary. I really would, but the portal will not--"

"Please, Calvin take me with you," She felt a terror formulating inside her when she realized he was suggesting that he wasn't going to take her with him. She moved closer to Calvin until her soft hip touched his leg, and she grabbed his hand. "I can't stay here any mo'." She was seconds from crying. "I see yous like me, and I like you the same. We can be a nice family, Calvin. I can makes you happy." She broke down, crying profusely. "Please, take me . . ."

Calvin felt terrible. His heart was twisted into a pretzel and was falling to pieces. He felt that burning pain in the back of his eyes growing uncontrollably. As she cried, Calvin embraced her, and whispered in her ear. "It's okay, Mary. Please stop crying. I would take you if I could." He realized this made her cry even harder. The more he embraced her, the more he felt himself becoming weaker. He pulled away because he couldn't do it. He was cursing himself a mile a minute for mentioning his plans to Jake in the first place! Deep down inside he understood why everyone wanted out of this hellhole, but he wasn't their messiah!

Mary turned around and bowed her head in her lap. She was crying quietly now, hating herself for believing Calvin cared about her.

Why did she let him fool her with those fake smiles!? She was confused because he wasn't responding to her tears the way she expected.

After three minutes of silence, Calvin heard a distinct noise materializing at a distance. Calvin focused his attention on the noise and noticed it sounded like pounding horse hooves rapidly getting closer.

Mary raised her head, wiping her eyes. She hastily rose to her feet. "Somebody's coming." She headed toward her cabin with Calvin in pursuit. "There's somethin' wrong 'cause nobody comes out here this time of night."

Calvin realized she was right. Since he'd been here no one ever came to the plantation this time of the evening. When Mary continued pass her turn leading to her cabin, he said, "Where are you going?"

"I wanna see who is it 'fore I goes inside."

They trotted over to the cabin closest to the big house and peeked around it.

Calvin saw it was a man on a horse about fifty yards away and was rapidly approaching. He had a lantern in his hand. Staring at the approaching figure, Calvin felt a disturbing premonition coursing through his body. He didn't believe in ESP, but this weird feeling was making him reconsider his stance on this topic. As the man on the horse drew closer to the plantation, certain features becoming more visible, Calvin sensed the presence of an enemy -- an incomprehensible but keenly felt evil.

CHAPTER # 10

Demetrius rushed inside the house when Ramanda opened the door. He headed straight for the living room where the digital electronic player was located, while talking excitedly. "I think I got something concrete. You were right about Eric." He turned on the digital electronic player and inserted the microscopic chip. "This is a recording of Eric and Diana entering the lab with a strange man."

"It's about time," Ramanda said as she stood watching Demetrius. "It's been well over a month you been investigating."

Dameeka came rushing down the stairs and stood next to Ramanda. "Is it good news?"

"I think so," Ramanda wrapped her arm around Dameeka's shoulder, drawing her closer in a motherly fashion.

"What the hell!?" Demetrius was baffled beyond description when he saw no image on the screen. He fast forwarded the device and adjusted various dials without any improvement.

"I guess that means this is a false alarm," Ramanda said to Eric's back. "What happened?"

Demetrius sighed as both hands landed on his hips. He stared at the digital electronic player in deep thought with a dumbfounded expression. After a moment it became apparent what had happened. He turned and faced Ramanda and Dameeka. There was a record scrambler system somewhere in the vicinity of the lab. It was a device that prevented any camera or audio equipment from recording, and would allow the operator to view and even hear what was taking place, but it would not record. The system was very sophisticated and extremely expensive.

"So, what was on the recording?" Dameeka asked.

Demetrius looked downward and gave her an expression, which said she couldn't be serious. He looked at his watch. "Shouldn't you be on your way to school? I think this is grown up stuff."

Ramanda was seconds from blowing up. "I told you she has a right to hear everything that involves her father. Now, don't make me repeat myself again, Demetrius. Is that clear?" She saw him reluctantly nod his head. "All you have to do is avoid profanity and any other derogatory issues unhealthy to the ears of a child her age."

Dameeka looked up at Ramanda with loving eyes and a smile. Then she gave Demetrius a stern stare that clearly said how do you like those apples Mr. always trying to shut me out of the show and treating me like a fart!

Shaking his head in disbelief, Demetrius threw up his hands as if to say he gave up. "All right. Last night--or rather this morning, Eric and Diana entered the lab with a strange man. When they left, the man wasn't with them."

Long pause.

Ramanda saw this was something she obviously was supposed to understand, but it wasn't clicking. "And?"

"I believe they transported him without authorization. If my hunch is correct, that man might be going back in time to deal with Calvin." He paused. "Eric might be trying to cover his tracks by preventing Calvin from getting to the Backlash. The man looked extremely dangerous. He--he had that unmistakable look I've seen--"

"Okay, okay." Ramanda said, noticing Dameeka's eyes growing wide with fright. "I think we see where you're going." She gave him a screw face that said he was supposed to sugarcoat or delete the dangerous parts. "So, what do you got planned next?"

Demetrius thought hard about the question. Going to the board was apparently not an option, since he had no evidence to support any of his

93

claims. There was really only one thing left for him to do. He headed toward the door. "What are you doing tonight, sis?"

"I'll be here as usual."

"When I get off work, I'll come straight here. I'll let you know what the plan is then. I wanna check a few things out first."

Before Ramanda could open her mouth, Demetrius disappeared out the door. She and Dameeka looked at each other and shrugged their shoulders.

Larry Drugan's saddle sores were flaming as he bounced along the dark, deserted dirt road. The waning moon and the stars had the sky to themselves. Larry was mumbling all sorts of curse words because the last time he made a stop to acquire directions to the Gilbo Plantation, he was told it was about a five-hour horse ride in this direction. That red neck lying ass motherfucker said five hours, but he'd been on this fucking dirt road for almost eight hours! At least that's the way it felt to his ass cheeks. If he could turn back, that poor white trash, son of a bitch!--What did he say his name was, Jeffro?--would get a taste of this nice hot laser beam!

Twice Larry wanted to stop and make camp, but everywhere he laid his eyes seem to be thick uninhabitable underbrush. Had he stopped four hours ago, he could have successfully found a suitable place. He sighed so hard with a flaming fury boiling inside him spit flew from his mouth and landed on the back of the horse's neck. When he reflected back on all the shit he'd been through during the past five days, he knew when he got his hands on that motherfucker Calvin, he was going to make sure he took every drop of his rage out on him. Should he savor the moment by torturing Calvin or just blow the sucker away with a flick of a finger? He'd figure that out when the time came. However, he felt at the time would determine his method of extermination, but right now he would go for the slow death option.

That first night he transported here he was filled with an adventurous joy. Even after he arrived at the Jackson's Plantation and found out the owner, Sam, recalled numerous people talking about a strange, foreign nigger who assaulted a couple of white men, Larry was still happy about this whole situation. Sam allowed him to sleep in the barn. The following morning, Larry purchased one of Sam Jackson's "pretty brown horses" and headed for the seashore market, the place where the strange black man was taken. The one-day ride, in a southeastern direction, went smooth. When Larry arrived in town, and started asking around, he easily discovered Calvin was sentenced to lifetime slavery.

After the workers at the auction block told him Calvin was sold to someone named Dick Gilbo, Larry laughed in the faces of the men and alienated them all because they thought he was laughing at them. He couldn't understand why they didn't see the humor in a name like "Dick Gilbo." His happy mood changed when he found out the Gilbo Plantation was a two-day horse ride. After leaving the auction block, he browsed around the town, watching the people and buying various foods from the makeshift restaurants.

By the time the sunset, Larry was in a Saloon having stiff drinks of Moonshine and good old fashion corn liquor. When he realized he was drunk, but not too drunk to walk relatively straight, he decided to call it a night. Just as he was about to enter the nearby hotel, realizing he was drunker than he thought and was feeling as rowdy as a hillbilly, Larry clashed with the three men who encountered Calvin. They wanted to know why Larry was snooping around asking a lot of questions about that strange nigger. They told Larry they were the ones who Calvin had assaulted as if Larry really gave a rat's ass.

While in the midst of an exchange of words, Larry realized the men came to rob him. They repeatedly called him an up-north scalawag and an abolitionist and rudely tried to look inside his knapsack. For whatever reason, they were convinced Larry was a friend of Calvin's and was there to rescue him. As the red beard man repeatedly called Larry a "nigger lover", Larry escorted the three around to the back of the hotel and into a wooded area. He was shocked at how they didn't realize what he was doing. Man, were these some dumb motherfuckers! On the way, he scanned the immediate vicinity to make certain there was no one else around.

When he pulled the weapon in response to their demanding him to turn over his money, Larry saw the men thought he was giving them the laser. The red beard man reached his hand out and got a big surprise as his hand disappeared. With flinching speed, while the laser gun was turned on full blast mode, Larry cut down the other two before their screams even registered inside their throats. The surrounding air had a smell of burning flesh and all three were cut into pieces with major portions of their bodies disintegrated. Larry simply left their bodies where they landed, rented a room, and slept comfortably.

The next morning as he started his journey he saw the entire town was in a frantic uproar after the three bodies were discovered. Some of the rumors of what killed the men were so ridiculous Larry wanted to slap some goddamn common sense into these whispering idiots. The only rumor that made any sense was the one claiming the men were struck down by lightning from God. Larry smiled because if he wanted to he could make all these people bow to him as if he was their God. That sounded lovely, and if he didn't have the mission on his mind, he might have gave into the temptation.

Larry was pulled from the reverie when the horse suddenly slowed down. For the first time he realized he had been pushing the horse at top speed for a long time, and hadn't provided it any water either. The horse stumbled violently and Larry saw the ground rushing up at him. With reflective speed, he catapulted himself out of the saddle and away from the horse while going into a dive. He hit the dirt awkwardly, felt a sharp pain scurry up his shoulder, and lodged itself in his neck. Dirt slipped inside mouth and covered his face.

Larry rolled a couple of times and came to a stop on his back. He laid there for a couple of seconds, cringing in pain from the shoulder injury while spitting out the hard, crunchy dirt. Raising his wounded arm to see if there was anything broken, his anger was mounting. Already he was calculating how much extra money he was going to charge Eric for this shit. Bruises and excessive pain was not in the deal and, when they occurred, the customer had to pay extra. He wiggled his fingers, bent the arm at the elbow, and noticed it wasn't broke, but it was definitely going to be sore after a good night's rest. He hastily checked the Micron watch, saw it was intact and got up from off the ground with the knapsack still hanging from his uninjured shoulder.

Wiping the dirt off his clothing, he went to the horse and saw it was dead. He was instantly reminded of the stories he heard about horses running themselves until they dropped dead. So, it was true after all.

With the moon and stars as his only source of light, Larry continued onward. About ten minutes into his long stride walk, he came upon an old weatherworn sign with faded paint that was supposed to provide some sort of directions. Upon closer observation, he was able to decipher the words. It said "Gilbo's Estate. Ten miles." There was an arrow pointing in the direction Larry was headed.

CHAPTER # 11

Calvin entered his shack, sat down on the mattress and began checking the items inside the twine feed sack. It was literally pitch black and it took his eyes a moment to adjust. He began pulling out items, whispering their names as he laid them next to him: "two jugs of water ... shoes ... two pair of pants ... shirt ... five candles ... machete ... pistol ... two bag of bullets ... matches ... map ... black pepper ... smoked rabbit meat... three peaches ... four apples ... spoon ... two folding pocket knives ... two quills with ink ... and seven sheets of paper." As he put the items back inside the sack, he felt odd, as if he was missing something. When Calvin got to the shoes and the black pepper, he put them on the side.

Last night, after the arrival of the man on the horse, who according to Jake was an overseer from the nearby Dawson Plantation, Calvin decided he had to make his break as soon as possible. Whatever that overseer told Dick, Calvin sensed something was wrong. This morning, he noticed Dick was looking at him strangely. Later on in the day, when Harvey suddenly started doing the same thing, his mind was made up. His journey would begin tonight, May 17th. He intended to leave in two more days because he wanted to get into the cellar of the big house and get another gun Jake assured him was down there. But whatever that strange man told Dick, Calvin was not going to wait around to find out, thus, his mind was firmly locked into the position that it was a now or never situation.

The moment the plantation began to settle down for the night, Calvin had been on the move. Earlier, before the candles were turned out, Jim Roof wanted to practice some more karate moves, but Calvin politely told him he was feeling very sick and stayed inside his shack. Mary Sue wanted to talk, but he told her the same thing. He was glad

Jake had not come around because he knew Jake would have detected what he was up to.

Calvin thought about how he was going to just up and disappear without even saying good-bye to anyone, and for a moment, the thought made him feel terrible. But after he thought about his daughter, Dameeka and his future wife, Ramanda, he realized he had to get to his real family. He owed nothing to these people here. Then, when Eric's face flashed across his third eye, and he realized Eric might be in the process of becoming the first credited time traveler, Calvin was able to forget about Jim and Mary as if they hadn't even existed. Now, he had to tame the anxiety because no matter how fast he got to the portal it would open according to a set time schedule.

Calvin put on the pair of black leather shoes he took from the tool and weapon shack, and noticed the things were far too small. He rose to his feet and almost stumbled as he limped around the shack in pain. He sat back down on the mattress, dug inside the bag and found one of the folding knives. He carefully cut the toe areas out of the shoes, put them back on and walked around the shack in them again. Yeah, that was it. Then he went to the sack, put the knife back and retrieved the huge two-pound bag of pepper. He scooped a handful of the pepper and began rubbing the stuff all over his body from head to toe. He sneezed four times, but constricted them, forcing them to come out silently.

He stood in the dark with his hands on his hips looking around the shack, wondering why it still felt like he was about to leave something behind. After quickly recounting all the items inside his head, he concluded this feeling was nothing more than last minute jitters. He had everything he needed.

Suddenly, the sound of boots treading across the dirt yard outside was heard. Calvin was about to panic. What should he do!? He frantically ran to his mattress and laid down, pretending to be asleep. His senses were concentrated on the noise. The footsteps were heading straight for his cabin. Who could be lurking around at this time of the night!? Calvin wondered because it had to be at least two o'clock. He could hear the pounding of his heart in his ears. Calvin saw shadows through the holes in the wall, creeping forward.

The cabin door opened and Calvin remained in a lying position. It was Dick. Calvin's anxiety rapidly grew.

"Get yo' ass up, boy!" Dick said, standing in the threshold. "I seen it in yo' eyes, boy! You know 'xactly why I bought yo' black ass and I aims to get my money's worth." He unbuckled his pants and approached. He stopped and sniffed the air. Black pepper!? He sneezed and resumed his approach.

Calvin's heart was thundering in his chest. Damn! He didn't want to do what he knew he was about to do! But he really didn't have a choice in the matter. He inconspicuously opened his knapsack, pulled the folding knife and flicked it open. He slowly rose into a sitting position. Tonight he was leaving and nothing was going to stop him! "Who's gonna play the woman's roll? You or me?"

Dick stopped with a smile. This was easier than he thought. "I'm doing the taken, you give. We do it that way first. Then we do it the other way around after that." He felt himself becoming erect as he hastily took his pants off and tossed them aside. Licking his lips, Dick moved slowly toward Calvin.

When Dick was within reaching distance, Calvin sprung to his feet. He grabbed Dick by the neck and flipped him backwards to floor. Dick struck the ground with a huge, bone-crushing thud. Sitting on Dick's chest, Calvin placed the blade of the knife to his throat.

Dick was aghast. "What is you doing, nigger!?"

"Shut the fuck up and listen carefully." Calvin said through gritted teeth. All the suffering this piece of shit caused Jim danced vividly inside his mind. With perfect English Calvin said, "I'm a man. I don't fuck other men!"

Dick began thrashing under the weight, trying to grab at Calvin. His face was purple with rage and frustration.

"Stop!" Calvin pressed the knife so hard against Dick's throat blood trickled out of the cut. Dick instantly stopped resisting. "You want me to cut your throat, motherfucker!?" Calvin felt the need to play with Dick's head. "Does your wife know you like men? Do your neighbors know you like being fucked by other men? I bet they don't. Since they're so-called Christian folks, I don't think so. Now, you got a choice here. You either chose to live and promise to leave me the fuck alone or I kill you right here and now?" Calvin knew he was lying. There wasn't gonna be any choosing around here tonight, but he had to see just how arrogant Dick was.

Dick turned beet red. He was furious. The anger interfered with his ability to formulate his words. No nigger he owned would force him to agree to shit! And he wasn't gonna let Calvin even think he could get away with this. "Nigger, you dead! You just killed yohself, nigger! How dare you even thank you can threaten me?! You better let me up right now and I'll go easy on you."

Calvin was right. Dick was as arrogant as a twisted and diseased-minded tyrant. He had a knife to this idiot's throat and his superiority complex was so blinding he didn't have enough intelligence to talk to Calvin in a respectful manner. Calvin sighed loudly as he wondered why Dick waited so long to make his move!? "Listen, Dick. Does anyone know you came here?"

Dick huffed and puffed with anger, but remained silent.

Calvin continued with a teasing tone. "I'm almost certain you made sure you was not seen or heard when you snuck out here. The way you tiptoed to my cabin, I think that's quite obvious. What if you just happen to suddenly disappear? Who's to say I did it?" Dick moaned nervously and it made Calvin feel good. "I'm sure no one would suspect me or any of the slaves here. Hell, people might even assume you just up and

101

disappeared; especially since you and the wife are having major marital problems and you're in debt with so many people."

Dick was now sweating profusely. Why is this nigger talking crazy like this!? A strong sense of regret and realization seized his entire being. He cursed himself because his intuition told him to leave this particular slave alone, and he'd been following his first mind, but tonight he couldn't control himself. Plus, he didn't know this nigger spoke perfect English. This revelation frightened him tremendously because it was common knowledge that educated niggers were dangerous. He now saw it was true. "Listen, Calvin. I'm sorry. It won't happen no mo'. I promise." When he heard Calvin giggle, he panicked. *He's gonna kill me! Oh, God No! Maybe Harvey will hear me if I screamed loud enough!* Dick hysterically drew a huge blast of air into his lungs, about to unleash an ear-shattering scream. "HHHEELP---"

Calvin cut the scream short with a firm sweep of the knife. The blood and air that spewed from Dick's severed throat wound shot into Calvin's face. For safekeeping, Calvin stabbed Dick twice in the neck where the jugular vein is located. Blood sprayed from the puncher holes like water escaping an angry high-pressure water hose.

Calvin rose to his feet and stared at Dick's flinching body, which jerked convulsively. Blood squirted out of his neck as gurgling sounds escaped through the open wounds. Calvin was surprised he felt not even a moment of sorrow for killing Dick. It was not a moral question for him; it was a do or die situation. This was survival in every sense of the word. Dick would have killed him without uttering an afterthought if he had let him go. Only a fool would have let Dick live after violently warding off one of his homosexual advances, and a fool Calvin was not.

It took Calvin an hour to get a shovel from the tool shack, dig a three-foot deep hole, bury Dick inside his shack, and covered the mound with his mattress. The excess dirt was thrown outside in the back of the shack.

Calvin ran back in his shack, scooped up his knapsack, put each arms through the custom-made straps, and turned the knapsack into a makeshift backpack. He picked up the shovel and crept out the shack. His heart pounded with anxiety as he tiptoed pass the slave cabins on his way to the open field of watermelon and pumpkin patches.

When he was beyond all the shacks, Calvin started jogging toward the wooded area. The root of his need to hurry up to the woods was that feeling of being exposed while moving in this open area where there was nothing to hide behind. The faster he moved, the faster he noticed the bare, naked feeling subsided.

He arrived at the wooded section, breathing slightly hard. Wiping the sweat from his forehead, Calvin maintained a fast pace, stepping over vines, scrubs and bushes. About ten minutes into his forward movement, he realized the underbrush was getting thicker by the minutes. He stopped, hid the shovel in the underbrush and continued. When the vegetation reached the point where he could barely move, he stopped, flung his makeshift backpack off, pulled the machete and put the sack back on. Slashing and cutting his way through the tall grass and thick underbrush, he realized his muscles were beginning to ache as the minutes turned into an hour.

Then, suddenly, it all came to an end, almost as if he had penetrated a wall. He was still in the wooded area, but the trees were spaced apart from each other much more than earlier. He picked up his pace with the machete still in his hand.

A half hour passed, and he saw the forest was thinning out greatly. Suddenly, he heard something in back of him and his heart almost jumped clean out of his chest. He bolted for cover behind the nearest tree. Quiet as a trapped animal, Calvin listened intently, but didn't hear anything other than the normal sounds of the woods; owls, flapping bird wings, and crickets. He waited about four minutes and chuckled to himself as he concluded the sound was probably an animal scurry about. Maybe it was a wolf or a wild boar or something.

He continued onward. No sooner than he completed his twentieth step, he heard the noise again. That was no animal. It was human, no question about it. And whatever it was, it was trying to sneak up on him. Whoever it was, apparently was attempting to get close before commencing a surprise attack. Calvin inconspicuously flung his backpack off while pretending he didn't hear the noise. He stuffed the machete in the sack, dug through the items, retrieved the loaded pistol, and put the sack back on.

With the pistol now in his hand, Calvin abruptly ducked behind a tree and scanned the area behind him. He saw nothing other than trees and darkness, but he did hear the footsteps and noticed they had suddenly stopped a couple seconds after his abrupt movement. Someone was definitely behind him and Calvin's mind was skirting the edge of the panic zone. The crippling fear was mixed with an inquisitive eagerness to know who was following him. He was even angry with the prospect he had been detected. He was thoroughly baffled because he was certain no one followed him and he knew if it was Harvey or any of the other overseers they would have utilized the dogs to track him. They would not be trying to sneak up on him!

After a moment of being locked in deep thought, he decided to find out who it was. He looked around and saw numerous small pebbles scattered on the ground. He picked them up and started throwing them in the direction he was headed, hoping whoever it was would think he was walking and would continue to follow. Since it was very dark, whoever it was might be using the sound of Calvin's movement as his guide and sign to pursue. Tossing the pebbles at a speed assimilating the pace of his feet, he noticed whoever it was began walking again. It was working! Whoever it was drew closer and closer. When Calvin noticed the sound of the footsteps were about several yards away and still approaching, he knew at this distance he would be able to see who it was. He stopped throwing the pebbles and the pursuer stopped as well.

With the pistol drawn in the ready position, Calvin peeked around the huge tree trunk. What the . . . !? Rapidly blinking his eyes to make sure he wasn't seeing a mirage, Calvin slowly came from behind the tree. "What the hell are you doing here!?"

Mary Sue and Jim Roof were so startled they frantically fled away from Calvin and stopped a moment later when they realized who it was. They ran back to Calvin, looking scared out of their minds.

Mary Sue spoke frantically. "Please, Calvin, don't send us back."

"What are you doing here!?" Calvin's anger was about to burst at the seams. "I told you I can't bring you with me! What fuckin' part you don't understand!?" He looked at what they were wearing and couldn't believe they stupidly thought they could travel in this underbrush without shoes, long pants and sleeved shirts. They had nothing but the rags on their backs!? Already both of their feet, arms and legs were bleeding. "Where the hell are your shoes--and--and . . ." Calvin started pacing, with his hand planted on his head as if he had an excruciating headache. He wanted to send them back, but that would draw attention to him. A spark of fright suddenly exploded inside of him and he lunged toward them. "Did anyone follow you!?"

"No!" Mary said quickly. "We was watchin' everything. Nobody follows us."

Calvin didn't know whether to believe them or not. He stood staring at them. When he saw their suffering faces and their determined bodily gestures, he realized he couldn't send them back. If they were able to endure all those cuts on their feet and the scratches all over their limbs from the vines and brushes, it was evident they were going to continue following him no matter what he did. Calvin walked over to Mary and he was surprised when she raised her arm up as if to ward off a blow. His heart turned to silly putty. His anger mounted because it was evident she was so used to being abused and assaulted she assumed Calvin would hurt her as well. "It's Okay, let me see your feet." He said softly and kneeled, inspecting her cuts. "How's your feet Jim Roof?"

"I's ain't got but one cut and it ain't even hurts me."

Calvin smiled because he knew Jim was lying. He pulled his backpack off, and began searching for one of the pair of pants and the jug of water. He sat down comfortably and instructed Mary to do the same. He torn the pants into strips, washed Mary's cuts with the water and began wrapping them carefully. Just as he was wrapping the second foot, the distinct sound of barking dogs jolted him to his feet. He noticed Mary and Jim heard it also.

Calvin's eyes grew wide with terror. "Are you sure no one saw you!?" Calvin didn't wait for them to answer. "Come on, let's go!" He moved swiftly and ushered Mary and Jim to get in front of him. "We gotta run! Let's go!" Mary was limping very fast and he could see she was in great pain. Jim looked partially all right. Running while constantly looking in back of him, Calvin felt that sensation of doom hovering over his head. He was so angry he wanted to scream because the dogs were apparently following the scent of Mary and Jim.

Calvin sighed with fury as his rage boiled because Mary and Jim apparently did something to alert Harvey and the others. He thought about the black pepper, but there wasn't enough of it left to cover their scent and the mere thought of stopping to attempt to administer it was simply too frightening. Escape! Escape! Get away! Get away! Backlash! Backlash! was all his mind could think of at the moment. But reality quickly started to set-in. It told him humans couldn't out run canine animals and it was just a matter of time before the dogs would be upon them.

☼   ☼   ☼   ☼

Larry arrived at the Gilbo Plantation and was shocked when he saw a mob of men with torches and lanterns heading toward a forest. It was probably four o'clock in the morning and this commotion didn't sit well with him at all. Despite his hopes Calvin was still here, Larry's instinct told him all the ruckus had something to do with Calvin.

Just as he felt a barrage of curse words about to slip off his tongue, he realized this wasn't as bad as he initially thought it was. If the men were pursuing Calvin, there was a chance he might get hold of Calvin without conducting a search. They would either lead him straight to Calvin or bring Calvin to him; either way this mission was coming to a close. Larry was about to completely by-pass the big white house, but protocol told him to confirm his assumptions. He went up the stairs and knocked on the door.

A white woman with huge bags under her eyes opened the door. "Can I help you?" She looked surprised.

"I'm an investigator. I'm looking for a slave Mr. Gilbo purchased last week, I believe his name is--"

"Yes, his name is Calvin and they went after that ornery nigger right now. That nigger done ran off with two other niggers and they . . ."

Larry needed to hear no more and rudely walked away as the woman was still talking.

She looked at Larry walking away with dagger's in her eyes and muttered under her breath, "No good, low-life, disrespectful northerner." Then she slammed the door.

Larry entered the field and ran in the direction of the torches and lanterns emitting a very dim light on the dark blue horizon. He realized they had traveled a substantial distance in a very short period of time. Running at top speed, he reached inside his knapsack and pulled out the laser gun. There was no need in playing any more games and he was becoming tired of all this colonial bullshit. After the headaches he experienced during these last couple days, he now felt it was time to bring this little vacation to a rapid end. Plus, he was getting home sick and needed to see his girlfriend, Jamie.

He turned the laser gun's volume up to full capacity as he entered the forest area.

☼   ☼   ☼   ☼

With the pistol in his hand, Calvin felt like a broken leg rabbit on the brink of being eaten by a pack of rapidly pursuing wolves about to perish from starvation. Calvin wanted to increase his speed, but he couldn't; Mary and Jim's injuries wouldn't allow them to move but so fast and he couldn't leave them. He had to do something real fast because he could hear the dogs were minutes away. Looking in back of him for the hundredth time, he saw a galloping figure appear. He turned forward, looked ahead of Mary and Jim and saw a body of water; it was a river, maybe a stream or a brook. Across on the other side of the water was a strip of open land and just beyond was more wooded land.

They hit the water with a huge splash and their speed slowed down drastically. Calvin saw it was more like a huge stream; it was too small to be a river and the water wasn't moving in a forceful fashion. By the time they reached the center, the water had only reached just above Calvin's waist and seemed to maintain that level and then began to subside as they drew closer to the other side. Calvin flinched when he heard the dogs entered the water. He turned and saw there were five of them.

With lungs blazing with a fiery sensation, Calvin came out of the water and their speed picked up again as they headed for the trees. "Hurry! Go!" He urged Mary on who was directly in front of him. He saw Jim Roof was getting way ahead of them.

Suddenly, Calvin saw Jim slow down almost to a fast paced trot and what Calvin saw next almost knocked him silly. It slowed him down as well. The three men on horses came barreling out of the woods and stopped abruptly when they saw Jim, Mary and Calvin. Calvin turned and saw the dogs paddling in the water dogmatically. The dogs were only seconds from reaching the other side. Calvin turned back around and saw the three men were all carrying muskets and when they got a good look at Calvin, Mary and Jim they pulled their weapons. Calvin didn't know what to do; if he stopped, the dogs would pounce on them, but if they continued the white men would surely shoot them.

"That nigger's got a gun!" One of the men on the horse yelled.

"Stop or we'll shoot!" Another one shouted and took aim along with the others. "Drop it!"

Jim came to a full stop and Mary slammed into him. Jim wisely raised both his hands and was breathing extremely hard with eyes so wide they looked as if they were about to spring from their sockets. Calvin stopped with the pistol pointed downward. The thought of discarding the gun terrified him, since the dogs were now on the other side of the stream, rapidly approaching while their paws were kicking up dirt.

"I said drop that weapon, boy!"

Calvin quickly tossed it to the ground, and he braced himself when the lead dog leaped at him. Calvin swung a fist as hard as he could.

"YYEEEHH!!"

The dog screamed from the blow that landed smack dead on its wet nose.

The three men ignited with laughter as Calvin punched and kicked at the other dogs that arrived.

"I bet you the dogs'll win." One of the three men on horseback said.

"I got twenty cents on the niggers." Another one shot back. "They ain't nothing but dumb animals too."

The third one shouted. "You got a deal. I got thirty cents on the dogs. That's two 'gainst one for the dogs!" He laughed joyfully.

Calvin flung his knapsack off his back when the five dogs started surrounding them hesitantly while growling menacingly. Calvin noticed three more dogs had arrived dripping wet and growling with a maniacal ferocity. Now there were eight. He frantically pulled the machete just as a dog leaped at Mary. Calvin saw Mary strike the dog with both fists just as he brought the blade down upon the dog's back.

"YYEEEHH!!"

The dog yelled and was almost cut in half as blood sprayed from its body.

BOOM!

One of the men fired a shot at Calvin's feet. "Put that damn weapon down, nigger! You ain't 'posed to fight dirty!"

Calvin hesitated when Mary screamed for help when another dog locked onto her arm. The adrenaline that dumped into his bloodstream made him feel faint. Calvin hastily tossed the machete and ran for the dog locked onto Mary, but then Jim's bone chilling scream that came from the top of his lungs jolted him like an electrical surge. Calvin grabbed the windpipe of the dog locked on Mary and dug his fingers so hard into the dog's throat he chipped the nails on his fingers as the dog collapsed. The crunching sound of the dog's windpipe was loud enough to surprise him.

Then, suddenly, a dog had his leg. The pain was explicit. Jim Roof's hopeless and terrifying screams along with the explosive laughter of the three men were truly sickening. Calvin began pounding the dog's skull and then heard Mary hollering once again and Calvin realized approximately three more dogs had arrived. Where the hell are they coming from!? In between all the screams, terror-stricken confusion, and desperation drenched pandemonium, Calvin noticed Harvey, and the two assistants arrived fully armed and spoke to the three men standing at a distance. They all apparently knew each other.

One of the assistants whistled for the dogs to stop and they all stopped.

"What the hell are you doing!?" Harvey shouted. "Send 'em back! These niggers chose to run off and now theys gonna pay the price!"

The assistant yelled. "Get 'em!" and the dogs resumed their attack.

Calvin fought desperately with tears of rage rolling from his eyes as the men were having a good time, cheering, laughing and shouting happily. The dogs ripping, tearing and eating them alive were entertaining these sadistic bastards! But Calvin refused to give them the pleasure of seeing him died this way. He thought of things that would not allow him to succumb just that easy. That promise he made to his father resurfaced in his mind with the force of an atomic explosion and with one single punch Calvin crushed the dog's skull. As its teeth unlocked themselves from his arm and fell lifelessly to the ground, Calvin eyes were wide with rage and he didn't realize he killed the dog instantly. He noticed his fighting and killing skills learned during his short tour of duty in the U.S. Armed Forces coursed through his mind with reassuring clarity. He drew his fist back, about to pound the dog locked on his leg.

WHOOSH-BLLAMM!!

A beam of light streaked across the small river and shot right pass Calvin, missing him only by a foot.

With the dog locked on his leg and another one attached to the seat of his pants, Calvin forced himself to the ground, realizing this futuristic ray of light was aimed at him. He saw all the white men go into a terror drenched panic. The heat from the beam of light was so intense Calvin felt a blister instantly form on his right cheek as the dogs squealed even though the light had completely missed them as well. The smell of burning animal fur shot up his nose. When the beam of light struck the

111

tree about two dozen yards away, bringing it crashing to the ground, the dogs were momentarily scared out of their minds. Calvin instantly knew this beam of light was something from his time; military grade laser beams were so unique, if you had ever seen them once you would never forget them as long as you lived. When Calvin turned, he saw the white men were shooting at a man across the stream, lying on his belly taking aim.

WHOOSH-BLLAMM!!

The laser severed the head of one of the men on the horse. Upon seeing this, the other men panicked as they were pulled from a mesmerized state and jumped off their horses. No sooner than their feet touched the ground their horses were being cut in half as the laser beam did a wild dance of death on anything it came in contact with. The entire vicinity smelled like a barbecue of burning flesh.

Calvin went for the machete and when he got hold of it every dog in reaching distance was dismembered as he swung the weapon while inflicting several monstrous blows.

BOOM!

One of the three horsemen shot at Calvin. The bullet breezed pass him as he dove back to the ground while simultaneously dropping the machete and frantically crawled to the pistol he had discarded earlier. Meanwhile, the laser beam was sparking up the area and was competing with the light brought on by the crack of dawn sky that suddenly appeared. The screeching screams from the slave patrollers were truly ironic.

Calvin grabbed the gun and saw Mary retrieved the machete and was wielding it with grace against every dog that even thought about coming near her. Jim was standing behind Mary kicking at the dogs. Calvin took aim at the back of Harvey and pulled the trigger. His shot was drowned out by all the other gunfire, but he saw Harvey recoiled in great pain from the impact of the bullet and fell flat on his stomach.

"Mary! Jim! Get down!" Calvin saw Mary was in a standing position holding the machete, looking deranged with terror, hysteria and pain.

She obeyed and so did Jim. Three of the dogs had abandoned their attack and were fleeing toward the wooded area and Calvin took aim, but realized those dogs were only doing what they were taught to do. He let go of the aim because logic dictated if justice was to be commenced it had to be inflicted upon the ones who taught the dogs to do what they had done. And with that Calvin started looking for the two assistants, but he saw their bodies had been severed in half at the upper chest section by the laser. The sight was beyond grotesque.

When the last of the three horse men was struck by a laser beam that had cut clean through the body of a fallen horse, and disintegrated the man's forehead and most of the top portion of his head, Calvin knew it was time to go.

"Mary! Jim!" Calvin shouted. "Follow me! Do as I'm doing!" Calvin hastily slid onto his feet, frantically running in a crouched position toward the wooded area that looked like it was a mile away, but was actually yards away.

Larry stood with the laser in his hand. He saw he had killed all the white men with guns, but saw Calvin and two others running. Larry took aim and unleashed a laser beam. It missed completely. He tried it again with the same results. He sighed because they were too low to the ground to make contact. Larry started running at top speed keeping his eyes locked on Calvin who he saw was trying to get to those trees up ahead. He entered the stream, running at top speed. The water that splashed on his face was refreshing.

Calvin turned and saw the man with the laser gun rapidly approaching. Calvin's bent knee retreat increased and he noticed he had left Mary and Jim by a dozen yards. "Come on! God damn you! Hurry up!" Calvin forced himself to slow down and he let Mary and Jim get in front of him. He then turned and took aim at the man.

BOOM!

The shot apparently missed the laser beam wielding man, but Calvin saw it shook him up tremendously, causing him to dive head first into the water.

Calvin increased his speed and caught up to Mary and Jim. A few seconds later, Calvin turned and was surprised when he saw the man had made it to the other end of the stream. Calvin took aim and pulled the trigger.

CLICK!

The gun was empty and the shockwave of terror Calvin experienced in that moment was truly mind numbing. Calvin turned and saw with relief that the trees were feet away. Jim arrived and kneeled behind a tree and Mary joined him only seconds later. When Calvin arrived, he turned and saw the man take aim.

WHOOSH-BLLAMM!!

The laser hit the tree next to them and they felt the scorching heat burn the hairs on their heads even though the laser struck several feet from them.

"Run! Run!" Calvin screamed to Mary and Jim with the gun in his hand, hoping it would keep the man with the laser at bay. They were limping frantically into the woods. Calvin had to give them a huge head start because they were severely injured and bleeding all over the place. Calvin saw the man tried to stand and he stood while pointing the gun. He saw the man dove for cover. Yeah! It's working so far, he savored the thought with relief. The minute Calvin moved toward another tree a laser streak across the distance.

WHOOSH-BLLAMM!!

The tree Calvin was standing in front of moments ago came crashing down to the ground. Calvin scrambled for cover behind the fallen tree and realized it was about time for him to leave. His eyes were riveted on the approaching laser totting man. One . . . Two . . . Three! Calvin sprung to his feet and ran like he'd never ran before, ducking and weaving, zigging and zagging around trees.

Larry saw what Calvin did and bolted after him. When he reached the first fallen tree, he thought this was some kind of trick or something as he watched Calvin zigzagging as he ran deeper into the forest. With a smile Larry took aim, realizing all he had to do was time Calvin's crude maneuvers and this whole mission would be over. With the laser carefully pointed, his aim followed Calvin. Left, right, left, back right. Just when he was comfortable with the pattern of Calvin's movement, and as he pressed the firing button on the laser gun, a shot rang out from behind him, but he was certain the laser had struck Calvin.

CHAPTER # 12

Demetrius sat at Tina's dining-room table with a small stack of papers and a laptop computer in front of him while Tina sat across from him with a similar computer in front of her. After sharing his plan with his sister, Demetrius decided to visit Tina to get the first phase of his plan in motion.

Demetrius spoke while typing on the keyboard, "That Black Body radiation emitting around the Gallium Phosphide Crystal was not an accidental or natural occurring process. Somebody put it there."

"I can accept that theory," Tina stopped reading and looked up from the computer screen. "But what I'm having difficulty digesting is your conclusion that Eric and Diana are responsible . . . I just don't sense an evil vibe with them. We've all worked together for quite some time without any significant problems. I just don't see Eric wanting Calvin's position bad enough that he's willing to commit a serious crime."

Demetrius knew this was going to happen, since he initially felt the same way until he detected Eric's odd behavior and the deliberately altered components in the mainframe computer apparently put there with the intent to mislead. "Come here, let me show you something."

Tina came over to Demetrius, pulled up a seat next to him and sat.

Demetrius pointed at the screen. "I downloaded this configuration read-out earlier. As you can see, the alignments appear intact." He moved his finger downward. "What's this?"

Tina scrutinized the information carefully. She worked a number of universal time travel equations inside her mind, while comparing them to what was on the screen. Atomic spectra was increased . . . antiparticles placed in harmonic motion . . . before photons collapsed because of gravitation . . . electromagnetic fields mixed with Black Body radiation. Tina let all this circulate in her mind for another moment and suddenly a window opened. "Oh, shit!" She muttered when it all fell into place. Her mouth looked like the letter oh.

Smiling, Demetrius said. "Now, is that an act of premeditated concealment or what?"

Tina began nodding her head ever so slightly as she remained silent. Her deep thought process grew more evident through her bodily gestures. She was about to ask how did he know Eric and Diana were responsible for this, but that would be a stupid question because if it wasn't her or him, then it had to be Eric and Diana. "So they're making unauthorized time travels without any of those trips registering in the mainframe!?" She spoke as if the words tasted funny coming off her tongue.

"That's what I've been telling you." Demetrius started typing. "And that's not all of it . . . I also discovered a secondary return station. And it's completely unrelated to Timetron." Demetrius hit the enter key and information swarmed all over the screen. "Right now, I'm trying to determine where it's located."

"Oh, my God," Tina whispered to herself when she saw the confirmatory information. It was as clear as day. But how did they pull off a secondary return station intricately connected to the mainframe not on the grounds of the Timetron Lab without alerting anyone? That was no small feat. She rose to her feet with her arms crossed and a hand massaging her chin, concentrating with an intensity that resonated. "We have to do something. If we know Eric and Diana are committing time travel offenses, and do nothing, we'll be just as legally responsible as they are."

Demetrius sighed inwardly with relief. He needed Tina to set his trap correctly and he knew subconsciously he couldn't successfully commence with phase one without her. "So that means you're with me on this? I got a plan that--"

"I say we go to the board with what we have here and cut our losses. The board could send a rescue team to ensure Calvin gets to the Backlash portal. If we take matters into our own hands, we could subject ourselves to great liabilities, possibly even prison."

Demetrius knew this was coming. "I want to ask you a question." He waited until Tina gave a gesture indicating she was ready to hear it. "How do you think Eric got this position as the number two man on this project?"

Tina thought this was a ridiculous question. What is this, a joke!? "He acquired this position because he was the lead scientist at Continuum-tech and the Timetron board felt Eric would be a major asset to this project."

Demetrius typed on his keyboard and hit the enter key in a dramatic fashion. "Read this."

Tina began to read. She slowly sat down when the information started getting real good. Upon completion, she sat silently, staring off into space.

"Need I spell it out and connect all the dots for you?"

She turned and stared at Demetrius with a smirk. "I see you're full of jokes tonight . . . Well, I guess I'm in. Let's hear your plan."

☼   ☼   ☼   ☼

Eric's eyes flashed open as he scrambled out of bed when he heard the alarm to the secondary return station located downstairs in the basement of his five-million-dollar mansion.

Eric saw Diana, who was sleeping next to him, frantically jumped out of bed and hastily put on her pink terry cloth house robe.

Eric jumped in his house slippers and raced out of the bedroom with Diana stepping on his heels. He was almost salivating at the thought Calvin was finally out of the picture. Larry had been gone since

May 13th and it was now May 18th. The five-day wait was making Eric very nervous.

As Eric barreled down the stairs, and across a long marbled floor corridor, he felt like a kid racing for his Christmas gifts under the tree. He entered the basement and hit the light switch.

With eyes squinted from the artificial light beaming from fluorescent bulbs, Eric's anxiety transformed into terror. The return booth was empty and he rapidly moved toward it. As he drew closer, his mind ran wild, imagining all the things that might have gone wrong. The alarm went off, but where the hell was Larry!? If the secondary return station wasn't functioning, he was fucked up royally.

When he arrived, and peered inside the booth, Eric didn't know whether to be upset or happy. Larry was sitting on the floor inside the booth, cringing in pain. Eric frantically unbolted the door.

Eric spoke excitedly. "Is he dead!?" Eric reached inside, about to pull Larry to his feet.

"Get outta here!" Larry shoved Eric's hand away and struggled onto his feet on his own, limping out of the booth.

"Is he dead!?" Eric said, following Larry over to the counter. "What happened to you!?"

Larry felt truly embarrassed as he leaned up against the counter. "I was shot! What the fuck you think?"

Eric looked him up and down for signs of blood, but didn't see any. "Where? I don't see any blood."

Larry pointed at the floor of the booth.

When Eric turned and saw the blood on the floor, he realized where Larry was shot. "You were shot in the ass!? Is it life threatening!"

Larry blushed and spoke with anger. "If it was do you think I'd be walkin'! You fuckin'--" Larry's knees buckled and his head spun violently.

Diana grabbed his arm. "I don't think you should be standing. The bullet is still inside your body and moving like this may cause it to travel." She spoke to Eric. "We need to get him to a hospital."

"No!" Larry said. "No hospitals. What do you think the police will say if they find a fuckin' ancient bullet inside me?"

Eric nodded approvingly because Larry was right. "So, what are we gonna do about this injury? I'm not a surgeon nor is Diana."

"Get me to my partner. Get me to Ronnie's house. I'll be all right."

As Eric and Diana wrapped one of Larry's arms around their necks and moved him toward the stairs, Larry stumbled and fell crashing to the floor. He appeared to be either unconscious or dead.

Eric panicked because he still hadn't told him if Calvin was dead. The thought of Larry dying before he found out this information terrified him. "Larry! Larry, wake up!" He was about to slap his face, but hesitated when he saw his mouth move. "Larry, do you hear me?" Eric saw Larry's eyes slowly opened, and he grabbed his hand. "Is Calvin dead?"

"I . . . I think so--I mean yeah! He's dead! What do I look like, an incompetent fuck or something. Yeah, he's dead!"

Eric knew Larry was bull-shitting him. His first response indicated he wasn't sure and his tough guy ego wasn't going to allow him to admit he might have fucked up. "Okay then . . . Where's the body part or a piece of hair we agreed you would bring back?"

"Yoh, man, Calvin is dead! Under the circumstances, I couldn't get the fuckin' piece of hair or cut off a fuckin' finger. Shit happens, man."

Eric kneeled on one knee. "Listen, Larry, I wanna hear everything that happened, all the way up to the point when you killed Calvin. Please tell us the truth because this is a matter of life and dead." He was about to threaten him with reducing his fees if he got caught in a lie, but he realized he still might need this guy.

Larry explained everything up to the point when he aimed the laser as Calvin ran away, and just as he pressed the firing button, a shot rang out and he felt the bullet strike him in the right butt cheek.

When Larry started explaining how he had turned and killed the man who shot him, Eric cut him off and said, "Okay, Okay, we understand that part, but what happened with Calvin, did you go and see his dead body?"

"I couldn't because more dogs popped up! And when I tried to go see Calvin's dead body, another motherfucker took a shot at me. That's when a mob of more slave patrollers came right at me. I tried to knock off as many of them as I could, but it was a lot of 'em and the blood from the bullet wound was bleeding too much. I had no choice but to come back. But, I know I hit that bastard, I'm telling you."

Eric sighed and when he saw Larry was messing up his floor with all the blood, he decided it was time to go. "I think we'd better get you to wherever you're gonna get yourself fixed up."

It took them five minutes to get Larry in the car. As Eric got the Mercedes ready, Diana ran back inside and grabbed her and Eric's clothing. They hastily got dressed and were breezing down the highway.

From behind the wheel, Eric spoke to Larry, who was lying flat on his stomach in the back seat on top of a huge plastic garbage bag. "This friend of yours, Ronnie Neal, do you think he'll be interested in going back to make absolutely certain Calvin is dead?"

"I told you I think I got him!"

"Well, Mr. Drugan, I have a major problem with your statement you 'think you got him' instead of you 'know you got him'. This is no disrespect to you in any way, but I must be certain this man is dead. I'll pay him whatever his price is . . . Do you think he'll be interested?"

"If the price is right, there's a good chance Ronnie'll do it . . . Since we're on the issue of money, I guess you got my other half?"

Eric sighed loudly. "The deal was you had to kill him. You were supposed to bring back a piece of Calvin's hair or a body part as proof of his death, and after that, then you would get--"

"Listen, man," Larry said with venom in his tone. "I want my god damn money. And I got some issues to air with you any fuckin' way and it's gonna cost you extra. I'm tellin' you. I know I killed him. If you got a problem with--"

"I tell you what I'll do Mr. Drugan . . . If you can convince your friend Ronnie to take this job and he brings back the proof of Calvin's death, I'll triple what I owe you and pay Ronnie exactly what you're getting."

Larry liked that. After calculating the total amount, he began to see this as an offer he couldn't refuse. *Hey, wait a minute--this guy must be desperate to offer to pay such a high price.* The thought of squeezing Eric for more money entered his mind. *Nah, ain't no need in being greedy.* Then he realized this was all a waste of everybody's time because he was certain he killed Calvin! His aim was a bull's eyes and he knew he didn't miss! He suddenly came up with a solution; all he had to do was tell Ronnie to first make sure Calvin was dead and then find out where he was buried, dig him up, chop off a finger or two, and snatch a handful of hair, and they'd be financially okay for at least a year. "Mr. Seabright. I think you got yourself another deal."

"You sound as if you know for certain your partner will take the job. Do you really think he'll take it?"

Long silence.

"Well, that's hard to say," Larry felt compelled to make him sweat a little. "But, I do believe I can talk him into it."

An hour later, they arrived at Ronnie Neal's place; a huge loft located in an old ghost town looking, abandoned industrial district just on the outskirts of the city.

Eric had major doubts about Ronnie being an effective hit man when he first laid eyes on him. He was short, simple looking and wasn't intimidating in any way. Shit, Eric knew he could take this guy in a fistfight even if he had a missing arm and a broken leg. But, after Ronnie spoke, and when he saw the level of intellectual stability mixed with a rare and roguish ruthlessness, Eric realized he erroneously judged a book by its cover.

Ronnie made a phone call to a friend who was a doctor, and while waiting for the doctor to arrive, Larry told Ronnie the story that lead to his current bullet injury, and then asked him would he be interested in completing the contract. Winking his eye inconspicuously, Larry gave Ronnie their signal to pretend not to be interested. After some great acting, which involved convincing Ronnie to take the job, Larry felt damn good when he was able to increase Ronnie's fee to $80,000 up front and $80,000 upon completion of the job.

CHAPTER # 13

Calvin sat on the back of a brown horse staring at the empty grasslands up ahead and all around him. Moving at a slow pace, Jim sat in front of him while Mary was seated in back of him with her arms wrapped around his waist and the side of her face propped comfortably against his back. It was a clear, windless day with clouds rolling across the sky and the sun was beaming boldly, maintaining a comfortable 78-degree temperature. It was May 21st. Four days had passed since they escaped the dogs and slave patrollers and Calvin was still baffled by the man who was shooting the laser beams.

The more he thought about that very close call, the more his desire to inflict a severe and painful justice on Eric grew. It didn't surprise him that Eric would send someone here to kill him, but what did shock him was Eric sent a killer with a laser gun!? This was beyond dangerous and skirted the realm of sheer stupidity!! If such a high-tech device got into the hands of someone from this time era, it could literally discombobulate the future and possibly alter major future events. What if various technologies came before their time? He realized all the scientists from his time were unable to answer this basic question with absolute certainty, but they all agreed (as he did) that it would have detrimental effects. How stupid could he be!?

Calvin couldn't believe he could endure so much pain and suffering, and still be able to think as clearly as he'd been doing these past four days. Mary and Jim surprised him by the way they withstood those throbbing, agonizing bite wounds. Calvin had seven dog bite injuries while Mary had nine and Jim had thirteen. The laser induced burns were not of a third degree nature, but they were quite painful and Calvin thought Jim would never stop asking him a million questions about the laser beams. Calvin was in a constant state of fear for Jim's life because four of his wounds had become infected. At first Calvin thought it was rabies, but when he noticed he and Mary hadn't come down with an infection, he put rabies at the bottom of the list.

But, obviously, the question of rabies could not completely be ruled out because the incubation period of this disease was extremely variable--it ranged from 10 days to 2 years or more. With this in mind, Calvin felt an overwhelming dread looming over him along with that sense of extreme hopelessness because they had no medicine to treat rabies. So far none of them showed any rabies related symptoms, such as fever, uncontrollable excitement, pronounced spasms of muscles of the larynx and pharynx, extreme salivation and thirst, difficulty swallowing water (hydrophobia: fear of water), convulsions, exhaustion and paralysis. Calvin was driving himself crazy looking for these symptoms and he saw a case of stress related ulcers about to come to fruition. Along with the ever-present threat of the laser gun totting hit man on his mind, ulcers were practically a sure thing.

The only thing that was working in their favor was the fruit and nut trees all over the place, and the fresh water. The cool mountain streams were in plentiful amounts. By keeping the wounds clean, and bombarding their bodies with bioflavonoids, vitamins and minerals from the fresh fruits and good quality proteins and oils from the nuts, they were able to keep their immune systems strong and functioning effectively. But four of Jim's injuries weren't responding to the natural treatments and this had Calvin on edge.

The first day after the attack was the hardest day of the four. After getting only four hours of sleep, not only did they come across two plantations and had to go around them by turning north, then resuming their westward travel, but they clashed with a river. Calvin's calculations told him it was the Ocmulgee River, and this was no lightweight body of moving water because it was at least 500 yards wide and the water moved aggressively in a southerly fashion. The dilemma of crossing it stumped Calvin so thoroughly he decided to sleep on the matter with hopes that a rested body and mind would help him solve the issue.

Sure enough the answer came to him the next morning. The solution was obvious: They had to build a raft. It took Calvin and Jim three hours to build the three by four foot raft that came apart when they got just beyond the middle section of the river. Calvin was so glad Jim could swim or else he would've had a major catastrophe on his hands. With Mary locked in his embrace, they made it to the other end and continued their westward journey.

On the second day, they came across another plantation that had a huge barn with an attic containing all sorts of supplies. Under cover of night, Calvin, Jim and Mary entered the barn and retrieved a new wardrobe for each one of them; shoes, pants, shirts, straw hats for Mary and Jim, and an elegant black suit and a matching derby for Calvin. Calvin was dressed as elegant as the Duke of Earl. The only things missing from this outfit were the gold cuff links and a cane. This suit was truly a blessing because now they could move more freely, since Calvin became something (pretending of course) he never thought possible: a slave owner.

The plan was simply; if they were stopped by anyone, Calvin would simply tell them he was a free black man and Jim and Mary were his slaves. He knew if he traveled these southern areas claiming to be a free man, and Jim and Mary pretended to be his slaves, this might allow for more rapid mobility. Since Calvin spoke perfect English, and when compared to any slave patroller, Calvin was an academic and intellectual giant, he sincerely felt the ruse could work. It was truly amazing what the power of clothing could do and Calvin saw this concept in action when they came across a white couple riding a horse-drawn wagon. From the couple's response, no one could convince them Calvin was not a free man from the way he was dressed and the manner he greeted them.

On the third day, they clashed with another river, the Chattahoochee, but this time there was a Ferry Service. From Calvin's calculations, he realized this river constituted the divider that separated Georgia and Alabama. This Ferry Service was useless because the old white man with a boat just as old as him was charging a fee for carrying each passenger across, and Calvin had no money. Hiding in the nearby bushes, Calvin sat staring at the Ferryboat and the white man. Since his mind was made up (he was not swimming across the river nor planning to build another raft) Calvin focused only on how to get them on that Ferry. They had nothing of value to sell, nor was it wise to simply force the man at gunpoint to sail them across, which would no doubt ignite a massive manhunt for three blacks.

Calvin sighed helplessly. Then, he stuffed his hand in his suit coat pocket, felt the broken pocket-watch and an idea hit him. Although the watch looked relative new and was cheap looking, Calvin knew with the right salesmanship, he could convince the Ferry man this was a special, rare watch worth ten times its weight in gold--maybe not ten times, but definitely three times its obvious value. As Calvin headed toward the Ferry, the wave of doubts ran rampage in his head, but he ignored them. Calvin was shocked when the plan had worked without even blowing the watch's worth out of context. The minute Calvin said, "Me and my niggers need to get across and I got this watch--" The old man simply said, "Let's go" and snatched the watch out of Calvin's hand.

After walking for four straight hours in the blazing hot Alabama sun, Calvin saw a pasture with several horses grazing on the land. Riding horses wasn't new to Calvin, but taming a wild one was. If Calvin's bunions and corns weren't screaming for a break, he might have ignored the horses all together. It took two hours to convince one of the horses to let them get on its back. With the blankets they used to sleep on serving as a saddle and a twig tied to a rope serving as their reins, Calvin savored the relief to his feet and saw Mary and Jim were even more grateful than he was. That was yesterday and old Betsy (the name Calvin gave the horse) was still holding up.

Last night, after they set camp in a wooded area and got a small campfire started, Calvin noticed Mary was becoming bolder with her affectionate gestures toward him. Calvin understood why she was so deeply infatuated with him. She merely wanted to show her gratitude, but he held back the urge to respond to her open invitations. Ramanda had flashed in his mind each time he felt himself becoming weak and his hormones were about to take control. Also, the thought of breaking Mary's heart by misleading her into believing there was going to be a future between them also kept him pretending not to notice what she was doing.

But her boldness had become very intense last night because she became very physical; she kissed him passionately while rubbing his genitals, as he laid on the blanket almost in a deep sleep. At first Calvin thought he was in a dream and went with the feeling, but when he opened his eyes and realized where he was, he pulled away. He rolled over and tried to go back to sleep. When she continued her sexual endeavors, Calvin simply laid on his stomach. He could hear her crying quietly and it hurt him deeply. He wanted her just as much as she wanted him, but he couldn't make this situation more difficult than it already was!! This lead him to thinking about what he intended to do with Mary and Jim once he got to Oklahoma, since there was no way he could take them back to the future with him. He'd decided to get to his destination at least a couple weeks before the Backlash opened, build a small ranch or a simple home for them and hope they could survive without him. He knew Mary and Jim were well versed in farming and hunting, which was enough to put him at ease since these survivals skills were enough for them to sustain themselves.

As they moved along the waist high grass, Calvin shook loose of these memories of the past four days when he saw several indistinguishable figures suddenly appeared up-ahead about a hundred years away. It was a large group of people and it looked like they weren't wearing shirts. A few paces later and he saw clearly who they were.

Jim saw them as well and spoke, "Look! Them is Inguns!"

Calvin stared at the crowd of approaching Indians, and saw these weren't the regular peaceful type. They all wore war paint on their faces, and two of them possessed bow and arrows, while three others carried muskets and the other dozen or so were brandishing tomahawk hatchets and spears. Calvin's memory bank was suddenly running on high octane as it snatched snippets of information from way down inside the archives within his mind. These particular Indians were either Creek or Cherokee. The history lessons indicated these two tribes were the dominant groups in this region: Eastern Alabama. However, they weren't known to be violent, but they were territorial. As the Indians drew closer, Calvin realized they might have inadvertently wandered onto the Indians land without permission. The way the Indians approached, they didn't appear to be coming to celebrate. This was no peaceful welcoming committee.

Calvin looked around the immediate area to see exactly where they were, and his heart leaped in his chest. *Oh, shit!* They were trampling over an Indian burial ground! Hidden amongst the tall grass were graves scattered about and each one had a huge tree branch planted at the head of the dirt mound with a feather or some sort of relic attached, which apparently were grave-markers. Calvin was about to maneuver the horse to the right, but instantly realized they were surrounded by graves.

Mary looked around and then in back of her. "We's in a Ingun cemetery." Her voice was saturated with fear.

"Just relax," Calvin said. "It was an honest mistake. They'll understand."

A moment later, they completed trampling the graves and moved past two trees that had huge animal skins hanging from the branches. Calvin realized they were exiting the burial ground. Up ahead the Indians had stopped and were waiting for them to arrive.

Moments later they arrived, and Calvin was surprised because all the Indians were brown skinned. Calling them red people was clearly inaccurate. When an Indian wearing animal skin pants, no shirt and a colorful headband held up his hand, Calvin brought the horse to a stop. Then, suddenly, this Indian and another one who was similarly dressed, but had on traditional Indian Chief head-wear with huge feathers approached while all the other Indians started running. It took a few seconds for Calvin to realize they were surrounding them, placing him, Mary and Jim in the middle of a circle.

The Chief spoke to Calvin in his native tongue and when Calvin didn't respond, the Indian with the colorful head-band said, "Do you speak Cherokee?"

"No." Calvin said.

The Chief spoke again, but this time he appeared upset.

The translator said, "You must come down from your horse when you speak."

Calvin obeyed. He scooped up Jim and hoisted him down to the ground, and then did the same with Mary. He jumped down and stood looking at the two, while Mary and Jim nervously looked at the surrounding Indians.

The Chief spoke, and then the translator said, "You have angered the spirits. You have violated the resting place of the dead and their spirits are now restless because of what you have done!"

"I'm very sorry," Calvin said, "We didn't realize this was a burial ground because, as you can see, the grass was very tall and concealed the graves. Had we known this was a burial ground we would have never violated such a sacred place."

The translator told the Chief what Calvin had said.

The Chief frowned and folded his arms across his broad chest, staring at Calvin, Mary and Jim. Then he screamed angrily, which caused the surrounding Indians to start yelling war cries.

Calvin was startled and went into a defensive Kung Fu stance, while pulling Mary and Jim close to him. Even Betsy became agitated as well.

The translator spoke when the cries came to a halt. "Your assault on the spirits is unforgivable. This is the resting place of our great warriors. When they are disturbed in this manner, tradition says there must be a battle match. You will fight one of our warriors. If you win, you can go--"

"But why!?" Calvin said pleadingly. "It was an honest mistake. Had we known this was a gravesite, we would not have--"

The Chief spoke with intense anger.

The translator said, "You either accept this offer or you all will died. You--"

"I have severe injuries that won't allow me to fight. See." Calvin pulled up both his pants legs, showing them the wraps covering his injuries. He then took off his suit jacket and rolled up both of his shirtsleeves. "I have too many injuries to fight--"

"You will fight or you all die!" The translator shouted, "You lucky we are giving you a fair and honorable opportunity to make right the wrongs you have inflicted upon our great spirits."

Calvin thought this was sheer madness as he looked into the eyes of the surrounding Indians, realizing every single one of them were warriors in every sense of the word.

The Chief clapped his hands together and up stepped an Indian warrior who was positioned behind Calvin.

Calvin turned around and saw the brave had a tomahawk hatchet in his hand. He was slightly muscular with long black hair and a horrible

131

scar on his left cheek. The killer instincts in his eyes were as lethal as snake venom and it further announced that killing was his specialty.

The Chief spoke again, and the other Indians rushed toward Calvin, Mary and Jim. Calvin was about to unleash a barrage of punches and kicks, but then he noticed they were just clearing the circle for the fighting match.

When the brave moved slowly toward Calvin, sizing him up, waving the hatchet in a real threatening manner, Calvin handed Mary his hat and suit jacket. He then shouted to the translator, "How is this fair and honorable? He has a weapon and I don't."

The translator spoke to the Chief, who yelled something to one of the nearby Indians. This Indian then stepped forward and tossed Calvin a tomahawk identical to the one his opponent possessed.

It landed two feet from Calvin and he hastily picked it up without taking his eyes off his opponent.

YYAAHH!!

The Indian screamed as he charged at Calvin, swinging wildly and with maniacal force . . .

☼   ☼   ☼   ☼

Two nights ago, at about the moment Calvin, Mary and Jim were entering the barn that had an attic full of clothing, Ronnie landed a few meters from the spot where Larry was demolecularized back to the future. His response was similar to Larry's initial reaction, but was more inward. He too had heard of all the advances in time travel technology, but that science was like space travel because only the super-rich and the extremely powerful were allowed to dabble into those affairs.

As his senses gradually adjusted to the abrupt change from the interior of the time travel booth to the dark, hot, cricket infested Georgia night, Ronnie realized he suddenly heard barking dogs. The sound was at a distance, but as he looked around, familiarizing himself with his new location, he could sense they were drawing closer.

He pulled his electronic compass from the same knapsack Larry possessed only days ago and determined where west was and walked casually in that direction. He put the compass back and pulled the laser gun because he was now heading directly toward the barking dogs. Ronnie instantly realized there probably was a search team still in the area, and their dogs apparently picked up his scent. He had no intentions of going back, and since west was where he was going, whoever or whatever was in his way would simply have to get trampled over. It was as simple as that.

Ronnie turned the laser beam volume up two notches shy of the max. All the shit Larry had told him about these laser guns and all the hype he'd been hearing for years had him anxious to see the laser at work.

About three minutes later, he saw five hounds galloping right toward him. He took aim and hit the firing push button.

WHOOSH--BLLAMM!!

The laser lit up the whole area with a bright orange-yellowish light and one of the dogs looked like it disintegrated. The dog's body parts were splattered all over the immediate area as if it had come in contact with dynamite. The four remaining dogs did a remarkable about-face, retreating with amazing speed. If Ronnie were the joking and laughable type, he would've gotten a damn good laugh out of the scene.

Ronnie was totally enthralled with the way the laser felt when the stream of light shot from the weapon. Such a feeling could cause an addiction in no time he instantly realized. With glee circulating swiftly through his bloodstream, Ronnie took aim and repeatedly pressed the firing button. Trees were severed, crashing to the ground. After pressing the firing key six times, he realized he only succeeded in killing two additional hounds; a fallen tree crushed one of them.

About five minutes of continuous walking, Ronnie heard the mob of men approaching. He took cover behind a huge tree trunk and could hear them saying things like: "the light came from over here", "where's them damn dogs!?", "'member now, shot to kill, boys", and "if it moves, shot it!"

Ronnie pulled the infrared night goggles from his knapsack, put them on and smiled broadly when he saw the huge mob. He counted twenty of them. Just when he was about to take aim, he saw another ten appear on the far right. He wondered if the laser energy crystal could last through this sort of massacre that was forthcoming. Then, he remembered he had another laser in his knapsack, and in any event, Eric assured him the second one was provided only as an extra-added precaution (Eric even described it as an overkill) because one laser gun could fire two years' worth of beams if the weapon was fired fifty times each day. He liked this concept of being over-prepared.

He sighed happily and went to work. Each Hilly-Billy looking man he hit with a beam was killed instantly and they either had gaping holes in their bodies the size of a soccer ball or were dismembered. Everyone who tried to run was sliced down and Ronnie was amazed at the level of terror the men displayed in their zeal to get away. The men were either too stupid to simply take cover and lay low or they were scared completely out of their minds and into a suicidal retreat. But Ronnie could understand the fear they were experiencing because he stared death in the eyes on several occasions. There was no question when death was right upon someone, the mind registered only one thing: Get the fuck away from whatever the potential source of your demise!

By the time he was almost finished with the mass killing, he saw six of the men finally dove behind trees. Ronnie's stomach churned with nausea from the thick, penetrating and gruesome smell of burning human flesh. He couldn't comprehend why the hell the damn lasers were burning the men so intensely. It dawned on him for the first time;

maybe the damn thing was turned up too high. But he did remember Larry had told him he had kept the laser gun on its maximum level when he was here. He sighed because he wasn't in the mood for any cat and mouse games, and so he aimed at the base of the tree where one of the men hid behind, assuming he was merely wasting time because there was no way a laser would cut through a tree trunk that size. It was at least four feet thick, but he aimed carefully and pressed the firing key.

WHOOSH--KABLAAM!!

The laser ripped through the tree trunk as if it wasn't even there. The man stumbled from behind the tree as he tried to run and Ronnie saw his right arm had disappeared and half of his upper chest was also gone. The man collapsed after taking several terror-drenched steps. Through the goggles Ronnie nodded approvingly at the horrible sight.

When the other five men realized there was nowhere to hide, they loss all elements of control as hysteria gripped them. As they ran, oblivious of the laser beams they thought were lightning bolts from God here to punish them for all the diabolical and wicked deeds they had done throughout their lives, Ronnie wanted to thank them for making his job easier. Each one received a burning laser beam as the giant holes appeared in their backs, while two of them were severed in half.

With a smile, Ronnie was about to take off the night goggles and put them back inside the knapsack, but his professional instincts told him to keep them on. He headed west, inspecting his work with pride and his chest poked out in a dignified manner.

☼   ☼   ☼   ☼

Calvin jumped away from the hatchet and saw an opportunity to inflict a devastating wound to the Indian's back, but he held back. It didn't take a genius to figure out that if he killed this Indian they would likely kill him. All that "fair" and "honorable" talk was exactly what it

135

was: "bullshit." The Indians on the sideline were screaming war cries in a nerve-wrecking fashion and Calvin struggled to block out those shrieks. The brave he fought was almost insane with anger and Calvin saw this emotion was his greatest enemy because each time he swung with excessive force it caused him to stumble, thus, stupidly leaving himself opened for a deathblow.

The hatchet breezed pass Calvin's face and then his body as he ducked and weaved the violent sweeping motions of the tomahawk. Calvin knew there was no way he could maintain this defensive tactic consisting of bobbing and weaving much longer because it was already wearing him down tremendously. Breathing exhaustibly, he realized if he didn't do something soon, there was a chance the brave might get a lucky shot in.

KLAAM!

Calvin and the Indian's hatchets clashed and Calvin jumped away as the brave tried to grab him. Calvin unleashed a snap kick that made contact with the brave's arm that held the hatchet. The brave almost lost his grip on the weapon and the look on his face indicated just how truly surprised he was.

Calvin stepped away and felt his right foot became entangled in a twig or vines on the ground. Terror flashed through his whole body as he fell clumsily and saw the brave charging at him as he hit the floor.

BLAAM!!

The tomahawk tore at the ground just as Calvin rolled away from the murderous blow. He sprung to his feet and saw another opportunity to strike the brave, but again held back.

Calvin started bouncing in a dancing manner, about to show the brave what the Ali-shuffle was all about. When the Indian charged at him, Calvin tried to do a fancy move, but miscalculated the direction the brave was going to swing.

"AAHHH!!"

Calvin screamed when the hatchet sliced across his side in between his hipbone and the rib cage. In an instant, Calvin catapulted himself into a body roll when the brave went berserk with the hatchet. The brave smelled blood, assuming a kill was only seconds away and made it unequivocally clear he was going to capitalize on the blow he inflicted upon Calvin. He increased the violent swings of the tomahawk.

Calvin sprang onto his feet, and was running away backwards. Suddenly, a new, explosive surge of energy saturated his body. This was because he realized the injury was almost a coup de grace blow. As the blood trickled down into his pants, while still bobbing and weaving, Calvin decided it was time to stop toying around with this guy before his procrastination got him killed or severely injured. The thought of the other Indians retaliating if he out-performed their comrade entered his mind, but there was no other way to deal with this, he told himself.

BLAAM!!

Calvin spinning wheel kicked the brave in the face after perfectly timing one of his clumsy swings of the hatchet.

The Indians on the sideline suddenly became extremely quiet. When Calvin kicked the brave in the back of the head with a roundhouse kick and then planted a horse kick to his stomach, which brought him to his knees, cringing in pain, the sideline Indians' eyes were bulging in shock.

As the brave struggled back to his feet, and the crowd was in awe, Calvin kicked the hatchet out of the brave's hand as if he had kicked a football, in an effort to make a hundred yard field goal. The hatchet almost struck one of the Indians on the sideline.

The brave frantically tried to run for the tomahawk, but Calvin swept him off his feet with a spinning wheel sweep kick. The brave crashed landed on the hard dirt face first with earth trembling force and was dazed.

137

Calvin flipped him over onto his back, and sat on the brave's chest, making certain he restricted his arms and upper body movement with the weight of his body. Calvin raised the hatchet, about to bring it crashing down into the brave's skull.

The silence was so thick it was surreal.

Calvin held the hatchet in the air, and he noticed the brave started thrashing while futilely flailing his legs, but when he realized he was trapped, he became completely motionless. With a defiant facial expression, the brave braced himself for the inevitable. His chin protruded with intense honor and dignity.

Calvin turned and yelled to the translator. "I will not kill this man because his life is precious! . . . If the situation was the other way around, I would be dead! It takes a true warrior to let a worthy opponent live because killing is easy! Love, compassion and respect for life is often hard, but they are the marks of a true warrior!" Calvin flung the hatchet, rose from his seat, and headed for Mary and Jim. He saw Mary was clapping her hands with cheerful smiles.

The surrounding Indians maintained their position and were as quiet as an ancient tomb. After a moment, the Chief and the translator approached Calvin.

Calvin turned and saw the Chief instructing the translator to tell him something.

Reluctantly, and with humble gestures, the translator said, "The Chief says you fight as a true warrior. Your disrespect is forgiven. The way you fight is very strange, but very good. We would like to make right the injury you have." He was pointing to Calvin's side. "The Chief would like for you all to come to our home as guests."

Calvin was speechless, and when he looked at Mary and Jim for their views on the matter, they both had blank faces. Calvin saw no harm in accepting their offer because if they were going to kill him, it would have occurred by now. Plus, they needed medical attention for their bite wounds, and there were other things they could acquire from these Indians. He reasoned that in his current situation, he wasn't in a position to turn down any form of help, no matter how small it might be. He also sensed the Indians were very intrigued by his martial arts skills.

After a short pause, Calvin said, "We accept your offer." With a smile Calvin extended his hand for a shake and the Chief looked at it, baffled. But the translator reached over, grabbed Calvin's hand, and shook it firmly.

As Calvin, Mary, Jim and Betsy were escorted in a westward, but slightly northern direction, Calvin was scanning the faces of all the braves. When his glance fell upon the brave he defeated, Calvin saw that unmistakable expression of hatred and resentment. The desire for revenge seemed to emit from every crevice of his facial structure. Calvin pulled from the stare and wondered should he back down from this invitation. When his eyes landed on the Chief, his doubts disappeared because he knew if the Chief said he was a guest that was enough to keep this disgruntled brave at bay. At least that's what he hoped.

CHAPTER # 14

"Gradually increase the energy pitch!" Eric said to Demetrius, who was sitting behind the mainframe computer. Standing next to Eric was Tina, while Diana sat behind a computer a few feet away. From the control station, they were looking at the Time Machine.

The humming sound suddenly became louder. Seconds later, sparks from the base of the Time Machine appeared.

"Ignition in seven seconds!" Eric shouted. "Seven, six, five, four, three, two . . . one!"

Demetrius hit the send lever.

There was a tremendous flash.

Everyone's arms reflectively rose to their faces, shielding their eyes even though they were behind the protective glass of the control station.

When the light subsided, Eric turned to Demetrius. "Any visuals or audio?"

"No." Demetrius said, activating the keys on the computer keyboard. "It's the same as yesterday; fuzzy images along with distortion."

Eric held the boiling rage in check. *What the fuck is wrong with this god damn machine!?* They were scheduled for another meeting with the board, and Eric assured them the visual and audio components would be working. Since the board was just as eager as he was to see Timetron be the first to reveal to the world that time travel not only existed, but was completely safe and any subjects' journey was able to be monitored in all aspects. Eric understood Timetron's logic for wanting to make sure every aspect of this technology was intact and safe, but all this wasting time was eating him alive

Eric paced with jaw clinching tension in his face, wondering what the hell happened!? Weeks ago, they retrieved and installed Calvin's suggestions that caused the monitors to indicate the defects were rectified. This morning, Eric went inside the set-up program connected to the camera and audio recorder and the monitors again indicated everything was functioning correctly. It couldn't be sabotage, he concluded, because he made sure that he, and only he, was the one who made all final adjustments and repairs. This morning everything was intact, and even if Demetrius wanted to undermine the project, it would have been impossible.

Eric headed for the mainframe and stood over Demetrius's shoulder, looking at the screen for some answers. There were none. "Okay, pull him back."

The humming and flash ignited again.

When the commotion subsided, Eric led the group out of the control station and toward the Time Machine. Eric opened the Time Machine door and scooped up their new lab Monkey. "How was the trip, Charley!?" Eric saw the chimpanzee was excited and appeared to be in prefect health. Eric spoke to the others. "After we conduct a head to toe exam on Charley, we're gonna conduct another brainstorming session. We'll try it again after that." He headed toward the back section of the lab. "Be advised, it's gonna be a long night."

As Demetrius and Tina followed, Tina made eye contact with Demetrius and cracked an inconspicuous smile.

From the corner of her eye, Diana saw their little secretive exchange, and smiled inwardly because everything was going as planned. She couldn't wait to share the news with Eric.

☼   ☼   ☼   ☼

Calvin laid on a soft quilt inside a teepee, staring up into the darkness, feeling himself becoming weak again. Mary laid beside him, sound asleep. The sounds of the wilderness were like a serene song of chaotic tranquility. Calvin smiled when the memories of Mary's advances toward him during the past ten days here at the Indian camp skipped across his thoughts. She was maintaining a persistence that was wearing him down.

The third night at the camp, Mary asked Calvin why he wasn't interested in her. Calvin was about to explain to her that he was engaged to be married to a woman from his time, and didn't want to engage in any unfaithful activities, but held back. It was none of her business; plus he didn't want to start a process that might mislead her. Instead he told Mary he wasn't in the mood. He was surprised when Mary came right out and asked, "Why you don't like me, Calvin? Is it 'cause I was soiled by Harvey?" and then she started crying. Calvin vehemently assured her that was not the reason and comforted her as best he could without misleading her. Afterwards, he noticed she was content with making him happy and didn't care one bit if he wasn't interested (or pretended not to be interested). Twice Calvin came real close to giving Mary a serious run for her money in the sack.

But there was something else he was feeling for her and it had nothing to do with sex. It was making him very uncomfortable. Mary looked so much like Cookie and this was not making things any easier. He didn't want to believe he was falling in love with her because it scared him to even entertain the thought of allowing his heart to get caught up in this situation, since that could be very dangerous. But tonight he was feeling unusually sexual. Maybe it was the relaxed environment and the healthy foods he was consuming, or better yet, maybe some of the foods had aphrodisiac qualities. Whatever it was, Calvin was feeling in the mood. He sat up, propped the weight of his body on an elbow and stared at Mary. He felt himself becoming erect and wanted to touch her, caress her, make love to her, but with a struggle he pulled himself from the thought when Ramanda came to his mind.

TIME JACK   JOHN WHITFIELD

Calvin laid back down and let his mind resume its deep thinking process. The past ten days here at the Indian camp came into the mental picture and hovered there because this was a paradise compared to all the other places he'd come in contact with thus far. Calvin started contemplating whether he should leave tomorrow or hold off a couple more days? The date was May 31st, which meant he had about two months, exactly 63 days, to get to Oklahoma. He had covered a considerable distance so far and this accomplishment kept some of the tension at a minimum. But that voice of intellectual reason told him there were many miles to go and many unforeseen and unpredictable ordeals that lie in the way. Because of these thoughts, along with the possibility the laser gun totting hit man was somewhere out there searching for him, Calvin decided it would be wise to stay ahead. But it was hard to pull away from this place because he felt genuine happiness being here and saw Mary and Jim were having the time of their lives. Even the ointments the medicine man applied to their dog bite wounds were working with striking efficiency.

Calvin was extremely glad to see Jim Roof had even found himself a girlfriend. Although Quiet River was slightly older than Jim, her physical appearance did match his perfectly. The thought of breaking up their relationship didn't sit well with him. And with that in mind, he wondered if he could leave Jim here? That would sure take a strain off him. Calvin instantly made a mental note in his memory bank to ask Jim and Mary how they felt about this. If Jim was all for it, he would ask the Chief if this was possible.

Calvin rubbed his sore wrist and all those martial arts classes he was begged into conducting oozed into his current thought process. From the moment he touched foot in the Indian Camp, he'd been showing all the braves how to implement various Kung Fu kicks, punches and chops. Even the brave he fought, whose name was Burning

143

Feather, came to his training sessions held at the nearby Lake used as their main source of water.

He even showed them an old trick he learned from his war days, which enabled them to increase the speed in which their muskets and pistols fired. By filing down and rearranging various components inside the weapons, and by constructing a makeshift cartridge, the guns fired in a semi-automatic fashion. Calvin knew what he'd done could possibly disrupt the continuum balance, but knowing within the next century whites would annihilate just about all of these people, he had to do something, even though he knew enhancing the speed of their fire power wouldn't do a thing to change what was coming. But the gesture made him feel less pain in his heart and soul.

Calvin faded into sleep and the next thing he knew Mary was waking him up. After washing up and while he and Mary were eating, he realized his mind was made up. "How's your injuries?"

"They's alright," Mary sensed what was coming. She guessed it was good while it lasted. "They comin' along just fine."

"I have to continue west," Calvin laid the wooden bowl down. "If you want to come you're welcome. If not I can talk to the Chief and see if he'll--"

"I comin' with you, Calvin."

Calvin saw her decision was unequivocal. "Well, what about Jim? The way him and Quiet River are getting along he might be interested in staying here."

"Jim ain't gonna wanna stay here. He like me when it comes to being with you. Can't you see he likes you like a daddy?"

Calvin was about to tell her to slow down with all that daddy stuff. He liked the kid a whole lot, but he didn't want to start getting too attached. "Well, we'll let Jim decide."

When they spoke with Jim, they saw he was shocked by their inquiry. With squinted eyes, and a slight fear brewing in the pit of his

144

stomach, Jim said, "I's ain't stayin' here! Calvin, don't make I's stay here, please."

Calvin felt like a wicked demon and wanted to apologize to Jim, but instead he gave him something far better: a big hug. He pulled from the embrace, but held both of Jim's arms. "I'm not gonna leave you here if you don't want to stay. I just thought you wanted to stay because of Quiet River. I wanna see you happy."

"I's be happy with you and Mary."

It took them about a half hour to say farewell to just about all the Indians in the camp.

With two horses, Calvin on one and Mary and Jim on the other, they rode off with both horses piled high with various supplies; food, water, clothing, two muskets and two pistols. It was a sunny, beautiful day with clear skies as far as the eye could see. Dressed in his black suit and matching derby, Calvin's mood was in complete harmony with the weather. As they drew further away, Calvin continued waving good-bye to the Camp of about 75 proud, dignified and good-hearted Indians. But inside, Calvin sensed a danger rapidly closing in, all around him. He knew Eric's laser gun totting hit man was out there somewhere. He just hoped and prayed he was unable to follow his trail to this camp.

☼　☼　☼　☼

Ronnie stood next to an oak tree on the bank of the Chattahoochee River, watching the old boat with the matching conductor slowly moving across the river. His shiny black horse stood next to him. Several days ago, Calvin stood almost in the same location watching the same old man who was now transporting a group of people across to the Alabama side. Ronnie was waiting until the man was alone so he could have a talk with him. The river was too lengthy for anyone to swim across and it was logical to assume Calvin used this boat to get to the other side.

Ronnie was rather surprised his tracking endeavors weren't as stressful as he expected. All the little things like acquiring transportation (a horse), food, and camping sites were all falling in place nicely. Since he knew which direction Calvin was traveling, there was no wild goose chasing business to worry about. But he still didn't see why Eric thought it wasn't a good idea to simply send him to the area where Calvin was going and kill him when he got there. All that talk about killing him before he got anywhere near this "Backlash" was crazy, but Ronnie figured if Eric was willing to kick out all that cash, he wasn't going to complain. How the sayings goes, "the customer is always right", especially when he's "paying the cost to be the boss." In any event, Ronnie knew it wasn't going to be very difficult tracking a black man, a black woman and a young black child traveling west; not in this particular day and time, that's for sure. Thanks to Larry's information and the photo of Calvin in his pocket, he had a solid description to work with.

Ronnie headed for the old man as the empty boat cruised back to the Georgia side of the river.

As the leather skinned white man docked his huge boat, Ronnie walked right onto the vessel. "You mind if I ask you a couple of questions?"

The man looked at Ronnie with an expression that said he didn't appreciate his rudeness. "That 'pens on who you be." He wondered if the sheriff was sending a new face to snoop around. "I don't much care fo' you law men."

Ronnie cleared his throat because there was no way he could imitate this old man's accent, since it was heavily countrified almost beyond comprehension. "I'm not a law man. But I am looking for some people. Did three blacks; a man, woman and a kid come this way?"

146

"Sho' did," The old man sat down on a wooden crate. "Yep, it was three niggers, and they gave me a goddamn broken watch. I took 'em 'cross this here river 'bout five or six days 'go."

Ronnie nodded his head with a blank expression. Good, he was on the right track. "How much it cost to get across?"

"A Half Dime for you and a Dime fo' yoh horse."

Ronnie gave the old man ten Dimes, which almost gave the old geezer a heart attack because this was well over a weeks' worth of work. If he had known Ronnie was trying to get rid of some of these heavy, cumbersome coins Eric loaded him up with, the old man would have boldly asked for more.

After making it to the other side, Ronnie rode the horse until the sun started to set, and made camp just beyond some sort of cemetery. He could see it was an Indian burial ground by the feathers, animal bones and skins, and other relics attached to the grave markers. As Ronnie sat on a huge boulder roasting a frog he impaled on a twig over a small campfire, he heard approaching footsteps. He casually retrieved his laser gun, and waited for whomever it was to show his face. When he saw it was a white man with excessively thick facial hair, who looked like he was right at home in these backwoods, Ronnie decided to interview the man. "Hey partner. Come here."

The bearded man approached. "Howdy, name's Jesse Hogan." He extended his dirt covered hand, but Ronnie ignored it.

"You know this area well?" Ronnie laid the laser on his thigh as he spun the frog when one side became scorched.

"Sho' do."

Ronnie pointed to the tree stump a few feet away. "Have a seat." His tone was aggressive. He didn't like talking to people while he sat and they stood; it implied dominance versus weakness. He saw Jesse obeyed. "Have you seen three niggers; a man, woman and a boy?"

147

Nodding his head while speaking, Jesse said, "Yes, sir. Them dirty Inguns picked them up. The ones live over yonder." He pointed north.

Ronnie saw the man looking hard at his meal. "How far is it from here?"

"'Bout a five hour walk, but with that pretty horse of yours, you could do it 'bout a hour or two."

Ronnie gave Jesse half the frog and they silently ate. When he finished eating, Ronnie got on the horse.

"Hey, mister, I never got yoh name." Jesse said.

"You can call me . . ." Ronnie thought about the answer for a moment. "You can call me mister nightmare." He rode off into the darkness, while Jesse stood there, baffled.

An hour and a half later, Ronnie saw the dozens of teepees below, and realized the limited amount of moonlight was bright enough to enable him to make out the two Indians carrying muskets. He dismounted the horse and put on his night goggles to get an eagle's eye view of the camp. Ronnie wondered should he just go in there with a blazing laser gun, kill everyone in the camp and then find Calvin's dead body, or should he try to find out specifically where Calvin was sleeping, kill him without inflicting so much unnecessary blood-shed, and if Calvin had left the camp, squeeze someone to tell him when did he leave.

The answer to this approach was obvious and without further ado Ronnie headed for the camp.

CHAPTER # 15

Ramanda laid in her bed staring at the ceiling. Her emotions were not the only thing running high. Her patience and sense of focus were on a treadmill and the ugly faces of desperation and hopelessness were constantly forcing their way into the equation. But she had to be strong, not for herself, but primarily for Dameeka. She told herself this over and over again. On two occasions, she had to comfort Dameeka when she finally broke down in tears. Even though she'd been constantly telling Dameeka her father was coming home, Dameeka held on to the firm belief her father was forever lost. This was beginning to scare Ramanda because she knew family members had an innate detection system when it came to other family members, which had clairvoyant and supernatural qualities. At least that's what her psychic advisor had told her.

Ramanda rolled onto her side, and touched the spot where Calvin laid two months ago. Suddenly, she felt a rage start to boil inside her and she snatched herself from the thought of how long it's been. She wanted Calvin back so bad, she'd contemplated asking Demetrius to send her back to the year 1831 so she could personally make sure he got home safe. She suddenly sensed the tears about to start up again, and realized she was going to toss and turn all night long once again. She got up and did exactly what she said she wasn't going to do: take a sleeping pill.

Ever since that day Demetrius told her Calvin was transported into the past, she'd been having great difficulty sleeping at night. Since she was aware of the habit-forming nature of sleeping pills, she vowed to stop using them, but tonight she wanted to get a restful sleep.

Ramanda entered the bathroom, opened the medicine cabinet, found the sleeping pills and popped one in her mouth. As she turned on the water faucet, with the glass in her hand, she heard a noise. She

149

stopped in mid motion. It came from outside and sounded like a car door shutting.

When the car tires screeched, Ramanda almost panicked as she dry swallowed the pill and raced out of the bathroom. Ramanda didn't know why she instantly became so terribly frightened, but her instincts took control. It's probably nothing she repeatedly told herself in an effort to calm herself down as she entered Dameeka's room to make sure she was all right.

Ramanda hit the light switch, saw Dameeka's bed was empty and almost fainted right there on the spot.

☼   ☼   ☼   ☼

Ronnie heard one of the Indians shouting at him in his native tongue, and by the urgency in his tone it wasn't hard to conclude he was instructing Ronnie to stop. With the laser in his hand, Ronnie continued as if he hadn't heard a thing. When he saw the Indian raise his weapon, Ronnie pressed the firing key on the laser gun.

WHOOSH--BLLAMM!!--BOOM!

The laser beam ripped through the Indian's bare chest just as he squeezed off a wild shot.

Ronnie saw other Indians rushing out of their teepees and he introduced them to the thunderbolts from the underworld as each Indian thought of them when the lasers tore through their bodies. All the while Ronnie was looking for any black faces, and so far he hadn't seen one. A wave of gunfire ignited, causing Ronnie to go into a frantic dive as a bullet breezed pass his head. Lying on his stomach, Ronnie resumed the carnage. After killing an incalculable number of men and a few women (he'd stop counting after he killed the first eight), he suddenly realized he had to slow it down so as not to kill everyone. Conducting an interview now became imperative because from the way it was looking there were no black folks living in this camp, which meant Calvin left and as a result he needed to know specifics.

Ronnie saw a group of Indian women and children fleeing into a wooded area just beyond the camp. He rose to his feet, moving in a precautious instance, searching for survivors. Then it hit him. *What if they all spoke Indian? What if no one here spoke English?* He cursed himself for giving into the temptation to murder, maim and obliterate, since he probably killed the ones who spoke English. He entered a teepee and saw a woman and a small child cowering in the corner, crying in a state of terror.

Ronnie spoke calmly, "Do you speak English?" He couldn't understand a word the lady was saying. He was about to see the laser's damaging efforts at close range, but that little kid looked so, so . . . innocent. He turned, exited the teepee, and saw more people, including male Indians fleeing toward the nearby trees. Then he heard someone say, "This way, hurry" and then that same person transformed his speech instantly to the Indian language.

Ronnie raced toward the location, passing several teepees and almost ran smack dead into a toddler. With reflective speed, Ronnie pointed the laser, saw who it was and shooed the kid onward. Ronnie reached the last teepee, peeked around it and saw a man ushering the others in the direction of the nearby forest. Ronnie stepped from behind the teepee and shouted, "Hey you! The one who speaks English!" Ronnie saw two people turn. "If you run I will shot you with one of these." He pointed and fired at a teepee. It instantly caught fire.

The translator's knees almost buckled.

When a hysterical woman ran and the laser beam cut straight through her whole body, and the hot stream of light crashed into the nearby trees, the translator was frozen, mesmerized with a crippling fear.

"Do you speak English?" Ronnie moved slowly toward the man. "If I have to ask again you will disappear."

151

"Yes!" The translator screamed with tears flowing. "Please don't kill any more of my people, please!"

Ronnie smiled. He loved when people begged for their lives. He fought back a hard-on. "Where are the three blacks? The black man, woman and kid?"

"They're gone! They left this morning heading that way!" He frantically pointed west. "They're not here, they're gone! They're gone! Please . . ." He fell to his knees, falling completely apart.

Standing at a distance from the translator, while looking around for anyone who may be hiding, Ronnie realized he had to take this guy to a location where he could interview him without worrying about someone taking a shot at him. "Come with me. Don't make me say it again." Ronnie move back into the area where the bulk of the teepees were located.

When Ronnie turned and saw the translator following him, but was moving slowly, he shouted, "Hurry up!" He shot at another empty teepee, knowing it would serve as an excellent tactic to put some life in the English speaking Indian's movement.

When they were a suitable distance from the camp, Ronnie turned around breathing hard, "Now, I wanna hear everything about those three blacks . . . And if you leave out anything . . ." He waved the laser gun in the trembling man's face.

It took about five minutes for the translator to spill his guts, and everything else inside of him. Ronnie was even surprised when this terrified Indian told him the exact area where they were planning to stop for the night and even knew the town they were going to stop at in the next two days to purchase supplies. *Now this is why you gotta conduct interviews. Getting hold of this type of crucial information is well worth the effort*, he told himself rhetorically with an inward smile.

Ronnie looked at his watch and saw if he really pushed his horse there was a chance he could make it to the first location. He was about to kill the translator, but realized he was in a damn good mood. After slapping the translator, while calling him a "snitch", Ronnie kicked him square in the behind and sent him on his way. He then mounted his horse and raced out of the area with lightning speed.

Calvin was rudely pulled from his sleep when he heard the noise. He rose from the makeshift sleeping bag he had received from the Indians, and saw the noise had also awakened Mary and Jim. Even the two horses were irritated by the sudden noise. It sounded like approaching footsteps coming in contact with the brush. Calvin calculated the noise had come from a distance of about 50 to 100 yards.

After Calvin put on his pants and shoes, he whispered, "I'm gonna find out what that was." He quietly went to the knapsacks a couple feet from them and retrieved both pistols. He kept one and gave the other to Mary. "I'll be right back."

Mary grabbed his arm with a terrified expression and almost forgot to whisper. "We wanna come with you."

"No!" Calvin said firmly. "Keep the gun in the ready, and--"

The noise reappeared.

Calvin's head turned in the direction where the noise came from. "I'll be right back." Calvin tiptoed in the direction of the noise. Stepping into the tall grass surrounding their campsite, his hand trembled slightly as images of the man wielding the laser gun flashed in his mind. Suddenly, he realized it might be wise to simply pack up quickly and hit the road at an even faster rate. Then, he realized if it was Eric's flunky with the laser they would probably be dead by now.

Three minutes breezed by without Calvin realizing.

When he noticed he had traveled about a 100 yards, and still had not seen anything, he started wondering was he hearing things. *Nah, hell no! There was something out here.* They all heard it.   Even the horses heard it.

Another three minutes later, Calvin heard the noise in back of him and he frantically spun around. There was nothing behind him. Just when he was about to continue walking . . .

AAAHHH!!

The scream jolted Calvin into a frantic run back to Mary and Jim. With his heart thundering in his chest, he was waiting to hear the gunfire, but it never came. His mind was imagining all sorts of horrible things as he fled back to their campsite. As he drew closer and no additional screams followed, it made him even more terrified. The thought of Mary and Jim lying dead danced wildly in his mind. Just as he was seconds away, about to crash through the tall glass surrounding their camp, he slowed down when he heard Mary and Jim talking in a casual fashion.

With the gun pointed, Calvin barreled through the grass. When he saw the white man sitting on the ground talking to Mary and Jim, he was almost speechless. "Put your fuckin' hands in the air!"

"No, Calvin!" Mary said. "He ain't a bad man."

Calvin thought Mary had gone mad. This man was a complete stranger. "What's your business here!?"   Calvin said to the stranger, paying Mary no attention.

The thick bearded white man with sparkling blue eyes, and a pug nose, who wore buckskin pants and a cowboy hat rose to his feet. When he was fully erect, he looked like a natural born woodsman. "I was travelin' this here land and stumbled on to yo' little camp. I just stopped to say hello . . . The name's Clyde Jerkins." He stuck out his hand, but when Calvin didn't shake it, he wiped it on his pants.

Calvin's mind was moving at breakneck speed, trying to figure out how the hell this man crept up on them, what was he doing here and was he trying to trick them. "Listen, Mr. Jerkins, you're gonna have to do a whole lot better than that."

"Well, like I was tellin' Mary and Jim here. I'm what you call an abolitionist. I'm sho' you know what that is." He smiled proudly. "In order words, I fights fo' the freedom of black folks. I'm a fugitive because of my work."

As Calvin glanced at Mary and Jim who were smiling and looked convinced Clyde Jerkins was a friend, he realized he was beyond very upset with them. *How could they be so gullible? What if this guy is trying to pull a fast one on them?* For them to embrace, accept and open up to this man merely because he claim to be someone who's fighting for the freedom of slaves is crazy. Then he realized Mary and Jim couldn't read or write and had been born into slavery. How else would they respond; especially when a white man approached them acting like a true friend? "Well, Mr. Jerkins' I--"

"Please call me Clyde, I would greatly appreciate it."

As Calvin stared at Clyde, trying to figure out should he believe him, the history of John Brown popped into his mind and Calvin realized this guy looked a little like him. After a moment Calvin instantly ruled out Clyde being John Brown because John Brown didn't become heavily involved in abolitionist work until the early 1850's and never reached this far into the Deep South. "You say you are a fugitive because of your abolitionist work?"

"Yes, sir," Clyde said with a smile, now wondering why Calvin was so uppity. The way he spoke, Clyde was convinced he was definitely one of those free blacks from up north. "I was tellin' Mary and Jim I killed some white folks who owned a bunch of slaves. I personally cut all them slaves free. All together it was 'bout 50 of 'em. Even helped them all get to the free lands up north. Now, the law is after me and I just travel the lands down here in these Alabama backwoods, helping any black folks I come in contact with. The Lord has ordained me as his instrument against the evils of slavery and I live to fulfill this will through the grace of God."

Calvin didn't know how to respond, but it was going to take a lot more convincing before he would put his guards down. Since he never read any history about any rogue abolitionist in the Alabama region who was being hunted by the law, he was extraordinarily apprehensive. After a moment he realized there were countless major insurrections and bloody struggles against slavery that were strategically concealed and extracted from all the history books. With this in mind, Calvin became less tensed. "So, how long you been roaming this region?"

Clyde felt so good to be able to talk with other human beings he started telling Calvin, Mary and Jim his life story.

About two minutes into his story, Calvin cut in. "We're traveling west to a place just beyond Arkansas, now it's known as--"

"The Louisiana territory!" Clyde injected excitedly. "Yes, siree! I know 'xactly where it's at! I been there a few years back . . .

Calvin saw Clyde was very eager to do all the talking, and so he zipped up his lips and listened. Plus, this was an excellent opportunity to learn about this stranger.

About two minutes later, Clyde suddenly stopped in mid-sentence, and arched his head, listening. He saw Calvin about to say something. "Sssss!" His face transformed; an expression of wide-eyed surprise started taking shape. "Somebody's comin'! And they movin' pretty fast!"

Calvin heard it as well. He sprung to his feet and kicked dirt onto the campfire. "We gotta go!" Calvin knew anyone racing a horse this time of the night was someone he didn't want to see. And for some strange reason, he felt something was wrong. Goose bumps suddenly appeared all over his body as if some innate omnipotent force was telling him to get away because danger was rapidly approaching and the chills served as confirmation.

Within minutes, the campsite was packed up and they were about to get on the horses.

Calvin spoke excitedly to Clyde. "You're welcome to come along."

Clyde smiled from ear to ear. "Lawd have mercy! I sho' would love to ride with y'all good folks!"

Calvin and Mary hastily mounted Betsy, while Clyde and Jim hopped on the other horse, named Heckle. Heading west, they raced the horses at top speed, realizing the sound of the approaching horse was so close it was right upon them.

CHAPTER # 16

"No, we can't call the police," Demetrius said to Ramanda, while Tina sat on the sofa. Demetrius sat in the armchair and decided it was time to relax.

"This has to be the work of Eric," Ramanda said. "But why would he want to involve a child--"

"I don't think its Eric," Demetrius said. "It makes no sense for him to kidnap--"

"Then who the hell else can it be, god damn it!" Ramanda was about to start crying again. "She was under my supervisor and now I'm--"

"I agree with Ramanda," Tina said. "No one else could possibly have a motive to kidnap Dameeka. Maybe Eric snatched her to gain some leverage."

Demetrius sighed hard. "The reason it can't be Eric is because I have been monitoring all of Eric's conversations. The bugs I strategically planted on him indicate he--"

"Bugs!?" Tina shot back. "You never told me you planted bugs. What's the matter, you don't trust me? If I'm gonna be a part of this endeavor I want to know everything."

Demetrius didn't feel like arguing. "No disrespect, Tina, but some things are best handled on a need to know basis. As long as we're all working toward the same goal, I don't see why we're making an issue out of this . . . Eric's not going to bring any unwarranted attention to himself." he shook his head in disbelief. "Kidnapping Dameeka would be the stupidest move--"

"If it wasn't Eric, then who the hell was it!?" Ramanda was almost to tears. "This is crazy! I have to call the police. If I don't report this, I might be suspected of--"

"If the police gets involved," Demetrius said calmly. "This project will be placed in great jeopardy. Timetron is not going to allow that to happen, believe me. The government's hands are involved in this project and strings will be pulled if the local police becomes involved." He was certain it wasn't Eric, but he realized he should side with Ramanda and Tina for the sake of keeping the police out of this. "Let's say Eric is responsible. Do you think he would hurt Dameeka? I don't think so. He's trying to become the first documented time traveler and he is not going to throw that away by harming a child of one of his colleagues."

Ramanda struggled to keep her nervousness under control. "What the hell am I gonna tell her school when they start asking questions?"

Tina spoke, "Tell them you have to sign her out because of a family emergency. I have to agree with Demetrius. If the police gets involved Timetron is gonna pull strings, and I don't think Eric is stupid enough to hurt Dameeka."

"Well," Ramanda pulled herself together with a struggle. "That plan of yours better take effect soon because if it doesn't, I'm going to the police. In the meantime, I think we should come up with a way to find Dameeka on our own."

Demetrius held back his outburst because he saw his sister simply didn't realize the life and death situation she was about to not only drag herself into, but him and Tina as well.

Ronnie kicked the horse in the head as it laid on the ground breathing profusely. "You motherfucker!"

He was chasing two horses; each one carrying two people and suddenly his horse had stepped in a ditch. He heard the horse's leg snap like a dried-out piece of wood as he was hurled from the horse's back and hit the ground with an awesome impact.

With blood leaking from a cut over his right eye, Ronnie now paced. He wondered who the fourth person with them was. There was supposed to be three. But he was certain it was them and that brought a temporary smile to his face. The smile disappeared when reality set in. Now they knew he knew where they were and that also meant they knew not to stop at that town near the . . . river.

Shit! Ronnie sighed because that meant all his plans were now out the window. He relaxed, trying to think. When he noticed the horse was moaning in great pain, and the noise was distracting him, he pulled the laser gun, turned it down two notches and shot the horse's head off.

As the sun began to appear on the horizon, and the starlit night sky deteriorated with rapid speed, Ronnie started walking west, hoping an idea would soon surface. About twenty minutes later, it came. *Yes! That'll work.* He looked at the Micron watch and for the first time he wondered if this damn thing really worked. Well, if it didn't, he would soon find out.

He took several slow and deep breaths, bracing himself for the flash. He pressed the return button.

Eric was in the bathroom brushing his teeth when he heard the alarm downstairs in the basement. With a mouth full of toothpaste, he barreled out of the bathroom and entered the basement seconds later. He hit the light switch and saw Ronnie standing in the return booth.

Diana arrived breathing hard over his shoulder. "Wow! That was rather quick."

Smiling broadly, Eric approached and suddenly realized he forgot to spit out the toothpaste. He was so excited he swallowed it, wiped the corners of his mouth and snatched open the door.

"I guess mission accomplished." Eric was still smiling.

Ronnie stepped out with a wooden face. "No mission accomplished yet." He saw Eric's twisted facial expression and wanted to slap it off his face. "There was a few minor set-backs, nothing to worry about. All I need you to do is transport me to--"

"What the hell are you talking about!?" Eric shouted. "I can't just transport you whenever I want! Timetron--" He caught himself, realizing what he was about to say was none of Ronnie's business. He calmed himself down, realizing there was no need in dwelling on the past. The object was to fix this problem and keep moving. "Sorry for that outburst. Now, what happened?"

It took Ronnie a minute to explain what happened. "Now, all we have to do is transport me back to a couple of places in that region to see if Calvin stopped at any of those locations. If he did, then you can transport me back a few days earlier and he'll meet his maker."

Eric was extremely apprehensive about this plan. All of that bouncing back and forth could create some difficulties, but there was no other available plan he could think of. Not to mention, all of this constant, back-to-back time traveling could inevitably have a detrimental side effect on Ronnie's genetic integrity. The second this thought registered Eric kicked it aside, since he really didn't give a shit about Ronnie's wellbeing. He turned to Diana. "What do you think?"

"It's gonna take us a couple days, but it sounds like a plan to me."

Eric turned back to Ronnie. "Let's do it." Eric led the way.

From a distance of about a quarter mile, Calvin stood near a huge mountain, looking at the Mississippi town located about a mile across the border. It was hot, humid and a haze hung in the atmosphere. The sweat was pouring off the dark brown skin of Calvin's face. Mary, Jim and Clyde were nearby, watching and sweating as well.

After the stranger chased them on horseback in Alabama, Calvin decided not to stop at any of the towns in that state, since he suspected whoever was chasing them acquired that information from someone at the Indian camp. Another motivating force which kept Calvin on the move was Eric's laser gun wielding hit man who was likely working overtime and could pop up anywhere at any time. They had been traveling nonstop for eight straight days. It was June 9th and all of their most basic supplies had been consumed days ago. Stopping at this town was not a matter of choice, it was an issue of necessity.

"I'm going in there." Calvin said. "What's the attitude of the people in this town, Clyde?"

"Just like all the white folks in these parts; mean, hateful and abominations of God's grace."

Calvin assumed that meant blacks were treated worse than animals, which obviously was not unusual. "It'll probably look better if Mary and I go." He gave Mary a glanced. "You feel up to it, Mary?"

"If'en that's what you want, Calvin, I'll go with you."

"Clyde, hold it down until I get back." Calvin said.

"Just make sho' you got yo' pistol close-by," Clyde said with his arms folded across his frail chest. His ego was flaring up again and was eating him alive. "I would go in there instead of lettin' y'all do it, but these folks know who I am and what I stand fo'."

"I understand, Clyde," Calvin said, sensing Clyde's guilt. "That's why I didn't ask you. Don't worry, I have my pistol." He patted the gun tucked in the back waist of his pants. "We'll be back before you notice we're even gone." He cracked an insincere smile at Clyde and turned to Jim. "You fine with this, Jim?"

"I's wanna come with y'all." Jim pouted.

Calvin ruffled his nappy head. "I promise you can go with me the next time." He saw Jim nod his head. "We'll be right back."

Calvin and Mary headed for the town. It took them twenty minutes to reach the inner perimeter.

When they entered the inner most area of the town, Calvin noticed the whites were looking at him strangely. But after scrutinizing their expressions, Calvin realized it was because of the suit and derby he was wearing. A black man dressed like this was indeed a rarity. He could also tell they were very dangerous because of the envy and jealousy resonating from their stares. He could also see it in their gestures, which clearly stated: "Who the hell do this nigger think he is walking up in this town like he owns it!"

Calvin's eyes doted across the wooden, shabby buildings, searching for a hardware store or any store that carried supplies. There were barbershops and numerous grocery stores, but no hardware store. He didn't want to ask anyone anything, but when he realized he might have to walk around in circles looking like he was lost, he was re-considering giving in to the idea of asking someone. Then he saw a lawman, probably the sheriff or a deputy. Normally lost people would ask the police for assistance with respect to directions, but this guy looked truly evil. He had Klu Klux Klan written all over every part of his body. Asking him was apparently out of the question.

Calvin saw a white man dressed in a brown suit with a large mustache approaching. Just when he was about to ask this man for directions, he saw the store with the sign that said "Sam's Supplies." When he passed this man, he suddenly felt a strange vibration. Calvin turned around to get another look at the man. Something about him was not quite right. Come to think of it he looked totally out of place. And what was that feeling he just experienced? Looking at the man's back, Calvin shrugged and forced himself to continue on his way to the store.

When he arrived on the wooden platform, Calvin turned and saw a couple staring at him. Mary looked nervous and petrified. He grabbed her hand, squeezed it tight and said to Mary, "Relax, it's all right. Let's go inside." He was about to enter, but stopped abruptly when he saw the wanted poster plastered on the side of the door. Mary bumped into him as he read it quickly, squinted his eyes in deep confusion and entered the store. He instantly realized he was unable to conceal the shock that just invaded in mind.

Ronnie turned and looked back. When he saw Calvin and the woman enter the store, he did an inconspicuous about-face and casually moved toward the store. He wondered why Calvin responded as if he had suddenly recognized him or had become agitated when they locked stares with each other. Was it the fake mustache he was wearing? He needed this disguise because of all the crazy stuff he'd done here when he was bouncing back and forth in time, looking for Calvin. He put his mind to rest on the subject when he remembered Calvin had never saw him before.

Ronnie sighed because he wanted to laser beam the shit out of Calvin right there on the spot, but there were about six-lawman roaming around. Since he promised Eric he would stop killing innocent people from this time era, he couldn't gun Calvin down in the middle of a crowded street, in broad daylight. His word was the most precious and most valuable thing he had, and there was no need to treat it like dirt, especially when a little patience and ingenuity could get the job done. As he reached the platform of the store, he also looked at the poster and then entered.

☼　☼　☼　☼

"Listen, Mister," Calvin said humbly to the shop owner. "I simply would like to buy a few items and we'll be out of your hair."

Wearing a dirty green shirt with a clean shaved ancient face, the shop owner said with countrified force. "I ain't gonna tell you again, we don't serve niggers in this town. Whether you free or not."

Calvin turned when he heard someone entered the store. His heart flinched when he saw it was the man with the mustache. That same weird internal vibration instantly returned.

Ronnie stared at Calvin as he walked over to the countered and stood less than a yard from Calvin. Ronnie spoke to the shop owner. "What's the problem with serving black folks, Sam?" His imitated country accent was a complete absurdity.

Calvin eased away from the man as the shop owner responded to his sarcastic remark. Calvin now knew for certain this man wasn't right. He was faking the accent and Calvin's scientific mind came back to life. He analyzed his inner response to this man's presence as if it was under a magnifying glass. He realized the gallium phosphide chemical proponents within Time Travelers from the same time era, if two or more came in contact with one another, could spark chemical reactions in some subjects. Calvin concluded he had just undergone one of those chemical reactions.

Calvin wanted to reach for the pistol tucked in the back waist of his pants. Why on God's earth did he put the damn gun in the back instead of the front!? Within seconds he realized grabbing the gun in time to use it was out of the question. His eyes nervously darted around, and when they landed on the shotguns hanging on the wall behind the counter, Calvin wondered could he get to one before this guy opened

165

fire? *Impossible! Nobody in the universe was that fast!* Calvin fought to control the panic provoking stress growing with every passing second.

Calvin decided he had to try something. "You know what, Sam? Forget it! We'll go somewhere else!" He hastily headed for the door, while shoving Mary along.

"I wouldn't do that if I were you, Mr. Thompson." Ronnie said teasingly as he pulled the laser gun.

Calvin stopped instantly. Shocked, he turned around, realizing the man knew his name. He was even more shocked when he saw the laser gun.

Suddenly, running footsteps on the wooden platform were heard outside, rushing toward the front door. The sheriff entered the store with a shotgun in his hand with one of his deputies on his heels.

In an instant, Calvin moved as fast as he could, but he sensed it was too late.

CHAPTER # 17

Eric hated these executive board inquiries at moments like this. Sitting in the end seat on the left next to Diana, Eric tried to quiet down his anxiety as the board sat on the platform, seated in a neat row of seven, getting themselves ready to chew out the behinds of their project workers. Eric turned his head slightly and saw Demetrius, who sat next to Diana, looking a little too calm. Next to Demetrius was Tina, who was reacting appropriately for this occasion.

The visual and audio components were not functioning at all and Eric had nothing of substance to report to the board. When James Simpson, who sat in the center of the row, spoke, Eric was jettison into a state of attention.

"This report is very disturbing, Eric." James was glancing down at the document in his hand. "Is there any reason why the audio and visual components are, as you said here, 'irreparably flawed'?"

Eric cleared his throat and swallowed hard. "I believe the problem may lie within the audio and visual equipment, sir. I say this because all control devices indicate the recorders are functioning correctly, yet when we transport, nothing reads on the monitors. My team and I have examined every possible variable up to this point."

There was a moment of silence.

Karen Koenigstein, who sat in the second seat from the right, said, "I would assume you came to this conclusion based on the detection of an identifiable defect, as opposed to drawing an assumption merely because you were unable to rectify the matter."

Eric felt a nervous sweat formulating under his armpits. A few days ago, he examined the internal workings of the camera and recorder and they both were working perfectly. "I conducted a perfunctory examination of the equipment, and based on what I saw, the camera and recorder did not have any detectable defects. However, without specialized instruments to have each component meticulously analyzed, it's practically impossible to say with absolute certainty the problem does not stem for one of these inner components."

The entire board stared at Eric for a long moment.

Keith Wilson, who sat in the first seat on the left, said, "Eric, I'm sure you are aware of the critical nature of this delay. And please understand that we do appreciate your hard work and efforts, but this board needs a publicly documented, appropriately accredited time travel. Continuum-tech and a few other labs are gaining upon us. With this in mind, we have decided to enforce a deadline. If this board does not receive confirmation that all devices are functioning by June 30th, we are going to replace you and your team."

Eric's heart felt like it was stabbed with a burning hot dagger. He was shattered. The punch-drunk feeling was so strong it nearly brought tears to his eyes.

Demetrius shifted in his seat and smiled inwardly. Diana wanted to fling a few curse words at the board for ignoring all their hard work. Tina felt her career slipping from her grasp and could have wrung Eric's neck for getting rid of Calvin; if he were here none of this would be happening.

Mark Phillips, who sat next to Keith, said, "Linda Welch is on standby, and she has already displayed an eagerness to come onboard." He stared at Eric because he knew Linda was an old friend of his. "As you know, she's one of Continuum-tech's heavyweights."

Oh God no! Eric thought as the terror took hold. He thought he had finally got away from that trifling bitch. With a struggle, Eric pulled himself together.

Sydney Smith, who sat in the first seat on the left, said, "The investigation into Calvin's disappearance has taken a turn. This board has received several anonymous letters indicating that Calvin's disappearance was the work of sabotage." He saw the anxiety-ridden expressions on the faces of all four scientists. "Relax. We are fully aware of the possibility that those letters could be nothing more than lies or rumors. They may even be from our competition, trying to disrupt our endeavors. This is why we're bringing in an independent investigator. He'll be working closely with you all, and I advise you all to cooperate fully."

Eric trembled inside. A million terrifying things suddenly scrambled through his mind; his brain felt like a volcano about to explode. He forced himself to breathe deeply, and said, "With all due respect to this board, I vehemently object to this course of action. Now that we have a deadline to meet, it's going to be very difficult to work at optimum level if we're going to have someone breathing down our backs at such a crucial moment in our endeavors."

Demetrius, Tina and Diana all voiced their agreement.

The board whispered among themselves. A moment later, James said, "Your objections have been noted. The independent investigator will be held in abeyance for two weeks. In the meantime, this board is looking forward to some tangible results before our next meeting. This meeting is now adjourned."

☼   ☼   ☼   ☼

Calvin dove into Mary. As they hit the floor, Calvin saw he had injured Mary by the way she grimaced. The laser beam just missed Calvin by a foot, but he still felt the burning sensation on his back. He frantically scrabbled behind a wooden rack while shoving Mary along.

At the moment Calvin dove, and the laser beam tore a hole in the wall behind him, the sheriff fired his musket at Ronnie, who was already seeking cover behind a group of barrels. The bullets rip through a barrel, spilling its content all over the floor. The strong, penetrating smell of whiskey fumigated the area.

169

Calvin frantically retrieved his pistol, realizing his back was still scorching hot and the smell of burning material grew thicker. When he felt the flame on his back touched his skin he almost shot to his feet, but instead he frantically rolled onto his back and smothered the fire. While all this was happening, gunfire was going off and the laser beam was blowing huge holes in the wooden walls.

The mixture of burning wood and other material along with the smell of the whiskey turned Calvin's stomach. Peering from behind the wooden rack, Calvin couldn't see Eric's hit man.

BOOM!

The deputy took a shot at Calvin. He was crouching in front of the threshold of the door while the sheriff was inside the store kneeling on one knee; he was hiding behind a turned over table that once had leather saddles on top of it.

The sheriff yelled, "Drop your weapons right this minute! That means everybody!"

Ronnie yelled from behind the barrel of whiskey, "Hey Calvin, why don't you do as the good law man said. If you come on out, we can prevent all these people from losing their lives . . . I'll kill you quick, don't worry, okay."

Calvin peeked around the rack again, and saw the deputy sticking his head in and out. "Sorry, Mister whoever you are, I'm not in the mood for dying right about now."

"Ahh, ain't that a pity," Ronnie said. "Because in that case, I'll just have to show you that you can't hide from me. There's nothing in here you can hide behind and be safe from my wrath." Ronnie wasn't certain where Calvin had scrambled to, but he knew where the sheriff, his deputy and the shop owner were. "Keep your eye on this." He turned the laser gun up to one notch shy of the max. He quickly rose to his feet, fired at the counter where the shop owner was hiding and shot back down just as the sheriff and his deputy opened fire.

There was a bright flash, an explosion, a mangled scream and then silence. The sheriff and his deputy were so perplexed they thought they were dreaming. They could not understand how it was possible for a man to shot lightning bolts from a tiny black box.

The deputy yelled to someone outside. "Go get some backup over here, goddamn it!"

When the laser beam struck the counter, Calvin flinched because the counter was only a few yards from him and Mary. Plus, the heat and the impact of the laser ripping at the counter were devastating. He embraced Mary, who was on her stomach trembling. "It's gonna be all right."

Mary grabbed Calvin's hand and held onto it.

Ronnie sprung into a standing position again, fired a laser and hit the deck just as fast.

The laser cut through the table where the sheriff hid. Although the laser beam was not a prefect shot, it was close enough to disintegrate half of the sheriff's head, killing him instantly.

Calvin again flinched when the laser made contact with its target because he could hear the beam literally slicing through everything that it touched.

Again, Ronnie sprung to his feet, and fired at the side of the door where the deputy was positioned. The size of the threshold was enlarged substantially when the laser struck the wall. With a severed right leg the deputy crashed to the ground screaming as the beam almost struck a nosy pedestrian who was standing far too close to the store.

When the crowd outside saw the laser beam cut through the wall, they panicked and fled farther away from the store.

Ronnie shouted to Calvin. "Come out, come out wherever you are." Ronnie sang teasingly. "So what's it's gonna be, Calvin? Am I gonna have to simply shoot up the place until I get you or are you gonna come on out of that hiding place, so we don't have to drag this thing out

171

until more law men come. I'll murder 'em all and because you ain't come out it'll be your fault. And after all that, I'll disappear just like that." He snapped his finger.

Calvin remained quiet, knowing he was trying to determine his location.

"Hey, Calvin, you know what else? That daughter of yours, Dameeka, man, is she a pretty little thang. You should've heard her scream when I drilled her with this nine-inch cock of mine!"

Calvin felt like he died when he heard this remark. Something exploded inside of him, and the sensation was interfering with his breathing. The anxiety mixed with pure rage and galvanizing disbelief nearly brought tears to his eyes. He rose and fired a shot at the area where the voice came from. With watery eyes, he flew back to the floor. "You motherfucker! I'll kill you and everything you ever loved, if you harmed my child!"

Ronnie almost burst out laughing because Calvin fell for the oldest trick in the book. Find out the name of a love one, tell the target you're fucking them and low and behold they fall apart like a stale piece of crumb cake. Eric showed him several pictures of Dameeka; she was a cute kid. But Ronnie was not into the business of murdering or traumatizing kids and he saw Eric felt the same way.

Ronnie moved up a little, getting in position because now he knew exactly where Calvin was located. He was planning to spring up and fire as many lasers as the futuristic weapon would take to disintegrate that entire area. He braced himself. On the count of three . . . One . . . Two . . . Three!!

☼   ☼   ☼   ☼

Earlier, Clyde sat on a huge rock, eating an apple, watching the town. Suddenly, he saw people running. Since there were buildings blocking the area where the people were headed, Clyde became very agitated. When he heard the muffled sound of gunfire, and suddenly saw people running in the opposite direction where the mob was initially headed, Clyde decided it was time to go inside the town. Plus, his gut instinct told him the shooting had something to do with Calvin and Mary.

Clyde rushed over to the horse, Heckle, hastily retrieved his two pistols, checked to make sure they were loaded and then crammed his pocket full of extra bullets. "Come on, Jim, this is yoh chance to ride that big ole horse by yoh-self. Hurry now." Clyde climbed on Heckle's back, and smiled when he saw Jim mounted the other horse, Betsy, with acrobatic grace. "Listen up now, I need you to watch these horses when we gets about right over yonder by that house right there." He pointed at the first house on the outskirts of the town. "You just wait right there until Me, Calvin or Mary gets back." When Jim nodded, he raced the horse.

When Clyde arrived at the location, he jumped off the horse, and waited for Jim, who was only seconds behind him. When Jim was in place, Clyde ran toward the excited looking white people and blended in the crowd. A couple of seconds later, he saw the root of the commotion was at the hardware store. The adrenaline rush was strong because it was confirmed; this event definitely involved Calvin and Mary. As Clyde increased his pace to a frantic fast walk, he was hoping and praying he wasn't too late to help them.

Clyde nonchalantly broke away from the crowd and headed for the back of the hardware store. So far no one recognized him. He ran to the back, turned the corner and saw six men. As they turned around at the same time, with wide-eyed recognition, Clyde drew his pistols with blinding speed.

"Well if it ain't the ole Bank robbin' nigger lover." The potbelly white man, who had a beak of a nose said.

173

Two of the men frantically reached for their pistols.
BOOM!!--BOOM!--BOOM!--BOOM! . . .
Clyde gunned down all six of them, dropping them with the precision of a highly seasoned gunfighter. Clyde retrieved two pistols from the dead men, tucked them in his waist and slowly entered the back door. The moment he entered, he heard a strange humming sound and a thunderous eruption, almost like a muffled explosion. By the time Clyde tiptoed through a back room to the customer service area, he heard a man talking about his dick being nine inches.

He peeked around the corner, saw the man was still talking while kneeling on one knee. He was wearing a brown suit. The way the man spoke told Clyde instantly he was not one of the locals. The man mentioned Calvin's name and was standing behind barrels of whiskey; on the side of him was a shelve full of kerosene canisters. A few feet away were two drums of gunpowder. Clyde's glance swept across the store and he was thunderstruck by the amount of damage to the walls. He instantly wondered who the hell was firing a damn canon in this place!? He didn't see one outside, and it was obvious a big ole canon couldn't fit inside here.

Clyde saw the man waving a little black box in his hand and instantly realized Calvin was telling the truth when he said there was a man from the future trying to kill him with a la . . . *What did he call it!?* . . . *Oh, yeah, a laser gun!*

Clyde saw Calvin spring to his feet, fired a shot, ducked back down, and then shouted, "You motherfucker! I'll kill you and everything you ever loved, if you harmed my child!" A barrage of mixed emotions struck Clyde; shock, happiness and bewilderment were the strongest ones. But what really angered Clyde was this man had said he had violated Calvin's daughter. Clyde couldn't fix his mind to believe a grown ass man would sexually assault a child, not unless Calvin lied when he told him he had only one daughter, who was 13 years old, which was highly unlikely.

Clyde saw the man was bracing himself to spring up and shoot one of the laser things. Clyde carefully aimed his gun with his bad hand (the left one), and was about to pull the trigger.

The rapidly approaching footsteps behind him, forced Clyde to pull from the aim, swing his arm around and squeeze off a shot into the chest of a man wearing coveralls.

WHOOSH!--BLAAM!!

The laser beam tore through the wall just above Calvin and Mary. The scorching heat caused Mary to scream.

BOOM! BOOM!

Clyde fired two shots at Ronnie.

In response, Ronnie fled the area, and was now out of Clyde's sight.

Clyde wanted to scream because he could tell his shots had missed.

WHOOSH!--BLAAM!

The laser beam shot pass Clyde. "Ahhhh!" He yelled as his reflexes jolted him backwards. The flaming heat burned his face, almost blinding him. His facial hair was burnt; including his beard, eyebrows and eyelashes. Even his cowboy hat was smoking. Clyde peeked around again and confirmed what he saw early: Canisters of kerosene and a couple drums of gunpowder. He frantically retrieved two match sticks, ripped the entire sleeve off his shirt, found a piece of wood lying next to him, wrapped the cloth around the wood, and lit the cloth. He aimed and pumped three bullets inside two of the canisters and tossed the lit piece of cloth.

"Run, Calvin! Run!" Clyde yelled. "She's gonna blow! Run! Run! I'll cover you!" Clyde started firing shots in the direction where the man was earlier. He saw the huge flame was seconds from engulfing the kerosene canisters. When Clyde heard rapid movement where Calvin was located and a laser beam ripped across the store and tore a hole through the wall near Calvin's location, he fled, realizing Calvin wasn't going to make it.

KABOOOM!!--KABOOOM!!

CHAPTER # 18

Eric and Diana sat at a secluded table at Perius', one of the most elegant (and most expensive) restaurants in the entire region. The elevator music added a classical touch to the atmosphere. They were waiting for their dinner to arrive, and were dressed appropriately for the occasion.

Eric had a glass of red wine in his hand. He spoke quietly in between sips. "I don't know why I let you talk me into this. We should be at the lab trying to crack this case."

"Eric, for crying out loud," Diana said, "We need this break. Has it ever crossed your mind that maybe we're missing critical issues because we're overworking ourselves?"

Eric sighed, realizing she was making a lot of sense. Fatigue and brain-fog due to over-taxation of the mind was a well-known cause for senseless blunders, oversights and absurd human errors. But, there was too much at stake with too little time to make things right. "Since we're in this relaxed environment, maybe it'll help us find some answers to these issues."

Diana shook her head in disbelief. "I give up. Until we straighten out all these issues, our love life, and any other life will be on hold. Okay, let's brainstorm the issues again . . . Better yet, let's talk strictly about solutions. You first."

Eric felt guilty and her sarcasm was touching him way down to the core, but she was right about one thing; everything was going to be on hold until they straighten out these issues. "Look at it on the good side." He reached across the table and caressed her hand. "When all this is over and done with, wedding bells will be ringing from here to Kingdom come." He smiled awkwardly and saw his crude attempt to liven her up was a flop. He let her hand go and thought deeply for a moment. "I think it's time to reel Tina in . . . We need to know exactly what Demetrius is planning."

"I agree with that. It's time to force Tina to get onboard with us because it's evident Demetrius is up to something of a tremendous nature, and I doubt it involves sending secret letters to the board."

Eric felt the nervous tension churn in the pit of his stomach at the mere mentioning of those anonymous letters. "I would love to know what was written in those anonymous letters, and who the hell wrote them . . . I agree with your analysis; Demetrius or Tina wouldn't send letters to the board. They don't know of any specific evidence of foul-play and they're both smart enough not to engage in speculation." He paused for a moment. "Once we lock Tina in we'll know for certain whether or not it was anyone of them . . . We gotta find out who the hell sent those fuckin' letters and what the hell was said."

"Well . . . Since the board used the word sabotage to describe the contents of those letters, it's fair to assume we might have a situation on our hands and may be powerless to stop it."

Eric was about to respond, but the waiters appeared with their trays. The standard dressed waiters sat the plates of Lobster Tetrazzini, Vegetable soup Du Jour and sautéed caviar in front of Diana and Eric and left.

They ate in silence; Eric finished first, filled his glass with more wine and sipped as Diana took three additional minutes to finish her meal.

"We need to find out the identity of this Independent Investigator." Eric said.

Diana saw it in his eyes. "No, we don't. And I don't think you should get any ideas about venturing into that matter."

"We've went this far into these turbulent waters, it's too late to turn back. If we start pulling punches now, we'll regret it."

Diana thought hard about the issue. "If this person suddenly and mysteriously drops out of the picture, don't you think that'll attract some attention?"

"Perhaps . . . But this is a top-secret project, and has class A1 priority status. Timetron wants this public time travel as much as we do, maybe even more. Without clear evidence their hands will be tied. No matter what happens, as long as we get rid of Calvin, we're home free."

"As long as we keep it clean, let's go for it." She poured herself more wine. "What we need to be wrecking our brains on is rectifying those audio and visual problems."

"I'm gonna make a request that Timetron replace the audio and visual equipment."

Diana whistled. "Timetron may be desperate, but reckless with money they are not. Do you realize how much money that's gonna cost? Imagine what would happen if that doesn't fix the problem? Linda Welch will not only be sitting in your Captain's chair, but Timetron might even try to hit you in the pocket."

"That's why I'm putting up half the money." Eric said with a half-cocked smile.

"Eric," Diana grappled for the right words. "Those systems will cost tens of millions of dollars. Half of the cost could consume everything you have."

"Yes, I know," Eric went into a silent reverie. His father's vile statements invaded his being: "You're nothing! You will never be the shinning jewel of this family!" Eric frowned and welcomed these degrading memories because they drove him. Those remarks made him realize he was going to succeed and nothing was going to stop him. *Nobody!! And no amount of money!!*

The text messaging on Eric's cell phone shattered his daydream. It vibrated violently as he pulled it from the cellphone pouch fastened to his belt and saw the signal was from the secondary return station at his mansion. He sprung to his feet. "It's Ronnie." He said excitedly. "Pay the check and I'll get the car. Hurry!" He hastily headed for the door.

"I thought we agreed not to send any letters to the board!?" Demetrius said forcefully as he leaned against the living room wall with his arms crossed. "That meant any form of letters, anonymous or not!"

Tina was truly offended. "What, you're accusing me!? I didn't send those letters to the board." She sighed irritably. "I know this is not what you called me over here for!?"

Ramanda spoke with her hands on her shapely curved hips. "And I know damn well you're not accusing me!? I wouldn't know where to send such a letter even if I wanted to."

Demetrius was perplexed because their responses were genuine. "Well, if it wasn't one of you, and it wasn't me, who could it be?" Demetrius shook his head, trying to make sense of this enigmatic ball of confusion. "No one else besides us suspects Calvin's time travel was the work of foul play . . . This is very disturbing because this may force Eric and Diana into a desperate situation . . . This is something we don't need right now. It's gonna compel them to look at us. As a result, they're gonna take extra precautions which means we'll have to work even harder." Demetrius sat on the sofa as he realized the last thing he needed was for Timetron to send out an Independent Investigator.

Ramanda was turning into a nervous wreck. She was becoming lonely and afraid to sleep in this house alone. At night, she heard footsteps right outside in the backyard, and other strange noises. She felt embarrassed when she was about to tell Demetrius and ask the both of them if they heard or saw anything unusual these last few days. She'd been so hard on Demetrius throughout her life, she would look like a sheer hypocrite if she told him she was scared of noises or a boogie man creeping around. But, what if the kidnappers were planning to snatch her also!? Her ego nipped that possibility in the bud. She concluded it wouldn't matter, since she was ready for whoever it was. She slept with a gun under her pillow and kept it close by at all times. "Listen, Demetrius, I don't know about you and Tina, but I want Calvin and Dameeka back right now. If we don't find Dameeka soon--"

"Let's not start that again." Demetrius said firmly. "Please Ramanda. Wherever Dameeka is, she's safe."

Tina was becoming fed up with all this spying around and engaging in all sorts of conspiratorial acts at the work place. It was even more sickening to know they were pretending not to know of these clear illegalities. A child has been kidnapped for Christ sakes! And she was furious at the thought her job was in jeopardy and an Independent Investigator was going to be investigating them in the near future, which terrified her more than anything else. "Demetrius, I think it's time to pull back some. I understand Calvin deserves to be the one who gets universal recognition for being the first Time Traveler, but if Timetron does not get an accredited time travel out of us, we're gonna be out of the picture."

"What are you getting at?" Demetrius said. "Give it to me straight."

"Stop manipulating the audio and visual components. Let Eric get the credit. When Calvin gets back, it'll all straighten itself out. If those components do not become operable soon, we'll be out of a job. You heard the board. They're not selling wolf tickets."

"It was only an idea, a plan I was trying to bring to fruition. I tried to get into those programs and reconstruct them, but it didn't work. I guess after we installed Calvin's suggestions, they were apparently inadequate. These flaws are not my doing. I'm just as confused as you are."

Tina didn't know what to believe, but based on Demetrius' response and his sincere facial expression, she knew it was time to start looking for a new job and that scared her silly.

Later that night, after Demetrius and Tina left, Ramanda sat at her computer preparing an inventory report for the clothing store she worked as the manager. It was about 11:30, and she was still brooding over the fact she sacrificed watching the news in order to finish this report. Suddenly, she heard a noise outside. Her heart fluttered as she nervously reached over and picked up the gun lying on the desk. She slowly rose on to her trembling legs.

Ramanda tiptoed to the window, eased the curtain to the side and peeked out. Trembling while her heart thundered in her chest, she carefully scanned the area.

Her eyes grew wide with debilitating fear when she saw a person wearing a green sweat suit with the hood covering his or her head and had on sunglasses. He or she stared at Ramanda, and then slowly pointed and poked a finger at her as if to scold her. In terror, Ramanda jumped away from the window as though she was retreating from a scorching hot oven. Breathing rapidly, she slowly approached the window again, peeked out and saw the stranger was gone.

Eric raced the Mercedes down the highway heading toward the mansion. As he spoke to Diana, he turned onto the final road leading to the mansion and the headlights landed on someone standing in front of the mansion gate. As the vehicle drew closer, Eric saw the person was wearing a green outfit--a sweat suit, the hood was on and he or she was wearing sunglasses.

"What the hell is this?" Eric said as the person fled.

Diana looked at the main gate, but missed the person. "What the hell is what!?"

"There was someone in front of the gate wearing sunglasses." He shook his head. "It was probably that damn Ronnie snooping around."

Diana glanced over at Eric as he pressed the dial on the remote control and the main gate began to open. "I thought the Basement door was locked?"

Eric realized she was right and began looking around to see where the stranger in the green sweat suit ran to. "You're right, it's locked. It better be locked." He parked the car and got out.

Leading the way, Eric raced inside the house and headed straight for the basement. When he turned the doorknob and saw it was locked, the anxiety was turned on full blast, but the thought of receiving good news wiped the person wearing the green sweat suit out of his mind.

Eric entered the basement and saw Ronnie lying on the sofa watching TV while eating a sandwich.

"Well, it's about time," Ronnie mumbled with a mouthful of food. "I been waitin' damn near forty-five minutes."

Smiling, Eric said, "Please tell me he's dead?"

"He's dead." Ronnie saw Eric was enthralled with happiness and couldn't wait to burst his bubble. "But you gotta transport me back because I gotta get--"

"What the hell happened this time!?" Eric struggled to remain calm, but that was not going to work; unauthorized time travels were not wise activities to engage in at a time like this. As Ronnie began to explain what happened, Eric's mind was thinking of other things. With the board talking about deadlines and Independent Investi---He suddenly realized the stranger he just saw could be the Independent Investigator.

Even though the board said they were going to hold back, that didn't mean they wouldn't try to catch them off guard.

Eric felt the acid in his stomach begin to bubble, and the taste of bile appeared in his mouth. He realized he had to calm himself down and concentrate because he didn't hear a thing Ronnie just told him. "Hold up, wait a minute, let's have a seat." He sat on the sofa and so did Ronnie. Diana sat in the nearby armchair. "Repeat that again, please."

Ronnie sighed loudly. "I need to go back and get the hair and the finger." He made no attempt to conceal his nasty attitude. "There was an explosion. I couldn't hang around. But there was no way Calvin could have escaped. Since the deal was to bring back a finger and a piece of his hair, I gotta go back to get that stuff. But rest assured, that motherfucker is dead. I waited until seconds before the explosion, and I never saw him reach the door." He saw Eric's doubtful expression. "And even if there was a fire, I'm sure teeth will do just as good."

Eric stared at Ronnie impatiently. Screaming and yelling was not going to fix the problem, so he swallowed his rage and stayed calm. "Let's go. I hope you're right this time."

As Eric exited the mansion, leading the two toward the car, he was searching diligently for the person in the sweat suit and sunglasses, but he or she was nowhere to be found.

CHAPTER # 19

The bouncing motion caused by the moving horse was a sure way to prevent falling to sleep behind the steering strap. Add a case of bleeding saddle sores and even a comatose drunk wouldn't dare doze off into the dream world. This was an excellent analogy of what Calvin was experiencing as he led the way down a dirt road with thick underbrush and jungle like trees lining the sides of the path. With Mary's arms snugly wrapped around his waist, they rode Betsy, while Clyde and Jim rode Heckle.

Calvin hadn't done any significant talking for the past seven days since escaping that explosion at the Hardware store, nor did he stop moving onward for any extended period of time. If it wasn't for the purpose of sleeping, urinating or defecating, stopping was considered a violation. The thought of Dameeka needing his help, but his not being there to help her, was slowly transforming him into a very dangerous man. He never thought he could fix his mind to engage in the insidious act of plotting and planning all sorts of exotic ways of killing another human being; what Eric had caused to happen to his daughter not only made such activities possible, but utterly guaranteed. If Calvin ever got the chance to lay hands on Eric, he would kill him without question. After hearing what Ronnie had done to his daughter, he instantaneously felt his humanity break in half.

The date was June 16th, and as Calvin bounced along the dirt road, he thought about the August 3rd deadline, which was a ritual he engaged in at least four times a day. As usual, he felt that hyperventilating sensation stirring inside of him, slowly engulfing his entire being. With a month and a half left and hundreds of miles to go, Calvin's calculations told him he had to find a way to cover more distance in less time. But reality told him there was nothing he could do to defy the laws of nature and physics; horses could only move so fast, sleeping and eating was absolutely necessary and the terrain was wild and extremely obstructive. These realities kept him in a perpetual state of anxiety.

Calvin realized that day at the Hardware store would live in his mind for infinity. Not only because of what Ronnie revealed to him, but also because that daring get-away could go down in history as one of the most brilliant and sensational escapes inspired exclusively by sheer ingenuity, or stupidity on the part of the pursuer. Thanks to those nearby laser holes in the wall, and his erratic response to Ronnie's remarks, Calvin was able to stomp out the unstable, laser-ridden wall behind him and Mary from a seated position just at the moment Clyde screamed "Run! . . . She's gonna Blow!" With two firm-stomps the wall collapsed, and just as the explosion ignited, he and Mary dove outside and were hurled several feet from the impact.

With minor cuts and bruises, Calvin and Mary headed for the initial location they started from, but met up with Clyde, who led them to the horses positioned on the outskirts of the town. After jumping on the horses, they fled the area. Moments later, a twenty man posse was pursuing them. If it wasn't for Clyde's impeccable knowledge of the Mississippi backwoods, they would have been caught and hung as sure as slavery made America a wealthy Country.

Calvin was now scanning the area for a campsite. The sun was taking a nosedive into the westward horizon with a blanket of dark blue sky trailing its path. About five minutes later, Calvin came upon a turn off in the road. A distance away there was a block of land covered with a bunch of trees that were considerably spaced apart from each other. Calvin stopped the horse, turned and spoke to Clyde. "This looks like a decent place to set camp," He pointed. "What'd you think?"

Clyde observed the area. "Nah, let's move further inside."

They continued. About ten minutes later, Clyde said. "Now, this here is 'bout as good a place we's gonna get."

With that said, they set camp as the sun began to slowly disappear completely. Within minutes, they had a small fire dancing and the rabbits, small birds and lizards they caught earlier roasting over the flames.

As they sat around the campfire in a circle, Mary next to Calvin, and Jim next to Calvin, and Clyde sitting next to Jim, they all ate in silence. The crickets, owls and howling wolves apparently couldn't wait to start their song and dance, since these sounds came to life before the sun was fully gone.

"Hey, Calvin," Clyde said. "Why is you blockin' us out like this? If we's a team, we need to talk to each other, don't you thank so?"

Calvin looked up at Clyde, surprised. He didn't respond.

Jim was so glad somebody saw this situation the same way he saw it. "Yeah. I's wanna see us talk like we's used to talk."

Mary eased over to Calvin and massaged his shoulder. "We's sorry what that mean ole man did to yoh little girl, but we's your friends, Calvin. We's startin' to thank you's mad at us."

"What I'm 'bout to say," Clyde said. "I hope don't get you mo' mad, but you's gotta stop moopin' 'round here likes you the only one with problems. How 'bout us? We's got plenty great big ole problems too, and you don't sees us actin' like you."

Calvin was about to lash out at Clyde, especially because Clyde lied to them about being an abolitionist who was on the run solely because of his abolitionist work. After a moment, Calvin decided to let him have it. "I wanna ask you something, Clyde."

Everyone became excited because Calvin was finally talking.

After pausing for a moment, Calvin continued. "I been wanting to ask you about that wanted-poster with your face on it." He saw Clyde respond in a way that said he didn't know what Calvin was talking about. "There was a poster with your face on it at that Hardware store in Mississippi. Do you mind telling us what that's all about?"

187

Clyde sighed while shaking his head. This wasn't a total surprise, but it did make him re-consider telling them the lie he had plan to convey to them. Since they were friends, he was going to be straight up. He laughed suddenly. "Well, I'll be . . . Okay, okay, I guess you got me. What happened is, I got low on funds. I'm a fugitive and can't go workin' 'cause the law is after me, yah know. And 'cause I needed money to survive, I had no choice. I only robbed two banks. Now, those men they say I killed in cold blood, tried to kill me, and I had a God given right to defend himself."

Calvin had grown attached to Clyde and decided to go easy on him. Plus, he saw Mary and Jim's sudden twisted facial expressions. Calvin would be the first to admit Clyde was truly a blessing in disguise, and the money he had in that dirty knapsack of his (probably stolen from those two banks he robbed) was definitely a lifesaver. Since Clyde was a very freehearted person, something Calvin was far from a master at, he had won everyone's heart, including Calvin's. And most of all, Clyde truly loved black folks, which was indeed the coup de grace attribute that told Calvin to be grateful, instead of trying to judge him. "Relax, Clyde, I'm just curious. Since we're a team, we have to be honest with each other."

Jim spoke, "Now that you's talkin' to us again, is you's gonna keeps talkin' to us, Calvin?"

Calvin smiled and ruffled Jim's nappy head. "Yes, I'm gonna keep talking to you all. I wanna say I'm sorry, and I hope you all forgive me. I really needed some time to himself. My daughter--" The mere thought of reiterating what Ronnie had done to her was simply too much and it choked him up. "Don't worry, I'm all right, now."

Mary massaged Calvin's leg. "You ain't gotta tell us 'cause we's understand, Calvin, that's why we's with you."

Clyde and Jim muttered their agreements.

188

After talking about all sorts of things for about an hour, Clyde started yawning, which caused Jim to yawn as well.

When Calvin saw the contagious nature of all this yawning, he said, "I guess our bodies are telling us it's time to hit the sack."

"Yes, siree." Clyde got up and began preparing his sleeping bag, and Jim did the same.

About twenty minutes later, everyone except Calvin was sleep. At least that's what Calvin thought as he laid staring at the starlit sky. The soft, incessant buzzing of voracious mosquitoes competed with Clyde's persistent snoring, which sounded like a rusty old buzz saw. Calvin wondered how he or anyone else was able to sleep with him making all that God forsaken noise.

As usual, so many things were on Calvin's mind as he was about to enter sleep. Suddenly, his father jumped in his thoughts. He realized his new attitude was in direct conflict with the promise he made to his dad while he was on his deathbed. He vowed he would continue his father's work and legacy and be the first time traveler. If that didn't happen Calvin knew he wouldn't be able to live with himself. A deathbed promise could never be taken lightly.

This promise made to his dad forced him to back paddle on how he planned to deal with Eric if and when he made it back to the future. Should he kill him on sight or leave it up to the system? Simple as it seemed, Calvin felt as if he was engaged in a great tug-o-war match each time the promise surfaced inside his mind. Deep down he knew what Eric did to his daughter couldn't be resolved by simply putting Eric behind bars. He could deal with Eric assaulting him, attacking him, twisting his whole world upside down, and inflicting pain of all sorts upon him. But to harm his child; that was the ultimate violation. Despite his belief that all people must obey the law to the fullest, he believed this situation was different. With all the money Eric possessed, Calvin knew that son of a bitch probably wouldn't spend a single day in prison. He

189

shifted his thoughts to something more digestible: getting to the Backlash.

Calvin heard movement and turned as he saw Mary dragging her sleeping bag over toward him.

With a wonderful smile, she whispered. "You mind if I sleeps next to you?"

"Of course, not," Calvin got up and helped her lay out her sleeping bag, and then laid back down.

Mary laid down and imitated Calvin, staring up at the stars with her hands cupped on her chest. After a short moment of silence, Mary said softly. "What's it's like where you from?"

"It's . . ." Calvin was surprised he had to think hard about this open-ended question before answering it. "I would say its paradise compared to this place. At least as far as black people are concerned."

Mary liked that word paradise because the Bible said it meant no hardship and suffering. "So is all the black folks free?"

"Yes, they are. Free to do whatever their hearts desire. With the exception of racism, it's a perfect place."

Mary couldn't fix her mind to picture such a thing. The only thing she ever known was slavery. "What's racism?"

Calvin thought about his potential answer for a moment. "It's a situation where certain people are treated unfairly because of the color of their skin, their gender, religious or political beliefs. Blacks in my time experience this sort of mistreatment, but they are free to a certain extent. There're no chains and no slavery like here."

Mary squinted her eyes because that didn't make sense. "How can it be a paradise if they bein' treated unfair?"

"Well, let's just say, it's a thousand times better than what you're going through here."

190

There were so many things Mary wanted to know, and now that Calvin was talking she intended to take full advantage. "You said peoples can go back in the past? How in the world they do that?"

Calvin turned and met Mary's soft brown eyes. She was not only in a very talkative mood, but was inquisitive. He resumed his original position. "You see all those stars up there. Well, beyond them are things, entities, called Black Holes, Wormholes, Cosmic Strings, Black Body Radiation, and Dark Matter. They are like time portals. Or things that assist time portals. Where I'm from, scientists can transform humans into compressed energy. We also have the ability to move this energy at speeds far greater than the speed of light. With a Time Machine, we are able to send people to almost anywhere in time, just by sending this energy into space to one of these Black Holes, Wormholes or Cosmic Strings and in turn the energy is sent back to earth, but to a different time zone."

Mary realized all this sounded like a foreign language. And it was definitely unbelievable. But there was something she always wanted to know, and Calvin could obviously provide an answer. "Them stars up there; what is they? I know they God's creation, but what is they? They look so pretty and bright."

"They're suns. Just like our sun. Because they're so far away they appear very small. They're huge balls of fire, burning gases like hydrogen and nitrogen." He was tempted to share his views on God and the universe, but changed his mind in order not to upset Mary.

There was a moment of silence.

"You wanna know a secret?" Mary whispered.

Calvin cracked a smile, wondering why she lowered her voice when they were already talking quietly. He whispered back. "Yes, I would love to hear a secret."

"I can read and write a little bit." Mary smiled proudly. "'Fore I was sold to Massa Gilbo, Massa Jefferson's daughter, Mary Ann, show me. I can read almost all the words in a book. Takes me long time, but I can read. I can even write my name too. Wanna see?" She shot into a sitting position.

"There's no need for you to show me. I believe you, Mary."

She laid back down. Mary spoke at normal volume. "I sho' miss Mary Ann. She was my best friend. That mean ole Massa Jefferson sold me 'cause of a debt he owed; a card game he loss and couldn't pay for. He almost loss every thang playin' them dog-gone cards. When I got to Massa Gilbo's place, I sees God punished me real bad 'cause Harvey come a runnin' for me. But I fight him. Even cut him with this big ole knife once. I fight him every time he came for me. Lawd God strike me dead if'en I'm lyin'. The wheals on my back even worse than yours, Calvin. You wanna see 'em?"

"No, that's okay. I believe you."

"He whooped me, and whooped me, and whooped me 'til I gave in." She suddenly became quiet, shaking her head in deep thought. Her voice was suddenly saturated with hatred. "I would've kill Harvey, if'en the Bible didn't say it was a sin. And I sho' came real close to killin' him many times."

Calvin saw Mary was becoming upset and decided to change the topic. He noticed Mary was very mentally sharp for a person without education. Another attribute similar to Cookie. He wondered how she would answer a philosophical question; one requiring an intense, innate view of the basic functions of life. "Hey, Mary, can I ask you something?"

Mary smiled. "Sho' you can, Calvin."

"What makes life worth living to you? Don't rush to answer. Really think about the question for a moment and give me an honest answer."

Mary stared at the stars, working the question over in her mind. About a minute later, she said. "I thank when we follows our dreams,

192

and keep tryin' to make our dreams come true is what makes life worth livin' to me.   But while we's makin' our dreams happen, we's can't become evil, mean and wicked like most white folks. 'Cause we don't wanna do the works and deeds of the devil. And even if'en our dreams are too big to come true, we's gotta try, try and keep on tryin' 'til we can't try no mo'."

Calvin was truly impressed. With the exception of the mean and evil part, she nailed his work philosophy down to a tee. "Wow, Mary, that's a beautiful way to look at life." But he noticed she left out some critical information. "Pursuing a dream is a powerful thing and I agree with you totally, but what is your ultimate dream? What dream you would like to come true more than any other?"

Mary couldn't believe he was asking her such a ridiculous question. "I wanna live in a place where I can be free." She saw an opportunity to work on Calvin's heart, and drove the main point home. "I wanna be free, Calvin. Any place where black folks ain't killed, whipped, hanged, burned and buried alive all the time fo' who they is. Anywhere I can be treated better than white folks treat they house pets." She wanted to crank out some tears for good measures, but all the terrible memories suddenly bombarded her mind and overwhelmed her with anger. She hated the reality of her bleak, miserable life.

Calvin was speechless. He was blown away by Mary's little speech. She indeed was a strong-minded woman with direction and focus. The sincerity in her voice made him feel guilty. How was he going to leave Mary and Jim behind, even after he saw how they were being treated? Boy, did he have to work on his selfish ways, he said to himself. But this was who he was; Calvin was for Calvin and he was number one in his life. He quickly shifted his thoughts to something less thought provoking, and as usual, he refused to come to terms with his glaring flaws.

A long sullen silence erupted.

Mary wondered if this was the right time to ask Calvin what he did to Massa Gilbo that night they escaped. *How did he make Massa Gilbo disappear like that?* This one question was all her mind kept asking. She assumed Calvin knew magic or was good with putting goofer spells on people. "Calvin, what did you do with Massa Gilbo that night we's 'scape?"

Calvin was surprised. He turned and locked eyes with Mary again. *So she saw what happened.* He always suspected they might have, but now he received confirmation. Calvin sighed and stared back at the stars. "Let's just say ole Dick Gilbo won't be purchasing any more slaves, nor will he be molesting any more young black children."

"How did you make him disappear like that? Did you put a goofer spell on him? I saw him go inside yo' cabin and ain't never come back out. I look inside yo' cabin 'fore me and Jim follow you and he was gone."

Calvin held back the urge to burst out laughing. *Goofer spell!?* He shook his head, not understanding Mary's superstitious inclination. "Let's just say he's resting in peace; in a nice comfortable, dark and quiet place. Instead of six feet under, he's about three feet under."

Mary thought about the remark and a moment later she realized what Calvin was saying. She knew what the term six feet under represented. Reading between the lines she concluded that he had buried Dick in the cabin. She went into a silent cocoon.

About two minutes later, Mary broke the silence. "Are you married?"

Calvin wanted to inform her that she was getting a little personal, but instead he turned and stared into Cookie--he meant Mary's eyes. "I was once married, but not anymore." He stared back up at the stars.

"What's her name?"

"Cookie. Cynthia Thompson." He was instantly catapulted into a world of heart-wrenching pain as the memories flooded his mind. His already guilt-ridden heart wasn't ready for this. He still believed he killed his sweet, kind and wonderful Cookie because he was too goddamn busy at the lab. He always said it over and over again that if only he could bring her back, he would show her how much he loved her. This was also another obsession that drove him to master time travel technology. He wanted to go back and change what happened, but based on the universal laws of time travel that was physically impossible, since no time traveler can occupy the same time zone with two different bodies, yet in the same body. In order words, a person cannot be in the same place twice. There can be only one person per time zone, and if an attempt was made to occupy a zone where the person already exist, he/she would kill themselves instantly. All the test runs conducted on lab animals confirmed this fact beyond question, but Calvin believed he would someday rectify that flaw; he had to.

Then, suddenly, Calvin started remembering all the specific instances of pain, suffering and neglect he inflicted on Cookie and it overwhelmed him. He struggled against it, but as usual it was just too much. The tears formulated and ran down the side of his face.

Mary saw his tears and she wondered should she try to comfort him. Numerous questions bombarded her mind. *Was it something I said? Is he crying because of his wife?* Mary hesitated and then said. "I'm sorry, Calvin, I ain't mean to hurt your heart." She moved closer to Calvin, laid a hand on his chest and allowed the side of her face to touch his shoulder.

Calvin turned, made eye contact with Mary and for the first time it hit him. His dream was fulfilled. With water filled eyes, he held the gaze and he could smell her sweet breath. In that fraction of a moment he saw a way to put out the fiery pain in his heart. He suddenly realized he had Cookie right here in his grasp, and once again, he was neglecting, ignoring, and taking for granted a beautiful black jewel any wise man would cherish. Before he knew it he reached his head over and kissed Mary.

Maintaining the deep French kiss, Calvin carefully rose and was now on top. With closed eyes, he gently swirled his tongue in her mouth and immediately she did the same with her wanting tongue. Calvin's shaft began throbbing so explosively it was about to burst through his pants, and a fire was circulating inside his body. His hands went on an exploratory mission, and he instantly saw that Cookie's--he meant Mary's soft and sensuous body was eagerly absorbing his touch. She was as wet and juicy as a waterfall and it even felt as soft as Cookie's. He had to explore even further, and his mouth kissed its way down to her erected nipples. They even tasted like Cookie's.

When Mary pulled him up to her and they resumed their deep kissing while Mary began taking her clothes off, Calvin followed her lead. Within seconds they both were buck-naked and breathing with sexual excitement. Calvin slowed himself down just before entering her because he knew if he started rushing, he would explode almost instantly. It had been a long time since he'd had sex, and despite the wet dream he had two nights ago, he was loaded with juices.

Locked in a kiss, he entered her. It was exceptionally warm and juicy. Despite his desire to take it slow, he started speeding. When he was about to explode he stopped, but Mary couldn't. He pulled out of her while squeezing his inner muscles and slowly the point of no return sensation abated. This time he moved slowly, and once he formulated a rhythm, it was like they were making sweet music together. She would slow down with him, and then speed up in unison. They were communicating without uttering one single word. Then she started moaning as she let herself go and Calvin maintained his slow, focused, rhythmic pace. Mary hips grind against his with a flaming urgency and then started thrusting up and down with a fury as intense as that of a machine stuck on full throttle. Her juices suddenly became noticeably abundant and served only to excite him further.

Calvin savored this moment because Mary even smelled like Cookie when she climaxed. He suddenly felt himself slipping; he couldn't hold it any longer because he realized there was nothing more delectable than the scent of a woman, who had been sexually aroused to the point of climax. Nature did a wonderful thing when it gave man an enhanced nasal sensory system geared toward appreciating such a magnificent scent.

He plunged gracefully into a watery world of unspeakable pleasure filled with a euphoric lust and a burning need for more, more, and more!! Breathing like he'd just ran a mile, Calvin came to a stop and laid where he was; on top of her. Their breathing was harmonic, and Calvin wanted to just be still, so he could appreciate the presence of such a wonderful gift. He resumed the kissing dance and knew this was true love when he felt himself growing, reawakening to a state of full attention.

With pulsating earnest, the intercourse re-ignited with explosive intensity. This time Calvin became creative. After experimenting with several different positions, ranging from doggy style to lying Mary flat on her stomach, Calvin came so hard it felt like he released every built-up drop of tension he had lurking inside of his body. When he closed his eyes for sleep, he experienced the most restful sleep he'd ever experienced while here in this time era.

The following morning, Calvin woke up in a good mood and saw Mary was happier than him. As he got dressed, Calvin thought about that hot, steamy episode last night and already he couldn't wait for the next round. But, then, something came to mind that made him feel guilty: Ramanda. He was so pained by his current unfaithfulness he had to sit for a moment and think. The skies overhead matched his inner turmoil. There were numerous clouds rolling across the sky and rain appeared to be inevitable.

What am I doing!? He mumbled to himself because he was allowing himself to become emotional attached to someone he couldn't be with and he'd just cheated on his future wife. Then, he put up his shield and started telling himself no one would know and that's all that mattered. *What Ramanda didn't know, wouldn't hurt her.* He'd cheated on Cookie; only twice and to this day nobody ever found out. The same would apply in this situation.

Calvin turned and saw Clyde kicking dirt on the campfire. Mary and Jim were somewhere in the woods, either using the bathroom or washing up in the nearby pond.

"AAAHHHH . . .

The ear-shrieking scream came from the direction where Mary and Jim were located.

Calvin and Clyde were jolted into a horror-drenched flee toward the continuous screams. Clyde was in the lead, but Calvin was gaining rapidly.

As Calvin approached, he saw Jim on the ground, clutching his leg, the calf. Mary was striking the ground with a long tree branch.

"What happened!?" Calvin went to Jim.

"That snake bit Jim!" Mary was almost to tears. "Kill it! It's right there."

Calvin rapidly began searching for the injury. "Where it bit you, Jim?"

"On my leg," Jim was crying. "I's don't wanna die, Calvin."

As Calvin examined the wound, Clyde stomped the snake's head.

Calvin was seconds from yelling at Clyde for killing the snake because it was just as much a victim in this situation as Jim was. Calvin hastily ripped a piece of his shirt sleeve and tied the makeshift constricting band around Jim's leg about two inches above the snake bite. It was not tight enough to stop pulsing of the blood, but it was loose enough for an index finger to be slipped between the band and the skin. Then, he pulled his pocket knife, struck a match, burned the blade, wiped it on his shirt, and slid the blade cross the small snake bite, and began sucking and spitting out blood along with the poisonous venom.

Meanwhile Jim was crying softly.

After five additional suck and spit episodes, Calvin shouted. "Get the horses and supplies. We gotta clean and bandage his wound." He saw Clyde jetted back to the camp, while Mary looked on in terror. "Jim, tell me how you feel? Do you feel strange?"

"I's feel sick. My stomach is hurtin'" Jim said weakly. "I's real tired now."

Calvin's heart was racing because Jim's weakness and other symptoms were not good at all. Calvin realized the poison got into Jim's bloodstream before he got to him.

Then Jim laid down and started convulsing and shivering.

Calvin knew something had to be wrong. "Jim, how many times did the snake bite you?"

"I's thank two times." He slurred.

Calvin frantically began searching his leg, found the other bite marks and implemented his suction treatment, but it was obvious the delay was going to have catastrophic consequences.

In a panicked state, Calvin saw Jim fall asleep and said, "Jim, please, don't do this." He stood and started pacing angrily. *This can't be happening!?* He realized this was going to delay his westward movement in a drastic way.

Clyde arrived riding Heckle, pulling Betsy along by her reins. "That was a cotton-mouth Moccasin, Calvin." Clyde spoke excitedly while dismounting Heckle while the horse was still moving. "It's poisonous." He saw Jim on the ground shivering. "We's gotta get Jim a snake bite serum."

Calvin forced himself to relax because getting excited wasn't going to help the situation. "Where are we gonna get a snake bite serum?"

"There's a town about five miles north," Clyde said. "If we's hurry, we'll be able to save ole Jim's life."

Calvin scooped Jim up and raced for Betsy. "Let's go, come on, Mary, Hurry!"

About an hour later, Calvin and the others arrived on the outskirts of the town and hid inside the wooden lands that surrounded it.

Clyde instructed Mary to get down from the horse, hoisted her down to the ground and said to Calvin. "So how I look?" He and Mary had shaved off all his facial hairs, and despite the bumpy ride they managed to accidentally cut Clyde's face only twice; once on the chin, the other on his left cheek. He looked like an accountant with a serious attitude problem.

"You look just fine," Calvin was still sitting on Betsy with Jim lying against him, looking unconscious, but was mumbling and breathing in a shallow manner. "You sure you don't need me to go in there with you?"

"Calvin, I'm tellin' you these here people in this Mississippi town are the meanness white folks ever walk the face of this here planet." His heart screamed when he remembered several incidents where blacks were murdered in a very gruesome fashion. And then he reminded himself these white people here in this town called Stringtown had literally took wickedness to a whole new level. "I'm sho' I don't want you to come. Now, let me hurry up." He raced the horse toward the town.

Within minutes, Calvin saw Clyde disappear.

Calvin and Mary gazed at each other with warm smiles. As they talked about Jim's health, Calvin and Mary both heard the noise. It was the unmistakable sound of rapidly approaching horses. They were about to flee for cover, but it was apparently too late because the twelve white men on twelve horses were moving very fast. They seemed to have popped up out of nowhere. The bunch looked like outlaws, and before Calvin was able to count them, he initially thought it was an army infantry division because the group appeared to be so huge.

Moments earlier, Daniel Spike and his manic marauders, as the folks in the five surrounding counties called them, were moving south. As they crossed a dirt road path, they turned their heads and saw Calvin, Mary and Jim. Daniel gave the signal and the high-speed charge began.

Calvin's hand was about to go for his pistol, but he changed his mind. Such a response would be suicide. He saw several of the men rode with muskets and Baker Rifles in their hands, and in any event, there were only five bullets in the cylinder of his gun.

The horses came to a stop and only one man dismounted his horse. Daniel's feet stirred the dirt when they landed on the ground.

The first thing jumped out at Calvin as the man approached was his eerie, green crossed eyes, which made him look truly insane and hideous. His drooping cheeks that flopped over his thick mustache served only to magnify the warped minded look and made him appear utterly abnormal. Calvin instantly noticed his voice was a perfect match when he said with a heavy drawl. "Who's yoh massa, boy?"

Calvin propped Jim's lifeless body against Betsy's neck and he came down from off the horse. "We're free blacks." Calvin retrieved the fake papers from inside the sack hanging from the saddle and handed it to Daniel.

Daniel snatched the document, and without reading it, he ripped it into shreds. He then flung the pieces of paper into Calvin's face. He

201

whistled loudly and the other men got off their horses. "What's your name, boy?"

Calvin wanted to tell him he should've read the fucking document, but remembered most people in this time era didn't know how to read. "Calvin Thompson."

Daniel nodded approvingly. "What's yoh name wench!"

Mary winced in terror and with lowered eyes, she mumbled. "Mary Sue."

Daniel moved toward Mary, examining her body up and down. "I sho' likes pretty black wenches." Daniel smiled and his marauders laughed explosively, howling remarks indicating they agreed with Daniel.

Calvin put his arm around Mary and saw she was shivering in complete horror. Calvin felt a rage boiling inside him because this evil eyed demon was planning to rape Mary, which meant he would die trying to defend her. Calvin had to tame his fear so as to be strong for the both of them.

"Listen here, Calvin. My name's Daniel Spike." He cocked his chest out as if Calvin was supposed to know this particular name and was expected to respond in a certain way. After a moment, Daniel said. "Oh, I see. You's one 'em uppity niggers, huh? Well, we knows how to deal with uppity niggers, don't we, Ray?"

"Yes, we do."

With a smile, Daniel said. "Listen up, Calvin. You, the wench, and the little nigglet is my property now." He laughed, and so did the others. "Now, get yoh nigger ass on that there horse you just got off, which is my property too, and let's go." When Daniel saw Calvin's facial response and his failure to jump at his command, he pulled his pistol, cocked the hammer and pointed it at Calvin's head. He spoke so coldly the icy depths of space would be considered a heat wave in comparison. "And you better not make me repeat myself."

CHAPTER # 20

Eric sat at the small table in the Timetron conference room, with Diana on his left, Tina on his right and Demetrius sat across from him. Eric was pondering a suggestion posed by Demetrius; it really had him on a mental mission. "I personally have no problem with that. Since the Gallium Phosphide Crystal couldn't be harmed in any way, I think it's worth the try. With the new equipment that'll be here tomorrow, it might even work. What'd you think, Tina?"

Eric saw Tina's uncomfortable gestures and he held back the devious smile. Several days ago, he confronted her with unequivocal proof showing she illegally purchased her bachelor's degree and lied on her resume she submitted to Timetron, claiming she was the Supervisory Scientist for Uni-trans, Inc., a small-time travel lab in Germany. Tina had an affair with the owner of the company in exchange for his presenting false reports and documentation on her behalf. Eric's private investigator, Mr. Brent Browsky, was also able to uncover an embezzlement scheme Tina and a few of her old friends were a part of and had stolen over a million and half dollars from "Genovac", a genetic engineering facility she worked for after graduating from Florida State University in Tallahassee. Since prison, the loss of her license, and a spectrum of other debilitating punishments would be inevitable consequences if she refused to "get on board" with Eric and Diana, Tina jumped on his proposition with gratefully open arms.

Tina was having minor difficulty concealing the turmoil that currently plagued her. Thanks to her plentiful experience with being on the edge she was able to express herself in a normal fashion. "Theoretically, it should work. In fact, I think we should try it now, and again tomorrow with the new equipment."

"Yeah, good idea," Eric said. "Does everyone concur?"

They all agreed and headed for the lab area.

As Eric adjusted the computers and other consoles inside the control station, while Demetrius was behind the mainframe computer, and Tina and Diana were getting Charley dressed for the trip to the 14th Century, he was trying to find logic in the information he came across concerning Demetrius. Two days ago, he instructed Brent Browsky to get him everything and anything on Demetrius and his sister, Ramanda. When Brent told him the two of them were like "meticulously clean angels", Eric heard bells ringing and saw red flags flashing. Such cleanliness was physically impossible because everyone had dirt hidden somewhere. There was a skeleton bone in every closet, and Eric aimed to find theirs.

Plus, from past experience, Eric knew people that had such so-called meticulously clean records were usually dirtier than the most unscrupulous career criminal. Brent suggested he implement a "sky is the limit search" and a "deep digging expedition" into their background, which would require assistance from the military, and various counter-intelligence agencies. Initially, Eric thought Brent was trying to squeeze him for more money, but now he was starting to realize this sort of background check couldn't hurt. Hell, it might even uncover something that could give him some additional leverage. He saw Demetrius was just too cool. *Something was going on with this guy.* Eric decided to give Brent the green light the minute he got to his secured cell phone.

Ronnie walked along the dirt-covered road; the main street of Stringtown, Mississippi. This hole in the wall type town had stores that looked like Jerry's Junkyard and the people were like uncivilized Vikings. Twice Ronnie came close to pulling the laser gun and setting a few of their asses on fire, but there was too much work that needed to be taken care of and engaging in unnecessary time travels wasn't going to sit well with his employer, Eric. He also noticed he felt like he was coming down with a cold, and he suspected it might be from the excessive time traveling he was doing. It was a dreary day and the forecast was in harmony with his mood.

Ronnie was still fuming from that earlier event and was even baffled by the fact Calvin and his crew had escaped that fiasco at the Hardware store. If he hadn't heard the people of that town talking about how Calvin, the black woman he was with, and "Clyde Jerkins" had escaped, he would have never believed it. Ronnie had obtained a wanted poster of this Clyde Jerkins character and saw this hairy face thief was a rogue white man with a cold heart. Ronnie got a good laugh when he saw the wanted poster called him a "Nigger lover" and he instantly realized this was the person who fired that shot at him when he was in the Hardware store.

After traveling back and forth into time like he done before, Ronnie realized Calvin and his mob were not making any stops at any of the towns they came across. Ronnie smiled when he recalled how Eric was so infuriated after they made ten back and forth trips and still came up with nothing. He always found pleasure in seeing other people under stress and irritated.

Now, as Ronnie was about to enter a Saloon, he realized this town was the most unlikely place Calvin would come across because it was a little too far to the north. But his gambling spirit told him there was something up with this town when he chose it five out of seven times after closing his eyes, twirling his finger in the air and jabbing it on the map. At least this tactic was better than playing that crazy ass eeny, meeny, miny, moe game.

Ronnie smelled the foul body odors the moment he stepped through the Saloon door. The stench struck his nose like a vicious kick in the face with a shit-covered boot; it made him want to vomit. The drunk, dirty cloth wearing men and even some women were a sight right out of a horror movie. He took a seat at the end of the bar near the window and asked the bartender for a scotch. He was about to request that the drink be put "on the rocks", but remembered ice didn't exist here yet. Thank goodness he didn't tell the bartender to put the drink "on the rocks" because he saw as stupid as this damn idiot looked he might have put a few real rocks inside his drink.

As Ronnie sipped on his drink, he saw a man on a horse rush pass in a very excited fashion. Although Ronnie didn't get a long look at the man's face, he suddenly got that strange feeling like the face was familiar. In an instance, he pulled the wanted poster from his pocket. He was about to rush outside, but maintained his composure. Looking at the poster, he imagined how this Clyde character would look if he cut off all that damn hair on his face. Ronnie sighed and put the paper back in his pocket, realizing he'd get a better look at the man when he came back this way. Since this was the only road in or out, Ronnie figure whoever it was had to come back this way sooner or later.

Clyde arrived at the location with the poisonous snakebite serum and almost fainted when he saw Calvin, Mary and Jim were gone. He jumped off Heckle and started searching around for horse tracks. When he saw dozens of them, a flash of anxiety surfaced. He didn't have to be told that Calvin, Mary and Jim were in trouble. Fighting to stay calm, he quickly thought up a plan, and realized he had to rush back to town, purchase a musket and then pursue. Whoever snatched Calvin and the others were riding with a lot of men, and following those tracks with only two pistols was insanity.

Clyde rushed back into town and rode right pass the Saloon, heading for the gun store at the far end of the town. He purchased a musket and a pouch of bullets. He also bought extra bullets for the two pistols he carried with him at all times.   Within ten minutes after entering the town, Clyde barreled pass the Saloon. He thought his eyes were playing tricks on him when he saw a man who looked very familiar standing on the Saloon platform porch staring at him as he galloped by. Clyde put this issue on the back burner, increased his speed, and began following the horse tracks.

☼   ☼   ☼   ☼

Earlier, Ronnie sprung to his feet and rushed out of the Saloon when he heard the horse approaching. He stood on the wooden porch like platform as the clean shave man dashed by. Ronnie felt that same vibe again. He wasn't sure what he was feeling, but he decided to follow this guy any way; especially since he had nothing to lose. It wasn't like he had a solid lead or anything close to it. He ran for his horse at the stable about two city blocks away, paid the caretaker for feeding and watering the mare, mounted it, and followed.

☼   ☼   ☼   ☼

Calvin didn't know what issue to allow to dominate his thoughts, as he, Mary and Jim rode Betsy. Mary sat behind Calvin with her arms wrapped around his waist while Jim was in front of Calvin with the back of his head laid sleepily on Calvin's chest.   Surrounded by the twelve bandits, Calvin felt a hopelessness and impending doom that grew with every step the sun descended into the west horizon in back of them. The most dominant issue at the moment was Jim. He had slipped into a deep unconsciousness and was sweating and shivering profusely.

The next issue was what these men were planning to do to Mary. Throughout this five-hour hike in an eastern southerly direction, Calvin became infuriated to the point he was moments from pulling his pistol and attempting to kill as many of these wicked creeps as possible. They all were talking about how they were going to "fuck" Mary's "brains out." With malicious intent, the men were trying to torment them and cause severe psychological damage. Despite the ironclad nature of his ego, Calvin had to admit they were succeeding in a very effective manner.

But the question that danced wildly in Calvin's mind was: *What the hell did they expect me to be doing while all this "fucking" was going on? They couldn't believe I would stand by and watch!?* If they expected that, which they obviously did, Calvin knew they were in for one vicious surprise. Thank God they didn't conduct a pat frisk on him and had only confiscated the musket that was in plain view tied to the saddle. Twice he caught himself praying for Clyde to pop up, but he quickly scolded himself because that sort of thinking would cloud his mind with unlikely expectations that would taint his will to fight with life and death intensity. The only good thing he noticed was the numerous military tactics learned many years ago were oozing back into his short-term memory bank with rapid fluidity.

When Calvin heard Daniel say to his men "start looking for a place to set camp", his heart leaped almost into his throat. He noticed Mary's arms wrapped around his waist tightened so hard it felt like a vise grip. The embrace had a unique force of a fear that was beyond any worldly description.

☼　☼　☼　☼

Clyde had been pushing Heckle at top speed for too long and so he was forced to slow down significantly. The trail he was pursuing was an easy tracking endeavor because of the many horses that apparently were moving together. Clyde continuously looked back because three times he saw someone behind him. When he would go downward into a slope in the land, he saw the man on his tail. Clyde had a plan, but was waiting until it got just a little darker.

Suddenly, he saw the bunch he was following and didn't know if this was good or bad because he still hadn't gotten rid of the man following him. Clyde didn't have to be a magician to know the man who stared at him strangely when he left Stringtown was the man who was now following him. But what Clyde wasn't certain of was what the hell did he want? Could he be a bounty hunter? A family member of someone he'd killed? Or could it be that man with the laser who was following Calvin all over the place?

Whoever it was Clyde knew he had to slow down tremendously because he didn't want to alert the band of men who must have kidnapped Calvin and the others. When he felt he had acquired a substantial distance from the group he was following, Clyde decided to put his plan in motion. He saw a section up ahead where the tree branches were low. Instead of ducking, Clyde grabbed hold of a branch, and twirled himself up into the tree. Heckle wisely continued onward. About five minutes later, he heard the horse hooves of the person pursuing him. The sound was rapidly approaching.

When he saw it was the man watching him from the Saloon porch, Clyde braced himself as he pulled his pistol. The second the man was almost directly under him, Clyde jumped.

WHAAM!!

The blow to Ronnie's head knocked him silly as he tumbled backwards off of the horse and crash-landed onto his stomach. The air shot from his lungs upon impact with the ground. Stars flared before his eyes as he struggled to his feet.

BOOM!--BOOM!--BOOM!--BOOM! ....

The four bullets tore at Ronnie's chest and stomach, shoving him backwards. Terror gripped Ronnie's mind, since it was clear he couldn't get to the laser gun and he was being repeatedly shot. With the assistance of the fear of death, and the pulverizing pain of the pounding bullets, Ronnie hit the switch on the Micron watch, just as the fourth bullet struck him in the stomach.

There was a bright, blinding flash.

Clyde was shocked. Rapidly blinking his eyes, he couldn't believe he had just seen the man disappeared. With wide-eyed bafflement, while looking around frantically Clyde muttered, "Well, I'll be goddamn!!"

Everything Calvin told him about being from the future and all that time travel stuff overflowed his mind as he walked over to the spot Ronnie stood only moments ago. After a moment, he pulled his attention back to Calvin, Mary and Jim.

Clyde saw the time travel man's horse had stopped once the man came off its back. Clyde mounted the man's horse whistled for Heckle and continued his pursuit. Less than two minutes later, he smiled when he saw Heckle racing back toward him.

Clyde dismounted the horse, checked the saddle pockets for anything of value, found nothing and got on Heckle. Realizing the band was far up ahead he pushed Heckle like he'd never pushed the horse before.

Then, suddenly, he heard and saw the flicker of gunfire on the dark blue night horizon. He mumbled curse words of frustration and fear as he tried to push Heckle even harder.

Calvin was lying behind Betsy's dead body, using it as a shield against the bullets pounding the corpse. Mary was next to him firing a pistol while Jim laid sprawled out, unconscious.

Moments earlier, when they came to a stop, Calvin laid Jim down on the ground, pulled the pistol with flinching speed and blew a hole in the forehead of the closest man to him and dove for cover. Betsy was shot three times by the return fire and fell crashing to the ground. Since he whispered his plan to Mary seconds before they dismounted the horse, she hit the ground the second she saw Calvin reach for his pistol concealed in the back of his waist, tucked between the pit of his back and the rope that served as a belt.

The Calvin dragged the dead man he shot moments ago by his shirt collar and positioned himself behind Betsy. Calvin sighed with relief when he discovered the man was carrying a pistol. He gave it to Mary and she started shooting without hesitation. She was a terrible shot, but he would definitely give her a big E for effort. Calvin guessed the fear of death or great suffering had a way of making people learn very quickly.

So far Calvin killed only two of the men and could hear Daniel cursing like a deranged psychopath who missed a month's worth of psychotropic medication.

Suddenly, Calvin heard gunfire coming from another direction and these shots were not aimed at them. A panicked-stricken commotion was also heard. He peeked over Betsy's dead body and saw some of the men trying to flee as if someone had opened fire behind them. A bullet struck the corpse and force Calvin's head back down. But he instantly sprung back up with his gun pointed.

BOOM! . . . BOOM! . . . BOOM! . . .

Calvin shot two men who came from behind the tree; their bodies recoiled from the impact of the bullets before dropping to the ground. Someone behind them was neatly picking off the other men. They were scrambling for a new place of refuge while trying to return gunfire, but were falling to the ground due to the barrage of bullets tearing through their bodies. Calvin wondered did one of Daniel's flunkies flip out and started killing his own comrades. Lunatics were known for such erratic, illogical and unpredictable behavior. Then it hit him. That could be Clyde. But when he realized they had acquire at least a several hour start before Clyde got back with the snake bite serum, he rejected out of hand that possibility.

BOOM!

Calvin dropped another man who came out of his hiding place.

Suddenly, he saw two men fleeing on his far right. Calvin took aim and pulled the trigger.

CLICK!

The gun was empty and he hastily scrambled to reload the gun. The bullets he took from his pocket clumsily dropped to the ground.

"Calvin!" A familiar voice yelled from the other side where most of the men were positioned.

"Clyde!" Mary shouted. "It's Clyde!"

"We're over here!" Calvin felt like the weight of the world was lifted from his back. He peeked over Betsy's corpse and saw a dark figure step out from behind the trees and tall grass while carefully inspecting all the fallen men. A few seconds later, he saw Clyde's buck skin pants.

BOOM!

Clyde shot a man in the back of the head who was crawling for his pistol.

Calvin rose with precaution as he finished loading his pistol and approached. He saw Mary get up. "Stay down!"

Mary dropped back to the ground as if a bullet was fired at her.

Calvin saw Clyde talking to one of the fallen men who apparently wasn't dead.

Clyde laughed with joyful vigor. "I told you, Daniel," He kicked the sole of Daniel's boot. "I'll get the last laugh." He howled with laughter.

Calvin stood next to Clyde staring down into those eerie green eyes of Daniel Spike, who was still acting as arrogant as a spoiled King. "You know this man?"

"Do I know him!?" Clyde's countrified accent was at an all-time high. "This is the poo' white trash that killed my brother."

Calvin was planning to talk Clyde out of killing him, but after hearing this he knew that would be a total waste of time. If he had a brother and someone murdered him, Calvin knew there would be very little anyone could say to stop him from acquiring retribution.

"You got the serum!?" Calvin said excitedly.

"I sho' do." Clyde dug in his pocket and handed Calvin the small glass bottle.

As Calvin raced to Jim, he could hear Clyde stomping and kicking Daniel. Then, that inner scientific voice started talking to him. It was telling him that he was wasting his time with the serum. A wave of tears tried to force themselves from underneath his eyelids because he suspected the voice was correct.

Eric stood a few feet from the secondary return booth, seconds from blowing a gasket. The rage was brewing beyond a high-leveled boil. He couldn't believe this fool ass Ronnie was putting him through so much unwarranted stress. With laser guns, all sorts of scientific information and 20/20 hindsight, how the fuck could he keep fucking up like this!? Eric was about to start pacing, but controlled the urge as he locked his stare on Ronnie and Diana.

"I told you," Ronnie sounded impatient as he held the bullet-ridden bulletproof vest in his hand. "I know the exact location, the exact time, and I know how they all look, including the crazy white guy, Clyde Jerkins." He tossed the vest onto the nearby sofa. "Now check this out . . . You can continue wasting time, bitchin' and complainin' about shit we can't change or we can keep this thing moving forward."

After a moment, Eric said, "All right, okay." He headed for the door and realized he couldn't continue putting up with Ronnie's fuck ups. It was coming to the point where he was contemplating firing Ronnie's ass because he was creating too many risks; every time they engaged in an unauthorized time travel, he was putting his entire career on the line. It was obvious the possibility of getting caught had increased substantially by that person in the green sweat suit, who was probably someone hired by the board to snoop around. When Diana told him she saw the same person jogging near the lab's outer security fence two nights ago, Eric knew this issue regarding Calvin had to expeditiously be brought to a swift closure.

As Eric exited the mansion, he was hoping that old well-known saying, "if you want something done right you gotta to do it yourself" wasn't going to apply in this case. But something, somewhere in the deep subconscious regions of his mind, was telling him it just might come to that.

CHAPTER # 21

Sitting behind the wheel of his red Corvette, Demetrius was parked across the street from "Glenda's Gorgeous Garments", waiting for Ramanda. He saw her through the plate glass window making preparations to close up shop. A moment later, he stole a glance at his watch. It was 8:30 pm, July 11th, and the streetlights had come on moments ago when the sun had set. Boy did they have to talk. His anxiety and stress levels were off the Richter scale.

About five minutes later, he saw Ramanda and her two assistants exit the store and lock up. As the two assistants headed down the street after bidding each other good night, Ramanda headed toward the Corvette. Demetrius saw the terror on her face because he almost never came to her place of employment, unless it was extremely urgent.

He hit the electric window switch as she arrived. "We need to talk. At a secure location . . . Follow me." He waited until she got in her car, a sky blue Cadillac Escalade, parked four cars in back of the Corvette.

Demetrius pulled from the curb and saw from the rearview mirror the Cadillac's headlights maintaining a close tail throughout the five-minute ride. He pulled inside the empty little league baseball field and found a parking space. Ramanda did the same as Demetrius exited the Corvette and headed for the bleachers, scanning the surroundings with eagle eyed precision; they were evidently alone.

Demetrius sat and twenty seconds later Ramanda sat next to him.

"There's been a lot happening in the last couple of weeks," Demetrius said. "Some good and a lot of bad."

"What's this secured location stuff all about?" Ramanda said. "Is there something wrong with our homes?"

"I think so," Demetrius propped both elbows on his knees, rubbing his hands together. "I spoke with Chris today. He said somebody's been snooping on us."

Ramanda was thunderstruck. Images of the green sweat suit person trampled through her mind. "Oh God. Did he find out who it was?"

"He told us not to worry. He claims he was able to stop a complete check."

"Did he say who it was?"

Demetrius shook his head no. "He assured us it's under control."

"And you believe him?" Ramanda was about to unleash a wave of reminders. After a moment, she decided to at least scrape the surface. "Don't forget the Strasbourg incident. Those were his exact words: It's under control."

"I didn't come here to engage you in an argument. So zip up that fuckin' mouth of yours and listen up. There's no one around, so you can come out of character for a moment."

Ramanda sighed.

Demetrius cracked a smirk. "Did you go through Calvin's computer files with--"

"There's nothing in those files. I checked them ten thousand times. My fuckin' head is spinning with all the shit I've been reading."

Demetrius pulled a piece of paper from his pocket and handed it to Ramanda. "There's a secret file somewhere within a file at his home computer. These might be the code numbers that open a hidden file that contains a code to the file we're looking for. Punch these codes in and see what happens . . . I was able to get inside Calvin's office while Eric wasn't doing all these unauthorized time travels and found these codes. I think we got something here from the way the codes were concealed within the configuration."

Ramanda was still enraged at all these setbacks. "Why don't we just wait until Calvin gets back? I was literally moments from getting him to share that stuff with me."

"There's no time. And what if Eric kills Calvin?" From the way Eric was going crazy with all these time travels, Demetrius was certain he hadn't succeed yet. "Also, Eric has got to Tina."

"As tacky as that dumb bitch is it's a miracle it took someone this long to unveil all her misadventures . . . I mean we really have to ask ourselves what kind of background checks are Timetron conducting."

"Timetron probably knew about all of her little skeletons in the closet. They wouldn't care if a serial killer was working for them. They care about one thing, and one thing only. As long as they become the first entity to prove to the public that time travel exist and is safe, that's all that matters."

"If Timetron knew about Tina, how can we be so sure they don't know about us?"

"You know Chris got eyes and ears all over; within Timetron and in probably every counter-intelligence agency throughout the World. If there was a problem, he would know. How do you think I got pass Timetron's security check?"

Ramanda was satisfied with the answer, but there were other unanswered questions. "How's Eric's accredited time travel coming along? I really feel Calvin deserves to be the first to do it." She sighed. "He worked so hard for it."

"Well," Demetrius agreed with that analogy; Calvin did deserve to be the first. "That's probably not going to happen. The new audio and visual equipment is working. I was able to manipulate the visual camera during our last couple of experiments, but Eric will eventually detect it. I would say by next week, Eric will become the most famous person on the planet and Timetron will be the entity responsible for it."

Ramanda felt like she wanted to cry for Calvin. He worked like a madman to accomplish what Eric just stole from him. Although she was trying to acquire certain information for reasons that weren't totally in Calvin's best interests, she did know without Calvin's endeavors time travel probably wouldn't even be possible. Then something else jumped in her mind. "Demetrius, I know I've asked you this before, but I need to know. Since this is a secure location . . . Did Chris have anything to do with Dameeka's disappearance?"

Demetrius eyebrows took a sharp dive as a result of the shock. "How would I know something like that? If he did, for whatever reasons, he definitely wouldn't tell me. But speaking from a logical standpoint, I would say he had nothing to do with her kidnapping. Her disappearance, as you can see, is jeopardizing our mission. Chris would do nothing to create this kind of heat. And in any event, what could possibly be gained from kidnapping her? When I asked him did he think Eric kidnapped Dameeka, he assured me Eric had absolutely nothing to do with her disappearance . . . It's sure gonna be hell to pay if Calvin returns and finds his daughter missing."

"That's exactly why I want out of this way before August 3rd."

"Well, break into that file and we can call it party time."

"What did Chris say about that person in the green sweat suit? I hope you didn't forget to mention it to him. Was it any of his people?"

"No," Demetrius was angry because Chris thought he was getting paranoid when he made the inquiry. "It's not any of his people. Are you sure you've seen this same person that many times hanging around the house?"

"Yes," Ramanda trembled inside because she was hoping it was Chris. "You know I would never joke around with anything like that."

Demetrius looked at his watch and rose to his feet. "It's time to get going. I suggest you get right on that." He saw Ramanda about to walk away. "What's up? Where's my sugar?"

They kissed for about ten seconds.

They exited the baseball field, got in their vehicles and drove off in separate directions.

About a half mile away, from the rooftop of a skyscraper, the person in the green sweat suit and sunglasses had been monitoring Demetrius and Ramanda's discussion with high-tech binoculars and a microscopic long range voice recorder system the size of a pack of cigarettes.

☼   ☼   ☼   ☼

Several hours later, Brent Browsky entered his hotel room, took off his suit jacket and tossed it on the bed. Brent was a big red headed Russian with double chins, and a stomach the size of a fifty-gallon drum. He was wearing heavy gum sole shoes, a flashy cheap suit and thought of himself as the epitome of a dirt digging private eye who could find any speck of grime on anyone unfortunate enough to come under his scrutiny.

After loosening his tie, he wobbled over to the phone and dialed Eric's number. "Hello, Eric," Brent said into the receiver. "Yeah, I got that stuff on those two. They're about as filthy as the asshole of a buzzard." He giggled. "I'll give you the details when I see you . . . Huh . . . After I take a quick shower, I'll come right over . . . See you soon." He hung up and headed for the bathroom.

As Brent was in the shower, the person in the green sweat suit and sunglasses approached Brent's hotel room. The full moon danced slowly across the night sky and the sounds of crickets were everywhere. He pulled a device from his pocket and waved it near the door. The locks clicked open. The person entered and hid in the closet.

Moments earlier, Brent heard a noise while he was under the water and turned off the shower, listening carefully. When no additional noise was heard, he turned the shower back on and continued washing under the huge slabs of cellulite.

Fifteen minutes later, he was dressed and headed for the door.

"Excuse me, sir." A voice sounding like a machine said from behind Brent.

Brent turned hysterically. His heart exploded in his chest. He saw a person with a dark green sweat suit with the hood tied firmly over the head and had on sunglasses. The person was pointing something at him. "Hey, what the fuck are you doing--"

ZZZZZHHH!

An invisible electrical wave struck Brent in the chest and he was hurled into a catatonic state. He instantly realized he couldn't move; couldn't even blink an eye, but he could see the person walking over to him. Brent felt his heart beat accelerating. Sweat burst from the pores on his forehead as the person dug inside his inner breast pocket and took the chip with all the dirt on Demetrius and Ramanda. After a pat frisk, the person spoke.

"You will not remember anything about this chip or any events connected to it." The person held the chip in front of Brent's eyes, and pointed the box at Brent's head.

Brent tried to scream as the electrical wave seared through his brain cells. In a standing position, he fell asleep, swaying back and forth ever so slightly on his feet.

The person in the green sweat suit and sunglasses nonchalantly exited the hotel room.

Five minutes later (although it felt like an hour to Brent), he snapped out of the trance and into attention. Brent stumbled and instantly felt the urge to sit-down. He looked around trying to figure out why was he dressed as if he was going somewhere? With squinted eyes, he took off his coat and shoes, wobbled over to the refrigerator, retrieved the two six packs of beer, and got ready to watch some Worldwide Wrestling.

CHAPTER # 22

"Another week ain't gonna make a big difference," Clyde said to Calvin as he stood near the door of the second-floor hotel room in a town called Pettus, located about fifteen miles east of what would eventually come to be known as Little Rock Arkansas. "The extra rest'll do Jim some good."

"We been here three and a half weeks, Clyde," Calvin was about to start shouting. It was July 12th, they had one more state to get through and the 22nd day deadline tumbled around in his head. "Jim is up and around. His energy is just about as it was before he was bitten." Calvin went to the window, looked out at the muddy dirt streets, and saw the people below walking in the rain in a nonchalant fashion. Lightning bolts rippled across the night sky and the thunder rumbled.

Clyde winked his eye at Jim and moved his mouth, instructing him to play along. "Hey, why don't we just ask Jim? Hey, Jim can't you use a little mo' rest, buddy?"

"I's—I--I." Jim stuttered nervously because he wasn't used to lying, and he especially felt very uncomfortable lying to Calvin. "I could use some rest, but if I's gotta go I's don't mind."

Clyde sighed and gave Jim a disappointed expression, realizing he wisely took both sides on this issue.

Mary frowned at Clyde. "Why you wanna stay here, Clyde? This ain't no nice place anyway."

Calvin wanted to let Clyde know he was aware of his gambling, drinking and prostitute chasing business, but he knew Clyde had a right to do whatever he wanted with his own money, even if it was stolen. Calvin turned around. "What if we stay here too long and that hit man shows up?" He smiled inwardly when he saw everyone's face cringed. "Even you said you saw him."

"Sho' did!" Clyde was excited now. "And I told you I shot the son of bitch four times square in the chest . . . I'll be goddamn if he's comin' back from that."

Calvin wanted to inform Clyde of the unfortunate fact there were bulletproofed vests and clothing where he came from and no military oriented person went into the field without them. He had another argument he knew Clyde could grasp. "Where I'm from there's hundreds, maybe even thousands of men like the one you may have shot and killed . . . Remember I told you I personally saw two different ones. Who's to say there isn't at least ten or even twenty of those men roaming around out there with those laser guns?"

Clyde was fed up with this back and forth debate. Plus, Calvin was making him nervous with that sort of crazy talk. "Listen here, Calvin. I'm gonna be straight with you. I'm leavin' this town in another week. Now, if you, Mary and Jim wants to leave without me, then be my guest. I told you I got some very important business to take care of."

"I hope it's not to rob that bank?" Calvin asked point blankly as he folded his arms across his chest.

Clyde felt insulted. "I told you I don't rob banks no mo'." He saw Calvin was very upset and realized he had a right to be. "Okay, I'm gonna come clean. I lost the money gamblin' last night. Every goddamn dime of it too." He saw Mary's eyes widen with uneasiness and it caused him to smile because he saw even black women understood the value of money. "And now, I gotta win it back with--"

"Clyde, forget the money," Calvin approached him. "We can find money somewhere else--"

"Give me one 'xample?" Clyde knew money didn't grow on trees and the stuff damn sure wasn't lying around in the streets. "'Cause if we ain't got no money, we gonna have some great big ole problems on our hands. Now, tell me where we gonna get money. If your plan is better

than mine, then we'll saddle up and hit the trail right this cotton-pickin'
minute?"

Calvin was speechless. Every suggestion that came to mind was
ridiculous. "I guess you're right . . . All I ask of you Clyde is to take it
easy with the booze, and please keep that trigger finger of yours under
control. The law men in this town are quite numerous and very serious
about what they do."

With a smile, Clyde headed for the door and spoke before he
exited. "Don't worry about ole Clyde 'cause I know how to take good
care of myself."

When Clyde disappeared out the door, Calvin sat on the bed
staring at the wall as Mary came over and started massaging his
shoulder. Jim came over and sat next to him.

Whispering, Mary said. "I agrees with you, Calvin, we should go
right, now! But don't you worry, 'cause we's gonna be outta here 'fore a
week. Once Clyde gets his money back he'll be ready to go."

Calvin laid down on the bed and stared at the ceiling. "I hope so. I
sure hope you're right."

Later that evening, Clyde sat at the card table in the Saloon with a
glass of rotgut whiskey on the table in front of him. He picked up his
cards from the table after a man called Lark, sitting across from him,
dealt the cards to him and the two other players. Lark was a tall, thin,
blond-haired white man who had a missing eye that was oozing pus. On
Clyde's right was Jacob, a medium built black-haired white man who
had a large beak of a nose and wore a big cowboy hat. On his left was
Frank, a heavy-set, clean shaven white men who had penetrating blue
eyes and smelled like he hadn't bathed in two years, but wore neat, clean
looking clothing.

223

There were three other card games in progress and the bar was lined up with people eager to get drunk. The glow of the dozen or more kerosene lamps provided an inadequate source of light that mixed with the clouds of tobacco smoke, creating the surreal landscape of a nightmare. The piano and harmonica players were taking turns keeping the customers happy with old country tunes.

Clyde's glance rose from the cards in his hands and landed on Lark. He wanted to tell this crazy bastard to get himself one of those eye patches because that gapping whole was turning his stomach. Clyde thought he could see Lark's brains, since the eyelid was also missing and the wound looked like a pus oozing factory of bacteria and disease.

Clyde downed his drink and yelled to the bartender. "Lemme get another shot over here!" Clyde accidentally dropped a card on the floor. As Clyde reached down under the table for the card, he saw Frank and Jacob hastily tuck the extra cards in between their legs, but Clyde saw the maneuver as clear as day. Clyde was about to flip the table over in a fit of rage, but realized he was probably out gunned and outnumbered. He came back up and showed them the card he dropped, pretending everything was all right. "Hey, where's my drink! . . . Who's 'ppose to draw?"

"It's your turn, Clyde," Lark said with a rotten tooth smile.

Clyde drew the card; it was a King of diamonds and he put it in his hand and threw a four of spade onto the table. As the others plucked cards from the deck, Clyde was inconspicuously counting all the men in the Saloon. For the first time, he noticed they all were watching him, despite the fact they were engaged in their own card games or were at the bar talking. There were about twenty-two sets of eyes inconspicuously stealing peeks at him. He didn't want to start freaking out since a logical explanation for the stares could be his newcomer status to this town.

As the game progressed, Clyde was getting angrier by the seconds. These low down, dirty, stinking scoundrels were playing the sham on him! Clyde struggled not to react impulsively. But when he realized they apparently stole over 500 hundred dollars of his hard-earned money, he'd made up his mind.

"Wait a minute," Clyde sat his cards on the table. "I got a damn Charlie-horse in my leg." He rose. The second he was fully standing he pulled both of his pistols.

BOOM!--BOOM!

Frank and Jacob's heads jerked violently with the impact of the slugs. Blood sprayed as they fell crashing to the wooden floor.

"Don't nobody move a muscle!" Clyde shouted, realizing time, motion and everything else seemed to have come to an abrupt stop. "Was you in on this, Lark!?" Clyde had one pistol aimed at Lark and the other pointed at the men near the bar.

Lark had both hands up in the air. "What in the devil's name are you talkin' 'bout!?"

Clyde walked over to Jacob's dead body and kicked his leg, displaying the extra cards. "Count those cards. What the hell's he doin' with all 'em extra cards! And look at 'em extra cards Frank got! You cheatin' rascals robbed me blind!" Clyde saw a man reaching for his pistol through his peripheral view.

BOOM!--AAHHH

The bullet struck the man's forearm. He screamed as blood sprayed on the nearby customers.

"I said nobody moves!" Clyde approached Lark as his eyes were darting everywhere, absorbing his surrounding like a multi-directional camera lens. "If I don't get my money you thievin' rascals stole from me, yous gonna join your friends on this here floor, Lark." Clyde placed the warm steel of the barrel on Lark's temple.

"Okay, okay!" Lark shouted. "Most of it's on Jacob."

225

"Well, get yoh ass up and get it!" Clyde kicked Lark in the ankle and hurt his toe despite the thick leather boots he wore.

Lark sprung out of his chair, frantically dug in the pockets of his dead comrade, and started handing money to Clyde.

Clyde tucked one of his pistols in his waist, snatched the bills from Lark and stuffed them in his pocket.

Suddenly, the sheriff silently rushed inside the Saloon with a musket drawn, quiet as if he was on tiptoes.

By the time Clyde turned his head, the Sheriff screamed. "Put that damn gun down!" He was aiming at Clyde's chest.

Clyde was about to try his luck, but when four deputies came right behind the Sheriff with pistols and muskets pointed at him, he dropped his pistols and raised both hands.

☼   ☼   ☼   ☼

The following morning, the frantic knock on the door catapulted Calvin, Mary and Jim clean out of their beds. Calvin and Mary shared the bed on the right side of the room while Jim utilized the one on the left, closest to the door.

With his mind disoriented with sleep and fright, Calvin grabbed his pistol and tiptoed to the door. "Who is it?"

"It's Ethan. The bellboy."

Calvin remembered the voice, unfastened the lock and snatched the door open. "Come in." He waved him inside, further recalling that this freckled face kid had taken a strong liking to Clyde and was very kind to them as well. Calvin closed the door and locked it once Ethan entered.

"I got some real awful news. Mr. Montgomery's been arrested for killin' two men."

Calvin felt a wave of mixed emotions, but he wasn't the least surprised Clyde got caught killing someone. "So what are they gonna do to him?"

The bellboy was baffled by the question. "Like they does with all folks who commit murder . . . They gonna hang him."

Calvin saw Mary and Jim were shattered and he realized his heart was crumbling as well. "Don't Cly--I mean Mr. Montgomery get a trial or something? I'm certain if he killed someone, he had a very good reason for doing such an awful thing. It could've been self-defense."

"They already had the trial this morning. The Judge sentenced him to hang in four days in the town square . . . And the only reason they puttin' it off so long is 'cause somebody says Mr. Montgomery ain't who's he claims he is. And they sent a rider to Mississippi to inform General Warps of the U.S. Marines. The General's comin' here to see if Mr. Montgomery is somebody else . . . I also came here to warn y'all that talks goin' 'round 'bout some of the town people comin' to string up y'all too.   They thank y'all Mr. Montgomery's property and they wants full retribution." He lowered his voice to a whisper. "When you's ready to go, I can sneak y'all outta here in my ma's wagon . . . Give me a holler when y'all ready." He headed for the door, and before leaving he turned and said. "I strongly suggest y'all move real fast now, yah hear?"

Calvin was so mentally twisted by the bombardment of all this devastating information, he simply sat on the bed with both hands massaging his head while Mary and Jim looked on in horror.

☼   ☼   ☼   ☼

Ronnie was on his horse, casually heading west. The blistering hot July sun invoked a thirst that ripped at his throat. He pulled his canteen and savored the drink of water. He had no idea where he was going, but he knew west was all he needed to know. Suddenly, on the horizon he saw a rapidly approaching man on a horse with a dust cloud on his trail. Dressed in a uniform, Ronnie saw the man was probably some kind of military man or something. After a moment, he thought he figured out who the man was by the time he was about 500 yards and approaching: The Pony Express.

It was apparent these information carriers and conveyors knew plenty of things, and Ronnie forced the man to come to a stop. Calvin saw the man had pulled his pistol.

"Howdy, partner." Ronnie said with his corny countrified accent while a smile tugged at his lips. "I ain't up to any evil deeds so you can relax. I'm lookin' for a white man and three niggers. Last I heard they was travelin' west and--"

"What's they names?" The Pony Express rider still held his gun.

"Clyde Jerkins is the white man and the nigger man's name is--"

"Ole Clyde was caught yesterday and he's fixin' to hang after General Warps confirms it's him."

Ronnie couldn't control the excitement in his eyes. "Where's Clyde now?"

"Pettus, Arkansas. If you keep on this here path you can't miss it. 'bout a nine hour hike nonstop."

"Thank you very much my good friend." Ronnie positioned his horse to take flight as the rider spoke with a knowing expression on his face.

"If you's a vigilante, I'm warning you, folks in Pettus don't take too kindly to people who takes the law into they own hands." And with that the rider left a dust trail behind.

Ronnie was about to tell the man to tell those folks in Pettus to kiss the crack of his ass. But, since he was headed that way, he decided to tell them himself.

Ronnie pushed the horse to its maximum speed.

CHAPTER # 23

The Time Machine hummed and the laboratory vibrated. Sparks flew from the base of the machine with great intensity.

The brilliant flash caused Eric, Diana, Tina, and Demetrius's arms to shield their eyes. A moment later, the glaring light subsided and so did everyone's arms.

"AHHH . . ." Charlie's voice crackled through the audio speakers.

Eric took a seat behind the mainframe and adjusted the controls connected to the cameras hooked up to Charlie. His heart raced. *Come on now, act right, goddamn you!* The fuzzy images on the screen were the same as yesterday and Eric wanted to scream. Then, he turned the contrast dials and when he saw the trees coming into focus, his eyes grew with delight and so did the sensation in his stomach. "It's working!" He shouted as his bowels got so weak he had to tighten up his butt cheeks.

Everyone rushed over, breathing over Eric's shoulder.

"Yes!" Eric cheered, causing everyone else to join in. He saw the picture becoming clearer with each second that slid by. Charlie was transported to a jungle somewhere in India. The year was 8,000 B.C. Charlie's squawking sounds as he walked about were music to Eric's ears. Eric saw Charlie was looking around at the trees and thick underbrush. There were four cameras attached to Charlie's backpack and uniform, providing Eric with the ability to see in all directions.

"Something moved," Demetrius said, pointing at the screen. "Right over there. Enhance the focus. Isolate and zoom in on whatever that is."

Eric happily activated the appropriate computer component. When he saw the huge snake, a boa constrictor, he said excitedly. "Bring him back immediately. We don't need any mishaps."

Demetrius hit the return lever. The humming, sparks and flash came all within seconds.

As they headed for the Time Machine, Eric said with a huge smile, "Let's pull out the champagne because we did it!" When he saw Diana's stern facial expression, he suddenly realized he was moving too fast because there were too many unresolved issues. But Eric was too enthralled not to ride this good mood for all it was worth.

☼   ☼   ☼   ☼

The following morning, July 13th, the Timetron board entered the lab with an entourage of expensive suit wearing executives and bodyguards with anti-social mugs replete with no non-sense gestures.

Eric realized some of these men he had never seen before, and he suddenly developed an even more intense respect and fear of Timetron. He also wondered was anyone of them the man in the green sweat suit he saw snooping around his mansion and the lab.

James shook Eric's hand and spoke in a fatherly fashion. "I hear you have some good news for us."

With a smile a little larger than James's, Eric said, "We want to demonstrate everything is working. And I'm ready to make that documented time travel."

The seven board members crammed inside the topless control station, while everyone else stepped outside the lab. It took ten minutes to transport Charlie to and from the year 20 B.C. in a place called Ephesus, a location in Asia Minor.

James patted Eric on the back. "This is wonderful, Eric."

The other board members congratulated Eric and his team.

"But we need to have a talk." James said as he exited the control station and headed toward the conference room. Everyone followed.

As Eric followed them toward the conference room, he sensed he wasn't going to like whatever it was they had to talk about. He truly despised the word "but". Not only because it signified on the contrary, but it always meant there was some bullshit about to invalidate recently accomplished advancements. What could there be to talk about, other than how they were planning to deal with the media, publicity, worldwide fame and fortune, the Noble Physics Prize and things of the sort? Eric's pessimistic friend inside his head was spitting venom like a WW II submachine gun on the beaches of Norway.

Upon entering the conference room, the board took their usual seats and Eric and his team did the same.

Keith Wilson cleared his throat. "Once again, we congratulate you all on a job well done. However, there are pressing matters that have come under consideration by this board, which compels us to reluctantly hold in abeyance any human time travels. That includes any publicity based actions."

Robin Choi interjected. "In other words, we are instructing you all to say absolutely nothing to no one regarding the success of your current work. Any human time travels are utterly prohibited."

"We are very sorry for this inconvenience," Albert Coppola said, "But we were forced to take this rather distasteful action in light of the contract we signed with Calvin's father."

Eric felt the tremors of shock slap him in the face. *This can't possibly be happening. Contract!? With Calvin's father!?* Eric was about to speak impulsively, and stomp all over their comments with a disrespectful outburst of monolithic proportions, but quickly snapped back into the world of reality.

"If or when Calvin returns," Karen Koenigstein said, "He shall have the first opportunity to be the first human time traveler. This was a stipulation in this contract. The exception to this provision is, if Calvin is no longer available, then and only then can we go forward. If, either due to death or incapacitation Calvin is not able to fulfill this trip, then control of the selection process reverts back to this board. Although technically Calvin is already the first human time traveler, he is not a scientifically documented traveler."

James said. "If Calvin makes it back before August 3rd, he'll be the first time traveler whether he conducts a fully equipped, official time travel or not. According to the definition of a time traveler, he merely has to transport and return intact."

"Excuse me," Eric fought to convey strict professionalism as he spoke. "If I'm not mistaken, this board made it unequivocally clear that if the audio and visual components were rectified, there would be an accredited time travel. It was also clearly stipulated that the law of chain of command would be strictly enforced. If the lead scientist was unavailable to partake in the journey, then his underling would be the next in line."

"Yes," Mark Phillips said, "However, as we just pointed out, there was a contract we inadvertently overlooked, and upon examining it, we saw we were about to violate the terms of this agreement. Indeed, thanks to an anonymous source, we were spared the embarrassment of trampling over a perfectly legitimate agreement."

"We understand your concerns, Eric," Sydney Smith said. "And if it's any conciliation, we assure you if Calvin doesn't appear within the next three weeks, then you will be the one." He smiled awkwardly. "In exactly 22 days, if Calvin doesn't return, you will be the most famous man to walk the planet."

As the board members left the lab, while spewing fake words of encouragement, Eric felt like there was nothing that could extinguish the raging fire lurking in his heart. He was not only overflowed with frustration and desperation, but he literally felt himself slipping. He didn't know where or what it was he was slipping from or into, but there was no doubt he was slipping. You're never gonna be worth shit!! His father's voice thundered inside his head. With a struggle, he held back the tears as he escorted the board members out the front door of the lab and into their limousines.

As Eric and his team waved at the disappearing convoy of limousines, Eric turned and headed back inside the lab. He didn't know what he was going to do, but he knew Ronnie had better not come back here with anything other than good news.

CHAPTER # 24

Ten minutes after Ethan came to the hotel room and told Calvin, Mary and Jim the unfortunate news about Clyde's situation, they saw a lynch mob approaching the hotel. In a frantic haste, they exited the hotel and followed Ethan's instructions. They rushed to the outskirts of town and wait near the woods. Ethan arrived twenty minutes later. Calvin could not believe Mary and Jim wanted to go on a suicide mission to save Clyde.

"Get on the wagon!" Calvin hissed at Mary and Jim, who were adamant about not leaving without first trying to save Clyde. "I told you, there's nothing we can do." Calvin was standing at the rear of the wagon as Ethan sat in the driver's seat waiting.

"But we's gotta try, Calvin," Mary pouted. "He needs us, and we's can't leave him to die like that."

"What part you don't understand!?" Calvin said. "This is suicide. If you don't know what suicide means, it's when you do something that gets yourself killed. Self-murder!"

"Clyde saved us, 'member." Jim said. "Only mean, hateful folks would let a friend die without tryin' to save him."

Calvin was jolted by Jim's comment. He felt this low blow way down in the pit of his soul. He thought hard about what Jim had just said and his conscientious started kicking him in the backside for being so selfish, self-centered, conveniently forgetful, and uncaring. Jim's comment also reminded him of something his father once said, "True friendship is not measure by what a friend does at times of tranquility and peace, but it should be judged by what he does during times of great turmoil and confusion. If you want to know if someone is a true friend, see how he acts when you need him most." Calvin had to admit Jim was right; only a mean-spirited person would abandon a friend in dire need of help.

Calvin leaned against the wagon with his arms folded across his chest. How in the hell were they gonna save Clyde when he was in a jail surrounded by dozens of musket totting, trigger-happy lawmen? On top of that, how in the world could they (black folks), who were now being hunted by the town's people who were under the misconception they were Clyde's property, save a white man from being hanged by other white people? Calvin realized this dilemma was a brain buster right out a Ripley's believe it or not scenario involving impossible phenomenons.

Calvin sighed. "Okay, we'll try to save Clyde." He saw the happy expressions on their faces and in their bodily gestures. Calvin yelled to Ethan. "I don't think we're gonna need a ride right now."

Ethan smiled. "Poo' Mr. Montgomery is sure gonna need y'all help. Ain't much I can do, but if I can help, you can count on ole Ethan."

Calvin thought for a moment, and all the military maneuvers circulated through his mind. Then, suddenly, a plan appeared. "Hey, Ethan, can you get us some dynamite or gunpowder?"

"Hey, wait a minute, now," Ethan came down from the wagon and stood facing Calvin. "I can get some dynamite and gunpowder, but I can't help y'all kill any mo' folks. This is my home, if y'all ain't noticed."

"No, no, we're not gonna hurt or kill anyone," Calvin became very animated as he explained the plan to Ethan. He saw Ethan's attentive head nods, and when he saw that naughty little boyish smile on Ethan's face, Calvin knew he had him. "You see. No one'll get hurt."

"But what if they all don't fall for the trick?" Ethan said. "And what if y'all go inside and there's one of 'em law men still in there somewhere, then what?"

"I'll have to get the draw on him, and tie him up. Not a single shot will have to be fired as long as we follow the plan." Calvin knew all this sounded good, but even the most well thought out plan very rarely unfolded without complications and this made him extremely nervous. "So are you in?"

Ethan pretended to be thinking hard about this proposition, but all the while he knew he was all for it. "Well, I guess so. Mr. Montgomery was a kind, God-fearing man who don't deserve to die. As a fellow Christian, I'm duty bound to help save his life."

As they got on the wagon, and headed toward the barn about a half mile away, Calvin wanted to tell Ethan that Clyde was as about as religious as an old horny goat. But, he figured if this image of Clyde was what motivated and inspired Ethan to do the right thing that was all that mattered.

☼   ☼   ☼   ☼

The moment the sun was firmly out of the way, and the moon took control of the night sky, Calvin, Mary, Jim and Ethan headed for the town. Ethan rode the wagon with Jim hiding in the back under a sheet of tarpaulin, while Calvin and Mary were on foot. When they reached the outermost perimeter of town, they split up; Calvin and Mary took a southerly detour while Ethan went in a slight opposite direction, heading for an abandon stable.

Moments later, Calvin and Mary stood on the side of an abandon, decrepit, termite-ridden house. The smell of decaying vegetation resonated from the building. Calvin assumed the house might have once been a storage facility for farm goods. In the shadows, they watched the jail where Clyde was held, and saw two men standing out front with muskets. Calvin had his pistol in his hand and so did Mary.

Whispering, Calvin said to Mary, "I'm gonna check the back. Keep your eyes on 'em. I'll be right back." Calvin ran back into the nearby woods, and maneuvered around the backyards of the nearby houses. He came upon a location where he could see the back of the jail. With a smile, Calvin saw no one was positioned in the back. He ran back to Mary. "There's no one back there."

236

Pointing, Mary said, "Look! Three mo' just came over."

Calvin saw there were now five men with guns in front of the jail. He knew, at the moment, this was nothing to worry about, at least this is what he was hoping and praying.

Ten minutes shot by and Calvin started getting nervous. The signal was taking far too long. *It should've occurred at least five minutes ago!* He felt Mary massaging his shoulder, since his tension was becoming highly visible. But he knew this was Mary's way of taming her own anxiety. He turned and gave her a kiss on the cheek, knowing this would get her back on track. Watching the jail, Calvin started rocking from side to side as each minute seemed like an hour.

KABLLAAM!! . . . BABLLAAM!!

Calvin flinched when the explosions suddenly ignited. He turned and saw the flames dancing on the northern horizon. When he saw four of the five lawmen fleeing toward the explosions, he began whining up his confidence, telling himself this was a piece of cake. People instantly rushed out their homes and places of business to see what happened. After Calvin saw two additional lawmen rush out of the jail, and fled in the direction of the explosions that had transformed into a full-scale fire, he stuffed the pistol in the waist of his pants. He nonchalantly headed toward the jail; Mary was dead on his heels with her pistol concealed behind her back.

As Calvin headed toward the lawman that was looking at the fire with his back to him, he heard what sounded like a rapidly galloping horse. He turned and about a quarter mile away he saw a man was entering the town from the main road. When he saw the man had binoculars to his eyes, a wave of terror grabbed Calvin by the throat. *Binoculars didn't exist during this time! Or did they?* Whatever the answer was, his instinct compelled him to walk faster. He kept his eyes on the man on the horse. Just as Calvin pulled his pistol, he saw the man on the horse raise his hand, pointing as he increased the horse's speed.

WHOOSH!--BLAAM!!

The laser beam streaked pass Calvin just as he pushed Mary backwards while simultaneously diving for cover.

The laser beam ripped a hole in the wall of the jail, causing the lone lawman to open fire on Ronnie while he sought cover behind a water barrel.

As Calvin and Mary shot to their feet and rushed inside the jail, Calvin saw the futuristic hit man's horse was struck by the lawman's bullet. The horse took a hard nosedive, flinging Ronnie to the ground.

With amazing grace, Ronnie did a body-roll behind a wooden water trough near a barbershop and fired at the jail just as Mary entered.

The moment Calvin entered the jail he saw a panicked-stricken lawman running toward him from the back. Reflectively, Calvin was about to squeeze off a shot, but he saw the man's facial expression did not display any danger toward them. Calvin moved behind the nearby wall, just in case, with his pistol behind his back and Mary clearly out of harm's way.

"What the hell's goin' on out there?!" The overweight red-faced lawman shrieked as the gunfire appeared to increase as if more men with muskets had arrived. Meanwhile, the laser beams were blowing small holes in the walls of the jail and the screams from somewhere outside were mounting with skin crawling effects.

Calvin saw an opportunity; the lawman apparently thought he and Mary were fleeing from the pandemonium right outside. Calvin spoke just as excited as the man, in a countrified fashion. "Lawd God, they's shootin' out there! Please help us, mister! Please!"

When Calvin saw the law man had come right up to him and stopped within reaching distance, he continued, "Go on out there and see for yo' self, Mr. Lawman! Look!" When the man obeyed, frantically heading for the door, Calvin grabbed him when his back was to them. He put him in a sleeper hold. The man thrashed wildly, his feet and arms flailing frantically as if he was trying to flip Calvin off his feet, but within seconds he was sleeping like a newborn baby. Calvin gently laid him on the floor, retrieved the keys and headed for the back screaming. "Clyde! . . . Where are you, Clyde?"

Clyde was sitting at the foot of his bunk, listening to all the gunfire when he heard someone calling his name. He sprung to his feet, and was filled with something far more powerful than joy. "I'm back here! In here! In here!"

Calvin followed Clyde's voice and realized this place was much bigger inside than it appeared on the outside, or at least that's the way it felt. He turned a corner and saw Clyde rattling the bars as if he was trying to shake them loose.

As Calvin frantically unlocked the cage, while Mary was behind him looking scared silly, Clyde spoke jubilantly. "I knew y'all wasn't gonna leave ole Clyde. No siree!"

Mary wanted to say, "If you only knew."

The cage flung open and Clyde rushed out, "Where's my pistol? You know I needs my pistols." He took the one Mary handed to him.

"Come on," Calvin led them toward the back door. "That hit man is out there." He looked back and saw Clyde's shocked expression.

After running down a corridor, Calvin came to an abrupt stop. He was lost. He wasn't even aware he was shouting. "Where's the back door, Clyde?! It's gotta be around here somewhere!"

"How the hell am I 'pposed to know!" Clyde shouted back. "They had me in a damn cage!"

There was a sudden tremendous explosion that unhinged them all. It came from the front of the jail and was so loud and forceful it felt like the entire front section of the jail was blown away.

Calvin resumed their desperate retreat, leading the trio down another small corridor. As Calvin saw a door up ahead, he simultaneously heard a crashing sound behind them. Calvin kept running and arrived at the door seconds later. He saw a chain and pad-lock prevented it from opening.

"Step aside!" Clyde moved Mary and Calvin out the way and pointed the pistol at the pad-lock.

BOOM!--BOOM!

Clyde kicked the door, but it didn't budge because the bullet didn't penetrate the lock.

"Watch out!!" Calvin yelled in terror as he dropkicked Clyde to the other side of the corridor when he saw the hit man appear at the other end of the corridor.

WHOOSH!-BLAAM!

The laser beam just missed Calvin and Clyde as they went in different directions, but the piercing heat scorched the hair on their heads. Mary squealed from the searing and excruciating heat. The laser made a hole the size of a soccer ball in the center of the door and had smoke oozing from it.

BOOM!--BOOM! . . . BOOM!

Calvin and Clyde opened fire.

With a slight hysteria forming, Calvin saw they were trapped. He forced himself to stay focused. Peering around the corner, Calvin could barely make out anything in this dimly lit corridor. The small kerosene lamp hanging from the ceiling swayed back and forth, creating a pendulum of swirling shadows. He turned, examined the hole in the door, and a plan was instantly formulated. He saw Clyde across from him positioned inside a room. He turned and said to Mary. "Stay here." Calvin did a body roll over to where Clyde was positioned and, as he expected, a laser beam was fired, but missed him and ripped another hole in the door.

"What the hell are you doin'?!" Clyde whispered, and fired a shot down the corridor.

"Just relax," Calvin took several deep breaths, peeked around the corner and body rolled back to the other side. The laser again just missed him and blew a hole in the door. The heat caused by the laser beams raised the temperature in the immediate area by at least twenty degrees.

When Clyde saw the holes appearing in the door, he caught on. "Make room over there!" Clyde did a sluggish, half-cocked roll.

WHOOSH!--BLAMM!--AAHHH!!

Clyde screamed when the laser beam shot pass him, apparently a little too close for comfort. Although it missed his forearm by inches, a patch of skin was burnt to a crisp. When Clyde made it to the other side, he was clutching his arm, cursing profusely.

"Calvin!" Ronnie shouted from down the corridor. "Why don't you just come on out and stop all this nonsense."

Calvin couldn't believe this guy was this arrogant. "Hey, what's your name?"

"The name's Ronnie Neal." Ronnie shouted back. "Why should it matter, you're gonna be dead very soon. Then again, I guess you do have a right to know the name of the person who killed you."

"Do me a favor, Ronnie," Calvin was peeking around the corner and saw Ronnie was peeking as well. "Tell Eric I said he's gotta come a whole lot better than this."

"I take that as an insult," Ronnie shouted indignantly. "What'd you tryin' to say? I'm not capable of killing you?"

"If you are, you can bet your ass I'm not gonna sit quietly and let you do whatever you wanna do to me." Calvin was hoping this little stale tactic would give the town's people time to regroup and commence some sort of attack. Calvin exchanged several more questions and answers, and then he heard the crowd outside.

Ronnie turned when he heard the two men coming up behind him. In a smooth, swift motion he aimed and fired the laser. A hole appeared in the wall in back of where the man stood behind. Instantly, the man unleashed an ear-shattering scream when he realized the hole in his stomach.

The moment Calvin heard Ronnie fire the laser and the scream, he moved with lightning speed. Calvin ran and kicked the door covered with laser holes. His leg went through the door, and he hastily pulled his leg back inside. He dove for cover, assuming Ronnie would fire a shot after hearing the commotion. Calvin peered down the corridor, saw the bright flickering lights from the laser beams and heard Ronnie was thoroughly preoccupied with the newcomers. When he heard the several gunshots in that direction, he knew Ronnie's attention was fully distracted now. This time Calvin charged at the door and slammed his shoulder into the section above the padlock and chain. He was catapulted outside into the backyard and stumbled face first to the ground.

Mary and Clyde raced through the door the second Calvin barreled outside.

Running at top speed, Calvin led the trio toward the open grass plain up ahead. The pasture was spread out for about 200 yards. When they were a substantial distance away from the jail, Calvin ushered Clyde and Mary in front of him. He looked in back of him every couple of seconds or so.

Just when they were running across the open grass plain, where there were no trees or anything else to hide behind, a laser shot pass them. It struck the trees about 100 yards in front of them. They all cringed from the searing heat.

Calvin suddenly realized they were better off inside the jail; at least they had something to hide behind. Out here in the open they were like sitting ducks. Stopping to engage Ronnie in an exchange of gunfire was totally out of the question. "Don't stop! Run!! Run like this!!" Calvin ran in a zigzagging fashion as he heard a barrage of gunfire behind them. He saw Clyde and Mary followed his instructions. Calvin braced himself, anticipating the laser lacerating into his back.

They were almost there! Just a little further! His legs were pumping with frantic force. He prayed whoever was shooting at Ronnie would continue for just a few seconds longer, but no sooner than the thought registered in his head, the shooting in back of them stopped. Then, suddenly, as if his innate super-consciousness detected a catastrophe about to occur, an image of his father's face flashed across his mind. He heard his dad's last words just as the violent burst of flaming hot yellowish orange energy took him down to the ground.

CHAPTER # 25

Dameeka laid on the bed watching her personal roller Television (a screen that rolls down like a window shade). She couldn't remember ever having this much fun in her life. She burst out laughing, giggling joyfully as the crazy clown on the screen was being struck in the face with huge cherry pies. But what she liked most of all about this place was, she didn't have to go to school, and learning no longer required being in a classroom. When she first discovered this form of acquiring knowledge, she thought it was some kind of evil joke. It was the easiest learning process ever known because all she had to do was look into some amazing machine with swirling lights and the lesson for the day would be inside her head. The day she stared into the swirling lights, and suddenly realized she knew things that would normally take days to learn, the whole experience shocked her immensely. Indeed, it was too good to be true, she had repeatedly told herself, and vowed never to return home again. She burst out laughing again at the clown. Suddenly, her personal nanny, Shirley, appeared on the roller television screen.

The hologram oozed out of the screen, hovered in midair and stood at the foot of the bed, "Dameeka, it's time for bed."

Now this was what she hated about this place. "Shirley, there's only five more minutes, and then the show goes off!"

"Sorry, you know the rules," Shirley floated back inside the screen and the television went blank. The screen rolled up into its compartment in the ceiling.

Dameeka scooted under her covers with a serious screw face. This place was real cool, but why couldn't it be a place where she could get away from adults telling her when to go to bed, when to eat, when to study her lessons. As she turned the lights off merely by snapping her fingers, she wondered when they were going to create a machine that would enable humans to simply look into some swirling lights and get all the rest and sleep the body needed without going to bed. And most of all, when were they going to be a time when kids would call all the shots.

☼   ☼   ☼   ☼

"You will be the most famous man to walk the planet!" Those words of executive board member, Sydney Smith, echoed in Eric's mind as he laid in bed staring into the dark. Sydney's voice churned like a penetrating echo chamber, and was commingled with Diana's rhythmic breathing as she slept.

Eric allowed the unfortunate news to drag him into a rut and the only cure seemed to be good news. Deep down he knew all wasn't lost as long as Calvin didn't make it back. The odds indicated he would soon be the man, but he wanted to be the man right here and now! Ever since the meeting ending, he'd been calling Ronnie every foul word in the dictionary. Out of nowhere, Diana's words suddenly circulated in his present thoughts; she was right! He was becoming his own worst enemy. His pessimistic attitude and self-defeating thoughts were as toxic as high-grade cyanide. If you believe something strong enough, you will make it happen, be it subliminal or premeditated. *Yeah! That was actual fact! Sort of like a self-fulfilling prophesy!*

With a smile, Eric felt his mood suddenly developing into something very pleasing. He imagined himself receiving the Noble Physics Prize! He began thinking about all sorts of events with a happy ending, allowing only issues that made him feel good to enter his mind, and he instantly felt a euphoric wave grip him. He took his good mood a few steps further, and allowed his hormones to spark up. Earlier, as he was getting ready for bed, Diana made it clear she wanted to have sex, but he insisted he wasn't in the mood. He rubbed his genitals for a moment and saw he could go a round or two. Shit, it might even do him some significant good, he realized.

He undressed, flung his pajamas on the nearby chair, rolled over and began fondling Diana's soft, succulent breasts that perked up instantly. She squirmed in pleasure and released a wanting moan. *Damn!* He smelled her breath and quickly turned his face away, fearing the odor would shatter the mood. He moved quickly, holding his breath and got on top of her and began sucking her nipples while she quickly began pulling her panties down. Eric flipped her over on to her stomach and stretched out on top of her. He began maneuvering himself, poking and probing for the jackpot spot.

"Whoa!" Diana said when he was about to plunge into the wrong hole. A moment later, she wiggled her rump and sighed in relief when he slid inside her.

Eric kissed her neck as they developed a rhythm, Diana raising her hips from the mattress when her spot was rubbed the right way. After about fifty delicate strokes, Eric felt himself becoming too excited. He tried to slow down, but Diana's thrusting hips demanded no such thing; she had reached the point of no return and Eric was powerless to navigate the ride any longer. He felt her muscles spasm around him. "Together! Let's come together!" Eric slurred through his moans and groans, as he exploded inside her while Diana felt electricity surging through her body.

She clutched the pillow and closed her eyes in bliss.

"AAWW!" The laser tore into Calvin's shoulder, flinging him clean off his feet into a forward lunge. He hit the ground, tumbling, but body-rolled back onto his feet. The pain from the blood dripping wound exploded in his head with burning intensity as his speed increased.

They entered the woods as laser beams ripped and tore at the surrounding trees. Smoldering leaves, branches and chips of wood rained down all around them. The smell of fresh burning wood and leaves filled the air.

"Turn right, Clyde!" Calvin shouted when he saw Clyde was headed the wrong way. He knew Ethan and Jim would be waiting and wondered would it be wise to lead this laser gun wielding creep toward them. Should he find a way to deal with this guy right here and now? Or should he keep running and hope the town's people would keep him preoccupied long enough for them to escape? Running seemed like the only logical thing to do.

Calvin turned when he noticed the laser beams had stop striking the trees. From a distance, he saw the bright streams of flaming hot light being fired in a different direction and were commingled with the small flicker of gunfire.

Calvin's burning lungs were screaming for more air. He saw Mary was moments from passing out. "Come on, Mary! Keep going!"

Mary was breathing extremely hard, gasping for air. She was forcing her stumbling feet to continue running. "I can't! I can't--" She stumbled forward and crash landed to the ground, scraping both hands.

Calvin smoothly snatched her back to her feet and dragged her along. He wanted to scoop her up into his arms and carry her the rest of the way, which was about another 500 yards, but his exhaustion was too overwhelming.

Clyde was the first to make out the wagon up ahead. "There it is!"

Calvin saw Ethan and Jim sitting in the back as they rapidly approached. Jim became excited when he saw them approaching and Calvin was glad Jim wisely instructed Ethan to get into the driver seat and get the wagon moving.

They mounted the already moving wagon and flopped on the floor, breathing with maniacal force.

Calvin shouted. "Let's go! Speed it up! Faster!" Ethan's foot dragging response was pissing him off. Why in hell is he acting like this was some kind of joke? "You gotta move much faster than this, Ethan!"

"Go!" Clyde shouted. "Let's go, god dam it!"

"Okay, alright," Ethan struck the horses' backs with a soft tipped whip. The wagon jerked into a faster speed, gradually increasing.

Ronnie spun around with his finger locked on the laser gun's firing button. The beam of flaming hot energy swept across the immediate area like a raging sword of lightning, cutting, ripping, severing and disintegrating anything that dared to across the laser beam's path. Where the fuck was all these motherfuckers with guns coming from?! Every time Ronnie began pursuing Calvin, shots rang out and bullets whizzed pass him. The two graze wounds, one on the side of his head and the other on his right leg, told him it was time to get into a much deadlier frame of mind, or else he might lose Calvin again, or even worse one of them might get off a lucky head-shot.

He pulled the other laser gun from his backpack, turned them both to full blast and had a field day with everything in sight. If it moved, he shot at it, was the golden rule at this moment. By the time he finished, he saw Calvin had made it across the open grass field and had disappeared into the heavily wooded area up ahead.

Ronnie ran back through the battered corridors of what used to be the jail, heading for the front. He stepped out the door, looking for a horse. He disintegrated a man who looked suspicious. He saw a black horse and bolted for it. After mounting the horse with acrobatic grace, he galloped frantically in the direction Calvin headed.

Calvin kept his eyes locked on the rear. With his heart booming in his chest, his exhaustion was still out of control. The wagon bounced and rattled savagely, and he saw Mary was heaving as if she was about to throw up. He helped her to her feet. "Do it over the side of the wagon, Mary."

The second her head was over the side, the vomit exploded from her mouth.

Calvin massaged her shoulder with his uninjured arm. Suddenly, the pain sparkled in his shoulder and Calvin quickly turned his head, examining the injury. The hole in the shirt was covered with blood. The wound was a badly scorched burn, but it wasn't of a third degree nature. It even smelled like burning flesh and it turned his stomach at the thought of smelling his own cooked flesh. Just by thinking of the wound, the pain became exquisite. Calvin turned and saw Clyde reloading his two pistols and hastily began doing the same.

"Mr. Montgomery?" Ethan turned his head, facing Clyde in the back and shouted over the nerve-racking noise of the fleeing horses. "Where's we goin'?"

"West, my beloved Christian brother, west." Clyde got back into his Christian preacher mode. "That's all you--" Clyde saw the horse and the man rapidly coming up the rear.

Calvin saw it also. "Ethan, can you make this thing go any faster?!"

"I'm pushin' 'em 'bout as fast as I can!" Ethan lashed the whip, but the horses were not built for speed. "If I goes any faster--"

A laser beam shot pass the top of Ethan's head. The heat not only mesmerized him, but it jettisoned him into a panic. "What the hell was that?!" Ethan's eyes were wide, and he frantically began lashing at the horses' backs with desperate energy. The speed increased. Each time the wagon hit a bump in the road, everything in it was momentarily airborne.

Calvin made Mary lie flat on her stomach. Clyde was in a kneeling position, taking aim. Jim didn't have to be told to lie flat on his stomach. The bouncing from the fleeing wagon inflicted a severe beating on their bodies and prevented Calvin and Clyde from aiming their pistols with the appropriate accuracy.

WHOOSH!--BLAAM!!

A laser beam struck the ground near the wagon and splattered a huge cloud of hot dirt into the air. Calvin and Clyde instantly got on their stomachs as well and began firing their pistols.

WHOOSH!--BLAAM!!--"AAAHHH"

Another laser beam was fired. Calvin saw it breezed right over their heads, and heard a scream. A warm liquid splashed on him. Before he turned to see what had happened, the wagon started going wild. Calvin turned and saw Ethan was gone. He wiped the back of his neck and saw it was blood.

WHOOSH!--BLAAM!!

The laser beam struck the right back wheel of the wagon, causing the wooden box to go into a savage spin. The horses went wild and made the situation worse. Suddenly, the wagon flipped over and tumbled violently. The screams of the horses commingled with the cries of Calvin, Clyde, Mary and Jim were like a symphony of hellish horrors.

They crashed landed into a tree.

Calvin was hurled by the impact and hit the ground with a sickening thud. Severely dazed, he frantically stumbled to his feet. "Let's go!" He turned and saw Ronnie approaching. Where was his gun?! He lost his gun!! Looking all over the wreck site with hysterical energy, he saw his gun and reached for it, but a laser beam struck the nearby tree. Calvin ignored the sparks and flying chips of wood, grabbed the gun, aimed and squeezed off three rapid shots.

Ronnie's horse squealed from the bullet that struck its head and went down hard. Ronnie was violently slammed to the ground.

Calvin ran to assist Mary and Jim, who were crawling out of the rumble, looking seriously beat up. Through his peripheral vision, Calvin saw Clyde on one knee, shaking his head to clear his mind from the daze.

"Is anyone hurt!?" Calvin helped Mary into a standing position. "Mary, you alright?"

"So far as I can tell, I am."

"How about you, Jim!? Can you run!?"

"I's okay, and I's can run too."

"Run! Go that way!" Calvin shouted while pointing. He locked his stare on Ronnie who was still lying down, appearing to be unconscious. Calvin could sense he wasn't dead and the temptation to run up on Ronnie and pump five bullets into his head was very strong, but the fear of him suddenly getting up and unleashing one of those laser beams was even stronger. He turned and saw Clyde limping toward him with his gun in his hand.

"Let's go over there and finish him off?" Clyde's excitement was at an all-time high.

Calvin grabbed Clyde's arm. "I don't think that's a--" He saw Ronnie move. "Let's go! He's getting up--"

"We oughta finish him off--"

WHOOSH!--BLAAM!!

The laser beam streaked across the open space, just missing Clyde by inches. The heat was so intense it knocked Clyde backwards and off his feet. Calvin fired two shots and the gun registered empty. He saw Clyde was back on his feet. When another laser beam struck a tree trunk, it catapulted them both into a desperate retreat.

Calvin ran through the thick underbrush, ducking and weaving the trees. He could hear Mary and Jim up ahead.

Clyde was turning and firing shots every couple of minutes.

Calvin dug in his pocket, retrieved a handful of bullets and hastily loaded his pistol. The underbrush and wild growing limbs from the trees were so thick Calvin had to swim through the stuff. This was working to their advantage, since the vegetation prevented Ronnie from hitting them with a laser.

Five minutes later, Calvin caught up with Mary and Jim. Calvin touched his pocket, felt the eight bullets he had left and spoke to Clyde. "How many bullets you got left?"

Maintaining the fast-forward pace, Clyde tucked one of his pistols in his waist and patted his pocket. "Maybe a dozen or less."

Calvin felt a wave of hopelessness sweep across his subconscious. That pestering voice of realization started talking and wouldn't shut up. It told him Ronnie had a laser gun, bullet-proofed clothing, and was adamant about killing them. Everything Ronnie possessed was superior to the items they possessed. Logic indicated it was just a matter of time before they would succumb to Ronnie's pursuit.

Calvin's heart jumped a beat when he saw the thick jungle like vegetation had come to an end. He slowed his pace, scanning the area. About 100 yards in front of them, he saw what looked like a mining camp. With the help of the glow from the moon and the stars, Calvin could easily make out the wooden frame lining the entrance of the shaft and the three mining carts. The shaft was bored into the side of a hill and looked like the entrance was on a downward slope. There were two wooden shacks not too far from the shaft.

Looking around frantically, with the sound of Ronnie's footsteps thrashing through the underbrush, drawing closer, Calvin saw there was nowhere else to flee.

Clyde pointed his pistol at the location where Ronnie's footsteps were heard, then whispered. "He's coming up on us fast." He fired a shot into the wall of vegetation, and noticed Ronnie stopped moving.

"Let's go inside this shaft." Calvin increased his speed, running with the others on his heels. When he reached the front, Calvin came to a stop and quickly examined the area. There were mining carts and three sets of tracks similar to those of train tracks. The entrance was huge enough to fit five mining carts. Just as he expected, the tunnel proceeded in a downward fashion into the earth.

Calvin entered, breathing hard with his gun in the ready. Mary, Jim and Clyde were on his heels. The darkness felt like it had swallowed them up. Without the moonlight, the difference was striking. Moving rapidly down the rock tunnel, Calvin felt his eyes slowly adjusting to the darkness. Suddenly, he noticed there were things lining the walls and he went to investigate.

Crossing the tracks, Calvin was hoping these objects on the wall could be of use to them. When he arrived, Calvin saw lanterns hanging from the tunnel wall and right below on the floor was a crate of sulfur sticks (matches). The smell of turpentine was thick in the air. Calvin grabbed one of the lanterns, kneeled and retrieved one of the matches. He was about to strike the match, but hesitated, realizing the light would tell Ronnie their exact location. After further analyzing the surroundings, Calvin decided this darkness was too much. Plus, they had to see where they were going.

Calvin struck the match on the tunnel wall. The small flame lit up the area like an explosion. He touched the flame to the wick inside the lantern, and the immediate area was drenched in a flaming light. Calvin's eyes darted every which a way. The first thing caught his sight was all the items lined against the tunnel wall (small drums of kerosene, picks, shovels, sledgehammers, and a few unidentifiable objects).

"Watch out!" Clyde shouted when he saw Ronnie arrived at the entrance.

Calvin, Mary and Jim put their backs to the tunnel wall.

Calvin's eyes were taking in the surroundings with the rapidness and efficiency of a computerized microchip. He saw down into the declining tunnel there were turns; other tunnels connected to this main tunnel. When Calvin saw the crate of dynamite sticks near one of the turns, he lit up with enthralling joy. *There ain't a bulletproof vest in the world that's explosion proof, bet that!* With amazing clarity, his military knowledge of setting trip-wires came back to him with blazing speed.

Calvin stepped away from the wall.

WHOOSH!--BLAAM!

The laser beam struck the tunnel wall, flinging pebbles, dust and sparks everywhere. Clyde dove for the ground while Calvin put his back to the wall. Mary and Jim got down on their stomachs.

Calvin was about to put out the lantern and suddenly remembered all the lighting fluid and dynamite lying around. "Shit!" If a laser beam struck any of these items, the whole area would go up in an explosion. He had to move faster than fast. He nervously put out the lantern. "Hey, Clyde! Come here, hurry!" Calvin whispered. When Clyde arrived, he told him the plan.

Whispering with a baffled tone, Clyde said. "I don't thank setting off dynamite in this area of the shaft'll be a good idea."

"Well, what'd you suggest?" Calvin whispered, realizing Clyde was right, but knew full well they had no other options.

"I ain't got a suggestion." Clyde saw movement and squeezed off a shot. "But I know we gots to be real far away when that stuff goes off, 'cause there's probably dynamite all over this here section."

"Listen, I need you to hold him back. Keep him busy. I'm gonna rig up a trip-wire. When I'm almost finished I'll call you." Calvin instructed Mary and Jim to grab a handful of the matches and escorted them toward the crate of dynamite.

It took Calvin ten minutes to set the trap. "Clyde!" Calvin whispered in between the gunshots.

When Clyde arrived, Calvin attached the trip-wire to the match connected to the fuse of the strategically placed dynamite. The dynamite fuse was stretched out from wall to wall, raised off the ground about 7 inches, and was connected to several sticks of dynamite on each side.

Calvin led the group further into the shaft, making a left turn down the first sub-tunnel. This tunnel seemed to be more sloped downward than the main tunnel and there was a strong breeze circulating the air. Calvin was carrying the crate of remaining sticks of dynamite. Mary carried two lanterns and Jim had one. When they were at a safe distance from the main tunnel, Calvin lit a lantern. The glow of the light revealed horror-stricken expressions. He could literally feel the tension steadily growing as he crossed his fingers, waiting for the explosion.

Ronnie approached with caution. He wanted to kick himself in the ass with a set of spiked, steel toed boots for dropping his night-vision goggles and didn't even realize it. It had to occur when Calvin shot his horse and he was knocked unconscious. How hadn't he noticed he dropped them!? There obviously was no turning back now, so he forced himself to stop brooding over the loss. A shot rang out, and the bullet whizzed pass him just as he ducked. The slug struck the tunnel wall and splattered dust and pulverized rocks.

He saw a lantern was lit. The light was dim and he was about to fire a laser beam, but another slug whizzed pass him. He thought about charging at them and opening fire with both laser guns, but the thought of one of them getting off a lucky head-shot compelled him to be patient and precautious.

In any event, Ronnie knew they did not have an unlimited supply of bullets. Most of all, he had all night and they foreclosed their avenues of getaway by entering this mine. *Stupid motherfuckers!* He was repeatedly forcing them to waste bullets by abruptly moving toward them, making sure his head was safe from bullets. Twice he was struck by a bullet and cringed in pain. He should have worn padding under these bulletproofed clothing, he repeatedly scolded himself.

After a couple more shots were fired, one of which struck Ronnie in the chest, he heard them running deeper into the tunnel. His mind was prepared for a long-haul situation, and so this cat and mouse game didn't faze him one bit. In fact, he decided he was going to enjoy this challenge.

When he heard no more sounds, and the silence was almost overwhelming, Ronnie continued forward. He moved several steps at a time before pausing to listen. He moved again and his foot became entangled in a piece of rope or some kind of wire. From his peripheral vision, he saw a spark. The sight and sound of the fizzing fuse was unmistakable. The situation registered in Ronnie's mind with profound crispness.

With terrifying speed, Ronnie turned and ran back in the direction he came while his index finger slammed down on the control dial on the Micron watch.

KABLLAAAM! . . . BABLLAAAM!!

Calvin felt the ground under his feet sway as if a giant was trying to topple the mine. The dozen or more rapid blasts caused rock and debris to tumble down upon their heads. Calvin was totally perplexed by all those explosions. He had only used a couple of sticks of dynamite. Where were these dozens of other explosions coming from!? Suddenly, Clyde's earlier remarks about dynamite being all over that area answered his question.

Calvin and the others were running deeper into the tunnel with their arms warding off the falling debris, but they instantly realized wherever they went the tunnel seemed as if it was caving in.

A huge ten-pound boulder struck Calvin's injured shoulder. He screamed with ear-piercing force, instantly causing a colloquy of other screams. Then, Calvin saw a humongous bolder crash down on Clyde's head and he just knew his friend was dead. Amazingly Clyde brushed it off and kept running. Calvin's eyes flared up with utter shock. It was humanly impossible to withstand a blow to the head from something that big! But this mental shock was short lived because the falling debris shoved that phenomenal event to the back of his mind.

THUUM!!

A tremendous earth-shaking rumble brought the massive commotion to a rest. The first thing Calvin noticed was the small breeze circulating through the tunnel had suddenly disappeared. Calvin was afraid to even fix his mind to imagine what might have caused the breeze to stop, but subconsciously he knew the answer. It made him tremble. *Relax; it might not be that*, he repeatedly told himself as he moved down the tunnel back toward the entrance. "Is everyone all right?"

When everyone indicated they were okay, with the exception of minor cuts, bruises and contusions, Calvin increased his speed toward the main tunnel, with the lantern held in front of him. Calvin jumped over rocks and boulders. The others followed him. His heart thundered in his ears because that breeze wasn't supposed to stop like that. As he approached, a noxious gas attacked his nose. It suddenly felt like sandpaper was being scrapped on the back of his throat.

Jim started coughing, which ignited a chain reaction of other coughs. They all were coughing with terrifying force.

With the lantern raised about eye level, Calvin was moving so fast he crashed into the barricade of rocks and almost broke a knuckle in the process. Calvin sat the lantern down and stood staring at the wall that sealed them from the main tunnel. With a truly stupefied look, Calvin was so shocked he felt the crevices of his brain freeze up with high-octane terror. The noxious gas no longer had an effect on him, even though his lungs were now burning. Too many horrifying realities were suddenly over-flooding his mind.

Calvin dropped to his knees and wept. The coughing returned and was accompanied by stomach pains and a treacherous headache. He did not want to believe his eyes or his nose. They were buried alive, and were being exposed to a poisonous gas, which meant one thing and one thing only: They were dead.

CHAPTER # 26

General Warps, with his thick scruffy looking facial hair, his cold blue eyes and his medal-laden uniform, sat high on his sparkling white horse. With a light kick, he urged the mare into a cantering gallop and led his 40-man infantry division along the slope of a ridge. He was on his way to Pettus Arkansas.

On the horizon, the sun was raising and he was still upset he was awakened from his sleep, but he repeatedly told himself Clyde Jerkins' capture was indeed worth the interruption. Ole Clyde had become big news throughout the south in the last couple of months and had graduated from being a bank robber to a mass murderer. Even more shocking, Clyde was traveling with a gang of runaway slaves, and a strange white man who had some kind of thunderbolt gun, that shot lightning rods. Rumors! If there's one thing consistent about most folks in these parts, it was their unrelenting ability to blow things out of context and twist the facts. *A thunderbolt gun that fired lightning rods!? Give me a break, please.* He wondered if these folks realized just how stupid and insane they sounded!?

Normally, General Warps didn't get involved in such local affairs, but when a group of people leaves a trail of almost 200 hundred dead bodies, the entire U.S. Government was obligated to take action. This sort of mission also required the use of all available resources, which was why General Warps sent a rider to the Arkansas U.S. Marine Base instructing Colonel Bush to meet him at Pettus with no less than 50 troops. Since the Pettus messenger man made it clear Clyde's gang was still at large, General Warps knew extra precautions were imperative. He just hoped he got there before Clyde's gang attempted to break him out.

When the sun was in its 7 o'clock position in the sky, and already the heat was blistering, General Warps saw a rider appear at a distance up ahead. A few seconds later, he saw it was an infantryman. General Warps knew what the news was without being told.

General Warps waved a hand, bringing his troops to a stop when the messenger was right upon them.

"General Warps, sir," The messenger said respectfully. "My name's Lance Corporal Payne here to inform you of some very unfortunate news--"

"Let's get moving." General Warps waved his troops back into motion. "Clyde Jerkins escaped, huh?" He saw Corporal Payne's shocked facial response. "I know you didn't expect a few local law men to hold ole Clyde while his gang is on the loose, did you?"

The Corporal shrugged as he rode alongside the General.

The speed of the galloping horses increased.

With a legal-size envelope tucked under his/her arm, the person in the green sweat suit and sunglasses pulled the motor scooter in front of Timetron's main headquarters. The huge 70-story skyscraper was made of glass and had "Timetron" in big letters above its main entrance. The sun was at its high point, beaming hot rays upon the land below.

After locking up the motor scooter in the messengers' parking zone, the person headed for the main entrance. When he/she entered, the cool air from the air conditioner brought forth a sigh of relief from the hot July sun. Looking at the directory near the elevators, the person found James Simpson's location, got on the elevator with two men dressed in sleek business suits and pressed the 47th floor.

When the elevator arrived at the 47th floor and the door slid open, the person hesitated for a second and then stepped off the elevator. The person made a right turn and approached the secretary. Without saying a word, the person laid the envelope on the desk in front of the blond hair, high cheek boned woman and then handed her a "Unicom" messenger receipt.

She looked up at the person, and thought the messenger had to be one of those punk-funk kids. Wearing sunglasses inside a building had to be some kind of fashion statement she concluded. But upon closer observation, she realized it was a white man and he was apparently too old to be into punk rock. "Who is this for?"

The person picked up the envelope, repositioned it so she could read the label and laid it directly in front of her.

The secretary looked down and the statement "extremely urgent" was the first thing that jumped out at her. Then she saw it was for James Simpson. She signed the receipt, handed it back to the white man, and watched him exited the office. Hesitantly, she decided this was a basis for interrupting Mr. Simpson's important meeting and headed for the conference room.

The secretary tapped softly on the door, entered with a smile, gave James the envelope and exited. She was hoping and praying what was inside the envelope was really urgent because James gave her that look which said he was going to chew her ass out for not obeying his instructions; he had explicitly ordered her not to "interrupt this important meeting."

"Excuse me for a moment, please," James said to his fellow board members as he opened the envelope, emptied the contents onto the table, and saw the computer chip disk and a type written letter. After reading the letter, James looked up into the eyes of the six executives with a strained expression. He broke the long pause with a loud sigh and said. "I think we have a very serious problem on our hands . . .

Eric stood gaping down into the secondary return booth with bug-eyed disbelief mixed with a furious rage. When he realized the blood was pouring out of Ronnie's wounds onto the booth floor, he snapped out of the trance. "Diana, get the first aid kit! Hurry!"

Eric snatched the door open, reached in and delicately dragged Ronnie out of the booth.

"Take it easy, man," Ronnie was clutching his left wrist, trying to stop the bleeding due to the four missing fingers on his left hand.

When Eric saw Ronnie's right foot was missing as well, along with innumerable cuts and scratches on his face, he sensed this bastard fucked up again. His anger rose to a seething level. "Did you kill him!?" Eric spoke calmly, but forcefully because the rage was so overwhelming.

Ronnie didn't answer. He was grimacing in pain as Diana arrived with the first aid kit.

Within minutes two tourniquets were put in place; one attached to the wrist and the other around the leg.

As they carried Ronnie on a stretcher to the car, Eric said persistently, "Did you kill him?"

"I don't think so," Ronnie felt like a bumbling idiot and a complete loser. He hated feeling this way. His urge to vent on someone was powerful, and he wished it could've been that motherfucker, Calvin! But his injuries were making him so tired. The loss of so much blood was taking its toll. "Take me to my crib. We'll talk then." He almost dozed off as they placed him in the back seat of Eric's car. Ronnie dug in his pocket and pulled out the poster of Clyde. "This is the reason why that bastard Calvin is getting so fuckin' lucky." He handed it to Eric.

Eric took it, got behind the wheel, started the car and examined the poster closely just before driving off.

During the ride to Ronnie's house, Eric was gritting his teeth, struggling with the reality that indicated he now had to result to extreme measures. He was so infuriated he thought about simply pulling to the side of the road and kicking Ronnie's ass out. There was nothing else he or Larry could do for him. Even if they had other friends to complete the job, Eric was no longer interested. With less than three weeks to stop Calvin, he needed guaranteed results. Suddenly, the thought of kicking Ronnie out on the side of the road grew stronger. The only thing stopped him was the thought of being responsible for Ronnie's death, while Larry was still roaming around.

After carrying Ronnie inside his loft on the stretcher, and Larry made the call to their personal doctor, Eric gave them fifty thousand dollars cash, thanked them for their services and was about to leave.

Larry grabbed Diana by her hair and she screamed. With a short-lived struggle Larry placed the gun to her head, which tamed her instantly. "We want every dime you owe us. 200 grand."

Eric's heart quivered with genuine horror. *What the hell is this!?* Every cell in his body surged with a terrifying fear. "Larry, come on now, let's look at this realistically. The job isn't complete. Ronnie admits he didn't kill Calvin." He looked over and saw Ronnie was unconscious. "He didn't bring back the finger or the piece of hair. The deal was clear, if you kill--"

"Give us the rest of the money or she dies," Larry said with a deadly calm. "All the shit we went through, we deserve every fuckin' penny you owe us . . . Not only will I kill this beautiful little lady of yours, but I'll go public and tell every media company everything."

Eric saw his career and all the years of hard work crashing down the drain, becoming irretrievably lost with every word that rolled off Larry's tongue. "Please, Larry, don't hurt her. I thought you guys were honorable hit men?"

Larry laughed. "Honorable hit men!? What world are you from!? This is all about money my man, no more no less . . . Now, if you think we're playin' fuckin' games with you, go on and do somethin' stupid." Larry smiled and caressed Diana's breast. "We brought back some relics from the past to prove it." He saw Eric's pained facial expression and he nodded over to the table on the other side of the room.

Eric turned and saw the table was covered with all sorts of items, bullets, posters, clothing, tools, and God only knew what else. He was slipping even faster than before.

"I also did a little homework," Larry traced the barrel of the gun down Diana's chest, passed her stomach and stopped between her legs. He imagined himself conducting some homework on Diana. "Those carbon 14 tests will prove where all that stuff came from. The choice is yours." He cocked the gun as Diana unleashed a wave of fake tears.

"Okay, I'll give you whatever you want. But I swear to God, I will kill you if you touch her."

With a smile, Larry said. "Touch her like what? Like this?" With his free hand, Larry grabbed Diana's crotch, trying to stick his middle finger through her pants and into her vagina. Then he began massaging the area where he knew her clitoris was located.

When Eric saw Diana's eyes about to roll up into her head, he jumped forward with clinched fists.

"Go ahead! Play like you superman motherfucker!" Larry worked his hand up to her breasts and maintained his degrading fondling mission while he spoke. "Now, I suggest you get moving. If I see one cop, you know what time it is. Don't worry yourself too much, because I know how to treat a woman." He laughed again.

Eric felt an indescribable steam rolling off his body. His mind snapped in half because too many bad things were happening to him all at once. His iron will had to compensate, since becoming weak was something inconsistent with his very existence. He had to throw Larry off guard and spoke softly, almost nerdy like. "Larry, if you have any morals, I beg of you not to--"

"Don't worry, I'll make sure she's well taken care of, now go get that 200 grand and save this sweet, juicy girl of yours." He licked her face.

Eric swallowed hard as his eyes became watery. "I'll be back for you, Diana. I love you." He raced out of the loft, ignoring Larry's snide remarks.

As Eric entered his car, he realized his whole life had just changed. He had killed before and swore he would never do it again, but that vow was officially nonexistent. That day would live in his mind forever. He often told himself it was an accident, trying to go along with what everyone thought, but his subconscious mind wouldn't allow it. When he was a teenager, he shot and killed his best friend during a hunting trip. Eric hated David because he had all the girls and used to always tease him about not having girls. He was now trying to remember how good it felt when he blew David's head off with the 12-gauge shotgun. This sensation would get him into the appropriate frame of mind. He sighed when the feeling came back vividly.

As Eric maneuvered the Mercedes onto the highway, he wondered could Brent obtain him a silencer for the gun he had. Brent was the best investigator he'd ever seen, but he wasn't a murderer, nor would he condone such an act. Eric realized if Brent knew a murder was about to transpire, he might even report it to the authorities. Despite all this, Eric decided he had to at least give it a try and was hoping Brent's lust for money would help him keep his mouth shut.

Then, he remembered Brent was now trying to regain his trust because of what he did with that investigation into Demetrius and Ramanda's background. That amnesia game Brent played on him had Eric fuming, and as a result, he had threatened to cut Brent off for misleading him into believing he had acquired the information on the two when in actuality he hadn't. *Well, now he would get his chance to make things right!* Eric wiped a runaway tear from his face and realized he was going to enjoy personally killing Larry and Calvin as well.

CHAPTER # 27

Calvin turned and saw Mary had collapsed to the ground while Jim was clutching his throat. Clyde wisely had a handkerchief covering his nose and mouth. Through his coughing spell, Calvin tried to think of a way to get out of this tomb, but the mental images of his daughter, his father and the promise, and even Ramanda were interfering with the process. He hastily ripped a piece of his shirt, rushed to Mary, and was shocked when he found she was unconscious. Terror gripped him when the thought crossed his mind she was dead.

With frantic speed, Calvin tried to find Mary's pulse, but Jim suddenly passed out and struck the back of his head on the tunnel wall. Calvin dropped Mary's arm and rushed to Jim, still coughing profusely.

Clyde was helping Jim when Calvin arrived and so he rushed back to Mary. He checked her pulse and discovered it was very shallow. Suddenly, an idea struck him like a blow from a wrecking ball. "Clyde! Pick up Jim and follow me!" He picked up the lantern, scooped Mary up into his arms and raced deeper down into the tunnel. With Clyde less than a stride behind him, Calvin was still coughing. He went about twenty yards pass the crate of dynamite, and laid Mary down and saw Clyde do the same with Jim.

Calvin raced back up the tunnel with the lantern raised in front of him and stopped at the crate of dynamite. Through a dry and painful cough, he said to Clyde. "This is very dangerous, maybe even suicidal, but it's our only chance . . . Grab a handful of 'em. Hurry!" With four sticks of dynamite in his hand and a pocket full of matches, Calvin ran up toward the barricade.

Clyde had five sticks of dynamite and was right behind him coughing every step of the way. Twice he stumbled when he felt like he was going to faint, but the fear of dying kept him going strong.

Calvin sat the lantern down. "Dig!" He frantically began pulling rocks from the pile and tossing them in back of him. "Focus on one area until you make a decent size hole."

Seven minutes later, Calvin and Clyde planted the dynamite. Just when Calvin struck the match, Clyde grabbed his hand and said. "What if this whole damn place comes tumblin' down on our heads!?"

Calvin wasn't trying to hear any more debates because sooner or later they both would be unconscious from smelling this gas. "Ready?" Calvin shoved Clyde away and lit the fuse connected to the four sticks of dynamite he planted. As he went to the other five sticks Clyde planted, Clyde took off. Calvin lit the fuse and ran after him.

Calvin was no more than thirty feet away from the barricade when havoc struck; he felt nauseous, saw stars hovering crazily before his eyes, and his bowels were even becoming loose. He tripped and fell. Through a comatose vision and an oxygen-deprived mind, he saw a blurry figure (Clyde) rushing back for him. He felt himself being snatched onto his feet and into a foot-dragging flee.

Calvin felt like he was swimming through quicksand as he fought the sudden afflictions. Only after he realized death was looking him in the eyes, he was able to garnish enough energy to move faster, but the effort came a little too late.

KABLLAAAM! . . . BABLLAAAM!!

☼   ☼   ☼   ☼

Eric pulled the old brown Buick Skylark to a stop in front of Ronnie's loft. He pulled the nine-millimeter from the front of his waist, injected a bullet in the chamber and took the safety off. He put the gun back, pulled the 12-millimeter from the back of his waist and did the same. Looking around the area carefully, he hoped when he started shooting the cover of night would help them get away. His nervousness came to life like rushing water bursting from a shattered dam.

Earlier, as he approached Brent Browsky's home, Eric realized he would be wasting valuable time trying to get a silencer and decided to deal with it as the cards unfolded. But what really changed his mind was the thought of another man having sex with Diana, his future wife. These heart-wrenching mental pictures were killing him in a unique way.   And what drove him even further over the edge was the indisputable fact Diana's current pain, suffering and humiliation was basically all his fault. How could he walk her into this shit!?

Eric reached over, picked up the brown paper bag filled with exactly 200 thousand dollars in big bills (100, 500 and 1,000 dollar bills), and exited the car.

When Larry opened the door, Eric saw he was smiling broadly with the gun in his hand. He stepped aside for Eric to enter. Upon stepping pass the threshold, he smelled sex in the air and almost lost it completely.   When Eric saw Diana crying, he rushed to her. As he moved toward her the bag was suddenly snatched from his hand.

Diana forced her fake tears to flow a little harder as Eric approached.   The electricity that still surged through her body, in particular, between her legs was very unique.   She always knew a man not suffering from premature ejaculation syndrome could make her feel like this.   She was upset it had to come to an end.   Her embarrassment grew when Eric embraced her because if he had heard and saw how much she enjoyed that explosive sexual episode with Larry, moaning, groaning and hollering in pleasure, he would have completely disowned her.

As Eric tried to comfort Diana, he saw Larry had took his eyes off them and was peering into the bag at the money with a huge deranged looking smile on his face. Eric saw his opportunity and just as he was about to pull the gun . . .

The doctor came from the back. "I think our friend Ronnie's about ready to rock and roll, Larry."

Eric made eye contact with the chubby, thick eyeglass-wearing doctor, but the smell of Diana's vaginal juices snapped his mind completely. He pulled the nine-millimeter, took aim and squeezed the trigger.

BOOM!--BOOM!--BOOM!--BOOM! . . . BOOM!--BOOM!--BOOM! . . .

Larry's body jerked and trembled from the impact of the four slugs to his chest. As Larry crashed to the floor, Eric spun the gun, now aiming at the doctor, who was in a state of sheer petrification. Eric felt a tremor of excitement pass through his veins as he cut off the doctor's statement: "Oh my God" with three shots. The doctor convulsed from the impact of the bullets; his head snapped from the slug that struck him just below the right eye. He landed with a sickening thump.

Eric was enthralled because his aim was still as good as it used to be when he went hunting and spent time at the firing range. The kick of the weapon and that thunderous sound literally made him feel good! And he noticed it was like riding a bike; you never forget; you only get a little rusty, that's all.

Breathing like a mad man, Eric walked up to Larry and pumped two more shots into his forehead, causing his already dead body to flinch violently from the impact. He saw huge chucks of flesh had splattered across the room.

He turned and Diana rushed toward him. She hugged him and Eric was about to ask her did he touch her. But, based on the look of her clothing, the smell and the tears, that was evident. "Pull yourself together, Diana." He saw she instantly snapped out of the humiliation and was ready for action as if the tears were nothing more than a front. "Get a rag and wipe everything we touched. Hurry!"

Eric rushed toward the back room, as Diana bolted into action. When Eric entered the room, he saw Ronnie had scrambled out of bed and was dragging himself toward the closet. "Well, well, you're one real rough and tough cookie, aren't you? Now, where do you think you're going?"

BOOM!

Ronnie screamed when Eric's bullet tore through his right buttock.

Eric thought he heard commotion outside as he aimed at Ronnie's lower back. He fired another shot and Ronnie recoiled, but didn't holler this time. Eric aimed for the back of Ronnie's head, pulled the trigger, but the gun registered empty. He tucked the gun in his waist, pulled the other gun from his back waist and fired three rapid shots into the back of Ronnie's head. The grotesque sight of Ronnie's bullet-ridden head made Eric feel like he was on top of the world. *Nobody fucks with me and lived to boast about it, not even professional hit men!*

Eric barreled out of the room. "Let's go!" He snatched up the bag of money, headed out the door with Diana behind him. They ran down the stairs like a lightning bolt. Before exiting the building, Eric carefully inspected the immediate area. When Eric saw everything was in order, he headed for the car. They hastily walked to the car, got in and drove off casually.

When they were about ten blocks away, police sirens suddenly screamed and flashing lights appeared in back of them. Eric and Diana were startled almost into a terror-induced coma.

Over the loudspeaker, and cop in the passenger seat said. "Pull it over."

☼   ☼   ☼   ☼

Calvin felt himself gliding through the air as if he had wings. The impact of the explosion upon every part of his back, his buttocks, the

271

back of his head, and even the back of his legs, felt like a scorching hot tennis racket had swatted him with savage force, flinging him down the tunnel. It felt like he would never land, but when he did, he violently tumbled about ten feet before coming to a complete stop.

The pain seemed to touch every part of his body and his mind was far beyond weary. Calvin shook his head and his senses were activated. The breeze from the circulating air struck Calvin's senses like a nuclear explosion. The fresh air smelled sweet and had a powerful rejuvenating effect on his entire being.

Calvin heard Clyde moaning and sounded like he was struggling into a standing position. Breathing deeply, Calvin struggled to his feet and saw Clyde limping toward him.

"I think it worked," Clyde limped pass Calvin, heading back to the barricade.

When they saw a huge four-foot by six-foot hole was bored straight through the barricade, Calvin and Clyde raced back, scooped up Mary and Jim, and exited the sub-tunnel. The daylight almost blinded Calvin and Clyde when they stepped outside of the mineshaft, and into the stifling heat. Their entire bodies, including their faces, were covered with a black dust.

Calvin was so thirsty and tired, he wanted to simply lay down somewhere, anywhere and sleep for two weeks. He spoke hastily as he headed west. "Let's move from here . . . The mine workers might pop up any minute."

Moving quickly Calvin sensed Mary was breathing. He raised her face up to his ear and heard she was breathing.

About five minutes of the high-speed walking, Clyde spoke with clear stress in his voice after he did to Jim what Calvin had done to Mary. "Calvin, I thank somethin's terribly wrong with Jim." Even the mere thought of saying Jim wasn't breathing scared him.

"He's breathing isn't he?" Calvin remembered that terrible fall Jim suffered and realized it was a severe one.

"I--I don't thank so," Clyde said nervously.

Calvin nearly leaped out of his skin from realization. He hastily propped Mary against a nearby tree, and took Jim's limp body from Clyde. He laid him down on his back and placed his ear near Jim's mouth and nose. He frantically checked his pulse. "No! Jim! No!" He started mouth-to-mouth resuscitation, and began pumping his chest, trying desperately to restart Jim's heart.

With eyes glistened with tears, Calvin worked feverishly on Jim for ten minutes, refusing to believe Jim was dead. Calvin was about to commence another round of resuscitation and chest pumping, but Clyde grabbed him, and said, "He's gone, Calvin. Let him be. Ain't nothin' you can do to bring him back. He's with God now."

Calvin flopped into a lying position next to Jim's dead body and cried quietly, staring up into the sky. For two straight minutes he laid there thinking of how he was going to make Eric pay for this. He heard Mary waking up; he rose and went to her. Reaching out for her hand, Calvin saw she wanted to get onto her feet, so he pulled her into his arms. "Mary, how you feel?"

"My head is achin'," Mary swallowed and her throat screamed from the fiery pain. "My throat is hurtin' too . . ."

Calvin's urge to hug Mary was great and he gave into the temptation. How was he going to break the news of Jim's death without hurting her? He knew Mary had become so attached to Jim she thought of herself as his mother. He knew how it shattered him and could only imagine how the unfortunate news would affect Mary. There was no way of not breaking her heart, and since time wasn't in their favor, he gave it to her straight. "Mary, Jim is dead."

"Dead!?" Mary responded as if the word was foreign. When it sunk in, she screamed, broke away from Calvin's embrace, and raced to

273

Jim's dead body.   She was crying with an animation truly unique to black folks.

Calvin let her vent for about five minutes. Afterward he pulled her from Jim's body. "We gotta go, Mary." He wrapped his arm around her and started walking. "Clyde, bring Jim's body, we're gonna bury him when we're out of this area."

"Let's go buddy," Clyde muttered as he wiped a tear away from his face, scooped up Jim's body and followed Calvin and Mary.

Two hours and a half passed so quickly, Calvin didn't realize they covered a distance of ten miles.   However, he noticed his thirst was mounting, and was certain he saw a couple of mirages as a result. Twice he had to carry Mary when she couldn't walk anymore and was pleading with him to stop.   After what happened in the town of Pettus last night, there was no doubt in Calvin's mind there were going to be a posse, law men, bounty hunters and all other entities into the business of catching outlaws scouring the land for them. If they didn't get at least twenty to thirty miles away from Pettus, they would be courting with catastrophe.

Clyde noticed Jim's body was becoming very stiff. Rigor mortis was setting in. This condition was brought about by the coagulation of protein in Jim's muscles, accelerated by the heat of the blistering sun and by his pre-death activities, which caused undue exertion and fatigue. From the stiffness of Jim's body, Clyde knew it was time. "Hey, Calvin, I thank it's time we put our little buddy to rest."

Calvin stopped, looked around and saw the area would do. "Mary, see if you can find some wood, maybe a couple of tree branches, so we can make a grave marker." He turned to Clyde. "I guess you and I can start digging."

With bare hands, they began digging next to a healthy looking bush. The smell of the dirt had a strong, damp richness, which indicated it was high quality soil. Twenty minutes later, they made a hole about four feet deep and was the size of Jim's body. Calvin wondered was this deep enough to prevent wild animals from digging Jim up? He knew six feet was standard burial depth, and decided to continue digging until they were about six feet.

Mary found two large branches and some vines. After she tied the two branches together, forming a cross, Jim was buried and the cross planted at the head of the grave. Clyde preached a eulogy that dealt with the genuine greatness of children and rattled off Matthew 18:1-14 with remarkable precision and flawlessness. He equated Jim to the "child" Jesus claimed was "the greatest in the kingdom of heaven."

They bided Jim Roof farewell and continued west.

A half hour later, they saw a strawberry bush and they feasted happily. Right across from the strawberries were peach trees and they had a couple of those as well. It didn't take long for them to realize the fruits weren't doing any justice to quench their thirst, but did give them some energy. They continued west with unrelenting vigor.

Suddenly, Calvin saw the forest they were moving through was starting to thin out. Then, suddenly, he realized he heard a body of moving water and followed the slashing sound in a northwestern direction. When Calvin saw the stream up ahead, he bolted for it. Diving into the water head long, he slurped the water into his mouth with an urgency that was frightening. Clyde and Mary did the same. They drank until they could drink no more.

They resumed their westward travel, and about an hour later, they came across a huge plantation. As usual, they went around it and continued. A mile farther, they clashed with another plantation and did the same. This went on for the next fifteen miles comprising of four additional plantations. At this point, the sun began to creep into the western horizon. The question of whether they should set camp was a real brainer for Calvin because they had lost everything. They had no sleeping bags or blankets, and the few matches Calvin had were still wet from when he dove in the stream and forgot to take them out of his pocket. Plus, Calvin didn't feel they were at a safe distance from Pettus.

They decided to continue traveling west. As they walked across the darkened countryside, Mary suddenly screamed and fell tumbling to the ground.

Calvin and Clyde went to her with frantic haste.

Calvin was aghast. "What happened Mary?" He saw Mary clutching her ankle, and the first thing jumped in his mind was another snakebite incident.

"I stepped in that hole." Mary pointed. "I thank I messed my foot up real bad." She grimaced in pain.

"Can you walk on it?" Clyde said as he kneeled, looking at her ankle.

"I don't know," Mary gestured for Calvin to pull her onto her feet. When she was standing on one foot, she slowly put the other foot on the ground and applied some of her weight. "Ahhh!" She screamed again when the pain shot up her leg.

Calvin helped Mary sit back down. "Move your foot just a little." When he saw Mary was able to move her foot, while cringing in pain, he knew there were no broken bones. He slowly massaged her ankle. It was badly sprain and she wasn't going to be able to walk on it for a while. Calvin was about to explode with rage. It took all his energy not to throw a temper-tantrum. *Shit! Why now!?* He had two weeks left and God only knows how many miles to go.

Calvin shot to his feet and stared out into the darkness, realizing he wasn't going to make it to the Backlash. With deep breaths, he held the hyperventilating sensation at bay. They had no horses, no food or water and now he had to carry Mary. *Goddamn it!* He sighed loudly. He turned, kneeled, scooped Mary up gently and started walking. Giving up was not a word in his vocabulary.

They walked for about a half hour through pit darkness. The trees and underbrush grew thicker with each step. Just as Calvin's arms started burning with fatigue and exhaustion, he saw something up ahead. He slowed his pace, realizing they were on a hill. Calvin stopped at the edge, peering down into a valley. High up on a hill covered with trees, they saw the farm like ranch below. The place was littered with horses, cows, and roosters running around freely. There was also a pigpen, a chicken coop, a barn and a storage facility for the farm's harvest.

Calvin sat Mary down on the ground.

Clyde spoke excitedly, "With all 'em horses, I knows these folks won't mind helpin' a poo' preacher man such as himself with a ride."

"Wait a minute, Clyde," Calvin saw the place also had a couple of watchdogs roaming around. "I don't think that's wise. All the people in this area probably know your face. Don't forget there's posters plastered up all over the place."

"So what do you suggest?" Clyde said with a huge smile. "We go in with guns blazin' and help ourselves to whatever we want?"

"I didn't say that," Calvin saw that evil little twinkle in Clyde's eyes and didn't like it at all. "I think we should develop a plan that doesn't involve us exposing ourselves."

"Well, one thang we know for sho'" Clyde said. "We needs plenty supplies, like water containers, blankets, shoes, bullets, and at least two horses. And some bandages for Mary's ankle . . . And I don't know 'bout y'all, but I could sho' use some sleep."

Calvin nodded, agreeing with everything Clyde mentioned. "I think we need to first find out how many people are on this farm, what we're up against, and if there's a way to sneak pass those dogs."

"Why don't we draw the dogs to us," Mary drawled. "Get rid of 'em, then takes what we want and get away fast?"

It was a rather crude plan, but it was a practical approach, Calvin realized and saw it got Clyde to thinking while nodding his head. The only thing Calvin saw as a problem with Mary's scenario was they would probably have to kill the dogs. He hated when animals were hurt and punished because they were simply obeying humans. "Anybody got any ideas how to get rid of the dogs?"

Clyde pulled his two pistols. "I gots one bullet in each one. That's two dogs."

Calvin sighed angrily. "If we fire a shot, that'll wake up the whole farm! Shooting is the last thing we wanna do. What if the owner has guns, and we provoke a shootout and don't have any bullets?"

A penetrating silence swept over the three as they were hurled into deep thought.

Calvin decided to look at the whole farm from a military maneuvering perspective. He walked over to the edge, folded his arms across his chest, and stared down at the ranch. The northern perimeter was the weakness zone because the dogs didn't roam that area much, but the problem with that was this location was the storage house. The horse stable and the main house were the locations of most concern, but were guarded by four German Shepherds. As Calvin pondered the situation, he heard a noise.

Calvin's heart almost jumped clean out of his chest because whatever or whoever it was, it was apparent it was right upon them.

"I strongly suggest nobody moves," The deep, hard countrified voice said from behind them.

When Calvin turned and saw the two white men brandishing muskets, his knees became weak and unstable.

The other white man who wore suspenders said. "Put yo' hands up in the air real slowly. If you ain't know, this is private property."

With a racing heart rate, Calvin saw Clyde about to do something stupid. He crossed his fingers, praying Clyde would hold his head because whatever he was about to do . . . It obviously was not going to work.

CHAPTER # 28

Demetrius had to rapidly blink his eyes to make sure he heard Chris correctly. With the phone clamped to his ear, Demetrius spoke through the shock. "But how could they know all that!? You said all these records were inaccessible! . . . Don't you think I know that!? . . . How long do we have before the ax comes down, that's all we need to know?" Demetrius started to pace and stopped with a facial expression stronger than shock. "Are you fuckin' kiddin' me!? That's just enough time to pack our shit!" He sighed with excessive force. "Okay, okay. I'll call you when I get to the zone. Later."

Demetrius slammed the receiver into its cradle and ran to his bedroom. He packed within minutes and was rushing out the door. As he closed the door and jammed the key in the lock, he saw something near the bushes through his peripheral vision. Demetrius turned his head, while activating the lock and saw a white man in a green sweat suit with the hood covering his head. He had sunglasses covering his eyes and was stepping from behind the bushes. The man was pointing a little black object at Demetrius, and his bland, almost bored facial expression was startling.

Demetrius raised his hands assuming it was an FBI agent. That son of a bitch, Chris told him he had at least an hour or two to make moves! Demetrius was about to open his mouth to ask to see the man's badge, but the electrical shockwave crippled him. Demetrius realized he couldn't move, nor could he scream; he couldn't even blink his eyelids, but he could see, hear and probably feel as well.

With a desperate struggle, Demetrius tried to move, but it was as if his spinal cord was severed and his brain couldn't communicate with his body. Looking at the man with bug eyes, Demetrius was baffled into a state of sheer terror and the urge to scream increased ten folds when the man walked away and disappeared down the walkway.

About a half hour later, Demetrius wanted to cry when the FBI vehicles pulled up in front of his house. As if that wasn't bad enough, the moment the four agents got out of their cars, approaching with weapons drawn, he was suddenly released from the spell and was finally able to move.

☼　☼　☼　☼

Ten minutes after Demetrius was handcuffed and placed in one of the government vehicles, while a dozen agents ransacked his house, Ramanda turned her sky-blue Cadillac Escalade onto the street. She got a terrible surprise when she saw all the commotion in front of Demetrius' home. She hit the brakes and now knew why Demetrius didn't show up at the location. In an attempt not to provoke any suspicion, Ramanda casually found a parking space and killed the headlights. She put the car in park and watched.

Oh, God, what went wrong!? She asked inwardly as she looked on in terror. She nervously wondered did the agents see her when she drove onto the street? When she saw the agents continuing what they were doing, not once looking her way, Ramanda knew they weren't paying her any attention. If they got out of this fuck up, she was going to kill Chris! She decided conclusively. He said they had an hour or more! *How the fuck could this happen!?* Ramanda was fuming with a fury mixed with fear, anxiety and bafflement because this was not supposed to occur even from a worst case scenario analogy! Working the second back up and escape plan inside her mind, Ramanda knew she was on her own now. She put the vehicle in gear, about to maneuver the car out of the parking space.

TRUUM!--"AHHH"

Ramanda screamed and almost jumped out of her skin when the man in the green sweat suit and sunglasses snatched open the passenger side door and took a seat next to her. In terror, she saw the man was white and his skin looked synthetic. It gave her the creeps! She also saw he had a small black box in his hand and had it aimed at her chest.

With a trembling voice, Ramanda said, "What do you want!?" She was about to scream for help because the thought of death loomed largely in her mind.

Without saying a word the man in the sunglasses pressed a button on the handheld device and Ramanda felt like she was being electrocuted. Cataclysmic bolts of electricity raged through her body. She tried to scream, but nothing came out of her mouth. Summoning every drop of energy in her body, she again attempted to unleash a screeching shriek. That's when her eyes almost sprung from their sockets because he waved the box in front of her face and she could literally feel the electrical wave surging through her brain cells.

"Go to the agents," The man said with a mechanical voice. "Tell them who you are." He then got out of the car and disappeared into the shadows.

As Ramanda put the gear in park, she couldn't believe her body was following these insane instructions. It was like a puppeteer was pulling strings and she was powerless against its will. Fighting hysterically against this invasion of her being, Ramanda felt like she was undergoing an out of body experience similar to the ones people claim to have undergone just before dying. It was almost as if she was watching her herself from the vantage point of an observer and could do nothing to stop herself.

Ramanda closed the car door and headed for the entourage of FBI agents, trembling, screaming, kicking and thrashing inwardly every step of the way.

The following day, Eric, Diana and Tina escorted the Timetron executive board out the front door of the lab to the fleet of Limousines, and collectively waved as the convoy cruised away.

As Eric re-entered the lab, he was still trying to re-group from all the crazy news he was just exposed to at this meeting. He turned and spoke to Diana and Tina. "It's time we have our own little private meeting." He led them to his office four rooms down from Calvin's old office, entered and they all took seats.

Eric sat in silence for a moment, realizing whoever created the saying "when it rains, it pours" knew exactly what he or she was talking about. An example of this reality quote was that night last week when he was pulled over by the police after he shot and killed Ronnie, Larry and the doctor. This event was what he would call a good/bad situation. Good because they got away, bad because he lost the money and the guns. For the past ten years, he'd thought dirty cops were a thing of the past, but that night he discovered the media was lying through their teeth. He was still pissed off because he had to bribe the cops with the money after they found the guns. But now as he reflected on the situation, looking at it for what it was worth, including all the variables and possible outcomes, he had to admit it was well worth the loss.

Eric sighed because the thought crossed his mind again. Did Brent turn over that information on Demetrius and Ramanda to the board, instead of giving it to him? He felt it in his bones this is what Brent had done and he wondered how much Brent got for the information and why he reneged on their agreement? Eric put an end to these pestering reveries with a small struggle, leaned forward and propped his cupped hands on the desk. "It's amazing how they were able to evade Timetron's security checks." He looked over at Tina, shaking his head. "Let's hope you survive such a search, Tina. I've pulled a few strings since you been onboard, but let's keep our fingers crossed anyway."

Diana spoke with a disbelieving tone. "The board wasn't telling us everything, that's for sure. I even wonder if they got all their facts right. How does an ex-Albanian counter-intelligence agent, who acquired his expertise from Israeli, Russian and British spy Networks slide right through the most sophisticated background checking system in the world?"

"Money." Eric said point blankly. "And knowing the right people in the right places also helps tremendously. They said he was trying to steal this technology for some unknown lab in Spain. I would assume it was the Spanish Government behind this conspiracy. The amount of money Demetrius was paid was a sum only a government could throw around like that."

Tina smiled, whining up for a joke. "Demetrius is one shrewd man to sic his wife on Calvin like that. And he knew she was with Calvin in the most intimate ways." She shook her head. "Now, that's a man who is either insanely serious about accomplishing his mission or the pervert of the century."

"Like I said before," Eric pulled a file from the top desk draw. "Money . . . There's no limit to the things people will do to attain it. That's why I made sure very early in life to always keep plenty of it. That's enough of Demetrius . . . Tonight is gonna be a busy night. I'm going back in time to deal with Calvin."

"Eric." Tina said. "Weren't those two men who couldn't get the job done professional killers?"

Eric saw clearly where this was going. "Yeah, they were."

"No disrespect, but if Calvin evaded them, what's to say, he won't evade you as well?"

"The difference between me and those so-called hit men is that it's my ass that's on the line. No one is gonna deal with this at the same level of seriousness as I am . . . And, I should've known this from the start, if I wanted this done right I would have to do it myself. I'm just upset I'm finally making this decision with only two weeks left before the Backlash opens.   Now, it's strictly extreme measures all across the board."

"I'm going with you," Diana said. "Two intelligent heads are better than one."

Eric gave Diana a loving smiled. He wanted to reach over and give her a huge kiss.   When he saw Tina's surprised facial response, he said. "You, Tina, is gonna be our navigator commanding the controls. After we construct another secondary return booth at my mansion, I guess you can move in . . . Have you ever been inside a mansion that's a prefect structural mixture of contemporary, Gothic, Colonial, and Romanesque?"   When he saw Tina cracked a smile, he added. "And don't get any unfaithful ideas. I didn't get where I am by not taking extra upon extra precautions; especially when it comes to those who may harbor an animus toward me because of pressure moves."

That evening, Eric was behind the control station, setting the coordinates. "The location Ronnie transported from was about here." He pointed at the screen. "I think it'll be wise for us to transport to this location, but a few days later.   Also, hitting it right on the buzzer is too risky. We don't know if they were being pursued. Since this location was inside a mineshaft, we'll move the landing over just a little. We'll pick up the trail from there.   Obviously, he's going west; we know that for certain."

Eric rose to his feet and grabbed his knapsack identical to the one Larry and Ronnie possessed; it contained all the things theirs had and much more. Wearing typical 1830s attire, Eric was about to exit the control station, but turned and said. "Remember, Tina, re-adjust the time so Diana and I appear at just about the same time."

"I heard you before, Eric," Tina said. "All you have to do is say it once." She smiled when Eric gave her that look.

Eric turned and gave Diana a kiss. He exited the control station and entered the Time Machine. Seconds after Diana fastened the hatch, and re-entered the control station, the humming sound came to life with an intense eagerness. *This is it!* He was finally getting a taste of time travel, something he'd been waiting to do for most of his adult life. If it were for worldwide recognition it would be even far more thrilling. But that was forthcoming in the near future.

The humming increased, the sparks flew and then the sudden flash came.

Eric felt like he had faded into oblivion and suddenly awoke in a forest. He stumbled slightly and saw it was so dark he could barely see his hands before his eyes. The sweet smell of the fresh leaves from the trees and the nearby plants and flowers were remarkable. The crickets were talking and this whole forest seemed to be alive with life even though it was late at night.

Seconds later Eric saw the huge, almost blinding flash. He raised an arm to shield his eyes and a few feet away Diana stood, looking quite confused.

Eric pulled out his compass and found where west was located. "Let's go." He took the lead and Diana followed. About two minutes later, he could feel his eyes slowly adjusting to the darkness enough to make out the nearby trees, the tall grass they were moving through and the bushes. With the help of the light from the quarter moon and the clear sky, he saw movement up ahead. Slowing down his pace, Eric suddenly noticed the horses. He counted four of them; one of them was white and seemed to almost glow in the dark.

Eric increased his speed as he turned and spoke to Diana. "Our first hurdle is out the way; we got ourselves some horses." When Eric stepped through the tall grass and onto a piece of land that appeared not to have grass, he tripped over something that felt soft.

"Hey!" The man's voice said. "Watch where you're walking!"

All the surrounding troops in the camp shifted and continued sleeping.

When the man saw Eric and Diana, he shouted. "Where'd y'all come from? What are you doing here?!"

The whole camp of about fifty U.S. Marines jumped out of their sleeping bags, grabbed their nearby weapons and began lighting their lanterns.

Colonel Bush sprung to his feet, pushing the sleep out of his mind in the same fashion as he would reposition a cup on a table. He pulled his pistol. His hawk bill nose, beady blue eyes, stone chiseled face covered with poke marks and drooping square jaw resonated with inquisitivity. *This had better be damn good!* The dream he was just experiencing was the best one he'd had in months! There were naked dancing girls, plenty booze, and it felt like it wasn't a dream at all.

Eric rose to his feet. When he noticed the dozens of lanterns were being rapidly lit and the area was engulfed in light, he felt like a kitchen counter roach caught out of its nest and was dead center on the counter right under a spotlight. Diana stood next to him with an equally shocked expression. The thought of retrieving the laser gun from the knapsack was extinguished when he heard guns in back of them being cocked.

"Who the hell are you?" One of the troopers said as he approached with his pistol pointed at Eric's chest.

Eric's brain froze up, realizing there were over two-dozen guns pointed at him and Diana. His eyes darted and swept across the area. By the looks of the matching uniforms it was evident this was an army regiment. "I'm--we're--we," Eric stammered. "We're heading west and accidentally stumbled upon your camp. We're very sorry for the disturbance--"

"How did you get in this area?!" Colonel Bush shouted, approaching from behind them. He stopped in front of Eric and stared him in the eyes. He was about to blow a gasket until he saw Eric directed his eyes to the ground. Looking a high-ranking official straight in the eyes was considered the ultimate disrespect in Colonel Bush's book. "Where did they enter from?"

"From right here, sir." Private Smith pointed.

Colonel Bush got up in Eric's face, their noses almost touching. "How did you walk pass my soldier on guard duty? Was my man sleeping on the job?"

Eric was stuck like ultra-crazy glue and couldn't believe another human being's breath could smell so awful. "I—I--don't know, sir." He hoped the use of the word sir would lighten this man's heart.

"You don't know!?" Colonel Bush had his pistol pointed downward. He turned and yelled. "Tell Private Barnes to get his ass over here pronto!" He faced Eric and Diana with an evil smirk. "If you got this far into my camp, you gotta know if you walked in here without anyone stoppin' yah."

Eric was searching for something to say in response, but nothing entered his mind. After a long pause, Private Barnes arrived.

"Private Barnes, reporting, sir!" He shouted and stood at attention.

Colonel Bush walked over to Barnes, inspecting him closely to see if he had the look of sleep in his eyes or on his face. He looked fine. "How did these civilians get pass your post? They came from your perimeter, son!"

"Colonel Bush, sir." Private Barnes said with confidence. "No one came pass my post, sir, but I did see a huge flash of light, sir. It happened no more than five minutes ago, sir."

Colonel Bush walked over and began inspecting Eric and Diana. "What's your name?"

"Uh--Eric, uh, Simons. The lady's name is Diana . . . uh . . . Holmes."

"What are you doing in this area anyway? Hasn't anyone told you this place is under Martial Law?"

"No, sir," Eric said quickly, wishing he had his laser gun in his hand.

"Well, guess what?" Colonel Bush walked around and spoke to Eric and Diana's backs. "You just violated not only a perfectly legal curfew, but you also snuck pass my soldiers, which tells me you and this here lady is up to no good." He turned and shouted to a soldier. "Detain them and confiscate all their belongings . . ."

CHAPTER # 29

Calvin sat on the brown horse with Mary behind him; her arms wrapped around his waist. Clyde was on another brown horse listening carefully to Vernon Wright, one of the white men who caught them on the hill eight days ago.

"Reverend Weatherford," Vernon said humbly looking up at Clyde with his straw hat to his chest. "We sho' would like for y'all to re-consider." His wife Jane walked over and stood next to him. "A man of God is always welcome to stay at our house as long as he want."

Clyde loved all this attention. "My child, the Lord has called upon me, his loyal servant, to carry his word west." He looked up from Vernon and glanced across at Billy Wright, standing on the porch with his arms crossed. He had a look that said he was no longer convinced of Clyde's holiness. Yes, it was time to go before he would have to kill ole Billy, Clyde said to himself.

Vernon saw Clyde was looking at Billy and said, "Don't pay Billy no mind Reverend Weatherford. That boy ain't nothing but a mean ole heathen with a--"

"Please, don't say that, my fellow Christian Brother," Clyde said softly. "Billy is one of God's children. Christian love is the force that will bring Billy 'round. I must leave now. Although my helpers and I would love to stay, we can't keep the word of Christ from touching the lives of those in dire need of God's love. However, I would like to leave y'all with some words from the Bible . . .

As Clyde preached on, Calvin was still a bit perplexed by the awesome effects the Christian faith had on people of this time. He knew from studying history that Christianity was very influential in this era. But the way Vernon and his brother, Billy, responded that night when they caught them on the hill when Clyde simply uttered a few verses from the Bible, and told them he was a traveling preacher, was beyond

289

surprising. They had embraced Clyde with open arms on face value, believing anything Clyde told them and invited him into their home as if he was Jesus Christ in the flesh. Calvin tried to pull the appropriate definition of this behavior from his head. A second later, it clicked: *Blind faith! Or better yet, gullible!* Whatever one chose to call it, Calvin certainly had no complaints, since it enabled them to eat, sleep, and get medical attention for Mary's ankle. It also allowed access to incalculable supplies, two horses and all of this as a "gift to the Lord."

The only thing that didn't surprise Calvin was the manner in which he and Mary were treated. While Clyde slept and ate in the main house, he and Mary were stuck in the barn. At first Clyde was about to make a major stink about this arrangement, but Calvin quickly talked him out of it, pointing out the benefit of being able to stay here. In any event, he and Mary didn't mind anyway because they understood the situation. In retaliation, Clyde brought them the best quality food and water and they ate like Kings and Queens. Calvin wondered what other punishment Clyde inflicted on them as a result of their racist behavior.

When it was all said and done, Calvin realized the eight-day rest in the barn enabled him to spend some quality time with Mary. When they weren't having sex, they talked extensively. Initially, all Mary did was brood over Jim Roof's death, which ceased only after Calvin sparked up conversations about the place where he was from (the future). When Mary asked why he always mistakenly called her "Cookie", Calvin reminded her about his wife, and how she looked so much like her. Finally, he also told Mary how Cookie died (allergic reaction to some incorrectly prescribed stress medication); how long they were married (14 years); how many children they had (one); and a few mundane things that only served to ignite the pain in Calvin's heart.

During this stay, Calvin felt his inner turmoil and apprehension increased substantially. He didn't want to admit it, but the truth of the matter was Mary was making him feel whole again. He was even more frightened because he was genuinely falling in love with Mary. She had slipped beneath his armor and touched him in tender places. Ramanda no longer sparked an emotion in his heart; she was fading so rapidly from his world, he felt like a hypocrite because he was already formulating plans to come back for Mary.

Calvin was so glad when Clyde ended his long good-bye and led the way, waving only once and looked back no more. It was July 25th and with only 7 days left, Calvin was a nervous wreck. He hoped Clyde and Mary had calluses on their hind-sides because if they didn't, they were going to have some soon when it was all said and done. He intended to ride nonstop; excluding watering the horses and the acquisition of sleep.

Twenty minutes later, they were traveling down a dirt road flanked by small bushes and small hills. The morning sunlight promised a day of sultry heat. Calvin started thinking about Dameeka. Stress ridden anxiety exploded inside his stomach, and as usual, these thoughts brought with them a mind crippling depression. His mind felt like it was on a ship caught in the middle of a savage thunderstorm, swirling, twirling, tumbling and swaying violently with so many issues.

The need to get home to his daughter was at the top of the list of issues, about neck and neck with the Backlash in regards to the degree of importance. Those words of the hit man, Ronnie, claiming he sexually abused his daughter was killing him slowly, chipping away at his humanity. Trailing this issue was keeping his promise to be the first time traveler, and not far behind was the question regarding what Eric was now up to. Where was the hit man? This matter was apparently up in the air because he was still uncertain if the trip-wire in the mineshaft had worked.

As Calvin looked on, observing the rolling clouds on the sky blue horizon, Ramanda and their planned marriage jumped in his mind. His conscience started beating him up. The first time you're away from her

291

and you allow the relationship to fall apart?!   What kind of man are you!? Talking all this eloquent stuff about loyalty, honor and trust and being faithful, and yet you can't even practice what the hell you preach! Man, you ain't nothing but a bullshit, jive ass brother with no discipline!! Calvin attempted to shift his thoughts to something else quickly, but his conscience wasn't finished. And you need to stop lying to yourself because you know damn well she's pregnant!

With that Calvin decided he had to spark up a conversation or else his mind wouldn't give him any peace. "Hey, Clyde, you got that map on you?"

"Sho' do," Clyde dug in the pocket of his sleek cotton shirt Vernon gave him, pulled the document, maneuvered his horse closer to Calvin and handed it to him.

Calvin unfolded the map, laid it on the back of the horse's neck, and examined it for a moment. He saw they were at least 70 miles away. He wasn't sure where the zone was, but he figured if he got to the center of Oklahoma he would be all right.

"So how is you gonna know when you get to the place you headed?" Clyde asked, bouncing along with the horse's stride.

"The Backlash has configured my genetic material. When it opens, and if I'm within several miles of the opening, I will get some kind of signal. I'm not certain of all the intricate details, but I do know my body will tell me something, that much I'm certain of." The bombardment of stress and tension instantly appeared in the pit of his stomach because his logical mind reminded him that nothing was certain with this Backlash. This system was an experimental component and there was obviously no way anything could be guaranteed. He was not even sure how long the damn portal would remain open. Terror started to grip him when those irritating questions re-surfaced: would he make it back? Would the Transport be as painful as the one that brought him here? Would it kill him instantly? The only issue he felt some degree of certainty on was, the Backlash zone. If or when the portal opened, it would cover a landmass of about forty miles and would be in a straight line, with one end in the south and the other end in the north. The issue of the portal's thickness wasn't much of issue, since as long as he was near the portal he would be sucked in.

Calvin was flung out of this reverie when Mary suddenly started heaving as if she was about to throw-up. He hastily stopped the horse. "What's wrong, Mary?"

Mary held her hand to her mouth. "I'm sorry, Calvin. It's--" she throw up her morning meal consisting of eggs, peaches, chicken and vegetable soup. "It's my stomach again."

Calvin hoisted her down from the horse.

As Mary walked away, finding a private spot to finish her business, Calvin saw Clyde had stopped his horse and was staring at him with a silly looking smile. "What the hell are you smiling about? This isn't a joking matter, Mary's sick."

Clyde laughed. "Damn, Calvin, you sho' ain't quite bright with the simple thangs in life, huh? You knows all that crazy mind twistin' stuff, but you know nothing 'bout the beautiful thangs about life."

"What the hell are you talkin' about?" Calvin gave Clyde a questioning expression.

"Open your damn eyes," Clyde said. "You 'bout to be a daddy."

The shock almost dazed Calvin like a blow from a titanium sledgehammer. Locked in a vicious moment of silence, it all came back. Mary had been throwing-up the last couple of mornings, but she insisted she had "a sour stomach" because of something she ate. Calvin actually sensed she was pregnant, but his keen ability to successfully engage in selective perception when he wanted to believe what he wanted to believe, enabled him to convince himself pregnancy was not a possibility.

"Pregnant!?" Calvin shook his head as Clyde burst out laughing again. Deep down inside, Calvin wanted to cry because all the rules had just changed.

☼   ☼   ☼   ☼

Eric made eye contact with Diana as they stood near a wooden paddy wagon that looked like a jail on wheels. Eric's knapsack was just confiscated and the men were trying to take the micron watches off both their wrists. There were four soldiers and Eric knew their escape attempt was now or never because sooner or later they would figure out how to get the watches off. Inconspicuously, Eric gestured to Diana with both arms, pretending he was grabbing something.

"Hold still!" The soldier fiddling with Eric's watch said forcefully. "You still ain't told us what the hell this thing-ga-ma-jig is."

Eric saw Mary shrugged her shoulders, squinting her eyes as if she was totally confused. He sighed impatiently. *Dumb bitch!* Why the hell did he bring her!?

"Hey, why's y'all two lookin' at each other like that?" A soldier on the sideline said as he raised his musket. "The Colonel already said we can shoot if y'all gets crazy." With a green tooth smile, he said softly. "I would sho' love to kill somethin' tonight."

The soldier working on Diana's watch sighed with anger and shoved her wrist away. "Sam, go get me one of 'em hatch saws."

Eric knew if they delayed one second longer it was over for them. He jabbed his index finger at Diana one last time. He thought he saw her nod her head, but it really didn't matter because if she didn't catch on it was going to be her ass. He was leaving and that was that. Eric frantically grabbed the man in a bear hug and screamed to Diana "Grab him! Hit the micron!" while he simultaneously pressed the control switch on his watch.

294

WHHHOSS!

Eric slowly opened his eyes. He was in the secondary return booth with the lifeless body locked in his embraced. He dropped it to the floor the moment he felt its heaviness. He turned and with relief he saw Diana was in the other booth with the dead soldier's face propped against the glass. The dead man's eyes were wide open and that frozen look on his face in the form of a terrified grimace gave Eric the chills.

Eric rushed out of the booth and so did Diana. Eric was talking fast. "Go get the car, while I drag out the bodies."

"What are we gonna do with them?" Diana asked, truly perplexed.

"What do you think?" Eric said as he dragged the soldier from the booth he transported back in. "We're gonna transport them to another time zone."

Diana took off out of the basement, barreled down a corridor, made a turn and ran pass the hall leading to the bedroom. Through her peripheral vision she saw movement. She stopped with skidding force and rushed back to see what it was. Peering around the corner, she saw nothing. As she resumed running she realized it looked like someone dressed in green was inside the house. After she deactivated the alarms, realizing the hidden sensory infrared beams were intact and there was no indication the alarms were tripped, she concluded her eyes were playing tricks on her and rushed out the mansion.

Eric and Diana entered the lab, dragging the two bodies. Tina was shocked beyond all imagination.

Tina spoke with a trembling voice. "What happened? You guys weren't gone a hot hour. And what is this . . ." She knew the answer by the clothing the men wore. "Oh, my God."

Within ten minutes, both dead bodies were transported back in time, but to different areas of the world. One was sent to China in the year 2000 BC while the other was sent to the Antarctic in the year 4050 BC.

"Listen up!" Eric said from behind the mainframe computer console, speaking excitedly. "If we don't get those laser guns back, we might be the cause of altering history so substantially we might even destroy ourselves." He turned to Tina as he rose to his feet. "Transport us back to the same location, but a few dozen yards away, very close to the moment we returned back here. In other words," He hit the key to open a file on the computer, "according to our transport log we arrived back here at 2:47 am, when we transport back set the dial for 2:57." He turned to Diana. "We're going in with blazing guns and we're not coming back until we get back everything in that knapsack." He rushed for the Time Machine while talking very fast. "When we get back, we're gonna devise a better strategic approach."

Before entering the Time Machine, Eric checked his two laser guns, and the night vision goggles. Diana did the same. Eric entered the machine, disappeared and Diana was seconds behind him.

From behind a tree, with his night vision goggles set high, Eric aimed the laser gun at a soldier who was approaching to inspect the two flashes of light. When the stream of flaming hot light tore through the man's body, Eric realized this felt better than the conventional weapons. Out the corner of his eyes, he saw Diana a few feet away behind a tree, with goggles on, unleashing lasers like a trigger-happy maniac with a new toy. Flaming sparks mixed with cooked chucks of flesh splattered from the bodies of the men upon impact. The screams of agony and terror were like nothing Eric ever heard in his lifetime.

The men who weren't struck down by the first wave of laser beams were so confused and terror-stricken by the sudden ambush they simply ran as if they were oblivious of where the lasers were coming from.

BOOM!--BOOM!--BOOM! . . .

Several shots rang out, forcing Eric to pull back behind the tree. One of the bullets whizzed pass his face while the others ricocheted off the tree trunk, scattering chunks of tree bark. The adrenaline rush made him shout with excitement. "Whoa!" The bullets continued for a couple of seconds. Eric saw Diana point the laser around the tree trunk and held down on the firing button on the laser gun. The blazing beam of light looked like a long sword as she waved the laser gun, sweeping back and forth across the targeted area.

Eric peered around the tree trunk. The area looked like an atomic bomb had ignited. Bodies were everywhere; even the horses laid dead with smoke oozing from their scorched bodies. There were fires scattered about the area; some over 500 yards away. He saw about five men running away. When he saw Diana take aim, about to cut them down, Eric shouted. "No! Can't you see they're no longer a threat to us?"

Diana's heart was thundering with excitement. Something came over her and she was apparently enjoying it. It was a force she couldn't quite comprehend, but it made her feel powerful and in control. She now realized why men got such a thrill out of warfare. The blood racing through her veins and the euphoric sensation induced by a mixture of fear, gratification and an intense desire to acquire vengeance on the male species drenched her mind with a delight that was almost as powerful as an orgasm. Diana slowly stepped from behind the tree, scanning the area. "Come on, let's get that knapsack. I see it! Right over there." She pointed.

Eric stepped from behind the tree. Through the night goggles, he couldn't quite make out what she was pointing at. He moved toward the laser-devastated camp, looking in all directions with head snapping precaution. The smell of all the burning human flesh was turning his stomach inside out.   Twice he held back the involuntary heaving sensation in his throat; a sure sign he was about to vomit. He couldn't believe the mixture of burnt human and horseflesh smelled like bacon. Ten paces later, Eric saw the knapsack. "Cover me. I need you to stay on this perimeter." He headed for the knapsack.

WHOOSH!--BLAAM!

Diana spun and disintegrated the soldier who was creeping up on her. The laser sliced through the tree and severed the top of the man's head.

Eric turned with flinching speed while kneeling and saw it was Diana. He continued onward, picked up the bag and looked inside. His heart almost jumped out of his chest when he saw the two laser guns and the sophisticated compass were missing. *Shit!* He turned and shouted to Diana. "None of the stuff is in the bag. We have to find them." The first thing jumped in his mind was the men he let live. A panic induced sweat appeared on his forehead as he literally started praying none of them ran off with those instruments. His eyes nervously scoured the area.

Five minutes later, Eric was almost in a state of desperation, still searching frantically. When Diana found the two laser guns under the mangled body of Colonel Bush, who had an injury in his stomach that went straight through his body, Eric wanted to kiss her.

"We have to find that compass," Eric said. "It has to be here." Again he hoped those men who ran off did not have it.

Meanwhile, a young soldier named Roland Wilburn was under the wagon resembling a jail on wheels. Lying flat on his back, Roland was literally scared out of his mind. He was hoping his little game of possum continued working. From the glare of the nearby fires, he was able to see the man and woman's faces as he listened to the two talk. He could also see those black boxes that fired lightning rods in both their hands and they were wearing some weird glasses that apparently enabled them to see in the dark. *How is it possible for people to see in the dark and shoot lightning bolts?!* Trembling as if he was freezing to death, Roland was terrified into a state of silliness, realizing the woman looked rather beautiful. He scolded himself for thinking such a crazy thought at a time like this. This woman helped to kill his whole company, and was obviously as dangerous as a black widow spider.

Eric was flipping the smoldering dead bodies over onto their backs or stomachs with his foot, while talking to Diana. "When we get back, we're gonna do some serious time hopping . . . I feel like kicking myself in the ass for trying to pick up Calvin's trail. Since he's going west, no farther than Oklahoma, all we had to do was bounce to every town in that direction. From here to the Backlash is about 100 miles." He moved a body and it came apart at the waist. "Damn it!" The thick gooey blood was all over his boot.

"I got it!" Diana shouted when she found the compass next to a dead horse with its head missing. Eric rushed over and examined it with relieved eyes.

"You ready?" Eric said with his finger about to hit the micron. When Diana said yes and mimicked him, he said. "On the count of three. One . . . two . . . three!"

Roland's eyes squinted from the intense explosion of light. But when the light was gone his eyes bulged with an indescribable shock. *Where did they go!?* His terror-twisted mind repeatedly asked this question over and over again. He started mumbling hysterically with his hands together, praying to God, begging him to continue protecting him as he walked through the valley of the shadow death.

CHAPTER # 30

On August 1, 1831, General Wasps sat high on his white horse, bouncing along with his troops following pursuit. The earth rumbled from the pounding of so many horse hooves striking the Arkansas plains. The late morning sky was a crisp blue and there were only a few sluggish clouds gradually passing overhead.

The General was stewing in the fury of having to continue his search for Clyde and those murderous niggers! Their death toll had risen so high General Wasps lost count at four hundred. This was insanity! he had said when he saw the devastation left behind in the town of Pettus.

That's when he sent a rider to inform President Andrew Jackson of the need to view this whole mission as a national emergency. Special emphasis was placed on his request to be given unlimited access to whatever manpower and materials he needed to neutralize this national security threat. Two days ago, he was enthralled when his rider returned with a presidential certificate granting his request. In an accompanying letter, President Jackson assured him additional military support was on the way.

General Wasps yawned and suddenly heard someone yelling from a far distance. He turned his head and saw a man stumbling and waving his hands; the lad was across the tall grass plain, about a mile away. With a raised hand and a pull of his reins, he brought his division to a halt. He turned and said. "Lieutenant Peterson, send someone to fetch that man."

Lieutenant Peterson sent two soldiers on horseback to get the man. Three minutes later, the two horses and three men arrived and the entire regiment was shocked when they saw the retrieved man was a fellow brother Marine.

General Wasps tried to conceal his shock as he spoke to the soldier who was half conscious from weary, fright and God only knew what else. "What's your name and rank, soldier?"

"Private Roland Wilburn, sir," he said hoarsely.

"Who was your commanding officer?" General Wasps continued.

"Colonel Bush, sir." Roland slurred. "Please, sir, I need water."

General Wasps nodded to Lieutenant Peterson who instructed a soldier to give Roland some water.

Roland drank greedily, spilling half the water on the saddle he sat on.

"What happened to you, Roland?" The General asked.

"They're all dead." Roland said and fell to pieces, crying like a lost child. "They killed them with lightning bolts--"

"Pull yourself together, soldier!" Lieutenant Peterson shouted, but held back his barrage of commands when he saw the General raise his hand, signaling him to stop and to let the soldier vent.

A minute later, the General said to Roland. "Where are they?"

Pointing, Roland said. "About twenty miles that way."

The General maneuvered his horse onto the tall grass and headed in the direction Roland had pointed. The troops followed. With Roland riding along side of him, the General said. "Tell me everything that happened."

It took Roland ten minutes to explain the massacre.

General Wasps wondered if Roland was suffering from too many hits to the head. *That story is sheer madness!* A man and woman shooting lightning bolts with a small black box!? And how could they see in the dark with strange glasses!? *Impossible!* This was the same crazy, farfetched story the people in Pettus were claiming and he simply refused to believe such hogwash! He sighed and said "How are you so sure they're on their way to that location?"

"Cause before that big bright light swallowed 'em up, they said that's where they was going."

The General shook his head, and said nothing else during the several hours ride. As they draw upon the massacre site, the devastating stench of dead bodies engulfed the entire land for miles. When they arrived and General Wasps saw Roland was telling the truth, he almost started spilling tears. The sight of all those fallen US Marines caused a pain that cut so deep. In that moment, General Wasps did something he did only once in his military career because of the potential for deviating from ethical behavior; he vowed to find and punish all those responsible, even if it meant sacrificing himself.

Calvin's saddle sores were yelling for a rest. Traveling nonstop (of course with the exception of sleeping and eating) for six days, they were now in the area of what would be known as present-day Oklahoma, rapidly approaching the Great Plains. Yesterday, they all collectively agreed to stop at the next available town. Calvin was on edge like never before because it was August 2nd, and the Backlash was scheduled to open tonight. The weather matched his mood. It was a windless, gray, overcast day with no hint of either sun or rain. The atmosphere was muggy, hot and sticky. It was an insignificant day on which to take a rest.

Three hours ago, Calvin had felt his first signal, in the form of involuntary twitches in various muscles in his body. As he drew closer to the Backlash zone, the muscle spasms increased. What surprised him the most was he expected to receive a bodily signal after the Backlash opened, but he realized this was even better because it served as a guide.

Watching the desert like plains grow with each mile they went farther west, Calvin felt bad because of all the stress he was putting on

Mary and his unborn child. He cursed himself because he had done the same thing to Cookie. Back then he worked the lab, day and night, while driving her up the walls with the lack of attention and intimacy. He always knew his selfish, self-centered, and obsession with fulfilling the promise to be the first time traveler was what drove Cookie to her grave. He basically stressed her out of her mind, which caused her to turn to medication. Because she was subjected to such unwarranted stress, Cookie was susceptible to incompetent, dangerous doctors who recklessly prescribed medicines on a constant basis.

Now, he was on a mission to get back to the future and was repeating history; stressing out his love ones. He was dragging Mary and his unborn child along a dangerous path replete with life-threatening conflicts at every turn all because he wanted to get back to the future. But, he couldn't stop his dogmatic onward push. He went this far, been through so many ordeals and refused to stop fighting now! He couldn't do it. He couldn't stop fighting. No way, no how! In the rational regions of his mind, Mary's remark about what makes life worth living sparkled to life and gave him that extra-added motivation. He had to try, try and keep trying until he could try no more.

A couple days ago, he came up with what he thought was a workable plan; he was going to transport back, acquire the accredited time travel recognition and return for Mary, even if he had to conduct an unauthorized time travel. But, he was scared; almost petrified out of his mind because there was simply no guarantee he would even make it back to the future.

The thought of leaving Mary and his child in this wild western region of the US, where gunslingers and the most notorious and infamous outlaws would soon roam the land was truly debilitating. Although at this point in history this region in the US was predominately occupied by members of the Five Civilized Indian Tribes (Cherokee, Creek, Seminole, Choctaw & Chickasaw) and was known as the Indian

Territory, many whites were present, and as usual, brought with them all their hatred for all non-Europeans.

As Calvin observed the high, short-grass plains phase into a prairie like landscape, he realized he was being pulled in two different directions and this inner turmoil was slowly driving him insane. Should he stay and protect Mary and his unborn child? Or should he enter the Backlash, and possibly make it back to his time? *Damn!* He sighed as they rode in silence.

Ten minutes later, Clyde shouted jubilantly when he saw the town suddenly appeared as a speck on the horizon. "There she goes! Just like the map said!" He increased his speed to a high-pitched gallop and Calvin did the same.

☼   ☼   ☼   ☼

Calvin flopped down on the bed in the hotel room. Mary cuddled next to him. The Tecumseh Hotel was like any other western type lodging establishment and certainly had its pros and cons. A benefit was, the white folks weren't completely bent on oppressing blacks and Calvin sensed this was only because there were not many plantations. However, this place was like a melting pot for an explosive mixture of sheer chaos and confusion, primarily because of the lack of any governmental structure. This area, that would eventually come to be known as Oklahoma, was not admitted to the Union until 1907, making it the 46th state of the US. This really got Calvin's blood rolling because law and order obviously had its benefits.

As they entered this town, Calvin saw Tecumseh was a jumble of buildings nested in a valley between two low hills. Beyond these surrounding low hills was a mountainous region that looked like an image right off a postcard. The sight was beyond breath taking. On the far western section, there were three Church spires that could be seen standing high above the rest of the structures. The entire eastern section was recently burnt down and covered a large portion of the town. About forty percent of the residents were white. The remaining inhabitants were Indians and Blacks.

Calvin reached over and gave Mary a passionate kiss. He saw she was falling to sleep already. Calvin laid back down, staring at the ceiling and couldn't believe Clyde was up to his old tricks again. *Some people never learn!* But what really pissed Calvin off was Clyde didn't even get a couple hours rest before running to the local Saloon to start ripping and running, and drinking and chasing prostitutes. If his ass got caught up into some nonsense again, Calvin decided conclusively Clyde would be on his own this time.

A minute later, Calvin turned and saw Mary was sound asleep. He got up, took her clothing off, and put her under the covers. Staring down at Mary, he saw her expression was serene. He couldn't believe he was actually planning to leave her here with crazy ass Clyde looking over her until he came back. Sitting down on the bed beside Mary with both hands to his head, Calvin was still struggling with the decision. As of yet, he still hadn't made a definitive choice inside his heart, but his mind was made up, and since it was very powerful, it was taking the forefront in the battle, likely to win by a landslide.

CHAPTER # 31

Eric and Diana sauntered into the Saloon and almost lost control of their cool and calm mannerisms when they saw Clyde Jerkins at the bar, wolfing down a drink while laughing joyously with a man and a fat woman.

As Eric headed for the empty table, he pulled the digital computerized photos of Clyde from his pocket. Eric had four pictures of Clyde; the original wanted poster, one with all this hair cut off, another with just the facial hair missing and the last with a thin layer of facial hair and a cowboy hat. Clyde looked just like the last picture.

Eric and Diana took a seat, trying not to stare. They looked around and noticed some of the people in the Saloon were staring at them. Eric determined, by the way the women were dressed (they wore long dresses that reached down to their ankles) the people in the Saloon were staring at Diana because she was wearing buckskin pants.

Eric whispered to Diana. "I don't know if it's wise to wait for him to leave . . . He looks like he's planning to be here for a while."

For the past two weeks, Eric and Diana had been jumping around throughout time, and Eric was in a state of pure desperation. They would transport to a location, ask the local people if a black man, woman and child, along with a white man had entered the town; if the people told them no, they transported back and continued this process. On the fourth transport, they found the Wright Ranch and spoke to Vernon and his wife, Jane. That's when Eric discovered Calvin was traveling with only the woman and Clyde. Eric assumed something happened to the kid. After twenty-four back and forth time travels, they landed here in this place called Tecumseh County, and low and behold, look who they found.

"I'm gonna get us a couple of drinks," Eric said to Diana. "I'll be right back." As he approached the bar, an idea jumped in his head. After ordering and obtaining the two glasses of whiskey, he sat down, slid Diana her drink and said. "What if we get this clown here to draw Calvin out?" He saw Diana squinted her eyes and twisted up her mouth as if she either didn't comprehend the comment or didn't like the idea. "I was thinking, what if we approach him, and make him an offer he can't refuse. We could offer him some gold to bring Calvin to that burnt down section on the east side of this town."

Diana thought about the suggestion for a moment. She nodded, realizing it was a practical plan, since Clyde apparently wasn't the most scrupulous of individuals. "Where we gonna get the gold? And how much you think will be enough to ensure he'll cooperate?"

"We can get the gold from that famous fortress," Eric began snapping his fingers to activate his memory. The name was on the tip of his tongue. "I can't remember the name, but we can find that out when we get back. Then we can time travel to that location, snatch the gold and time travel back here in a matter of seconds. As greedy as this guy is, he has a price and whatever it is we can get it for him. I think it'll work. With only hours left, we can't take a chance scouring the town looking for Calvin. He could sneak out right under our noses. This'll save us precious time and increase our chances for success."

"You think I should approach him?" Diana said and took a sip of the whiskey.

"Nah, I think he'll respond better to me. Don't forget, women in this time era don't have much authority." After he finished the glass of whiskey, Eric approached Clyde. He politely asked the man and the fat lady to give him a minute with Clyde. "Howdy, partner, my name's Eric Seabright." He stuck his hand out and Clyde shook it. "I'm from the US Department of Interior, and I was wondering if you would be interested in becoming wealthy? You look like you love gold. Shit, everybody loves gold. But, you my good man, look like you love it even more."

Eric laughed and saw Clyde didn't find the joke funny. He cleared his throat. "I have a proposition, a job I believe you can handle."

Clyde finished his rotgut whiskey and waved to the bartender to refill his glass. After it was refilled, and Clyde took another sip, he said. "How much gold are you talkin' about?"

After a moment, Eric said. "Two hundred pounds." Eric smiled when he saw Clyde almost choked on his drink. "I can get you a nice size chuck wagon to go along with it, if you would like."

Clyde wiped away the liquor that dribbled on his chin. With two hundred pounds of gold he could do just about anything he wanted, including disappearing into Mexico and never looking back again. "So what's the job all about? What I gotta do for all this gold?"

"I want you to kill that man you're traveling with, the nigger. I believe his name is Calvin." Eric saw Clyde's body tighten up as if he was about to reach for his pistol tucked in his waist. "Easy now. If two hundred pounds isn't enough, tell me how much is sufficient and it's yours. 300 pounds? 400? 500? Whatever you want, it's yours. Just say the number."

Clyde relaxed and allowed that prospect to circulate. He liked Calvin a lot, but he liked gold as well. After a moment of contemplating, while the liquor swirled through his system, he realized he liked gold a lot more than he liked Calvin. He looked Eric in his eyes and knew he was one of those men from the future. If he hadn't mentioned all that gold Clyde would've shoot him right here on the spot, but he needed some gold real bad. "If you can get me a thousand pounds of gold, I'll bring you his head, his nuts, his ass hole, and any other goddamn part you want."

"You got yourself a deal," Eric stuck out his hand and Clyde shook it. "Just give me twenty minutes and I'll let you take a look at half of the gold. When you're finished the job, you'll get the other--"

"I wanna see every drop," Clyde said point blankly, leaving no room for debate.

After a moment, Eric said. "Okay, I hope you don't try any funny business."

"I'm a business man and I know damn well if you can get yo' hands on all that gold, you gotta be a serious man . . . And a dangerous one as well." He looked Eric up and down. "Ain't gonna be no funny business comin' from me."

"Okay," Eric nodded. "This is what I need you to do. Tonight, bring Calvin over to the east end of the town, near those burnt-out houses. I'll paint a white cross on the wagon. Bring him over to the wagon, kill him right there in the street, and the gold is yours. If you like, you can check the wagon for the gold first, and then kill him."

"It sounds like a deal to me," Clyde wolfed down another drink, waved to the bartender, then said to Eric. "In about twenty minutes, I'll come on outside and take a peek at all that gold." He smiled drunkenly.

Eric gave Clyde a nod and headed for the door. Diana shot out of her seat, rushing after him.

They went to the other side of town purchased an old wagon, rode it back to the Saloon and parked it in the back of the establishment. They dismounted the wagon and activated their micron watches. With a thunderous flash of light, they disappeared. Exactly thirty seconds later, there were two almost simultaneous flashes of light. Eric and Diana both were standing next to a stack of gold bullion they stole from the U.S. gold fortress in Virginia.

After the gold was loaded onto the wagon and covered with a huge moth-eaten tarpaulin, Eric climbed into the driver's seat and hoisted Diana up. They sat silently for a few seconds.

Diana broke the silence. "Do you think we can trust this guy? Remember, what happened with Larry and Ronnie. The lesson I learnt from that ordeal was crooks, criminals and creeps can't be trusted."

"How right you are." Eric said. "I know you didn't think I was gonna leave it up to this guy to get rid of Calvin. We'll be waiting when Clyde brings Calvin to that location tonight. When he shows up, and you can best believe after he sees all this gold he will most certainly show up, we'll simply kill them both."

Private Roland rode his horse into the town of Tecumseh. Next to him was his riding partner, John Spivey. General Wasps assigned the two to scout and spy duty. They would go out ahead of the regiment and check all the towns for the people responsible for the massacres as well as for Clyde Jerkins. If they found nothing, they continued onto the next town. After checking five towns, and if there was no luck, they were required to return to the regiment and obtain a new schedule and route. At that point, the whole process started over again.

Roland was the perfect person for this job because he saw how the lady and the man looked. In addition, he was more than willing to avenge the death of all his fellow troopers. Dressed in civilian clothing, Roland carefully scrutinized the old shabby houses and shops and then up ahead he saw a huge chuck wagon. The distance made it difficult to make out the people handling the wagon. When he was about fifty yards closer, Roland saw there was a woman and two men. The woman was sitting in the driver seat while the two men were lifting a tarpaulin, looking inside the back.

Roland's heart started beating fast when he noticed the woman looked familiar. *Oh shit! It's her!* The only difference was she wasn't wearing those weird glasses! And she was still beautiful! He struggled to maintain his composure as he eased up to the wagon. When she smiled at him, Roland almost panicked. He awkwardly smiled back and just knew he blew his cover. Then, he saw not only the man who was with the woman that night his regiment was massacre, but also Clyde Jerkins. This was too good to be true!

Roland nonchalantly continued down the dirt street and turned at the next available corner. When he was out of their sight Roland spoke frantically to his partner. "That was them!"

"The three we just passed!?" John Spivey said.

"Yes!" Roland was about to bolt off, but turned and said. "I'll go tell the General, while you stay and keep an eye on them." Roland took off while his partner spoke. Roland was so glad the regiment was only about ten miles away because he was intending to ride his horse nonstop at full speed across the partially desert like plains.

Within forty minutes, Roland saw the slow moving monolithic convoy.

Roland was yelling excitedly before he brought the horse to a stop. "They're at the town! They're at Tecumseh! All of them!"

General Wasps waved and the regiment came to a stop. "Slow down, son. Now, say that again."

"They're at Tecumseh! All of them! The man and the woman that killed my regiment! And Clyde Jerkins! I saw them all with my own eyes, sir."

General Wasps immediately called another rider over, instructed him to head east and inform Colonel Stillwell, his back up regiment, to meet him at Tecumseh County as soon as possible. As the rider departed, General Wasps waved to the troopers. "Double time!" He shouted as he led the regiment with Roland galloping alongside of him.

Just around the time the sun was about to disappear for the day, General Wasps saw the town up ahead. He brought his regiment to a stop, and informed them he was going to break up into four groups. "Listen up troops." General Wasps shouted for all to hear. "I broke you up into four groups because I want this entire town surrounded on all sides. Group A will be positioned in the north, B in the south, C in the east and D in the west. I'll give you all twenty minutes to get in place, so I suggest you move quickly when this discussion is over. When you hear the bugle, that'll be my signal instructing the infantry units of each group to move in and to seize everyone in the town. Clyde and the two mass murderers are wanted dead or alive. Any resistance should be met with deadly force. The perimeter units will remain on the outskirts and I'm giving you all a direct order to fire upon anything or anyone if they refuse to obey an order to stop . . . Charge!"

By the time the sun had set, and the moon was inching its way into the cloudless night sky, the entire town was surrounded. The three bugle men were patiently waiting for the General's command, itching to signal to the troopers.

CHAPTER # 32

"Come on, Calvin," Clyde said, standing near the door of the hotel room. "It ain't gonna take but twenty minutes to show you."

"Even that's too long," Calvin was sitting on the bed with his elbows propped on his knees, still fuming because Clyde told him he would be back at the hotel before sundown, but was an hour late. "I'm supposed to be on the road right now. Right this minute! The Backlash is open. I gotta leave right this minute. I was waiting for you to come back, so I can tell you my plan. Why in the world you want me to look at something at a time like this?"

"'Cause it's important to me, Calvin, that's why!" Clyde shifted his weight to the other foot. "If you come on and stop wastin' time we could've been back by now."

"What is it you want me to look at?" Calvin said, realizing he was in an awkward position because he was planning to ask Clyde for a favor. If he didn't do Clyde a favor, then Clyde would be justified not doing him a favor. "I would like to at least know what it is, Clyde."

"Like I said, it's a surprise." Clyde said impatiently and decided to use a harsher means of persuasion. "Have I ever asked you for a favor before, Calvin?"

Calvin thought about the question and instantly realized Clyde never asked for a favor. The old make a person feel guilty trick, Calvin detected and within seconds he realized it was working. He answered by proffering a sigh filled with defeat.

"That's right," Clyde walked over to Calvin and stood a few feet from him. "The answer is no. I ain't ever asked you for nothin'. Now, all I'm askin' is for you to come look at something for me, and tell me if it's what I thank it is. I figure if I tell you what I thank it is first, it'll mess it all up because you'll already have it stuck in yo' head--"

"Okay! I'll go." Calvin sighed. Now he would have to push the horse at full speed, and would be cutting it real close. "The second we're finished looking at whatever this is, I'm getting on my horse and I'm leaving. I need you to stay here in this town for about a week and keep an eye on Mary for me. I was gonna ask you to do this earlier, but I was still working the plan over in my head. If I don't get to this Backlash real soon, all this hell we've went through to get here will be all in vain."

"I ain't got no problem keepin' an eye on Mary 'til you get back," Clyde was fuming because this put a major dent in his plans. Now he had to bring her with him to Mexico. "Now, is you comin' or what?"

Calvin rose to his feet, grabbed his knapsack containing all his belongs, tossed the strap over his head onto his shoulder and headed for the door. He stopped when he saw Mary following him. "Stay here--"

"I'm goin' with you, Calvin," Mary's statement was of such a firm and unequivocal nature that it was clear there was no debating the issue. "When we's finished seeing what Clyde wants us to see, I'll come back here with Clyde."

Calvin nodded his head.

Clyde was about to snap into a tirade because it wasn't supposed to go down this way. She was pregnant and shouldn't be around this type of stuff. He sighed and grabbed Mary's arm. "Mary, stay here and get some rest--"

"I'm going!" Mary snatched her arm away as she stepped around Calvin and lead the way.

Calvin looked at Clyde, shrugged his shoulders and exited the room.

Clyde gritted his teeth as the rage began to boil. He stomped out of the room, cursing under his breath.

They exited the hotel. The sounds of crickets and the distant voices of people inside their cabins merged together to form a weird symphony of nature. The constellations were firmly positioned on the dark, blue satin of the sky as the openings increased in the shifting clouds.

Clyde turned left with a lantern in his hand.

"Relax, Clyde," Calvin said with his arm around Mary, and the knapsack dangling from his shoulder. "You look like you just saw a ghost. Is everything all right with you?" A disturbing premonition suddenly surfaced in the pit of his stomach because Clyde never displayed this sort of jittery type of anxiety before. *What is he up to?* But this suspicion faded when all the things Clyde had done for him circulated in his memory bank. With an inward chuckle, he scolded himself for doubting Clyde's loyalty. Clyde was a violent, trigger-happy, liquor drinking, card playing, prostitute chasing, bogus Preacher-man, but a back stabbing disloyal friend he was not.

As they strolled along, Calvin knew this was a good time to talk to Clyde about a few things before he left; not that he really had to, since he knew Clyde liked Mary as much as Mary like him. Calvin was certain Clyde would look out for Mary even if he never asked. "Hey, Clyde are there any verses in the Bible that deal with friendship?"

Clyde looked at Calvin like he was crazy. "They's plenty verses 'bout friendship in the good book. Why you ask?"

"Well," Calvin examined what he was about to say. "I was wondering what does friendship means to you. Try to disregard the Bible for a moment, and tell me what friendship is to you?"

Clyde sighed. "I thank friendship is when people can depend on the person he say is a friend. And they help each other when they in need of help and there's no strings attached."

Calvin nodded approvingly. That was an excellent description. He just hoped Clyde remembered what he just said when he hit the road. He knew Clyde been drinking, and he also knew alcohol had a strange way of making people forget. "Was there anyone in your life you could honestly say was a friend to you?"

315

Clyde didn't like whatever Calvin was up to. He looked over at Calvin again with a questioning expression. "When I was 'bout yea big." He demonstrated by putting his open hand about as high as his waist. "I had a Pal name Charley Woods and 'fore he died, that was the best friend I ever had. Ole Charley Woods was the kind of fella that would--" Clyde came to a stop when he saw the wagon with the huge white cross painted on it. He began looking around. "So who's yo' best friend?" Clyde started examining the surrounding burnt structures as Calvin spoke.

Calvin answered without hesitation. "My father was my best friend. My father was the best. He was a scientist and was the first person to break the most debilitating hurdles in the field of time travel. After he died I--"

The sound of bugles suddenly came from all four directions.

Calvin felt a nervous tension building because those horns sounded too military for comfort. He turned and saw Clyde staring at the wagon and he knew something was not right.

As Clyde dropped the lantern, and pulled both of his pistols, he turned to Calvin and said, "I'm--"

BOOM!--BOOM!--BOOM!--WHOOSH!—BLAAM . . .

Several minutes earlier, General Wasps had a talk with the scout, John Spivey, who remained behind while Roland raced to inform the regiment. "Are you sure this is the location of the man and woman that killed those Marines?"

"Sir, yes, sir."

"How about Clyde Jerkins? Where is he?"

"I don't know, sir. I was able to follow only one. The man and woman seemed to be the ones of most concern, sir."

"Good choice, private. You're gonna show Lieutenant Peterson and his company where they're located."

"That would be my pleasure, sir." John saluted both the General and the Lieutenant.

Lieutenant Peterson shouted to the company of twenty soldiers. "Let's move out soldiers!"

The crowd of troops began jogging toward the town.

General Wasps waited until he saw Lt. Peterson and his team had arrived in the town, and with a wave of the hand, the three bugle blowers played their tone, facilitating the signal, which ignited the onslaught of infantry troopers.

Eric and Diana stood near the ground floor window peering out at the street. The smell of chard wood was so potent in the air, it seemed like the house was just burnt down only days ago. It was about as dark as grandma's dusty old closet; the moonlight helped some by emitting a dim light that slipped through the cracks of the houses, casting a unique bluish glow upon the area. The huge rats squealed and Eric was tempted to have some target practice with a few of them. Right in the line of their vision was the wagon with the white cross painted on it, containing a ton of gold. Eric wondered how was Clyde going to travel any serious distance with that raggedy wagon, since the wheels were already about to collapse.

Eric leaned on the wall as he continued watching the street. "As long as we been waiting here we might've been better off searching the town for Calvin."

Diana stood next to him, scanning the street. "Too late to start second guessing the plan. Don't worry he'll be here. Since we're counting the seconds it seems longer than it really is."

Eric saw movement and repositioned his head. His heart flickered with excitement. A few seconds later, he saw a dog scurrying by. "I still think we should've killed that guy who kept following us around earlier. He didn't strike me as a man who was about to rob us. He seemed like a professional, like he was up to something much more sinister."

Diana remembered seeing this same man with another man earlier; both of them were on horseback when they were showing Clyde the gold. Despite all of this, she didn't see why Eric was making such a big deal out of him following them. They had laser guns, bullet-proofed clothing from their hats down to their boots, and the Micron watches. At the touch of a button, they could simply vanish into thin air if things got a little too uptight. In fact, in this world, under these circumstances, she felt they were practically untouchable and unstoppable. "Eric, honey, why even let that guy get under your skin? Whoever he was he sure can't hurt us."

"He's not under my skin," Eric shifted his weight to the other foot while leaning against the windowpane. "Actually, I'm just trying to keep some conversation go--" He saw three figures turned onto the street and were now approaching. With hysterical speed, he flung his night vision goggles up to his eyes. He smiled when he saw Clyde, Calvin and the woman.

Diana saw Eric's response and put her goggles on as well. "See. I told you it was just a matter of seconds." She rechecked the laser gun again.

Eric took aim. When Diana came up alongside of him and started aiming, he said. "We're gonna wait until they're near the wagon so we can get a close shot. Less room for a miss that way."

Lieutenant Peterson whispered to John Spivey as they moved through a burnt down section of the town. "Are you sure they're here?" The thought of someone living or even waiting inside one of these houses was sheer madness.

"Yes, right around this corner up ahead to the right," John said. "Once we make the turn its six houses down."

The huge mob of twenty soldiers followed with their muskets and pistols in the ready.

About three minutes later, they arrived at the corner. Lt. Peterson looked down the street in the direction they suspected the man and woman were located; he saw a wagon in the middle of the street. It had a white cross painted on it and there were dozens of additional burnt houses. When Lt. Peterson turned his head the other way, he saw three people approaching. He quickly pulled back, turned to the mob of troopers in back of him, put his index finger to his lips and quietly said, "Ssshhh."

When Lt. Peterson peered back around the corner of the house, he realized one of the men was Clyde Jerkins. He calmly and carefully aimed his pistol and opened fire.

As Lt. Peterson pulled the trigger, the only force guiding his emotions was the mental images of his two brothers, who died at the hands of this low down, wicked scoundrel! That day when he saw their bullet-ridden bodies back in Mississippi, he vowed his and only his bullet would be the instrument that would serve justice. It was the least he could do for his beloved family members.

CHAPTER # 33

The man in the green sweat suit approached the outer perimeter fence of Timetron Labs, examining its structural integrity. He walked toward the main gate and stood in front of the small-computerized box. The whole area was sensory activated and had its own self-contained security system. It was programmed to detect human activity, and to discard all animals such as birds, dogs, cats and any four-legged creatures. If a human touched the fence, it would send a barrage of specialized electrical volts through the invader's body, paralyzing the intruder for at least an hour. He thought this was a real nifty, primitive device as he pulled out his black box, punched in a code and waved it near the computer box.

The gate started opening slowly.

When it was opened enough for him to walk through the gate, the man entered and leisurely walked toward the building. He pushed his sunglasses back onto the upper bridge of his nose, observing the beautiful and well-groomed flowers, bushes and trees. When he arrived at the building, he inserted a new code as he waved the box.

The locks slid into the open position.

He knew Tina was inside and so he lightened his footsteps as he entered. The steady humming sound from the mainframe computer was a blessing because it would mask any small noises that would inevitably be made during this sort of endeavor. Looking around the place, he nodded at the cleanliness of the floors, walls and even the ceiling. Through his sunglasses, he saw a yellowish heat wave, which meant a human being was nearby.

He peered around a corner and let his eyes land gracefully on Tina, who had her back to him. She was working on something inside a tool cabinet about twenty feet from the Time Machine. The invisible waves from the glasses swept across her body. Directly on the lower left side of the eyeglass lens, a computerized listing appeared and started displaying most of Tina's genetic markers. Indeed, the computerized, wave sensory sunglasses had told him almost everything he needed to know about Tina just by the waves scrolling across her body.

He suddenly felt real bad for Tina because she was predisposed for breast cancer, and would begin to experience great difficulty within the next ten years if she didn't reconstruct her diet which consisted of the excessive intake of animal proteins and fats, the over-consumption of refined sugars and dairy products, while excluding fruits, fiber and vegetables. He wished he could give her some advice, but that wasn't permitted and he hated not being able to tell people about their genetic flaws, especially the ones people could change just by altering their diet or behavior. There were so many people with future ailments about to explode that could be neutralized by simply changing their diet and living a healthy life style. He couldn't believe so many people didn't notice all the poisons they were flooding their bodies with. Shaking loose of his health trip, the man in green went to work.

He approached Tina, letting his footsteps be heard clearly, since it really didn't matter.

Tina frantically spun around. With a startled expression she screamed when she saw the strange looking white man wearing sunglasses. She was about to flee to the back section of the lab, but the electrical surge shot from the black box and cut off the shriek, stopping her hysterical retreat with shocking suddenness.

He activated the dial that would allow her to hear, while also controlling the part of her brain responsible for involuntary responses so she would obey his every command. "Tina, go to the sofa in Eric's office. Lie there comfortably and do not come out until instructed otherwise."

Tina obeyed; she walked toward the room as though she was a zombie in a trance.

When she disappeared out of the lab section, the man in green entered the topless control station. It took him ten minutes to reprogram the secondary return coordinates. Now, all return landings and time travels would have to come through this Time Machine.

He exited the control station, found a comfortable chair in the conference room, rolled it out to the lab section, positioned it about fifteen feet from the Time Machine, sat down, and waited patiently.

He wasn't superstitious, but he crossed his fingers, and wished he could cross his toes as well because any extra-added luck was surely needed.

☼　　☼　　☼　　☼

Calvin laid on his back clutching his side with the pistol in the other hand. Bullets rained all around him. Little dust clouds were puffing into existence as the bullets struck the ground, whining and whizzing pass him as they ricocheted wildly. Mary was cowering next to him, lying flat on her stomach. He saw Clyde running toward one of the burnt-out shells that was once a house, returning gunfire with both of his pistols blazing at the soldiers about a half block away.

Through a dazed mind, Calvin was calling Clyde every name in the book of curse words because he had walked them into this death trap.

Seconds ago, just as the bullets rang out, Clyde's comments were cut off by the bullets that came from down the street; one of which had hit Calvin in the left side a few inches above the hip bone. When they all hit the ground, Clyde said frantically, "I'm setting a trap to catch them folks from the future! Let's go! I'll cover you!" and then tore ass toward the house across from them.

What Clyde failed to tell Calvin was he was also trying to get that wagon full of gold; have his cake and eat it too by killing two birds with one stone (kill the hit men for Calvin and become super rich with the gold).

"Calvin, you bleedin' real bad." Mary touched his hand, cringing when a bullet struck the ground.

Calvin noticed the injury felt like a flesh wound, but the blood was pouring out very heavily and steadily. "Yes, I know."

Mary flinched. "We gotta run! We can't stay here--"

WHOOSH--BLAAM!

The two laser beams ripped through the bodies of the three soldiers.

Calvin saw pieces of the men's bodies splattered into the air and he also saw his opportunity to get away. He sprung up, snatched Mary onto her feet and frantically took flight in the direction Clyde went, while squeezing off a shot at the soldiers who had now turned and were firing at the two people with lasers.

When Calvin barreled into what used to be a barbershop, the darkness enmeshed him, and was met with the scurrying sound of rodents. Clyde was nowhere in sight. He turned and saw the flicker of the lasers had lit up the area as if a gigantic strobe light was suddenly turned on. The responsive screams of the men were of a severe skin crawling nature and were loud enough to compete with the fusillade of gunfire. Calvin felt a wave of terror gripped him at the mere thought of having to deal with two-laser gun wielding hit men.

Calvin moved toward the backdoor with trembling knees and a nervous grip on the pistol. He saw the door was jarred opened. *Where the hell did Clyde go!?* His thoughts were cut short, and so was his forward stride, when he heard the frantic voices of approaching men who were apparently in an uproar as a result of the flickering lights from the lasers and the screams and gunfire.

Calvin grabbed Mary's hand and quietly took refuge inside a doorless room. He peeked out as his thoughts were racing about as fast as his heart. When one of the men entered, Calvin saw he had a gun in his hand and was conducting a search. Calvin realized there was only one way to deal with this situation. He took aim and opened fire. The bullet struck the man in the upper chest, violently shoved him backwards and then to the ground.

Another man tried to enter and Calvin shot him in the stomach. The man flinched theatrically and stumbled backward to the ground. A small stream of moonlight slipped through several cracks in the chard shop walls, and danced upon the two fallen men, dressed in matching uniforms. For the first-time Calvin's mind slowed down enough to realize these men were soldiers. His anxiety grew and the questions surfaced with explosive force: *What the hell are soldiers doing here? How many of them are roaming this area?* From his past experience, Calvin knew military groups moved in huge numbers and had the ability to dish-out soldiers at a truly eye raising rate.

Suddenly, a wave of angry gunfire went off in the back, where the other soldiers were located. The shooting went on for several seconds. After a moment of penetrating silence, Calvin heard someone shouting.

"Calvin!" Clyde screamed. "Where you at?"

Calvin raced to the backdoor, stepping over the two fallen soldiers. The flesh wound on his hip had stopped bleeding, but was beginning to throb. He slowly stepped through the threshold and saw about four other soldiers sprawled out on the ground. He looked up and saw Clyde, who was kneeling behind a wooded box, looking out into an open field. With anger in his stride, Calvin moved toward Clyde. After taking two steps, Calvin turned and said. "Mary, get their guns, and check their pockets for bullets! Hurry!"

Mary frantically obeyed the command.

"Next time," Calvin said through clinched teeth. "Let me know when you make these type of decisions!" He kneeled beside him, watching the open field and saw men on horses at a distance. He sighed angrily because he was hoping he could get out of the town this way, even though it was in a northern direction. "What the hell was you thinking, Clyde!? Why the fuck you walk us into a death trap, when all we had to do was leave this place! And on top of that, if we really wanted to deal with those hit men, we could've devised a plan far more effecti--"

"If it wasn't for all 'em goddamn soldiers," Clyde said, his face was purple with rage. "The damn plan would've worked!" He turned his head and examined the backyards of the establishments. They had to get moving. "I still got a way to make it work, but we gotta find a way to get behind them folks with the thunderbolt guns. Tell yah what I'm gonna do." It took him a minute to explain the tactic.

"No!" Calvin said point blank. He was seething with anger. "The Backlash is open and you're about to fuck this up for me. All this traveling is gonna be in vain, if I don't find a way to get out of here right now!"

"And what do you 'xpect me and Mary to do!?" Clyde said calmly. "I thought you wanted us to stay here 'til you get back? Don't you thank these military folks got this whole damn town surrounded?"

Calvin's rage stopped in mid-motion. Clyde was right. If the military were here, they would definitely surround the whole town and would not send in their entire group.

Clyde continued. "These military folks is here fo' us! Them hit men is here fo' us! If we run off, and gets away, they gone follow us. We's gotta deal with them once and fo' all. Ain't no other way!"

Calvin sighed. This wasn't the time for this! He had hours left and he was gradually becoming desperate. He would have to either leave now or be stuck here. In any event, there was no way they could fight two laser totting hit men and win, much less the military. *This is insanity!* "No! We can't do it! Let's just find a way to quietly sneak out of this town--" Calvin tried to grab Clyde's arm as he took off, clearly indicating the plan was not up for discussion. "No! Clyde! Come back goddamn it!" He sighed so hard spit threw from his mouth.

Mary walked over with an arm full of muskets and pistols. "I got us a whole bunch of good guns."

As Calvin hastily sorted the weapons, while checking to make sure they were still operable and fully loaded, Mary said. "I agree with you, Calvin, I say we go right, now!"

Suddenly, Calvin saw movement behind Mary. Just as he was about to knock her out the way, the shot rang out.

☼   ☼   ☼   ☼

Moments earlier, just as Lt. Peterson and his soldiers opened fire on Calvin, Mary and Clyde, Eric and Diana relaxed their aim. A mixture of anger, frustration and surprise began to formulate. Eric and Diana rushed out of the house to get a better view of the situation and mostly because their plan was down the drain.

"Where the fuck did they come from!?" Eric stared down the block at the men dressed in military uniforms and were firing their weapons. His night vision goggles picked up everything as if it was under a high-powered fluorescent light. Eric sighed because he noticed these men were US Marines.

WHOOSH--BLAAM!

The laser beam Diana unleashed ripped through the backs of two soldiers, which caused Eric to join in when he saw the others turned around and started returning fire.

As Eric fired the laser gun, he and Diana sought cover behind a wooden water barrel. "Ouch! Shit!" He shrieked when a bullet struck him in the chest. "Damn it!" The bullet was lodged in the bulletproofed fabric and he was surprised because the damn thing hurt like hell.

Although the bullet did not penetrate, it caused severe pain and Eric instantly made a mental note not to get hit by any more bullets.

Still rubbing his chest, Eric said to Diana. "Next time let me start the show, Okay? That way I won't get shot."

Diana smiled and paid him no mind because she was having way too much fun.

☼   ☼   ☼   ☼

Several seconds earlier, Lt. Peterson rapidly pulled the trigger on his Colt Sidehammer Revolver as he moved toward the three targets. His men were flanking him on each side and were also firing their weapons. Lt. Peterson ducked when a bullet breezed pass him and saw Clyde running toward the nearby store. His pistol roared lively as it followed Clyde until he raced inside the store. "Damn you!" Lt. Peterson muttered angrily because all the bullets had missed.

WHOOSH--BLAAM!

Lt. Peterson screamed when the heat from a laser beam brushed over his body. He dropped to the ground and saw the thunderbolt had struck one of his soldiers. The whole area had suddenly lit up as though a huge light was turned on. Sparks and blood was sprayed everywhere. The smell of burning flesh suddenly engulfed his surroundings.

When Lt. Peterson frantically turned his head, and saw a long yellowish orange stream of light strike one of his soldiers, while several others were already lying sprawled out on the ground, his eyes bulged. He saw his men were torn to pieces with smoke swirling from their wounds as if their bodies were mangled from a dynamite explosion.

Panic stricken, Lt. Peterson sprung to his feet and bolted back to the corner, stumbling over soldiers who had hit the ground and were engaging the two in an exchange of gunfire.

TIME JACK   JOHN WHITFIELD

As Lt. Peterson nervously peeked around the corner of the house, about to take aim at the two lightning bolt shooters down the street, he remembered Clyde had entered a store. He turned and ran toward the backyard section of the houses, hoping to cut him off.

☼   ☼   ☼   ☼

General Wasps saw the flashing lights coming from the interior of the town. From where he stood, it resembled lightning, but the flashes were on a much smaller scale and were far too persistent. He started pacing. His urge to go to the site to see what was going on with his own eyes was growing into an unbearable and unquenchable desire. All his West Point training told him that if he were to go to the frontline this would be unacceptable. But his frontline experience told him it would boost the morale and fighting spirit of his soldiers. However, in reality, it was the flaming urge to see that weapon everybody claimed shot lightning rods. What if he got hold of one of those things? There was no limits to the amount of fame he would acquire, and if he brought such a weapon to the President? *Wait a minute! There's probably no such weapon! Those flicking lights might be--It's probably--Some--It can't be . . .*

With a hard struggle, his curiosity won the match. He had to go see if such a weapon actually existed. "Corporal, I want you to pull two men from each perimeter group. I need an escort to the east end of this town." When he saw the Corporal's shocked expression, he said sternly. "That's an order, soldier."

The Corporal mounted his horse and raced away as General Wasps continued pacing. He was wondering what was taking Colonel Stillwell's back-up regiment so long to arrive? Even though he felt he had this assignment under control, he also knew the more troops meant the more chances for complete success.

☼   ☼   ☼   ☼

Calvin rose to his feet, pulling the trigger on the pistol as the soldier violently recoiled from the bullets entering his body. When the soldier crashed to the ground, Calvin turned and saw Mary on the ground curled up in a fetal position. In a state of panic, he kneeled. "Mary, are you alright!? Are you hit!?" His heart almost stopped when she didn't respond. He was uncertain whether the soldier's bullet struck Mary because the second he saw the soldier and as he heard the shot, he tackled Mary in a frantic haste. As they fell to the ground, he was already pulling the trigger.

He saw Mary was crying with her head tucked close to her chest and began massaging various parts of her body, searching for an injury. The gunfire in the background was maintaining a constant flow. "Are you hurt? What's the matter?"

"I can't take this no mo'!" Mary lunged up and hugged Calvin. This never-ending exposure to constant danger was taking its toll. She wished they could hurry up and get to the future. "I wanna leave this place, Calvin. Let's go right now! I wanna leave."

"Me too, Mary," Calvin caressed her soft body, and for a moment he was oblivious of the gunfire and the flicking laser beam lights. After a moment, he realized they were wasting valuable time and he pulled her away. "Please tell me, are you hurt?

"No, I ain't hurt, but we should just leave right now."

Calvin agreed with her approach whole-heartedly, since she had actually taken the thought right out of his head. But reality dictated that they had to first get beyond these current obstacles. "Let's move from here before someone else comes." He was about to race off, but stopped and hastily kneeled, grabbing a musket. After he stuffed two handfuls of bullets in his knapsack, and gave Mary one of the pistols, he started walking extremely fast while holding Mary's hand.

They were moving toward the west end of the town and Calvin realized this was the direction where he saw the two hit men. He quickly shook loose of the rapidly growing fear.

As they ran across a huge dirt street toward the backyard of one of the houses, he heard a massive wave of gunfire and saw Clyde up ahead. He was exchanging gunfire with someone inside one of the abandon houses. Calvin started running, while Mary was directly on his heels. When they arrived, Calvin kneeled next to Clyde and said. "What the hell is wrong with you, Clyde!?" Calvin saw Clyde was ignoring him as if he wasn't even standing next to him. "We gotta stick together! Don't run off like that anymore. If we work together, we'll stand a better chance of getting through this." Calvin pointed the musket and pulled the trigger. He saw the weapon had a nice healthy kick to it.

"Well, if you ain't gonna go along with my plan," Clyde said as he locked eyes with Calvin. "Then you might as well keep goin' on yoh merry way."

Calvin was shocked. This didn't sound like Clyde. He held his temper in check because arguing at a moment like this was suicidal. He let the snide remark bounce off of him. "Okay, you wanna kill these hit men, I'm with you, but you gotta promise after we do this, we'll get out of this town and get to the Backlash."

Clyde stuck his hand out. "You got yo' self a deal."

Calvin looked at Clyde's hand as if it was crawling with worms. Now, suddenly, he wanted to shake hands as if they were complete strangers or something. *Why the hell is he doing this?* Calvin shook Clyde's hard, callous-ridden hand.

Clyde turned and started firing his weapon.

Mary whispered excitedly. "They comin' from out in the field!"

Calvin and Clyde's heads turned at the same time. They both saw the movement hovering on the horizon.

Suddenly a shot rang out from the field, and almost instantaneously, the bullet struck the wall, just missing Clyde. They frantically kneeled to the ground. On one knee, Clyde returned fire.

Inside the house, the sound of rapid, frantic movement was heard. Calvin and Mary started firing at the shadows inside the house.

Eric was behind a turned over wagon, firing laser beams at a newly arrived group of soldiers. When the last of the ten man group was shot to the ground, he realized he was becoming totally frustrated with this little game consisting of hiding, shooting and hiding some more. He was even more agitated by the amount of soldiers that keep coming. They just obliterated a group of soldiers that tried to sneak up behind them from the west. It seemed like the more he and Diana killed them the more they came, almost as if by killing one, two would magically reappear.

"We gotta get to the back of these houses," Eric said to Diana, who was still positioned behind the water barrel. "He's gonna try to sneak pass us; we gotta cut him off."

Diana was so preoccupied with firing the lasers she almost missed what he said. "Lead the way and I'll follow."

Eric stepped into the street and headed toward the intersection where the dead soldiers lay. The sound of gunfire could be heard in that direction, but somewhere in the back of the houses. When they arrived at the intersection, they turned left on the dirt street and saw more soldiers. They put their backs to the nearby house. Through the goggles, Eric saw one of the soldiers was apparently someone of extreme importance by the way the other soldiers were guarding him. Diana took aim and Eric quickly shoved her hand, while whispering. "Wait a minute! Let's see what they're up to." Eric suspected they were looking for Calvin and Clyde and would lead them to one of the two.

Diana sighed. "Why are we wasting time? Let's just get rid of them, find Calvin, kill him and go home." She shook her head in disgust, since she couldn't believe how much Eric was complicating this mission.

A moment later, a massive wave of shots rang out.

Eric saw the group turned and rushed into the back section of the houses. Eric headed in that direction. "They're looking for Calvin and his bunch. Now, they're gonna lead us right to him. See, sometimes a little patience can go a long way."

They arrived at the corner of the building, peering around the house and saw the soldiers standing near a door exchanging gunfire.

Eric knew they apparently weren't shooting at each other and therefore that meant one thing. "Now, my trigger-happy maiden of destruction, you may relieve yourself."

With a smile, Diana stepped completely around the corner of the house, aimed and began unleashing lasers in a rapid-fire fashion, while rapidly moving toward the targets.

Eric followed with his laser gun in the ready, but let Diana have her funny.

Eric heard running footsteps behind him. He turned with the laser gun pointed as if his movement was a reflex. He saw about ten soldiers, three had lanterns in their hands. Eric picked them off so quickly they didn't know what was going on until half of them were dead with huge gaping laser holes in various parts of their bodies.

Lt. Peterson took cover, but the flaming hot thunderbolts went through the wooden cart and struck his arm. When Lt. Peterson saw his left arm from the bicep down was gone, he screamed. He tried to scramble away, but the next thunderbolt hit him in the back and everything instantly went black as if a light switch inside his head was flicked off.

Eric moved toward his targets as he fired the lasers, making certain he left none of the ten soldiers alive. For the first time, he felt the warmth of the laser gun in the palm of his hand and it made him feel strong and in control. When Eric turned back around, he saw Diana was right upon the fallen men they were initially pursuing. He jogged toward her.

Eric arrived, stared down at the big shot laid out with a huge hole in his stomach and saw the three stars on the lapel of his uniform. "Looks like we caught the biggest fish in the fleet." He pointed. "That's a General."

"That's strange." Diana said, peering into the house the soldiers were shooting inside of. She saw the vague contours of chard tables and chairs. "I thought Generals didn't get involved in front-line work?"

Eric shrugged, realizing he really didn't care one way or another about this dead General. "What'd you see in there?"

Diana waved her hand for Eric to be quiet because she suddenly saw frantic movement. She whispered. "They're rushing out the other way!"

"Let's go!" Eric rushed pass her and into to the establishment, running toward the front door, while kicking chairs and other debris out of the way. He rushed out the door and saw Calvin, Clyde and the woman running down the street.

Diana came along side of Eric and saw the three as well. "See, I told you we couldn't trust Clyde."

"Does it really matter?" Eric started running after them and Diana followed. "He brought Calvin to us didn't he? That's all that really matters." As Eric aimed the laser gun, he realized the bouncing caused by the high paced running was interfering with his shot. He started squeezing off sloppy aimed lasers, not caring where they struck, since he knew there was enough fuel in the laser gun to last for probably another two thousand shots.

A shot rang out and a bullet breezed pass Eric and Diana.

Eric recoiled unconsciously. The pain he experienced the last time he was shot was still throbbing lively. He fired another laser and saw Diana had finally began firing lasers just as the three turned a corner at breakneck speed. Eric noticed he was able to get off five shots before they hit the corner. He smiled because he suddenly realized it was just a matter of time before he would be on his way home and cracking open a bottle of champagne.

Moments ago, Calvin's legs were pumping frantically, despite the hip-wound. The strap of the knapsack bounced on his shoulder as if it had a life of its own. When a laser tore at the ground several feet away, Calvin turned and fired a shot. Mary was in front of him. Initially, she wasn't moving fast enough, but after the laser ripped pass them, and the scorching heat was felt, she increased her speed ten-folds.

Clyde spoke frantically through his deep exhaustion. "Turn left up here! The church is right around here! Make sure they see you go inside, Calvin!"

"I know!" Calvin's lungs were screaming for more oxygen and his hip wound was throbbing beyond description.

Clyde increased his speed and took the lead as they turned the corner. He saw the church, but turned and went into an alleyway on the side of the Church. Seconds later, Mary entered the Church and Calvin slowed his pace, waiting for Eric and Diana to turn the corner.

Calvin waited on the steps of the church until Eric and Diana came around the corner. Sweating and breathing extremely hard from over-exertion, Calvin fired two shots. He saw Eric and Diana scrambled to a stop and sought cover from the bullets. Calvin locked eyes with Eric and rushed inside the church. He hid on the side of the door as planned.

In the alleyway, Clyde felt like he was seconds from fainting. He was struggling to quiet down his breathing, which made him feel dizzy due to the restriction of oxygen into the lungs. In the dark, damp and smelly alleyway, Clyde braced himself as he heard the two laser totting hit men approaching.

The second Eric and Diana ran pass the alleyway, Clyde bolted out from the shadows with his two fully loaded pistols spitting flaming hot lead. He took special precaution to make sure his bullets struck the heads of his two targets.

Diana was on Eric's heels when the first bullet shot off her cowboy hat. She simultaneously felt a blow to the back of her head that resembled the impact from a baseball bat. It violently shoved her forward. At first, Diana didn't realize she was shot in the back of the head until her knees gave out and the pain exploded in her head seconds later. Since the bullet went straight through, it took a few seconds for her brain to realize it was severely damaged. She hit the church steps and instantly plunged into triple darkness. Unfortunately, this was a permanent nap and just before everything went black, Diana realized she was shot and apparently was going to die.

Clyde saw several of his bullets striking the other hit man in the upper back, but he missed the hit man's head because the hit man rushed up the stairs with his head down, completely out of sight. Clyde stopped shooting as the hit man rushed inside the church.

The moment Eric barreled through the threshold of the church, Calvin tackled him. Both their bodies glided in the air for a distance of several feet. They crashed to the floor in a bone breaking fashion.

Calvin's hands went straight for the laser gun. Once he got hold of the man's wrist, he started banging the hit man's hand possessing the laser gun on the floor. After four good solid bangs it slipped from his grasp and slid away.

Calvin felt a savage kick to his right eye. Stars exploded before his eyes. The blow almost knocked him unconscious. He knew it was Mary trying to help fight the hit man. While the hit man squirmed and threw half-cocked punches, Calvin screamed. "Mary! Stop! I got this!" He knew if she kicked him in his face like that again, he might pass out.

Calvin immediately went for the Micron watch. As he began to unfasten it, the hit man's thrashing became desperate. With his free fist, the hit man was wailing away at Calvin's head. The stars were swirling wildly from the blows to his head, but Calvin knew it was all worth it. He could feel the Micron about to become unfastened.

Clyde rushed in and pointed his pistol. Seconds later, his eyes started adjusting to the darkness. It took him a couple of seconds to carefully place his aim.

BOOM!!--AAAHHHH!!

The bullet struck Eric in the middle of his back. Eric screamed so loud everyone's ears began to ring. His hands reflectively tried to go straight for his back. Mumbling curse words a mile a minute, Eric felt a convulsing terror had gripped his mind because the Micron watch was no longer on his wrist. In a state of wide-eyed disbelief, Eric panicked, thrashing and kicking. "Get the fuck off me!"

Calvin flung the watch away, realizing the hit man's voice sounded familiar. As he and the hit men were wrestling on the floor, Calvin turned and saw Clyde pointing the pistol, his hand following them as they wallowed on the floor. Calvin could tell Clyde was about to inflict a headshot. "No! Wait Clyde!"

Clyde thought his ears were playing games with him. *What the hell he talkin' 'bout wait!?* This goddamn hit man's been trying to kill them and now he's talkin' about wait?! *He's out of his goddamn mind!* Clyde sighed and relaxed his trigger finger, but still kept the pistol pointed. But his ultimate concern and interest right now was he couldn't wait to get his hands on one of those laser guns. Clyde especially wished Calvin would hurry up with whatever he was going to do with this guy because that chuck wagon of gold was calling him.

Calvin ripped the night vision goggles off the man's face, sprung to his feet, and put them on. When he saw it was Eric, cringing violently from the bullet wounds, he didn't know if he should be shocked, happy, enraged or enthralled by the fact that he could inflict his revenge right here and now.

"Eric!?" Calvin felt a devious smile forcing its way into existence. "Now, isn't this one pleasant surprise?"

"You know him?" Clyde said with the gun still pointed.

"Do I know him," Calvin took the goggles off. "He's the one who sent me here."

"Well," Clyde braced himself, about to pull the trigger. "In that case, I'll just blow his damn head off and justice will be served."

"No!" Calvin pushed Clyde's pistol down. Calvin suddenly went into a penetrating state of silence. His mind was working like the good old days when he experimented with some of the most complicated time travel equations ever introduced to the human mind and it felt truly good. All sorts of things were flooding his mind, all competing to be the first to receive his attention. There were two Micron watches, which was the best realization of them all. Another pleasure provoking reality was, he now had access to the primer chemical since it was in both Eric and the other hit man's body and all he had to do was extract some blood and either ingest it orally or inject it intravenously. But the best thing about all this, he had Eric in the palm of his hand and boy did he have an excellent way to commence with justice.

With a huge conniving smile, Calvin walked over to Eric, grabbed a hand full of his collar and yanked him to his feet. "Whatever you got to say, you better do it now." He shoved Eric into the wall.

"Let's not get too excited here, Calvin," Eric said, still cringing from the bullet marks on his back. He just knew he had a cracked rib. "You gave me no choice in the matter. I tried to work with you and you know that. I made sacrifice after sacrifice and not once did you ever give me the credit I deserved. So you just calm down and relax."

"Do it look like I'm excited?" Calvin was still smiling. "I feel about as calm as a Gallium Phosphide Crystal in suspended animation."

Eric realized he was in a real fucked up position. Suddenly, it dawned on him; Diana was nowhere in sight. "Where's Diana?" He said in a panic-stricken tone.

"Diana!?" Calvin said with genuine distress. He was incensed, hoping Eric didn't drag Diana into to this madness. "Was she the other hit man? Clyde, where's the other one?"

Clyde was still shocked by the fact the other hit man's name was Diana, which obviously meant it was a woman. "I don't know where she's at right now, whether it be heaven or hell. But you can bet yo' breeches, she ain't in this world any mo', that's for sho'."

Eric couldn't control himself. "Where is she!?" His tears began to flow. "Please don't tell me she's dead?!" His legs moved of their own volition.

Calvin grabbed Clyde's arm when he was about to haul off and punch Eric in the face. Calvin followed Eric out the door. Calvin watched Eric scrambled to his knees next to Diana's dead body, crying like a baby. Eric rolled her over onto her back and began cuddling her.

Mary came along side of Calvin and he wrapped his arm around her shoulder and drew her close to him. Calvin's heart went out for Diana because he knew she was a victim of Eric's greed and wickedness. Calvin always knew Diana was the naive type and was infatuated with Eric's good looks and his money; she often allowed herself to be used and abused by Eric. But Calvin was surprised by Eric's response; his cries seemed genuine. Maybe he did have the capacity to love.

As Eric cried over Diana's corpse, his eyes were inconspicuously searching for Diana's laser gun. Although his heart was shattered by the loss, his survival instinct was even more intense. The thought of being stuck in this place was totally unimaginable. He knew Calvin wouldn't kill him in cold blood and therefore would probably leave him here, which was probably worse than death. But, he was enthralled because he could see his tears were moving Calvin. "Please, Diana." He screamed and turned the other way as he continued searching. "Oh God, no! Don't do this, please don't do this!" He saw the black box and his heart fluttered with excitement because it was about five feet away. "Oh, God she didn't deserve this!" Eric realized he could reach it by diving for it. He turned back around and saw Clyde still had his pistol pointed. *Shit!* He hated pain and he knew if he dived Clyde would surely open fire.

Calvin saw the specks of light on the horizon and realized it would be the crack of dawn real soon. He had enough of Eric's crying and now it was time for him to get things in order. He actually wanted to thank Eric for coming here and being so incompetent enough to allow himself to get caught up like this. He turned and spoke to Mary. "Go inside and get that back box and the watch. Be careful, don't press any buttons."

Mary raced inside the Church and began searching for the items.

Calvin turned and said to Eric. "Come on, it's time to go."

Eric pretended to be frantic with fright as climbed to his feet. "No! Please, don't do this!" Wailing with tears, he fell back to the ground like a belligerent child.

When Calvin saw what Eric was doing, and realized the laser gun was in the location where Eric was falling, he shouted while frantically reaching inside the knapsack for his pistol. "Shot 'em, Clyde!"

BOOM!--BOOM!--BOOM!--BOOM!--BOOM--CLICK!

Before Clyde's pistol registered empty, the five bullets ripped and tore at various parts of Eric's body, but none made contact with his head.

Eric flinched and cringed, jerked and recoiled, but the pain was bearable, since his fear was more powerful. He fell on top of the laser gun, grabbed it, and spun.

BOOM!--BOOM!--BOOM!--BOOM!--WHOOSH!--BLLAAM!

Calvin was carefully aiming his pistol at Eric's hand with the laser gun in it while pulling the trigger. Two of the shots struck Eric's wrist, catapulting the laser gun out of his hand. The other two bullets hit Eric in the stomach and the chest. The laser beam Eric fired went up into the sky.

Clyde hastily reloaded his pistol, watching Eric squirm on the ground in great pain. "Cause of stuff like this; that's exactly why I just shoot folks and ask questions later." After he had two bullets in the chamber, he cocked the hammer and aimed at Eric's forehead.

"No! Clyde!" Calvin shouted.

Clyde was aghast. He sighed angrily and threw his hands up in a state of frustration. "Why can't I shoot 'em, Calvin?! You see he just tried to kill us, even after we was gonna let him live!"

"Killing him is far too easy," Calvin said simply, since Eric deserved a punishment far more substantial than a quick death. He needed one that would linger indefinitely. Calvin wanted him to suffer the same way he made him suffer and there was no better way to inflict that sort of suffering than to leave him stuck here in this place for the rest of his life.

"Calvin, please," Eric whined. "Don't do this to me! I'll give you anything. Any amount of money you want."

Eric's mind raced desperately for a way to stop Calvin from leaving him here. Money obviously wasn't going to work by the look on his face. Maybe he could play on his sympathy and his conscience, make him feel guilty in some way? But, what could he use? Breathing hard, with sweat dripping from his face, Eric strained to find something. Then, suddenly, the answer popped into his head. Calvin's father. They always said they had that in common; strong fathers who wanted strong sons!

Eric pondered the approach at the speed of light and concluded he had everything to gain and nothing to lose. "Calvin, I know you can understand what's going on here. I've done all this because of my father." He cranked up a wave of tears and surprised himself when he saw the water dripping from his eyes. "He--he told me I had to be the first time traveler. He said if I didn't accomplish this task, he would disown me!" He cried even harder. "I--I love my dad—and--and I couldn't let him downnn . . ."

Calvin instantly felt genuine sorrow for Eric because he was striving to become the first official time traveler for the same reasons; to appease his father. Calvin knew exactly how powerful such a driving motivation could be. He suddenly remembered how his obsession caused the death of Cookie, and how it literally shattered his family life. Calvin sighed because Eric touched a major soft spot.

Clyde saw what Eric was doing and was itching to put a bullet in his brain. "Calvin, don't let this bastard slither his way out of his punishment." Clyde started searching for something that would snap Calvin back into the realm of reality. A moment later, it came to him. "Don't forget he's the one that sicced them hit-men on yo' daughter."

Calvin was jolted by Clyde's remarks. His eyes scrolled across Eric's face. He saw Eric's eyes suddenly grew wide. It looked like fear, but it could be surprise. Calvin's sad facial expression transformed into a vicious snare.

"What the hell is he talkin' about!?" Eric felt his lifeline rapidly slipping from his grasp. "Those men did nothing to your daughter! Calvin, you know I would never hurt a child. I love children. You know I've donated millions of dollars to institutions that help children. And--in any event, what could I possibly gain by hurting Dameeka?" He wasn't about to tell Calvin that someone kidnapped her. "Those hit-men were playing with your mind, Calvin. You know there's no better way to make a man slip up, make mistakes, than to make him think his love ones are suffering because of him. It's the oldest tactic in the book."

Eric saw Calvin's screw face started to relax and he went straight for the jugular vein. "Calvin, my dad made me do this. You told me yourself that your dad was your driving force, which I now can understand why you did all those foul things to me. And, you know fully well you've done some real terrible things to me, Diana, Demetrius and Tina. I forgive you and I'm asking you to forgive me. Look at it as we're both even now. Whatever I can do to make amends, consider it done. I'll even pull back and give you all the time travel credit . . . After this experience, Calvin I now realize that people must live their own lives. When fathers force their children to follow in their tracks, or to fulfill expectations that are not those of the child . . . they create monsters!"

Calvin was almost totally mesmerized by Eric's speech because it opened his eyes. He was following in his dad's footsteps, he was trying to fulfill expectations that were not totally his own, and his obsession did turn him into a monster. Calvin hated when that feeling of indecisiveness reared its ugly head because it made him feel vulnerable and weak. If he punished Eric for what he'd done, then wouldn't it be fair that he be punished for what he'd done to Eric, Cookie, his daughter, and the entire Timetron team? There was no question he adversely effected their lives, since he used, abused, neglected, ignored and manipulated anything that would help him complete his mission: Become the first official time traveler.

Calvin sighed, shifted his weight onto his other foot as the desire to punish Eric dribbled away and was replaced with guilt. There was a full-scale war going on between his heart and his mind. They were both pulling in opposite directions. *Don't be a hypocrite!* A voice in his head shouted. *Fuck Eric! He's a backstabbing snake and deserves everything he gets!* Another voice yelled. He needed something to help him decide, so he stared Eric dead in the eyes. He knew they were one of the few things that rarely told lies.

Calvin saw Eric staring down at the ground and said. "Look at me, Eric." When Calvin saw Eric's over-confident smirk, and that warped twinkle in his eyes, he made up his mind. Eric was about to stare at the ground again. "Don't look away!"

Calvin stared at Eric for a moment longer. He walked down the steps, confiscated Diana's Micron watch. He then walked over and picked up the laser gun. After walking back up the steps, and standing next to Clyde for a moment, Calvin said. "Clyde, keep an eye on him. If he tries anything stupid, do as you please with him." He turned to enter the church, but stopped when he saw Clyde's grin.

Clyde smiled because he just decided to shoot Eric between the eyes and simply tell Calvin Eric tried something stupid.

Before Calvin entered the Church, he said. "Clyde, I want justice my way. I deserve to see him punished on my terms. If we're friends, you'll do that for me." He entered the Church.

Clyde gritted his teeth as he stared at Eric. He mumbled a few curse words under his breath and reluctantly decided to let this low down scoundrel live.

Eric felt a wave of desperation swarmed all over his mind when Calvin's comment about seeing him punished on his terms registered. He desperately started thinking of another approach to convince Calvin not to punish him.

Inside the Church, Calvin moved toward the back and saw Mary on her knees praying in front of a burnt altar. He saw when Mary heard him approaching she picked up the watch and the laser gun, rose to her feet and approached him.

"Here they is, Calvin," Mary handed him the items. "Now, can we get outta here right now?"

"Yes," Calvin said. "I got a big surprise for you. I can now take you back with me, tonight." He smiled.

Mary did not quite understand. With squinted eyes, she said. "You gone take me with you, tonight!?"

"Yes, tonight."

Mary screamed with happiness. Her prayers were answered. Jumping up and down, she rushed to Calvin and hugged him, kissing him feverishly. "I knew you wasn't gonna leave me in this terrible place! I gots you' chile inside of me and I knows you's a good man. I love you, Calvin!"

"Okay, calm down." Calvin's heart felt a soothing wave of relief. "But first he gotta drawn some of their blood. After that you can come along with me."

Mary was rubbing her hands together. "Come on, let's go, right now!"

Calvin exited the Church and pulled his pocketknife. He walked over to Diana's body and kneeled. "Mary, come here. Kneel down here with me." She obeyed. "I'm gonna cut her wrist. I'm gonna drink a little bit of her blood, then you have to do the same--"

"No!" Mary sprung to her feet in utter horror. "I can't do that, Calvin. That's devil worshippin'."

Clyde chimed right in. "Sho' is Calvin. The good book forbids that kind a craziness. Peoples ain't 'posed to eat peoples, under any circumstance. And drinking blood's the same as eatin' peoples. It's right there in Leviticus."

Calvin was seconds from screaming, but he realized their observations made plenty sense. Drinking blood was a mild form of cannibalism. But, unfortunately, this was the only way to get the chemical primer from Diana's system and into theirs. There was no way to inject it directly into their blood streams, since hypodermic syringes weren't created until 1853. There was no other way besides drinking the

344

blood. He rose to his feet. "Well, Mary, you either drink some of the blood, or you will have to stay here until I come back in a few weeks. There's no other way to get the chemicals from her body into our bodies. If you wanna come with me, you gotta do this because the Time Machine won't transport you without those chemicals."

Mary thought about it for a moment. She sighed, hoping God would forgive her for what she was about to do. After another moment, Mary convinced herself he would understand she had no choice. "Okay, I'll do it. But when I get to where we goin', you gotta get me to a place where I can get baptized again."

"No problem." Calvin kneeled, slit Diana's wrist and let the blood pour into his cupped hand. He sucked in a mouthful of the blood. The metallic taste brought water to his eyes. He put his hand back under Diana's wrist and when it was full he allowed Mary to slurp the blood.

Mary gagged and almost threw it up, but she swallowed hard.

Clyde was shaking his head in disbelief. Then he realized it was time to make his move. "Calvin, give me one of 'em thunderbolt guns." He walked over to Diana's body and started taking off her clothes. She wasn't gonna need these bullet-proofed clothing anymore, Clyde concluded and knew exactly what to do with them. He spoke as he unfastened the clothes. "Since you and Mary leavin' ole Clyde, the least you could do is let me keep one of 'em thunderbolt guns, so I can defend myself properly." He smiled broadly.

Calvin knew he couldn't do that. "Stop that Clyde. Leave those clothes alone." Calvin knew if Clyde took this stuff, such an act could destroy or even reformulate history so substantially he could erase himself and everyone else from the world. He grabbed Clyde's arm, but it was jerked away. "Clyde, I can't let you do this. I wish I could but there's no--"

"I thought we was friends!?" Clyde sprung to his feet with Diana's shirt and jacket in his hand. "Why is it that I'm always the one doin' all

345

the goddamn givin' around here! I've put my goddamn life on the line for you so many goddamn times, I done lost count! . . ."

As Clyde rattled on and on about Calvin not understanding what constitutes a friendship, Calvin saw Eric sitting on the stairs smiling and enjoying this argument. Calvin was seconds from literally slapping that grin off his face. Calvin pulled from his pocket the Micron watch he got from Diana's wrist and examined it. His heart almost jumped clean out of his chest when he saw it was broke. He frantically stuck his hand in the other pocket, pulled the other watch and saw with partial relief it was okay. He sighed a breath of relief.

Then, suddenly, realization struck Calvin like an atomic explosion: only one of them could make it back with this watch. He had to find a seat. Just before he sat, he walked over and slapped Eric so hard, he felt his hand ringing with pain.

Clyde stopped in mid-sentence when he saw the thunderous slap and smiled. "Now, that's what I'm talkin' 'bout." He walked over and slapped Eric just as hard. "Go on Mary, get one in!" He saw her shake her head no. "Girl you don't know what you missin'."

Mary eased closer to Calvin and said. "Calvin, we should leave, right now."

Calvin sat on the church steps in deep thought. His mind was racing as he was trying to figure out a way around this dilemma. Could they make it back with just this one watch? After working various formulas in his mind, he realized if they both tried to get to the future with this one watch Mary could die in the process. Since his genetic markers were aligned to the Backlash, he could not undergo a transport with any other person during a normal transport. The experiment where a mouse was transported under these circumstances and the fleas that got on the mouse had died during the transport entered his mind as confirmation that it was too risky. There was no way he could take a chance and possibly kill Mary and his unborn child in the process.

After a moment, Calvin decided to use the watch himself. But after Clyde's comment pointing out his selfishness and his nasty habit of always forgetting the good things people had done for him entered his mind, his decision was changed instantly. Mary would get the watch and he would have to continue onto the Backlash zone. He started inwardly brooding over the fact the Backlash wasn't guaranteed and it was probably closed by now, but stopped himself upon realizing that at least Mary and his unborn child were guaranteed a safe trip. He chuckled to himself because had this been six months ago, he would've gone with his first observation without the slightest hesitation. Also, he noticed he couldn't seem to get Mary's common sense analogy about what makes life worth living out of his head. He would try to get back to the future and would keep trying until he succeeded.

A huge, thunderous explosion came from a distance and everyone, including Eric looked at each other with those knowing expressions.

"That was a cannon." Clyde said nonchalantly, without one shred of emotions.

Calvin was about to say he knew, but the military style bugle cut off the comment. He sprung to his feet. "That's officially our cue." Calvin turned with a screw face. "Eric, take off all those clothes. It's time for you to leave--"

"Wait! Please!" Eric rose to his feet. "Calvin, please don't--"

Calvin kicked Eric square in the gut, causing him to stumble backwards and to the ground. Calvin then said with clenched teeth and a tone that was drenched with a calm, no nonsense rage. "I'm not gonna say it again."

When Calvin walked toward Eric with the laser gun in his hand, he saw Eric frantically get up and started taking his clothing off. After he was stripped down to his underclothes and socks, Eric hurried toward the alleyway Clyde hid earlier. Just before entering, Eric stopped, turned and locked eyes with Calvin. He was about to launch another wave of pleas, but shook loose of the thought and disappeared into the alleyway. As he ran away, an indescribable sheet of desperation and despair gripped him, but it was nothing in comparison to the hatred, rage and bitterness he felt. Even more powerful than all the negative emotions combined was his vow to find a way out of this situation. He smiled wickedly because as long as he was alive there was always a way to solve any problem.

Earlier, Clyde was tempted to put a bullet in the back of Eric's head as he scurried away because he knew it was never wise to leave an enemy alive.

Calvin picked up Eric's clothes, the goggles, stuffed them in his knapsack and moved down the street. "Clyde, me and Mary sure hate to leave you like this. I guess it's time for us to--"

BOOM!--BOOM!--BOOM!--BOOM!--BOOM! . . .

A massive wave of bullets rained upon the Church and the nearby area, causing Calvin, Mary and Clyde to dive to the ground. Practically on hands and knees, they frantically scrambled toward the side of the Church. When they were safely behind the church, and the bullets came to a stop, Calvin and Clyde peered around the corner of the building.

Calvin's thinking process froze up and he nearly had a seizure of fear when he saw about a hundred soldiers marching toward them. It looked like a scene right out of a revolutionary war movie.

"Calvin, give me one of 'em damn lightnin' guns!" Clyde started firing his pistols down the street. "Hurry up!" He knew if he had one of those laser guns, he could easily get all that gold out of this town and into Mexico. "Whatever you gonna do, you better hurry up! Can't you see they comin' right at us! Give me the damn gun, so I can make sho' you and Mary gets away!"

Calvin felt a jolt from Clyde's last remark because he was right. If he and Mary were going to escape, Clyde would have to hold them off. Looking at the situation from all other angles, he easily realized none of those possibilities would work because there were simply too many soldiers to even think they could get away without someone holding them back. But what if he gave Clyde this weapon and he let it get into the wrong hands? What if this laser gun fell into the hands of a scientist, or the government?

As the soldiers drew closer, Calvin felt the solution becoming clearer with each step they took. "Clyde, listen to me. If I give you this laser gun, you have to promise me you will make sure this weapon never falls into the hands of anyone. When the fuel burns out you have to promise me you'll bury it or throw it in a lake or the ocean. Will you do that?"

Another barrage of bullets rained upon the Church.

"Of course! You got my promise! If that's what yah want, you got it, Calvin. Now, hurry up! Give me that damn gun!"

Calvin hesitated and his conscience started beating him up.

"Give it here!" Clyde shouted. "Hurry!"

More bullets rained upon the Church.

BLLAAAM!

A cannon was fired. Suddenly, the huge fifty-pound ball landed about twenty feet from them, scattering a tremendous dirt cloud into the air.

Calvin saw the devastating effects of the cannonball and shoved the laser gun to Clyde.

Clyde smiled from ear to ear.

"This is how you operate it," Calvin showed him. "Now, point and press."

WHOOSH!-BLAAM!

"Alright!!" Clyde cheered when he saw the laser beam shot from the weapon and struck two front-line soldiers. As Clyde looked for someone else to shoot, the other soldiers, in a panic-stricken haste, sought refuge behind buildings, turned over wagons, water barrels, while some laid flat on their stomachs.

Calvin gave Clyde a strong hug. "I'm gonna miss you my friend."

Mary hugged Clyde and kissed him on the check. "Bye-bye, Clyde." She felt like crying because she was going to miss him.

"Come on now! Y'all better get goin'," Clyde started blushing. He didn't like all this sentimental stuff. "It's been nice knowin' y'all and don't worry about ole Clyde 'cause I'm gonna be just fine!" That gold was dancing wildly in his mind.

Calvin peeked around the corner saw the soldiers' forward movement was halted by the laser blast. He made sure he had all the bulletproofed clothing (with the exception of a jacket that Clyde wouldn't give up), as well as the night vision goggles and then stuffed the futuristic items in his knapsack. He grabbed Mary's hand and ran.

They ran right out of the town and continued running for twenty straight minutes, searching desperately for a horse. Calvin knew without a horse, there was no way he and Mary would make it to the Backlash zone in time, since it could be miles away. Breathing hard, he noticed their high-speed run was transforming into a foot dragging fast walk.

With the sun about in its 7 o'clock in the morning position, Calvin turned around and saw the town in back of them had faded into a small image on the horizon. He turned back around and decided they were far enough and he began walking.

Mary was breathing and sweating profusely and stopped walking all together. She kilt over with both hands on her knees, sucking in air with excessive force.

They decided to take a five-minute rest. During this rest, Calvin re-calculated how much time he thought he had left and realization struck him like a slap to the face; if it was about 7 o'clock, the portal might be closing or already closed by now! With frantic haste, he spoke. "Come on, let's go!"

"I thought we said five minutes!?" Mary whined, still breathing hard. "That wasn't even three--"

"Come on!" Calvin pulled her into a fast walk.

Five minutes later, Calvin saw three men on horseback appear up ahead and he saw they were slowly approaching. Calvin realized he was desperate because he decided without any serious contemplation that he was going to get one of those horses one way or another.

As the men drew closer, Calvin saw they were not soldiers and that was good. Their three horses were laden with wares and Calvin surmised they were traders or men in search of gold. Calvin pulled the laser gun. After a moment, he realized the use of this weapon would be an over-kill. He put it back and something in the back of his mind told him to stop pulling punches, and go all the way. He ignored his intuition, retrieved the pistol from the back of his waist and put it in the front where he could reach it more easily.

With his hand on the pistol, Calvin saw one of the three white men was very old with thick gray hair and a Santa Claus beard while the other two were middle aged and clean-shaven. Calvin spoke just as the men were about to pass. "Excuse me, sir. We're in desperate need of a ride. We wanna know if it's possible if we could purchase one of your horses--"

"Nigger, who you thank you are, approachin' us good white folks like that!?" One of the middle-aged men said, inspecting Calvin closely. When he saw Calvin had a gun, he frantically reached for his gun.

BOOM!--BOOM!--BOOM!--BOOM!

Calvin pulled his pistol with remarkable speed and shot the one who reached first in the upper chest near the throat. With his trigger finger moving at break-neck speed, through the red haze, he saw a red hole appear in the chest of the other middle aged man as his torso jerked backward. The impact of the bullets flipped the man backwards off the horse. Meanwhile, the horses went wild, rearing up while screaming in fear. When the old man pulled his pistol and squeezed off a shot, one of Calvin's bullets struck him in the forehead, producing a red cloud in the back of his head as the slug entered and exited.

When the pandemonium-stricken moment came to a calm, Calvin was clutching his shoulder, cringing in great pain. He cursed himself for not opening fire on the men the moment they arrived. His curses grew ten-folds upon realizing he should have put on one of the bulletproofed garments he had in his knapsack. However, he was glad Mary moved away from him at the moment she heard the white man's hostile tone of voice and had hit the ground before the shooting started.

As Calvin examined the blood in the palm of his hand, he couldn't believe after all these months here in this time zone, he still couldn't get it in his head that white folks hated black folks. The only thing white folks in this time era felt obligated to do to black folks was to make their lives a living hell. Looking at this, he realized Clyde was truly one in a million.

Calvin and Mary took the sacks off two horses and each mounted a horse. They rode at top speed.

Calvin's injuries ached with agonizing force as the galloping motion re-awakened the throbbing in his hip. The blood oozing from his shoulder wound began to slow down about twenty minutes when they passed beyond the two foothills that appeared as a distant mountain when they were in the town. Now racing across the prairie like landscape, a nervous realization started to grow when Calvin received no bodily signal from the Backlash.

An hour later, still no sign came and Calvin again re-calculated the time for the thousandth time. A tear eased from under his eyelid because he missed the Backlash. The sun was now dancing overhead with blistering force and it made matters a million times worse. Earlier, he subconsciously knew it was game over. He had to be at the Backlash around sunrise, but as usual, he wanted to believe otherwise, so he psyched himself out.

Twenty minutes later, they were racing across the high, orchard-grass plains. Calvin was about to bring his horse to a stop and present the dilemma to Mary, but Mary's theory on what makes life worth living was hurled into the forefront of his mind. He had to keep riding; there was a chance he could he be off by a few miles or a couple of hours. It couldn't hurt to try. In any event, he had to find another town.

As Calvin was passing a wide grazing land with broad wheat fields, he wondered what he was going to do. He couldn't leave Mary here, or renege on what he promised her. And how was he going to send her to the future without him? If the Timetron board found out he sent a woman back from the past to the future, he would definitely be violating a spectrum of laws. Imprisonment would be inevitable if he ever made it back. He decided to continue riding until an answer came to him.

Twenty minutes later, the horse began to lurk forward as if it had hurt its leg. Calvin tugged on the reins bringing the horse to a fast pace trot. The lurking response went away. Then, suddenly, Calvin felt a tingling sensation growing all over his body, becoming so intense it was annoying. At first, he thought it was a side effect from his injuries, but upon closer inspection, he realized it was Backlash related. "Yes!" He shouted, enthralled with joy.

About ten minutes later, his vision became blurred. When his stomach started churning as if he was seconds from throwing up, and then he suddenly saw a huge grayish looking cloud up ahead about 100 yards away, he knew this was the closest he could get before the Backlash would swallow him up. He stopped the horse and got off.

Mary stopped her horse and dismounted. "Calvin, what's wrong, you look sick." She massaged his uninjured shoulder.

"This is it, Mary," Calvin was breathing hard because the Backlash was now literally trying to suck him into its realm. He pulled the

Micron watch from his pocket and put it on Mary's wrist with trembling hands. "Listen, Mary." His voice was quivering and he saw it was scaring Mary. "We're gonna walk about 100 yards into that small cloud right there." He pointed.

Mary turned and saw nothing. "What cloud? They ain't no cloud over there. Ain't nothin' but a big ole hill and some dry land."

Calvin realized he was the only one able to see the Backlash zone because it was constructed for his genetic markers. "Don't worry. I want you to walk with me to that area. When I tell you, press this button right here." He pointed at the control key on the watch. "When you press the button, you're gonna feel funny. Then there's gonna be a huge flash, but it won't hurt. You'll feel like you've suddenly gone to sleep and then you'll wake up in the future. You're gonna land inside a booth, and the moment the Machine whines down, the hatch door will open automatically. If no one's at the lab, step out and close the hatch door. This is very important so please remember this, Mary." He said it with deliberate force. "You must step out and close the hatch door behind you. If you fail to do this, I won't be able to get back until it's closed. You with me?"

"Yes, Calvin," Mary kissed Calvin again because she loved him so much. After a long moment, she let go of the deep kiss, "I understand. I step out and shut the door behind me. Yes, I got it."

Calvin grabbed her hand and they walked in silence. Calvin suddenly felt like he wasn't getting enough oxygen, his body grew weak. The fatigue was becoming unbearable. Once he almost stumbled onto his face, but Mary caught him. Just as he was five feet from the eye of the cloud, he stopped and said. "Mary, I love you." He kissed her again and then rubbed her stomach. "Press the button and I'll see you in the future." He backed into the cloud while watching Mary. Mary pressed the button. When the huge bright light came, she actually felt her body evaporate into a gaseous energy and then faded like a cloud of smoke unraveling in a gust of wind.

Calvin saw the flash and raised his arm to shield his eyes from the brilliant rays of light. With anticipation flowing through his veins, he moved deeper into the cloud. He could feel his molecules and atoms being ripped apart. It suddenly felt like his whole body was melting. Just when he thought this particular time travel was going to be as painful as the one that brought him here, he felt, saw, and even heard the thunderous flash and he disappeared.

CHAPTER # 34

Everything was swirling. All images were blurry and had no logical form. The lights were bright, oh so bright they were! Something didn't smell right; everything smelled too clean, almost synthetic like. But at least there was no pain. In fact, Calvin noticed he didn't feel the gunshot wounds at all, and noticed he even felt good as he rose from the lying position onto his feet and felt the weight of his body. Stumbling slightly, he noticed the ground he stood upon was made of some kind of special concrete. It was as clean and smooth as expensive white marble. The dizziness was gradually subsiding. He checked to see what had happened to his hip wound because he suddenly noticed it was no longer pulsating with pain, nor was his shoulder wound giving off any noticeable discomfort. He noticed the knapsack was still hanging from his shoulder.

"Oh shit!" He muttered when she saw the healed scar on his hip. Calvin started examining his surroundings looking for anything familiar. The images faded in and out of focus. His nerves flinched when he looked up at the sky and saw there was no clouds. The upper atmosphere, appearing as the hemisphere above the earth looked like a dingy bluish green with sunlight seeping through. It gave off a dreary, but sunny aura that was very hard to explain. He was outside, that much he was certain of, and he finally concluded the sky looked artificial. Blinking his eyes with his head locked in an upward position, he scrutinized the dome looking atmosphere for several long minutes and it all started to come to him. *No! It can't be!* His breathing increased. He was seconds from falling completely apart. *Please don't let it be!*

Calvin forced himself to calm down, since he had to make certain his observations and assumptions were correct. He slowed his rapid breathing to a slow pace and started walking. He noticed the buildings looked extremely weird. It was very early in the morning, since the streets were empty. He started getting very nervous because everything was too clean. In an effort to further calm himself down, he endeavored to convince himself he may have landed in one of those futuristic amazement parks and now he had to find his way to one of the exits or entry gates.

He stopped suddenly. The shock grabbed him when he saw massive high-rise walkways. There were hundreds of them and they looked like they were moving! It reminded him of that ancient cartoon the Jetsons.

His head turned with flinching speed when he saw movement coming from the sky. Something entered the dome like shield and it took him a couple of seconds for his eyes and mind to register what it was.

He collapsed to his knees and started crying.

"NOOOO!!" Calvin screamed because it was evident what had happened. He needed to see no more after he saw the spacecraft enter the artificial atmosphere, looking as if it had pierced through a wall of bluish green water. This was the first time he felt genuine pain on a universal scale. The agony ran so deep, he wanted to just roll over and die. There was no doubt he had gone way pass his time era. He was apparently catapulted farther into the future. He was also crying because Mary's poor heart would be broken beyond imagination. Not only that, he knew she probably would not make it in the time he was from without someone to help her. And because she had his unborn child in her stomach, Calvin cried even harder.

His head was suddenly flooded with so many painful realities his body trembled convulsively; he was moaning and groaning as if he was suffering in a vicious way. He failed his father. He wasn't going to be the first time traveler, at least not officially. What about Dameeka? How could he abandon his child!? What about justice? Whatever happened to what goes around shall surely come around? That little pestering voice inside his head also started reminding him that he was a monster. Isn't this a fair punishment? If it was good enough for Eric, isn't it good enough for you? He quickly put a muzzle on the inner voice because this wasn't the time for all these pain-provoking truths. After he went through an inward tantrum, brooding over all the failures that were evident in his life now, he rose to his feet and began to walk.

He needed to know how far he missed his time era. He walked for about ten minutes and came across a store. Looking inside the glass window, he saw it was some kind of appliance store. He touched the glass and his finger made the material stretch as if it was made of rubber.

"Please do not touch the viewing apparatus," A mechanical lady's voice came from somewhere Calvin couldn't begin to pinpoint the source.

Calvin continued looking in the window, scrutinizing all the space-age merchandise. After his eyes swept over a dozen items, Calvin saw a clock on the wall. And with a smile, he saw the month, day and the year. He quickly did the math and counted about two hundred years over the mark. The dread started resurfacing, but his will and optimistic attitude took control. Then, it hit him. Suddenly, he felt the urge to start walking again because it made him think clearly.

As Calvin walked along the clean, space-aged streets, pondering the possibilities of this sudden idea, and its potential for success, the excitement grew. *Yes! Yes! It could work!* But, a moment later, with a sudden and profound impact, reality hit him when he saw a flying garbage truck maneuver over a dumpster and the trash inside was sucked up like a vacuum. He didn't understand why this particular sight ignited this rude awakening, but it literally crumbled his heart. He continued walking, realizing the more he looked at the idea from a realistic and logical standpoint, the more he realized he was royally fucked up.

Mary opened her eyes. She could hear her heart beating in her ears. Her whole body pulsated to the rhythm of her heart. Even her brain, eyes, feet, hands and her private parts were throbbing. It wasn't a hurtful throbbing, but it definitely was a sensation she could not ignore in light of its profound abnormality. Outside on the other side of the little room she was in, Mary saw someone rose from a chair and was now approaching. It took a few seconds for her to realize it was a white man who was wearing some strange things over his eyes; probably the same goggles the hit men wore that enabled them to see in the dark, Mary concluded.

SSSSSSSHHH!

A hissing sound came from the Time Machine as the door (the "hatch" as she remembered Calvin refer to it) opened. Mary was momentarily startled, but she quickly realized this meant she must exit the booth.

As Mary pushed the door open all the way and stepped out, she saw the man had a scary looking smile on his face. His skin looked very odd and he had on a matching green outfit. He stopped and stood staring at her from about twelve feet. Mary did not know what to say or do. "Howdy, mister." Her eyes started taking in the surroundings, looking at all the machines, chairs, tool cabinets, the colorful walls, and the control station. She heard a constant humming that made the whole place seem like it was alive. Her eyes were bouncing about with a desperate urgency.

Then, she suddenly remembered and frantically turned and closed the door. Her heart started racing. The look of sheer terror grew steadily on her face because she failed to close the hatch door the moment she stepped out. She silently started hoping and praying she didn't mess it up for Calvin. She was about to panic as her mind started scolding her for not following instructions.

"Mary." The man in green said as if the name sounded like music to his ears. "My sweet Mary."

Mary turned around slowly with her mouth hung open and her eyes bulging. She blinked her eyes trying to make sure she heard this scary looking white man correctly. *Did he say my name!?* Then she realized he sounded familiar.

The man moved toward Mary with his white hand reached out, signaling to Mary to grab hold.

"Don't come near me!" Mary said frantically. "I'm waiting for Calvin. He's comin'!" She started trembling as she stepped away and couldn't stop the tears. When her rump bumped into the Time Machine, she gave the man her back and cowered with her hands covering her eyes, crying because she just knew she messed it up for Calvin when she took too long to close the hatch door. And she was so terrified of this white man, but had no idea why because he didn't present himself as a threat. In fact, she noticed he was acting like he liked her.

"Mary," The man said softly. "Turn around . . . Come on. I wanna show you something. Don't be afraid."

Mary suddenly realized the voice was so familiar. She turned around and allowed her arms to relax as they slid down to her sides. When the man started ripping his face off, Mary was about scream, but when she saw the black skin and the curly black hair underneath the covering, the shriek was instantly extinguished and replaced with genuine awe.

Mary's eyes bulged and she saw it was Calvin. But he was much older. The emotional surge engulfed her. It was truly a monolithic feeling of gargantuan portions. She leaped into his arms and squeezed him so hard with her head planted on his chest. Her tears of fear transformed into tears of love, joy and surprise. She reached up and kissed Calvin for several passionate seconds. She pulled away and said. "But, how you get here 'fore me?! You said you was comin' after me?"

Calvin kissed Mary for a straight minute, savoring her sweet, soft and succulent lips. When he finished, Calvin gazed into Mary's eyes, and then began rubbing her stomach with a silly looking proud smile. "Come over here and have a seat. I'll tell you everything."

They walked over to the sofa style crushed velvet chair and sat. Calvin smiled when he saw the velvet fabric and the softness of the sofa mesmerized Mary.

Brushing the tips of her fingers across the material while bouncing up and down, Mary thought this chair was the most wonderful item she'd ever seen.

Calvin wanted to embrace her again because her innocent, childish like behavior was turning his heart into Jell-O. After a moment he said. "This is a very long story and it may be a little confusing for you. I don't even know where to start . . . I'm now from the future beyond this future. I never made it back to this time zone. And both times it happened this way." He remembered when Mary appeared moments ago, he felt his memory reconstructing itself because he had successfully changed the past. And as a result, his new memory embraced all of what took place during this particular journey. During the first journey, Mary had died, which was the primary reason for his current endeavors. "You see, Mary, originally you had died before I made it to the Backlash." He saw her shocked expression and he nodded his head in a confirmatory fashion. "When I got to the future, I jumped right into the field of time travel. Your death along with our unborn child devastated me in an unimaginable way. I vowed to find a way to alter it. So, what I did was create a situation in that time era by altering certain variables. Just by adding a person, who would rearrange and affect certain events, even ever so slightly, I was able to change what had initially happened. I did this with an android." He saw Mary's eyes squint with confusion, and he realized certain words he was using were foreign to her, but he went ahead with his presentation. "That android was Clyde Jerkins."

"Clyde!?" Mary was beyond confused. "Clyde was android!? What's android?"

"It's a robot. A machine that's made to look and act human."

Mary shook her head unbelievingly because this was sheer madness. "How is it possible for people to be a machine?"

Calvin pulled his black box, punched in a code, and pointed it at the floor several feet from them. Before he pressed the button he said. "This is a hologram. It's not the actual android, but it is a clear representation of Clyde." He pressed the button.

Mary flinched when she saw the light shot from the box and Clyde appeared. His arms were crossed and he was looking dead at Mary. "Can it talk?" Mary was completely awe-stricken.

"Of course," Calvin activated another dial.

Clyde said. "Mary, why don't you stop messin' 'round with our heads, girl. Now, you come on over here and give Clyde a great big ole kiss on this here right cheek of mine." He pointed to his face.

Mary burst out laughing. It really was Clyde; complete with his heavy southern drawl and those no-nonsense mannerisms. "What about Jim Roof? Can you bring him back?"

Calvin felt the pain in his chest explode because he remembered Jim Roof as vividly as he remembered the two gunshot wounds. "Sorry, Mary, Jim is dead. There was no way to bring him back or to prevent his death. I guess it was written in stone for him to die because both times he died."

There was a penetrating silence as they pulled up images of Jim Roof.

Mary looked down at the face and hair covering on the floor that made Calvin look white. "What's that thang?" She pointed.

"Oh, that's a genetic appearance altering device. In other words, it's a high-tech mask. Sadly, in this particular part of the future, blacks still haven't acquired equal and fair treatment on a universal scale.

Racism, profiling and conspiratorial disenfranchisement of black folks are still rampant. Since whites move more freely, it was wise for me to become a white man."

Mary was deeply disappointed and felt the urge to cry because she wanted so badly to live in a world without so much meanness, hatefulness and downright senseless wickedness. She allowed her silence to speak volumes of what was going on inside of her.

Calvin broke the silence. "Where I'm from now, things have changed drastically. The technology is so advanced it's virtually indescribable. The earth has an artificial atmosphere, people have the ability to engage in inter-galactic travel, and all people are treated equally and fairly, even black folks. In fact, any activity that disrupts universal fellowship amongst all races is a criminal offense and the penalties are very severe. You'll see it all shortly . . . I also came back here because I needed to know if my ex-girlfriend, Ramanda was faithful." He sighed with a smile. "During my investigation, I stumbled upon some real surprising discoveries." He still was a bit shocked by the fact that Ramanda and Demetrius were spies trying to steal his works. What really devastated him was, Ramanda and Demetrius were husband and wife. "She got her justice this time around. I say that because during the earlier version she did something real foul and got off Scott free. Another reason I came back here, was for my daughter, Dameeka. You're gonna love her. And she looks a lot like you. I've told her so much about you and she's just dying to meet you."

Mary rose to her feet. "So when can we go?" The excitement in her voice was intense. "Let's go right, now?"

Calvin started laughing. As he rose to his feet, he saw Mary didn't find whatever he was laughing at funny. He laughed even harder when he saw the agitated frown wiggle onto her face. He kneeled and picked up the mask. "I'm sorry, Mary." He struggled to whine down the laughter. "Please forgive me, Mary, but that statement . . ." The memories affiliated with this comment coursed through his mind with remarkable clarity. "I tried to count how many times you said, 'Let's go right, now' when we were in the past, and you must have said it at least four dozen times. And yes, my sweet Mary we can go right now."

Calvin paused for a moment, locking eyes with Mary. He realized he was the luckiest man alive because he retrieved his rare, beautiful black jewel and did it against all odds and seemingly insurmountable obstacles. Not many people were able to go back and undo the past and Calvin deeply appreciated this blessing bestowed upon him.

As Calvin savored the moment, gazing into Mary's eyes, he realized now that time travel was more than likely be out of his life for good (he permanently loss his time travel license for engaging in this current unauthorized mission). He could finally slow down enough to enjoy life. No more me, myself and I missions; no more neglecting his family; no more selfishness, self-centered actions, uncaring attitudes, nor any selective forgetfulness. It was going to be living life for all it was worth, day for day, hour for hour, minute for minute, and seconds for seconds, strictly enjoying the finer things in life.

Calvin raised his arms. "Hug me. Better yet, give me the best kiss you got."

With a dazzling smile, Mary hugged him. Then, with her heart, body, mind and soul, she kissed Calvin as she closed her eyes.

Calvin savored the kiss as he pressed the main button on the device.

There was a huge flash and they vanished.

THE END

About the Author

John Whitfield, AKA Divine G, is the founder and owner of
Divine G Entertainment. He is a four-time PEN American Center award
winning writer and the winner of the 2008 Tacenda Literary award for
best play. He has written over a dozen novels and screenplays,
performed in countless plays, appeared in a Hollywood feature film as
an extra, hosted his own internet radio show, produced, directed and
starred in his debut short film, and worked with Lil Wayne as a
supervisory carpenter on his 2013 (AMW) America's Most Wanted tour.
John Whitfield is also a Youth Intervention Specialist currently working
with a non-for-profit organization called Council for Unity and has been
quoted by the United Nations and the New York Times.

Upcoming Novels from John Whitfield

THE TRIALS AND TRIBULATIONS OF BISHME CARLSON

(In bookstores Fall 2017)

The story of Bishme Carlson is one that epitomizes a tale of a man on a noble mission. After accidentally killing his family, Bishme vows to save as many lives as he can, especially young lives from the ravaging onslaught of HIV/AIDS. He pledges to start his own AIDS Prevention Organization, but there are many unresolved matters still haunting and hindering him; the most serious of them all is he's being followed by a stalker, a mysterious man who makes clear that his intentions are malevolent. Receiving his drive, energy and iron will to succeed from a statement his four-year-old daughter bestowed upon him before dying, Bishme confronts the life-threatening trials and tribulations while a tantalizing question looms omnipotently; will he survive and accomplish his mission or will he lose his life to a heartless foe?

FOLLOW THE SIGNS. . .

The Sequel To *TGONG*

Under the pseudonym Divine G

(In bookstores Fall 2017)

"Follow the Signs, they are everywhere" was the recurring dream world command Rayhiem Jones had been receiving all his life. In this sequel to *TGONG*, Rayhiem finally discovers the reason he's been experiencing the strange, recurring dreams. He was being groomed for a divine mission to save all life on the planet from a celestial virus lodged inside a meteorite sent to Earth by the Setphian Deities.

The Ausarian Deities (the Setphian's arch rivals) reveals to Rayhiem during one of his mystifying dreams that he must find the two people on the planet who has the cure within their bodies and get them to Phoenix Arizona within 13 days to make a celestial exchange or the entire planet will perish. But, Samuel Griener, the Setphian's General on the planet, and his very powerful and wealthy subordinates have no intentions of allowing Rayhiem to succeed.